Lady in Waiting

LADY IN WAITING

The Reluctant Brides

MARIE TREMAYNE

AVONIMPULSE
An Imprint of HarperCollinsPublishers

LADY IN WAITING. Copyright © 2018 by Marie Tremayne. All rights reserved. Printed in the United States of America. No part of this book may be used or reproduced in any manner whatsoever without written permission except in the case of brief quotations embodied in critical articles and reviews. For information, address HarperCollins Publishers, 195 Broadway, New York, NY 10007.

Digital Edition March 2018 ISBN: 978-0-06-274738-9
Print Edition ISBN: 978-0-06-274739-6

Cover design by Patricia Barrow
Cover art by Christine Ruhnke
Cover photographs © RomanceNovelCovers.com (woman); © Paul Briden/ Shutterstock (flowers); © antb/Shutterstock (manor)

Avon Impulse and the Avon Impulse logo are registered trademarks of HarperCollins Publishers in the United States of America.

Avon and HarperCollins are registered trademarks of HarperCollins Publishers in the United States of America and other countries.

FIRST EDITION

18 19 20 21 22   HDC   10 9 8 7 6 5 4 3 2 1

*To my husband, Gary, who after listening to me talk
about writing for years, kindly told me to get to it.
I love you.*

The Start of the Season
London, England
Spring 1845

The pit in Clara's stomach grew deeper as they rode farther away from their London townhome. She glanced uneasily at her sister, Lucy, who was seated beside her, looking pale and grim within the open interior of the hansom cab. The horse's hooves sounded loudly upon the road, and each strike against the cobblestone felt like a conspicuous advertisement of their plans, although she supposed it was only her guilty conscience that made it seem that way.

Still, Clara winced at the noise and reached over to tug the edge of Lucy's hood further down in an effort to better conceal her features. Her sister turned to regard her with her large blue eyes and an anxious sigh.

"I wish there was another way, Clara. You know I do."

Clara reached over to grip Lucy's trembling hand tightly in her own. "We've discussed this." Her eyes scanned the passing landscape and the darkened windows of the nearby homes, looking strange and haunted in the gloom. "This is the only way for you and Douglas to be together. You've already tried talking to Papa."

"Yes, I know," Lucy replied sadly, "but I am less concerned with Papa at this point and more worried for *you*."

Despite the extremity of the circumstances, Clara fully supported her sister's choice, even though she knew that when news of Lucy's elopement spread, the ensuing scandal would mean a . . . difficult . . . season for her, to say the least.

The cab rounded a tight corner and sent Lucy sliding into Clara, who took advantage of the sudden closeness to wrap her arms firmly around her sister. She planted a kiss on her cheek and leaned in close.

"Do not worry about me."

Clara knew Lucy had not taken this elopement lightly. She'd considered all the possible options and had tried approaching both their mother and father separately. Her sister had even contemplated an unimaginable future without the man she loved, weighing the likelihood of cementing a sensible but joyless marriage for herself during the season.

In the end, however, her love for Douglas had won out. Despite his lack of connections and fortune, the two were an incomparable match for one another, and over the past six months they had manufactured new and creative ways to see each other, even if it were only for a glimpse from across the street. It was simply bad luck that he was so far removed from their social sphere, a fact Lucy had often lamented since meeting the charismatic tradesman unexpectedly on a walk through their village. But he was proud of his lineage, he worked hard, and he was not shamed by the discrepancy of rank between them. Lucy couldn't help but love him for all the down-to-earth qualities that made him so different from the pompous, fluffy aristocrats of the *ton*.

They rode that way, arms wrapped around one another, until the gas streetlights of London had given way to the less reliable lighting of the roads that led out of the city. Soon the cab jerked forward, the driver's authoritative *whoa* and jerk on the reins slowing the horse's pace from his elevated perch. Lucy immediately sat up straight and Clara craned her neck, at last discerning the shape of a wheeled cart on the side of the road. They pulled over and a man stepped forward into the road, holding his lantern aloft.

"It's him!" cried Lucy, scrambling to gather her skirts.

The driver tugged on a lever to open the folded wooden doors by their legs, and Douglas rushed forward as Lucy nearly leaped into his arms, setting the yellow glow of his lamp swaying. He exhaled harshly in what sounded like anticipation and joy.

"At last—"

He set his lantern down on the ground to fully embrace her. Lucy's hood slid off her caramel-colored locks while they kissed with abandon, and Clara averted her eyes with a grin while disembarking. She noticed the driver had likewise chosen to busy himself by retrieving Lucy's bag from inside the cab.

They slowly pulled away to gaze at each other, then laughed in breathless disbelief at their moment of indulgence. Clara was happy to see that the earlier pallor of her sister's cheek had now been replaced with a glorious blush of color—further clarification that they were doing the right thing. She would do anything to see her sister that happy forever.

Douglas clasped Lucy's hand and glanced away from her to focus on Clara, his gray eyes shining with gratitude. "Thank you for bringing her."

Clara smiled. "I daresay she would have brought herself just fine had I been unavailable to assist. I've never seen a woman so determined in all my life."

His expression turned serious. "Will you be all right? Your parents—"

"All will be well for me, if you can promise all will be well for *her*," she said, tipping her head in her sister's direction.

"I see," he said, his warm gaze drifting downwards over Lucy's countenance. "Well, that is a promise easily kept."

A noise in the distance caught their attention, and Lucy quickly tugged her hood back over her head. Clara, too, ensured hers was in place as a carriage barreled past them in the empty lane. She sought her sister's eyes.

"I should be getting back, before Mother and Father find something is amiss."

Lucy came forward to hold her close, and Clara breathed in the sweet smell of her sister's hair. She was desperate to commit every detail to memory, for she had no idea when she might next be able to see Lucy. In spite of their brave faces, saying good-bye was hard, and both women were wiping away tears by the time they pulled away from each other.

"I'm not sure how we'll keep in touch." Lucy sniffed.

Fresh tears blurred Clara's vision. "It's probably better if we don't. At least for now."

She kissed her sister, then turned to place a kiss on Douglas's cheek as well. "Take good care of her for me," she whispered.

He gripped her shoulders. "Thank you, Clara. For everything."

She nodded mutely, then aimed a tiny smile at her sister.

Get in the cab, before you beg her not to go.

Clara was going to miss her so much. But she would take comfort in the fact that Lucy was living a life of her own choosing, with a man who truly loved her. Most women were not so lucky.

Clara would likely not be so lucky.

She turned with stiff, leaden legs and forced herself to board the cab. There was time for one last wave before the whip of the reins propelled the horse into action, and it was only when the cab pulled around on its return route that the gravity of what was happening sank in. Her sister was leaving everything, leaving all of them, leaving *her* behind for a new life. Tomorrow when their parents awoke, everything would be different. And even though she wasn't going with Lucy on her journey, Clara felt as if her life had just shifted in some massive, unchangeable way. A sudden panic closed in around her chest.

Desperate for one last glimpse of her sister, she lurched to the side of the cab and peered around the edge of the window, but the yellow glow of Douglas's lantern was already fading gradually away, taking Lucy along with it.

Sinking back into the seat, she battled her tears back into submission. She knew in her heart with all certainty they had done the right thing. But she also couldn't help but wonder, bleakly, if she had just contributed to her own ruin.

CHAPTER ONE

The End of the Season
London, England
August 1845

William, Lord Ashworth, was not going to the ball tonight.

Having finally made the decision, he reached up to loosen his white cravat with a sigh of relief. He strode to the sideboard to pour himself a brandy, seeking to numb himself from this acceptance of his failure. It was a pity. After all, he had endured the carriage ride from his country estate in Kent to make an appearance at one of the final and most fashionable events of the season. Were he actually to attend, it would have served to satisfy the *ton's* annoying demand to see the new Earl of Ashworth in the flesh, and perhaps quieted their rumormongering for a time. On the other hand, it could just have easily stirred the flames of gossip to unbearable heights. The *ton* was an unpredictable lot.

Sweat broke out upon his brow, and he unfastened the top button of his linen shirt before gripping the tumbler with shaking fingers and throwing back the drink, sending fire cascading down his throat. He uttered a groan, then slammed down the glass and only the sudden appearance of his friend, Viscount Evanston, stayed his hand from pouring another. In contrast to William's own state, Thomas looked crisp and perfectly at ease in his formal black-and-white attire. He glanced first at the decanter in William's hand, then with a raise of his brow, cast a critical eye at the state of his clothing.

"I wouldn't normally recommend attending a ball with your shirt open and cravat untied, but no doubt the ladies will approve," he said lightly, crossing the study to join him. The viscount's tone was teasing, but William did not miss the note of concern that was also present.

"I am staying home tonight," he said stonily.

His friend paused, then slipped the crystal container from his hands and replaced the stopper. "Come now, Ashworth," he chided gently. "Don't force me to be the responsible one. We waited until the end of the season, as you requested. You went through the motions. Accepted the invitation, traveled to London—"

William shot Evanston a leaden stare, silencing him immediately. "Yes, I went through the motions. As it turns out, that is all I can offer."

The disappointment that briefly flickered across his friend's face set William's teeth on edge. Inevitably, people would be upset by his inability to come out in society, especially after he'd finally relented for the event in Mayfair tonight. But even if he were to show up, there was no guarantee that the *ton* could be appeased. Any answer to their questions would be ruthlessly scrutinized for a sign that he was failing in some regard. A moment's hesitation could be the difference between projecting an air of self-assuredness and creating more fuel for their stories.

William knew there were fewer things more fascinating than an eligible lord who had suffered a calamitous loss, and for the past eighteen months he'd given them very little in the way of entertainment. Instead he'd shut himself away in the country, spending the time mourning three loved ones while recuperating from his own injuries, physical and other-wise. They would not take kindly to his absence tonight.

He closed his eyes wearily. They could all go to hell.

"Look, I don't care what you do," said Thomas, although the statement rang untrue. "And I certainly wouldn't bother yourself with what the *ton* thinks at any given point in time. But might I remind you that this was something *you* wanted to do . . . both for yourself and for your sister?"

Yes, William could admit that Eliza had probably been his most important consideration. Especially now that her house had been entailed to the next male in line for her late husband's estate. He needed to smooth their way back into society to make things easier for her, should she choose to re-marry. And he needed to represent the earldom in a way that would have made his father proud, and his older brother, too—though they were no longer of this world.

He swallowed hard against the inevitable memories that always lurked, ready to invade his consciousness. They were actually less like memories, and more like the reliving of a horrid tale that often insisted upon its own retelling.

The sickening tilt of the vehicle . . . the screeching of the horses . . . the last time he'd seen them alive, eyes pale in the gloom and wide with terror. His father reaching for him from across the carriage—

"William!"

William blinked to stave off the nightmarish recollection, and he could feel the blood draining from his face. Evanston must have noticed, for his gaze dropped down to the sideboard. Going against his earlier censure of William's drinking, the viscount removed the stopper to pour another drink while waiting for his reply.

"I would do anything in my power to make things easier for her," William managed at last.

His friend cocked his head. "Is this not in your power tonight?"

He seriously considered the question, then shook his head gruffly and looked away.

Evanston surveyed him calmly, then heaved a large sigh.

"I know you don't think I understand, but I do," he said, sliding the tumbler towards William, then retrieving a glass for himself. "But rather than viewing this as the aristocracy cornering you in a ballroom, you need to see it as a strategic move on your part, designed to—"

"I can tell myself anything I like," he said sharply, cutting him off, "and don't think I haven't tried. But I was *in the carriage* too, Thomas. My scars are not visible, but still they show. This isn't simply a matter of losing family and moving on. It's a matter of losing control, and of those selfish bastards finding any sign of my struggle so *vastly* entertaining!"

Throwing his glass down, it shattered loudly despite the carpet on the floor. The amber contents splashed out unceremoniously to soak the ground, and silence hung heavy in the air as he and Evanston stared down at the messy aftermath of his temper. William ran a hand impatiently over his face.

"Christ."

Thomas leaned casually towards the wall to tug on the bellpull. Then he came close again to grip William's shoulder.

"You will not be able to exert perfect control over every situation. This is a truth you need to accept."

William rolled his eyes. "Says the man who can command a room, and everyone in it, simply by entering." He sighed. "Besides, you know this is different."

"Not true," Thomas corrected. "It is more similar than you know. My success in navigating society comes from being adaptable. By changing course to suit what the situation demands, not the other way around."

"And given the reality of what this situation demands of me and my inability to provide it, I am changing course by *not going to this ball*."

Even as he spoke, he knew his friend was right. But being out among society was not the effortless exercise of his past. With no notice at all, he could get pulled back into the carriage to relive his family's final moments. It was a risk he was, quite simply, unwilling to take.

Evanston squeezed his shoulder, bringing him back to the present. A crooked smile brightened his face.

"Fine. Perhaps it is best for you to skip the ball tonight."

William laughed weakly in spite of himself. "I believe I already knew that."

"Not a word more," said Thomas with a shake of his head. "Only come with me to Brooks's. You can distract yourself at the card tables."

He scoffed at his friend's suggestion. "Surely you must be joking. To roam about London after declining to show at the ball? That would not help matters in the least."

"No, I suppose not." Evanston's grin lingered. "What about a woman? They can sometimes be the most effective kind of distraction."

William shrugged out of his black tailcoat, ready to make a biting retort, when his footman Matthew appeared in the doorway.

"You rang, my lord?"

He gestured to the crystal shards surrounded by a pool of liquor, now almost completely absorbed into the dark cerulean carpet. "I have made a mess, Matthew. Please have it cleaned up immediately. Also, please have Lord Evanston's carriage brought back around as he'll be leaving shortly."

The viscount's eyebrows shot up. "Have I done something to offend you?" he asked with a laugh, although clearly worried.

"Not at all, but it's obvious you've got other places you'd rather be," William answered heavily, "and I am suddenly very tired."

The two friends shook hands firmly. Evanston lowered his voice.

"Shall we return to Kent tomorrow?"

William hung his head in silence, his teeth clenched.

Thomas nodded succinctly. "Tomorrow it is, then. There will be other balls, William," he added reassuringly. "You'll see, all will be well."

And while he nodded in agreement, the Earl of Ashworth did not feel overly optimistic.

Clara sighed and folded her gloved hands carefully upon her lap while gazing longingly at the couples waltzing by on the dance floor. After her failure of a season, she had no delusions of actually securing a suitor, but what she wouldn't do for just a *dance* . . . she loved to dance.

As she had expected, the disgrace of Lucy's elopement had made association with the Mayfield family not only undesirable, but unthinkable. Dressed in all her finery, Clara had spent the duration of her season in the stuffy drawing rooms and ballrooms of London ignored, relegated to standing alone in corners or seated against various walls.

Well, not quite alone. Because of Lucy's chance meeting with her lowborn beau, her father was taking no risks. The constant watchful eye of her mother ensured there would not be a repeat of the scandal that had claimed her older sister, and this last great ball in Mayfair was certainly no exception.

It wasn't that Clara didn't have anything to offer as a prospective bride. She certainly had wealth as the heiress to the Mayfield banking fortune, and knew her looks were tolerable. So it had stung all the more when invitations to balls and soirées had dwindled, her letters received fewer replies, and more women went out of their way to avoid calling on her socially. Friends she'd known for years had turned their backs on her, even going so far as to shun her in public. She longed to rage at them for their bad manners and fickle ways, but sternly forced herself to smile instead, unwilling to expose her family to the additional ridicule that an outburst would bring.

The lack of gentleman callers was also not a surprise, but she hadn't grasped the dire truth of her situation until recently. By then, her parents had been left to calculate their mounting losses on this massive waste of a season, and Clara could finally envision the stark reality of her future—living as a spinster, alone and childless, with not even her sister to confide in.

Her head began to ache, and she stole a covert glance at her mother. Like Clara, Mrs. Mayfield was fair skinned with dark hair. They even shared the same dark eyes, and right now those eyes were staring unseeingly at the lavish gala before them. Not for the last time, guilt wracked through Clara. Her parents were good people. The *ton* was cruel and took an almost gleeful satisfaction in the Mayfield's misfortune, but she knew they were not selective. Any ill-fated family would have been shunned just the same, though this did not lessen the sting of it.

In fact, another target had emerged during the course of the evening. Clara had overheard a barrage of offended whispers between the lords and ladies in attendance, relating that the Earl of Ashworth had chosen not to attend tonight despite accepting the initial invitation. Aside from what they considered to be his unforgivable rudeness was their peevish discontent at being denied the opportunity to view the man, who had recently suffered an awful family tragedy.

It was mentioned too—by more than a few disgruntled women—that he was rather attractive, although Clara did not see these people as true authorities on the matter. Often enough, even if a titled bachelor was old and portly but still possessed all his natural teeth, they would consider him to be exceptionally handsome. Still, she did feel a sense of gratitude to the man for allowing her to share the hateful spotlight for a change.

Tired of overthinking the *ton* and their ways, Clara turned to her mother. "Would you like something at the refreshments table, Mama?" she asked, touching her arm lightly.

Her mother jerked, as if suddenly awoken, then smiled feebly at her. "Yes, that would be lovely. It is rather hot in here."

The pair rose to stand, and made their way into the refreshment room, which was currently empty, save one older gentleman, who was standing nearby with a steaming cup of negus. Clara couldn't bear the potent smell of the spiced port drink, and quickly directed her mother towards the lemonade and ices at the far end of the table. Glancing furtively in the man's direction, she realized she knew him. Gray head, no whiskers, slightly rotund physique. A widower. She had seen him often during the course of the season—he tended to leer at her when he thought her attention was occupied elsewhere. However, despite his seeming fixation on her, he had followed suit with the *ton* and remained distant, never once condescending to ask Clara for a dance. Yet his presence now put her on edge, the fine hairs on the back of her neck lifting as they might in the oppressive quiet before a thunderstorm.

Her mother leaned over. "Baron Rutherford," she whispered.

Clara nodded in confirmation and a shudder passed through her. His eyes alighted with recognition and he began walking towards them. She tensed her shoulders; there was nothing to be done except endure the uncomfortable exchange as best she could. Resolute, she pasted a waxen smile on her face and curtsied politely beside her mother.

He bowed. "Mrs. Mayfield, what a delight . . . and Miss Mayfield." He focused his attention on Clara, and she noticed an almost predatory gleam in his eyes. It was as if he were hunting in the woods rather than seeking a bride in a civilized London ballroom. "Why, you haven't been dancing. I won't stand to see you tucked away in the refreshment room during the final ball of the season. Allow me the honor." He extended a mottled hand.

It wasn't a request so much as a command. Clara could feel her eyes narrowing at his show of superiority, made worse by the indelicate reference to her lack of dance partners. Mrs. Mayfield flushed, but stood silently by, waiting for her daughter's reaction to this rare invitation to dance. While Clara longed to refuse the baron, it could not reasonably be done without fear of mortifying her mother, and her mother had been through enough this year already.

She tipped an icy smile in his direction. "If it pleases you, my lord," she forced out.

Accepting his proffered arm, they approached the dance floor. Clara glanced over her shoulder to her mother, who waved in encouragement, although the confusion in her eyes was somewhat less encouraging. She was probably trying to understand why a titled gentleman would now show interest in her daughter after a long season of snubbing her.

Rutherford led her out onto the floor, ignoring the flurry of disbelieving looks from those nearby, and launched into a waltz upon the first notes from the orchestra. His clasp on her waist was noticeably tight, as was his grip on her hand. Surprised, Clara glanced upwards to find him smiling hungrily down at her. The sight was disconcerting to say the least.

"My lord, is it absolutely necessary to—"

His hands tightened further, shocking her into silence in mid-sentence.

"Perhaps you are wondering why I might wish to dance with you now," he offered. "Particularly when an association with your family is considered so highly undesirable."

Clara's mouth fell open in offense. "I wouldn't want you to blacken your good name on my account. Pray, let me relieve you from such a *trying* act of generosity . . ."

She did not wish to create a scene, but her own sense of self-worth prevented her from blithely accepting his insults. She pushed against him again and he retaliated by jerking her closer. The cloyingly sweet smell of negus on his breath engulfed her and she turned her head to the side, gasping for air while trying to create more distance between them. All efforts were futile, though, and he continued forcing her to dance while leaning down to whisper in her ear.

"I have watched you these many months, Miss Mayfield. And I have waited. Tomorrow I will pay a visit to your beleaguered parents to make an offer for your hand. It is an offer they will accept, for the season has ended and your prospects are dire."

The baron whirled her around into a dizzying turn before she could respond, and her stomach lurched. Her eyes searched desperately for her mother, who was craning her neck to find them through the mass of dancing couples and frothy skirts. Clara knew that she was likely not able to see Rutherford's behavior from where she stood. She glared angrily up at him.

"Even were it so, I will never accept you as my husband."

He smiled. "Oh, you will accept me, my dove. Perhaps in time you will come to realize how very little control you have over the situation. It is of no importance, either way. In fact," he added, his voice lowering, "a little resistance might make things more enjoyable, if I may be so bold."

Shocked beyond belief, Clara wrestled out of his grip.

"You've had months to pay your courtesies, and this is how you choose to make overtures? With insults and threats and . . . detestable imaginings?"

The ladies and gentlemen surrounding them began to slow the pace of their dancing, immediately drawn to the commotion. Her cheeks burned at the unwanted attention, but it was minimal when compared to the fire of her sudden hatred for the baron. He took a step towards her. She immediately took a step back.

"I am not interested in making overtures, Miss Mayfield. You will consent to being my wife or your family will be ruined."

She scoffed. "I will consent to nothing of the sort."

The baron simply chuckled. As the music came to an end, he sketched a bow in her direction, and Clara spun on her heel, rushing off the floor into the relative safety of her mother's arms.

Clara paced fretfully in the parlor of the Mayfields' country home in Essex. Six weeks had passed since the night the baron had made his insulting offer—and yet the time since had been more awful still, something she wouldn't have thought possible.

Of course, she also wouldn't have thought it possible for her father to actually agree to marry her off to the baron, yet here she was on the eve of their wedding, the preparations having been hastened along by her husband-to-be. He was in the drawing room this very moment, preening and posturing before her parents in his penultimate moment of victory. As much as she loathed to admit it, he'd been right about everything. The state of her family's reputation being what it was, there had been no true alternative in the end. Rutherford had easily been able to force her father's hand, for denying the baron what he wanted could only damage the family further, while her marriage to him could repair it.

Her father chose to view the situation in a more optimistic light than Clara could, entreating her to give the baron a chance to prove himself a worthy husband. However, the season had afforded him many chances already, and he had shown plainly what kind of man he was.

Absently, she swiped at her cheek, then gazed down at the moisture on her hand. She hadn't been aware that she was crying. She'd shed enough tears to last a lifetime these past months, first with the loss of her sister, and now with the loss of her own free will. At least Lucy had found love—she reminded herself of that. But oh, the cost . . .

There was a discreet tap on the door. She rushed over to crack open the portal to reveal the white-capped head of her lady's maid, Abigail, holding a cup of coffee. Clara admitted her inside the parlor before they could be seen, then closed the door securely behind. Abigail set the steaming beverage down on a table and reached out to clutch Clara's shaking hands tightly in her own.

"The preparations have been made. My sister, Amelia, has agreed to provide a reference to the housekeeper at Lawton Park, although I did not give her the particulars of your identity. I only told her you were a capable housemaid from the Mayfield estate in search of work in Kent."

Clara regarded her anxiously. "And if they should turn me away?"

"I don't think they will," replied Abigail with a thoughtful shake of her head. "Amelia has commented on the understaffed conditions there for quite some time."

She chewed on her lip. "And the master there is kind?"

"From what I have heard, the Earl of Ashworth is . . . a bit of a recluse," Abigail replied. "But I believe him to be fair."

Clara nodded, but she had known this already. She had remembered the rage of his fellow aristocrats when he had backed out of the ball in Mayfair. His solitary ways were one of the reasons she'd even considered fleeing to his estate. Without the constant risk of having a master who enjoyed entertaining and throwing balls, safeguarding her secrecy would be easier.

Abigail paused in conflicted silence. "You'll tell me if you change your mind?"

Clara pulled her close in a familial embrace. Over the years, Abigail had become so much more than just a maid. She had become a close friend, and Clara would miss her almost as much as she missed Lucy. She hugged her tightly. "There's no chance of that," she whispered.

Another knock sounded on the door, causing the two women to spring apart. Clara smoothed her skirts and cast a nervous glance at Abigail.

"Yes?" she called out.

Mrs. Mayfield appeared. She gave a brief nod to the maid, and with a last departing glance at Clara, Abigail left the room. Her mother stared after her curiously.

"What was Abigail doing in here?"

Clara froze in panic for just a moment, before remembering her coffee. She strode to the table to retrieve the cup and saucer.

"She brought me coffee while I waited, Mama." She took a sip of the warm, lightly sweet drink. Clara had always preferred coffee, and this was perfect, just the way she liked it.

Cream with two lumps of sugar. It reminded her of how comfortable her home—her life—had been. Her heart clenched at the thought of leaving it.

She returned the cup to its saucer, the china rattling noisily in response to the trembling of her fingers. "Do you have news?" she asked, attempting nonchalance but feeling the full burden of her guilt.

"Yes, my dear," Mrs. Mayfield answered lightly. "They are ready for you in the drawing room."

Her heart began to race and her stomach roiled. It didn't matter that she had no intention of marrying the vile Lord Rutherford. Just the thought of seeing him, smirking and self-congratulatory, was enough to cause an adverse physical reaction.

She set her drink down on the table again. Otherwise, she might have been tempted to toss it in the baron's face. Extending her hand, she tried to smile at her mother.

"Shall we go in together?"

Moments later, they entered the drawing room. Both Mr. Mayfield and Rutherford stood to greet the ladies, although Clara did not approach the man or even look at him, electing instead to seat herself on the farthest edge of the settee across from his chair. She stared stubbornly down at her hands and an awkward silence ensued, which was finally broken by her father's rumbling baritone.

"Lord Rutherford," said Mr. Mayfield. "I am very pleased we could come to a mutually beneficial arrangement. Very pleased . . ." His great moustache absorbed any final murmurs on the subject.

Clara's fingers tightly gripped the dark emerald velvet upholstery as she listened silently, finally raising her gaze to evaluate the situation. Her fiancé sat opposite her, triumphant in his crisp attire that did nothing to conceal his bloated form. Mutually beneficial, Clara understood, was a relative term, one that excluded her entirely.

Baron Rutherford flicked an invisible speck off his perfectly pressed pants. "It seems we have, Mr. Mayfield," he drawled. "Your daughter will make me the happiest of men, I'm sure."

"Yes, my lord—such a handsome match," said Mrs. Mayfield. "It will inevitably be the talk of *le bon ton* . . ."

If there was to be any talk within high society about their match, it would likely not be flattering. Another titled old widower, his estate destitute after years of improvident financial decisions, finds a wealthy young wife to refill his family's coffers—almost certainly to drain them again.

What a tale for the ages, thought Clara.

It was strange to feel so helpless. Clara ached to confide in her sister, but the last thing she wanted to do was give Lucy any reason to worry on her account.

As if sensing Clara's despair, Abigail skirted by the door, giving Clara a nod of support as she passed. If their plans succeeded, it might allow Clara to live life on her own terms versus getting crushed beneath the baron's bootheel. It would also mean hiding in service until Lord Rutherford either remarried or died, but under these dire circumstances, she was determined to be eternally patient. Although if this scheme failed, which was a distinct possibility, it could mean a life of ill-repute—further ill-repute, rather—and destitution.

Or worse, returning home to be claimed by her enraged fiancé.

She sank lower into the cushions, wishing she could disappear. Every second felt more suffocating than the last, and while the men discussed the particulars of the arrangement, Clara passed time by studying the gleaming hardwood floor and the ornate golden rug that lay upon it. She knew her parents wished only for their remaining daughter to make an uneventful, but advantageous, marriage, to dispel the smoke of Lucy's scandal and return their lives to normal.

Rutherford had laid his trap well, silently waiting for its jaws to spring closed around Clara as if she were some unfortunate animal.

The baron's gravelly voice grew louder, disrupting her melancholy train of thought.

"You look lovely today, Miss Mayfield."

Before thinking better of it, she glanced up to see his mouth curved upwards in what could only be described as a leer. It did not surprise her that he was enjoying her discomfort. Clara merely disregarded his compliment with a dismissive raise of her brows. His steely gray gaze sharpened.

"So, my lord, the arrangements are all in place for the wedding," said her mother abruptly in an awkward attempt at conversation. "We've hired an orchestra, and the weather should be fine, so we will have tables and chairs on the back lawn—"

"That sounds delightful, Mrs. Mayfield," interrupted the baron without taking his eyes off his betrothed.

Clara's mother could certainly detect the simmering hostility, but persevered anyway. "Clara's dress is beautiful and just arrived yesterday. I had it made in Paris at this wonderful little shop . . . they even rushed to finish it in time. No expense spared," she said proudly. "White satin and lace, with tiny pearls . . ."

Mrs. Mayfield trailed off as she observed her daughter's increased pallor. Clara squirmed uncomfortably, aware that she had begun to sweat. She tried to discreetly wipe her palms on the couch. What would happen if she jumped up and started yelling gibberish while waving her hands about? Would they care that she had been driven to such madness? Even better, would it end this farce of an engagement?

"And what of you, Miss Mayfield? Are you *prepared*?" He was no longer even trying to sound friendly. Clara knew he wanted to intimidate her, but it was shocking that he was doing it openly in front of her parents.

"I prefer not to think about it," she snapped, and was rewarded with her father's sharp intake of breath, but she refused to feel badly for being impolite. Her only regret in all this was that her behavior vexed her parents, although they would be more than vexed by tomorrow morning for sure . . .

Suddenly Clara felt ill. She stood abruptly.

"May I be excused?" she asked, hoping not to cast her crumpets in front of the baron. He'd be certain to take that a sign that he'd won.

Her mother's brow wrinkled in a flash of concern before arching once more with a forced smile. "No, my darling," she replied in a soothing tone. "You must stay until we are finished speaking with Lord Rutherford."

Slowly, Clara sat back down on the couch and smoothed

her skirts, trying to hide her trembling hands. She looked up and caught the baron watching her every movement. It made her shudder.

"Forgive her, my lord. Clara has always been an unconventional girl," her father excused. "She takes great interest in matters of the estate. Why, I've often discovered her making rounds with my land steward, much to my dismay," he admitted with a chuckle. "But she does enjoy getting her hands dirty every now and then."

Rutherford scoffed. "She is a girl no longer, and will certainly not be getting her hands dirty on my estate. I expect her to behave as a baroness should."

Clara's eyes narrowed to slits. He would seek to control everything about her, she was sure.

Mr. Mayfield blinked, then continued. "Certainly, my lord. You will find Clara to be a cheerful and complacent bride despite the quirks of her personality. It may take time, but love so often does."

The thought of *love* with such a man made her skin crawl.

"She can be willful, but indeed wouldn't you say that is part of her charm, my lord?" added her mother.

Clara glanced at the baron, who trapped her gaze.

"Indeed," he said with a mirthless smile that shook her to her core. He rose abruptly, and Mr. and Mrs. Mayfield struggled to stand quickly as well. Clara stood hopefully, ready to dash out the door, but her fiancé stayed her with a look. "I'd like to have a word alone with my bride now, if you please."

Her father nodded and bowed, quickly escorting Mrs. Mayfield towards the door. "Certainly, my lord."

Clara shot a pleading look at her mother, whose brow furrowed slightly just as the door closed between them. She didn't think her mother fully grasped her abhorrence of this man. Attempting a brave countenance, she cleared her throat and faced Rutherford, who stared at her in barely concealed rancor. A jolt of alarm shook her already unsteady frame.

Perhaps a little politeness might hasten this meeting along. She attempted to switch tactics.

"Would you like a drink?" she asked lightly, approaching the sideboard.

His expression remained unchanged. "No. I would not." She did not hear him step across the carpet, but suddenly his voice was right near her ear. "I want my wits about me when you finally submit."

Immediately, all thoughts of politeness vanished. She whirled around. "Well then, I suppose you're giving up drinking altogether?"

His teeth clenched noticeably, but he only smiled. "It will take far less time than you think, pet. And I will enjoy every second." He regarded her. "Tell me, how does it feel to know you are already mine? Is it upsetting to see how eagerly your father accepted my proposal, as I'd told you he would?"

"I am not yours," Clara seethed, her fingers curling into fists. "And as for my father, I think he ended up having very little choice in the matter."

"By design. While you waited on the edges, hoping for someone, *anyone*, to court you during the season, I was watching in anticipation. Reveling in your every rejection." He closed the final distance between them and seized her shoulders in a punishing grip. "You will learn to yield. You will learn to be grateful. Especially in my bed—"

Before she could even flinch, he crushed his mouth against hers. Clara cried in revulsion and raised her fists against his chest, and once again she was surprised at the strength a man of his age could possess. She struggled to twist her face away, but he followed each way she turned. At last, he released her, and she took a step backwards to slap him soundly across the face. He instantly countered by grabbing her throat and squeezing tightly.

"You will learn to yield," he repeated slowly.

She clawed at his hand, struggling to breathe and eyes blown wide with panic.

"Stop," she rasped. "Please—"

The vice-like pressure around her neck was removed, and she fell against the wall, gulping in huge breaths of air.

"See?" he spat, tugging on his jacket. "You're learning already."

He proceeded across the room to throw open the door without giving her another glance. Clara massaged her neck, her thoughts hurtling wildly. She was supposed to be safe here. This was her family's drawing room, her home, where she and Lucy had played as children, and had grown into womanhood.

Her gaze flitted across the familiar paintings, her favorite green settee, the heavy patterned draperies beside the windows. It all felt wrong now, somehow. As if his violation of her here had challenged her very notion of home.

It needed to be safe. *She* needed to be safe.

Clara's resolve to flee grew stronger. Seeing what he was truly like, she couldn't help but wonder if Rutherford's previous wife had exited this world in an effort to escape his cruelty—or if he had sent her packing early.

She would not be lingering to discover the truth of it for herself.

Clara felt nearly blind in the darkness, but could see the soft rays of moonlight illuminate the gleaming satin of her wedding dress. It hung silently in the corner of her room like the hovering wraith of the bride she was to become.

She sat perched on the edge of her bed, had sat there for many hours, listening to the sound of crickets chirping outside. She had once thought the crickets' song sweet, but after listening tonight it somehow sounded sad; like the end of summer, like a hundred tiny good-byes.

Clara was wearing one of Abigail's dresses. Definitely not normal nighttime attire, but this was not a normal night. It was the end of a long struggle for her. The struggle of wanting to do right by her family, but incapable of sacrificing herself to the baron to do it.

She wished he'd been a different man. Maybe then she could have made peace with her fate. Remorse coursed through her. Standing, she went to her desk. She opened a drawer with unsteady hands and unfolded the letter inside.

I cannot do this. I'm sorry. I love you.
—Clara

The room became blurry with fresh tears as she refolded the note and pinned it to her wedding dress for her mother to find. She was careful not to damage the delicate fabric, for despite her complaints against the groom, the gown really was beautiful.

Clara loved her parents, and knew they had been devastated by Lucy's marriage. What was more, she knew they missed her, and longed to see the daughter they had lost. Their world would shatter one more time tomorrow morning upon discovering Clara's own flight from home, and while she wished to avoid causing them more pain and humiliation, she could not see how.

Leaning over, she retrieved a small satchel and her coin purse of saved funds. As she did, she caught sight of herself in her looking glass. Haunted eyes, her mother's eyes, admonished her in the gloom. Surely she didn't have the strength to break from the only family she'd known and loved. There was no guarantee that the strange world outside would have any more love for her, after all . . .

She touched the faint bruise the baron had left on her throat and turned abruptly.

She did not have the luxury, or the time, for second thoughts.

Shaking her head to clear it, she strode swiftly across her room and threw open the windows. The fragrant breeze of late summer engulfed her as she leaned out, one of her tears making the jump before she did to the carefully sculpted greenery below.

Chapter Two

Clara rubbed her aching hips as she jostled about the wooden grocery cart. It had taken time for her internal emotional storm to dissipate, but once it had, she had mostly enjoyed it, much to her surprise. True, the coach ride had been grueling, and the passengers with their various personalities—and smells—had been interesting and, at times, unpleasant. But each town they passed served as a reminder of the choice she had knowingly made for herself and the freedom that came with that choice.

Her companion was a grocery merchant named George. An older man, he'd proven to be an entertaining companion on her trip south into Kent. She'd been lucky enough to meet him upon her arrival in London, and he had easily agreed to convey her to Lawton Park as it was very near his own destination. During the trip, he had regaled her with tales of fanciful local lore, not the least of which was the story of how the current Earl of Ashworth had gained his title.

She had listened in horror as the old man told of the carriage accident that had taken the earl's father, older brother, and brother-in-law. In one cruel fell swoop, the family had lost its patriarch and its heir, leaving the only surviving son injured, traumatized, and contemplating how to run an estate he had never thought would be his responsibility or his burden. His now widowed sister had endured struggles of her own, raising her child in Hampshire alone while simultaneously mourning the loss of not just her husband, but also so many of her other loved ones.

As could be expected after such a tragedy, the new earl had withdrawn from society, choosing to reside exclusively at his country manor, seeming content to shun the outside world in favor of the solitude of his estate.

It was the earl who occupied Clara's solemn thoughts when the cart finally rolled into the bustling village near Lawton Park. She couldn't help but wonder about the man, and the isolation that was his constant companion. Was he a pale and sickly sort, withering away alone in his study? She couldn't bring herself to ask George, as any further interest in the details would seem like ghoulish indifference to this man's sufferings.

George tapped her hand with the reins and grinned. "We're nearly there, miss. Thought I'd stop in for a pint before we go the rest of the way," he said, nodding towards the pub nearby. "Would ye care to join me?"

The day was warm, and any further delay only meant prolonging her anxiety. Clara knew she was likely to be poor company because of it. She blotted the sweat from her brow and smiled at the merchant.

"No, thank you. I think I'll take a short walk instead."

He gave her a wink, his silver eyelashes glinting in the afternoon sunlight. "Suit yourself."

The man hopped down off the cart to land in the dusty street, helping Clara to disembark before continuing into the pub. Left alone there on the street, the feeling she'd been trying to ignore since running away came alive once again— the sense that she did not belong in this place. That her life had taken an unfamiliar and dangerous turn.

She placed a hand on her belly and took a deep breath. Soon, she would actually be inquiring for employment in the Earl of Ashworth's grand country house. It had not been an outcome she had foreseen for her life, but she was grateful for the chance, nonetheless.

Clara walked down to view the quaint little shops that lined the road, until reaching a small but plentiful outdoor market. Vendors called out to those milling through the stands, and she spent a good amount of time weaving through the people, her nervousness forgotten, fascinated at both their way of life and the wares they were offering. It was not an opportunity much afforded to a wealthy heiress under normal circumstances, and it was partly why she had so enjoyed her surreptitious outings with her father's land steward.

What coin she brought with her she would need to save, especially until she had secured a position at Lawton Park. She smiled apologetically to the vendors she passed and began making her way back to the pub. It had been nearly twenty minutes, and she couldn't imagine drinking a pint of ale could take much longer than that.

Clara walked back down the street, thoughtfully gazing down at the coarse, brown fabric of Abigail's dress as her walking boots pushed it out in front of her. She realized how much she would miss the flattering fits and sheer, silky fabrics of her old dresses. She supposed such a thing hadn't occurred to her before in her panic to escape the baron, and part of her felt ashamed at even having the thought so quickly after leaving her family. But still she felt wistful, thinking of the beautiful gowns, now hanging abandoned, in her armoire at home.

Frowning, she reminded herself that not only had all her efforts during the season been a complete waste, but her fine dresses had only succeeded in attracting the most vile man she'd ever met. Better to wrap up in a burlap sack and be free of him, she thought moodily, giving the ground an extra little kick.

The loud noise of an oncoming carriage startled her from her musings. The driver yelled in warning, yanking on his reins, horses whinnying frantically . . . and all she could do was stare at the approaching vehicle in panic, rooted to the spot.

There's no time—

Suddenly, she was knocked out of the way to land on the hard ground, with her rescuer tucking her tightly against his body to protect her from the brunt of the fall. He landed beside her with a grunt, and though his efforts had spared her the worst of it, the impact was still a shock. She curled up, her eyes squeezed shut, cradling her dizzy head in her hands.

"What on earth were you thinking? You could have been killed!" her savior raged, pushing away and rising swiftly to his knees. "You weren't even looking . . ."

The incensed timbre of his voice trailed off into silence while her head pounded madly. Clara heard him panting, then he broke off and swore before shifting into a crouch behind her. To her surprise, he reached forward to help pull her into a seated position. The feel of this stranger at her back with his hands warm and strong upon her caused her eyes to fly open. Pressed linen and a spicy, masculine scent radiated off of him with the heat of his exertion, and she found herself inhaling greedily.

A new awareness flooded her shaky limbs. One that made her wonder what would happen if she were to lean back and sink even farther against him.

"Try to relax," he instructed, sounding contrite. His hand stroked her back in what she guessed was an attempt to soothe her, but her body rebelled, spreading fire and chaos at even his lightest touch. Her breathing stopped as he leaned in closer. "You'll be all right."

She nodded, but it was hard to be calm with a man touching her this way, let alone one who smelled so delicious, with a deep voice that was affecting her, regardless of the circumstances. Clara turned within the circle of his arms to view him, sending her pulse immediately rocketing out of control.

He was the most handsome man she'd ever seen.

Clara gasped and pushed away. She forced herself up to a stand and he rose as well, slowly evaluating her as he did. She noticed with a touch of mortification that a small crowd had gathered during the mayhem, and her eyes flicked back to her savior. She could see by the quality of his attire, now covered in dust, that he was most certainly a gentleman. His dark blond hair was an intriguing combination of golden hues, and his large frame and serious brow caused her stomach to flutter in a way it never had before.

She'd been so busy staring at him that she jumped upon finding the dazzling intensity of his gaze was, likewise, focused on her. His eyes were not simply green, but some fascinating mixture of amber and peridot that made it very hard for her to think straight.

"I b-beg your pardon, sir—" she stammered, trying to ignore the stinging rush of her excitement.

A few laughs erupted from the group surrounding them, and with an annoyed wave of his hand, the group dispersed like scattering ants. He gazed at her earnestly.

"Are you hurt?"

Clara quickly took a mental inventory of her physical condition, discounting the accelerated rate of her breathing and the pleasurable heat that coursed through her limbs, as these things had nothing to do with the accident and everything to do with her sudden attraction to this stranger.

"No, sir," she replied. She continued to stare despite her determination against it.

His shoulders dropped in obvious relief. "Good. But be more careful next time. The streets can be dangerous, even in this little village."

"Yes of course. It was foolish of me not to be paying more attention. And thank you for . . . your help," she added awkwardly. Clara caught sight of a white cap on the ground, buried in an inch of dirt. Her fingers raised to touch her hair, verifying its absence, then she bent down swiftly to retrieve it. A hot tide of embarrassment flooded her cheeks and she dipped into a hasty curtsy in an attempt to end the conversation before she humiliated herself even further.

The man looked at her then, curiously, his lips parted as if to ask her a question. He stared as if transfixed, his gaze warm and alight with a hint of confusion. Then his mouth snapped shut and he gave her a terse nod. With an authoritative tug on his jacket to send a cloud of dust aloft, he turned on his heel and walked away, leaving Clara feeling strangely alone. She stood there, admiring the powerful athleticism of his build and his confident stride, somehow saddened at the thought of never seeing him again, when she suddenly remembered George.

With a start, she whirled around to dash across the road, after looking both ways of course. He was just exiting the pub, blinking in the midday sun as he looked for her.

"George!" she called, waving her cap. "I'm here!"

His eyes found her and they crinkled in confounded amusement. "Now this is a sight to behold! What have ye been doing while I was away that would put ye in such a sorry state?"

She laughed dismissively and swatted at her filthy skirts. "Nothing important. It was just a little fall."

Clara climbed back onto the cart for the final leg of her journey, her gaze unwittingly searching for a glimpse of the dashing stranger. To her considerable disappointment, he was nowhere to be found.

The first thing Clara noticed upon arriving at Lawton Park was the stunning splendor of the place. Surrounded by rolling green fields, a creek to the west and a lush forest to the east, the house itself was a jewel in an already immaculate crown. Abigail had attempted to describe it to her before, but had failed utterly. Such beauty and grandeur could not truly be quantified. Whereas her home in Silvercreek had been lovely, this grand estate was beyond comprehension.

Green ivy writhed and climbed the gold-colored stones of the house. It looked stately and dignified at this moment, but Clara knew in less than a month the ivy would transform into a dazzling autumnal red, surrounding the house in brilliant color. The lawn was flawless and immense. To the sides she could see perfect paths carved into gardens full of flowering shrubs, rosebushes and green hedges. Taking a leisurely stroll through these carefully tended grounds would be paradise, but of course, she would not have the freedom here to enjoy leisurely strolls.

She was jostled about as the cart trundled its way slowly up the drive, and the horses whickered as they sensed the end of their journey was near. George snapped the reins and the animals ambled towards the service entrance at the rear, where they pulled up under a beautiful old archway located between the stables and the house.

Clara stepped down from the cart and took a moment to ensure her hair was neatly tucked beneath her cap, now firmly re-affixed to her head. She found she was nervous and excited all at once, but she didn't indulge any sort of foolish thinking. This new way of life was going to be grueling and uncomfortable, more difficult than anything she had ever experienced. But at the very least, she would not be mistreated at the hands of Baron Rutherford.

And maybe, one day, she would see her family again. Maybe they could even forgive her for leaving.

Clara gave herself a shake. She certainly couldn't afford to bother with regret or thoughts of her family right now. She needed to secure employment at this grand house, and it was going to take a bit of convincing since she had no written character to submit to the housekeeper. All she had, and it wasn't much, was the anticipated referral from Abigail's sister, who was a housemaid at Lawton Park.

Of course, the girl had no idea who Clara truly was. Abigail had simply disclosed that a fellow housemaid was seeking new employment.

George turned to her. "Would you like me to bring you in?"

"Are you familiar with the staff here?" she asked, surprised.

He grinned. She could envision him as the handsome man he must have been in his youth, smiling in that same charming way.

"Miss, I come by here every Sunday with my wagon. Mrs. Humboldt has a weekly order for me, so I know these folks well. Now let me carry that bag for you."

He gently took the satchel from her hands, turned and limped along the gravel pathway with grace that belied his age. Clara followed him, her stomach suddenly twisting into knots.

They passed a glorious kitchen garden on their way to the

service entrance, and the air was deliciously scented with the smells of ripe vegetables and sun-warmed herbs. She caught sight of bright red tomatoes, bushy clumps of green rosemary, and the protruding tufts of carrots before she was descending stone steps towards the back entrance of Lawton Park.

Clara watched with trepidation as the large wooden door opened with a creak. A tall, lanky girl with large blue eyes poked her head out briefly, then swung the door wide open.

"George!" she exclaimed loudly. She threw her arms around him in a friendly embrace. "It's not your usual day. What are you doing here?"

"Well, I'm on a bit of a charitable errand today," he said, then stepped back to reveal Clara behind him. "Found this one in London needing a ride here to the estate, so figured I'd be of service."

The girl looked surprised, then said shyly, "Oh, hello."

"Hello. It's nice to meet you." Clara liked her immediately and smiled warmly at her.

"Well, are you going to let him in, Gilly? For God's sake . . ." came an annoyed voice from further inside. The girl jumped and instantly retreated the way she had come, into a massive kitchen and to the side of a solid-looking woman. They both stared at Clara from behind a wooden counter piled high with peeled root vegetables. Copper pots hung from hooks on the ceiling and a huge black stove dominated the entire wall at the far side of the room. Some kind of delicious smelling soup was bubbling away on its top.

"Now Mrs. Humboldt, I've told you about that language." George laughed as he followed Gilly into the kitchen. The cook rolled her eyes but smiled crookedly back at him in good humor.

"Can't help my natural way of speaking, George," said the woman. "I've been cursing since I was in my short skirts." She seemed friendly enough but her eyes were busily scrutinizing Clara. Feeling like a fish out of water, Clara clasped her hands together and focused her gaze at the floor. George interjected before the cook could ask a single question.

"Is Mrs. Malone around? She should be expecting this lass for the vacant housemaid position. Ah, there she is! Mrs. Malone!" he hailed, pointing Clara through the kitchen and towards a long hallway. A woman who was clearly the housekeeper paused, a silhouette in the dim light, and then turned towards them. Her black hair was neatly pinned in place and was matched by her equally well-ordered black dress. A large round keyring jingled merrily on her belt as she moved.

"Ah, George, what's all the fuss about now?" she asked. Her eyes settled on Clara. "Amelia's girl, is it? Gilly, go fetch Amelia, would you?" The woman smiled thinly at Clara as Gilly hurried down the hall. "My name is Mrs. Malone. I trust you had a good journey?"

"Yes ma'am, thank you for asking," said Clara politely.

"You can never tell about the weather in these parts," she said. "This close to the coast, we sometimes get an occasional rainstorm. And all you need when traveling by one of those rickety coaches is to have a wheel get stuck in the mud, or some such nonsense. Now why don't we go to my office and we'll discuss—"

They were interrupted by the sound of a door abruptly opening above them. Footsteps descended the stairs behind them, and both George and Mrs. Malone backed against the wall, dipping into respectful postures. She saw they were being joined by other domestics who, she could only assume, had been going about their business further down in the servants' hall.

They all either bowed or curtsied as a man finally came into view. Clara followed suit and curtsied, then looked up and tried not to choke as her breath caught in her throat.

It was her savior from the village, and he was the Earl of Ashworth.

A thrill raced through her and Clara swayed on her feet. *This* was the man who had decided against going to the Mayfair ball? If he had been there that night, she could only imagine how things could have turned out for her. He hadn't shunned her earlier in the street, dressed as a maid, but had instead treated her like a lady and even risked his own safety to help her. Was it too much to believe, then, that earl might have elected to ignore her sister's scandal and offer his hand for a dance?

Who knew what that could have led to, but instead, she'd been trapped into marriage by the abusive Baron Rutherford, forced to flee her home and seek safety by hiding as a domestic servant.

The injustice of it all was nearly overwhelming. She swallowed hard, trying not to be sick.

Lord Ashworth paused at the base of the stairs and tipped a nod to his staff. His broadcloth jacket was draped across his arm, still dirty from their misadventure in the village, and he glanced over those gathered before him, finally alighting on a brown-haired footman.

"Matthew, I'd like your assistance," he requested, handing over the jacket. "I've had a strange day indeed . . ."

Clara was mesmerized by the fit of his clothes and the ease with which he wore them. Had she envisioned a lord who had been defeated by life's cruel circumstances? This man was tall, with broad shoulders, sandy blond hair, and unfashionably golden skin, clearly browned from time in the sun, which she thought was quite appealing. The earl's features were unique and imperfect, yet perfectly put together. The sharp contours of his cheekbones accentuated his strong jawline, patrician nose, and light eyes, which were that unusual combination of gold and green. He was an active, healthy male, and although it was useless, she couldn't help but wonder again why *he* couldn't have found her in London.

And now it all made sense. Why the villagers had laughed at her addressing him as *sir* . . . the way they had scurried away at the annoyed flick of his hand . . . his powerful reaction to seeing her nearly trampled by a carriage . . .

Suddenly, their eyes met. With a start, she realized she had been staring and averted her eyes as a rapid blush flooded her cheeks with heat. His conversation with the footman faltered, then ceased altogether upon seeing her in his basement.

"You," he called out hoarsely. "Why are you here?"

Clara hadn't yet found her tongue, when Mrs. Malone saved her from certain embarrassment.

"This is the girl inquiring about the vacant position . . . a referral from Amelia, my lord," said the housekeeper as she gestured towards a buxom girl with curly red hair tucked up into a crisp white cap. The girl peered at Clara skeptically—not a good sign—then turned back to the earl.

"My lord," she said while bobbing a curtsy. "My sister, Abigail, has recommended her highly."

Ashworth turned back to Clara, giving her a thorough visual examination while the rest of the staff looked on. The crease between his brows grew deeper.

"Mrs. Malone, let's finish this discussion in my study upstairs," he said to the housekeeper, still staring at Clara. Finally, he glanced away and said to the footman, "We'll deal with my clothes later."

The staff resumed their places as he turned and began climbing back up the stairs. Mrs. Malone appeared taken aback, but shook off the expression and motioned for Clara to follow as she and Amelia started up behind him.

They exited the staircase and passed the telltale green baize door that was the physical separation between the upstairs and downstairs worlds. The boundary between the genteel and the unrefined. She trailed her fingertips along the soft fabric as she went by, remembering her home in Silvercreek and how she had always gotten in trouble for sneaking down to visit Abigail. But here, for some reason, she felt as if trouble awaited her upstairs, on the other side of the door.

Even in her anxious state, Clara noticed the interior of the house was just as breathtaking as the exterior had been.

Hardwood floors were polished to a mirror shine, intricately carved and dust-free woodwork framed the doorways, and exotic antiques and tapestries were artfully placed. Without a doubt, she knew that many of these items had been in the home for generations. The combination of luxury and thoughtful personalization made the rooms appear homey despite the vastness of the house.

The earl entered the study and seated himself behind a burnished oak desk. The room was decorated in muted greens and blues, with bookshelves lining one wall of the room. Clara would have loved to pore through those shelves of texts—reading had been a favorite pastime of hers back at home. With a pang, she realized she'd probably not have the chance, if she even managed to find employment here. Judging from the look on Lord Ashworth's face, that was not at all a certainty.

He gestured for her to stand between Mrs. Malone, who still seemed confused, and Amelia, who appeared sullen. She took her place before him, nervously fidgeting with the hem of her shawl. One slip of her tongue could ruin her best chance of escape and send her packing back to her parents and the baron.

Ashworth looked to Amelia. "You carry the referral for her?"

The girl curtsied and said, "I do, my lord. My sister, Abigail, up in Essex speaks well of her." Then looking at Clara with a touch of disdain said, "Although I personally know nothing about her at all."

Why did she sound so unfriendly? Was it possible that

Clara had vexed her already in the few minutes since arriving? She glanced over at Amelia and was met with a baleful stare. Panic shot through her. It seemed more and more likely this meeting would not end well.

"At which house does your sister work in Essex?" asked the earl.

"She works for the Mayfields of Silvercreek, my lord."

Ashworth nodded in acknowledgment. "Yes, I am familiar with that name. They are a reputable family, I believe," he said, looking to Mrs. Malone for her input, who lowered her chin into a succinct nod.

Meanwhile, Clara's emotions were locked in a fiery internal battle. It was difficult to hear her family discussed so soon after her tumultuous departure, but it was perhaps even more alarming to know that the earl was familiar with them. But of course, why wouldn't he be?

His eyes shifted back to the housemaid. "Thank you, Amelia. You may leave now."

The girl bobbed a curtsy and turned, shooting Clara a hooded glare as she left. When the door clicked shut, the earl turned to her at last. Amber light poured in through the west-facing windows, and she was instantly mesmerized by his eyes, so warm and vibrant. The color was like sunlight shining through a canopy of trees.

Her mouth went dry. How could the household staff possibly act normal around this man?

"What is your name?" he asked. His voice was low but his singular eyes were alert, watching her. He subjected her to the same visual evaluation she had received from the cook earlier, but instead of being embarrassed, she felt something else entirely. Self-conscious. Hot. The heat stirred wherever his gaze went, and his gaze seemed to be going everywhere.

She was about to make a fool of herself simply because he was *looking* at her.

He cleared his throat, waiting for her to answer. Of course she had come up with many names, any of them suitable for an alias. But in her current situation, with him staring at her, her mind had gone completely blank.

Think. Think!

Frantically, she glanced at the texts on the bookshelves for an idea, anything, that might work. A weathered copy of *The Iliad* caught her eye.

"My name is Helen," she said, then immediately winced at the irony of adopting the name of the most desired woman in history.

"I see. And Helen, am I to believe you have no character reference of your own? Merely the attestation of a housemaid from Silvercreek?" he asked incredulously. "Were you sacked?"

"N-no, my lord," she stammered, taken aback by the blunt question.

"Who was your employer?"

A bead of sweat rolled down her back, and she avoided his gaze by staring at the floor. "That information would be of no benefit since they chose not to provide me with a reference."

She raised her eyes just in time to see his eyebrows shoot up. The earl straightened in his chair while Mrs. Malone shuffled uncomfortably behind her.

"Why did you leave?"

Clara felt a variation of the truth might be the most believable lie to tell. "There was a disagreement between myself and the lady of the house. We chose to part ways, and she elected not to provide a reference when I left."

"Who are you to disagree with the lady of the house?" he asked, his voice a deep rumble.

She thought of her mother, and said nothing.

Ashworth was staring at her. He stared at Mrs. Malone. Then he picked up a pen and a stack of papers and began shuffling through them.

"No," he said.

With that, he lowered his head to focus on his work, effectively ending the conversation.

The single word reverberated through the quietness of the study. It took Clara a moment to realize he had just denied her employment. She and Mrs. Malone stood there, dumbstruck, then both began speaking in a panic.

"Please, my lord!" she beseeched. "I beg you to reconsider ..."

"My lord, normally you know I agree with you in all matters, but we are extremely understaffed at the moment . . ." added Mrs. Malone.

Ashworth glanced up sharply and they fell silent.

"I suppose," he said to Mrs. Malone, "you are going to tell me how we are supposed to hire a girl with no real references, other than the word of a housemaid and her own confession that she caused trouble at her last place of employment."

"I never knowingly caused trouble, my lord," she replied desperately, stretching her hands out in appeal. Ashworth leveled a finger in her direction.

"You. Stay quiet," he said fiercely.

She was taken aback by the force of his reaction. Tears pricked at her eyes and she swallowed hard, knotting her hands behind her back.

"Well," said the housekeeper, "you make an excellent point, my lord. However, the Mayfields are a reputable family and the maid there would be risking her employment by providing a false character reference for this young woman."

Indeed, Abigail had risked everything to provide this referral for Clara. She prayed they would not inquire further and put her friend's security in jeopardy.

Clara remained silent as the earl appeared to give consideration to Mrs. Malone's words. He did not look happy and, in fact, seemed resolved against glancing in her direction at all. After what felt like forever, he flicked his pen down onto the desktop and raked his hands through his thick hair with a sigh.

"How many staff are we in need of currently?" he asked.

The housekeeper ticked off her fingers as she explained. "We are short three, two housemaids and one head housemaid. I have been considering Amelia for head housemaid, which would still make us short on housemaids—and that's if we hire this girl," she said, shaking her head sorrowfully. "We need more servants, my lord."

He looked doubtful. "Lawton Park hasn't seen a ball or dinner party in years, how many servants can we possibly need?"

"As long as there is an earl in residence at this house," she intoned severely, "it must be cleaned and maintained. It takes numerous domestic servants to perform the tasks required, as it is quite large, even with the west wing shuttered." She glanced quizzically at him. "Until now you have been willing to trust my judgment on these matters. Has something changed?"

"No, no, not at all, Mrs. Malone. I have every confidence in your abilities." Again, he pointed at Clara, causing her to flinch. "It's *that* one who causes me worry."

Mrs. Malone nodded. "Understandable, my lord. Would it be acceptable if I took responsibility for this girl, then? Give her some time here to prove herself. I would not normally make this kind of request, but circumstances are such that we cannot continue the way we have for much longer."

Silence hung heavy as Ashworth weighed his decision. It was painfully obvious that he still wanted to refuse, but given the circumstances and the offer from Mrs. Malone, it would have been churlish. Clara tried not to take his rejection too personally, but if she were being honest, his objection to her seemed like something more than her lack of reference. It was almost as if she repulsed him somehow. Gone was the concern from earlier today . . . now he was all suspicion.

Clara sighed and stared down at her hands. Here she stood silently, her fate being decided by yet another noble gentleman. Would the course of her life forever be decided by powerful men? Sadness and resentment clashed inside her at the troubling thought.

The earl tapped his fingers on the desktop.

"Consider this the beginning of your probationary period," he said finally, meeting Clara's gaze. "If I so much as hear a word of displeasure from Mrs. Malone, or anyone for that matter, you are dismissed. If you do anything that upsets me, you are dismissed." His handsome face was severe as he said, "Do you understand?"

Relief coursed through her.

He had relented. The Earl of Ashworth was allowing her to stay, to work, to remain hidden from the baron. His words were harsh, but as far as she could tell, his expectations were reasonable.

"Yes, of course, my lord," she answered gratefully, relaxing her shoulders and emphasizing her words with a low curtsy.

Ashworth nodded begrudgingly. The seriousness remained etched in his face but his eyes betrayed some other emotion that she couldn't quite identify. It almost seemed like . . . anxiety? But what on earth could she have done to make him feel anxious?

Abruptly, he moved his gaze back down to his paperwork.

"Mrs. Malone, please get Helen settled in and show her to her room."

His words served as a reminder that she was now Helen from this point forward. She was bidding farewell to Clara Mayfield for good.

Fear crawled its way through her belly. The housekeeper inclined her head and stepped forward to touch her elbow, bringing her back to the present moment. "Yes, my lord. We will leave you now."

They turned and departed the study. Mrs. Malone carefully shut the heavy door behind them, and they winded through the hallways back to the servants' quarters, where the housekeeper led her to a doorway. Peering inside, Clara could see a murky staircase that would presumably take her up to the servants' bedrooms. Mrs. Malone stopped and turned to face her.

"Go upstairs to the top floor and wait for me there."

"Yes, Mrs. Malone," Clara replied. As she turned to enter the stairwell, she saw Amelia staring at her from down the hall. Then the housekeeper shut the door behind them, sealing Clara in the dimly lit enclosure.

Her inquisitive nature being what it was, she remained near the door. Amelia's annoyed voice was muffled but could be clearly discerned through the wooden barrier.

"So he hired her, after all," she said, unimpressed.

"Well . . . yes. But it was terribly odd," said the housekeeper. "That was the first time I've seen him act so unpleasant to someone."

"I suppose she didn't make a very good first impression," said Amelia, with a smug note of satisfaction.

Mrs. Malone paused silently for a moment. "Perhaps," she said. "Or perhaps it is something else altogether."

With that last vague remark, the conversation stopped. The housekeeper's footsteps faded, and after a moment Amelia let out an unladylike snort then walked away. And Clara was left there, alone behind the door, grasping to guess at what the housekeeper could have possibly meant.

Chapter Three

William knew he had just made a huge mistake.

He should have quickly and efficiently sent her packing and out of his sight. Because he wanted her—God, how he wanted her.

His attraction had been the only reason he'd been in time to help her earlier in the village. Had he not been staring shamelessly from his vantage point across the street, he might never have seen her stray off course and into the path of the carriage.

A *carriage*, for God's sake.

William closed his eyes in an effort to shut out the memories that threatened, ever near the surface, to encroach upon his sanity. Images that haunted every last one of his days and nights. He scrubbed a hand over his face and opened his eyes, his gaze immediately landing on the glittering decanter of brandy. He resisted the urge to pour a drink.

A frown creased his brow as he wondered what the odds had been of finding the woman from the village waiting for him in his own home. Not good, still there he had found her among his other servants, blushing and tongue-tied and painfully lovely. In an instant the feel of her, wrapped tightly in his arms, came roaring back. The pressure of her back as she leaned breathlessly against his chest, the dark tendrils of hair that swept like silk across his cheek, the soft curve of her waist beneath his hands . . .

In the end, he'd been forced to walk away, knowing that allowing himself to be held captive by those almond-shaped eyes for too long was an exceedingly bad idea.

And still, many times on his way back to the house, he had considered turning around to see her once more . . . to ask her a question that burned with a suddenness inside him, poised silently on his lips.

Who are you?

Regardless of her answer, he wanted her with a fiery need that he was not convinced would dampen in time, and this girl felt like the first thing that had mattered in months. There had been so much grief after the accident. He'd nearly drowned in it, and then he had just gone numb. Even if these feelings were simply the result of an inconvenient lust, at least they were something. A peculiar *aliveness* rushed through him now, and all it had taken was a chance meeting with this housemaid.

William rose from his chair and paced restlessly. Now she was living and working under his roof, and in some sort of hellish irony, he would have to endure each day as if none of it mattered. As if each time he saw her he wasn't imagining how she would react if he just hauled her up against him and kissed her.

Crossing to the windows, he let out a scoff. Who was he trying to fool? He was a broken man. Unable to even attend a ball without fear of making a scene, or behave as a proper earl should. He found himself often held prisoner by a kind of madness that seemed to come and go as it pleased, with little provocation or none at all. The only thing left for him to do was to retreat back to his country house to deal with the mortifying affliction without the prying eyes of the *ton*. Setting himself to rights and doing the job that had passed to him needed to be the priorities now. Too many people had died for them not to be.

William hung his head and pinched the bridge of his nose. Fantasizing about this maid would be his undoing, and he had certainly placed himself in one hell of a situation. He sighed.

I am an idiot.

In a flash of clarity, he decided that it wasn't too late. He would march back downstairs to tell Mrs. Malone that he had changed his mind and he needed Helen to leave. He would make up a reason, or give no reason at all. After all, it was his house and he could do as he wished. With a sense of relief, he realized he could boot her off the estate and things would continue normally, the way they had continued for the last year and a half.

He strode to the door, his hand hovering over the handle. Then his hand dropped and he walked back and leaned, defeated, against the worn edge of his desk. The idea didn't have as much appeal as he'd thought it would.

Since the accident, he had allowed himself very little in the way of enjoyment. Staying busy was easy when you were learning how to run an estate, so he had kept his head down and thrown himself into the work. Instead of attempting to persuade the *ton* that his earldom was well managed and he was moving past his grief, he simply chose to omit himself from their presence. Calling cards went unanswered, invitations were cast aside. He dealt with business matters efficiently but impersonally. This had served him well, until his failed attempt in London.

But there were long stretches of time where he found himself alone with his dark thoughts and remembrances, feeling as though he might go entirely crazy. Thinking about something else—even a blasted housemaid—would be a welcome change.

The earl rubbed the back of his neck, then pushed off his desk and exited the study. A walk outside in fresh air would do a good deal to clear his head, he told himself. He entered the sunroom and left the house through the open doors there. A chill washed over him as the night air came into contact with his skin, and it produced a welcome cooling effect on his overheated body. Slowly, he regained some of his usual clarity of mind.

Everything would be fine. He would avoid her presence, do his best to forget she even worked there. When forced to be near her, which shouldn't be often, he would ignore her entirely.

He was certain that with enough practice, he would no longer recognize the attraction he felt for her at all.

Clara's first evening at Lawton Park was going about as well as could be expected. Mrs. Malone had supplied her with the necessary uniform before showing her to her room. Servants' quarters were on the top floor of the house, men on the east side and women on the west, and her chamber was in the west garret. While small in size, the space wasn't altogether unpleasant, and contained a small bed, plain chest of drawers and a table with a pitcher and basin. A tiny mirror adorned the wall, and her window overlooked the front of the expansive grounds. Looking out, she noticed that the landscape was still primarily green. Only a handful of leaves had started turning their varying shades of gold and rust to signal the approaching change of season.

Once her belongings had been carefully stowed in the drawers, she sat down on her bed. For a moment, all was quiet, and then the stress of the day seemed to wash over her all at once. In the unfamiliar room, away from her family, the reality of her position sinking in, she started to cry. Sobs and gasps came unbidden and uncontrollable. She buried her face in her hands, helpless to do anything but surrender to the overwhelming tide of emotion.

After a few minutes, she gave herself a shake, her sobs giving way to sniffles. "There is no use in crying," she said aloud, pretending for a moment that she was talking with Lucy, trying to think what advice her practical older sister would offer. She swiped her tears away. "I must make the best of this situation, and I will."

She would've believed her own words more if her interview with the earl hadn't been such a disaster. But of course, having to be saved from the path of a speeding carriage, then turning up with no real means to recommend herself didn't exactly make for a strong first impression. It didn't help that she couldn't stop thinking about the way his body had felt wrapped protectively around hers, or the heroics he had taken to knock her out of harm's way. Truthfully, any male attention came as a surprise after being roundly ignored throughout the season—she only wished he hadn't retreated back into icy skepticism once they'd seen each other again at his estate.

Clara stood and stripped out of Abigail's worn dress. The room was stiflingly hot, but she shivered anyway as she slipped her new black servant's garb over her head and settled it over her hips. She fumbled over fastening the tiny buttons, a task she was not accustomed to, then she picked up her white apron and secured the strings around her waist. Finally, she gathered her heavy dark hair up into a simple bun, pinning it severely into confinement. As usual, it refused to cooperate and be tamed, stray wisps and curls springing free of pins. Even under Abigail's skilled hands, taming her hair had been challenging. Now it was impossible. With a sigh, she affixed her servant's cap over the bun.

It would simply have to do, she decided, as she quietly opened her door and crossed over to the servants' staircase. This set of stairs ran along the west side of the house, hidden from everyday view. Subtle doorways had been built into the structure of many of the rooms, allowing staff to slip in and out discreetly, so as to not disturb the residents. Mrs. Malone had given her a brief tour before delivering her to her bedroom, but Clara was sure she would get lost many times before the week was done. Lawton Park was massive, to say the least.

The candlelit sconces on the walls surrounding the staircase barely gave off enough dim light to help her navigate her way, and the windows were useless as night had now descended. The stairs were squeaky and old, and Clara wondered morosely if anyone had ever fallen down them before. Surely, at some point in this estate's history, they had claimed a victim. If not, she would probably be the one to take the honor.

She descended past the third floor, the second floor, the first, then came to a stop by the door leading to the servants' hall. It was getting late, and she didn't want to miss supper. She hadn't had a chance to eat since earlier that morning, but found herself lingering anyway. She supposed she was apprehensive about meeting the rest of the servants. Especially if Amelia's reaction to her was an indication of how she could expect them to receive her . . .

She could hear the muffled noises of people socializing and laughing through the thick wooden door. Gently, she turned the cold brass knob and pushed it open. Yellow light spilled into the stairwell, the sounds of conversation drifting more loudly now, from a room some ways down.

Clara stepped into the hallway and closed the door firmly behind her, being certain the noise alerted the staff to her arrival so as not to surprise them. The boisterous discussion stopped at once and she froze in place, only to be startled by a head popping comically into view from the dining area.

"It's about time!" exclaimed the young man. His bright blue eyes twinkled at her, and he had a pleasant, crooked smile.

Clara smiled back, grateful to see a friendly face. "Hello. Have I missed supper?" she asked.

"Almost," he said cheerfully, stepping fully into the hall. "But I talked them into keeping it out for a bit longer in case you were hungry." He held out his hand. "The name's Matthew. I'm a footman."

She stared at his hand, and after the briefest pause, she shook it. Matthew's grip was firm, his skin warm beneath hers. Clara tried to look as though this was something quite normal for her. It wasn't, of course. She was used to wearing gloves, for one, and certainly gentleman never shook hands so frankly with a lady. But there was something comforting about the rough hand clasped around her own.

"My name is Helen," she said, cursing the waver in her voice.

"Oh, we know what your name is," he replied with a laugh. "Word travels fast down here."

She followed him into the dining hall. Seated at a long, rough-planked wooden table were the servants of Lawton Park. She had heard Mrs. Malone's entreaty that the place was understaffed, of course, but even still she was shocked to see how few people the earl actually employed. There was no butler, which was unheard of for a country house this grand, and there was no lady's maid. Then again, she supposed, there was no lady.

"Are you settled in?" asked Mrs. Malone in a kindly way as she gestured for her to take an empty seat at the table.

"Yes, thank you," Clara replied as she hungrily surveyed the food that was laid out. It looked to be an assortment of leftovers from that day's meals. Cold sliced beef, cooked vegetables and pieces of rhubarb tart had never looked so good to her. Clara gladly piled up a plate and began eating, hunger overcoming her hesitation and shyness handily. Matthew grinned at her voracity and filled a glass with ale, jokingly sliding it over the table at her with one finger, as if afraid she might bite him if he got too close. She grinned in return, feeling suddenly more at ease, and applied herself to her meal.

Introductions were made around the table. There was Mrs. Malone, of course. The ill-tempered Amelia did not disappoint and scowled at Clara with only the briefest of nods.

Charles was the other footman, and Matthew's counterpart. His silvery blond hair was in contrast to Matthew's brown, but their height was the same which was, of course, the most important distinguishing feature for footmen—aside from shapely calves, or so she had heard. The kitchen maid, Gilly, was seated next to Mrs. Humboldt, the cook, whom Clara had met earlier. Now that Clara was a member of the staff, the elderly woman had relaxed, nodding at her with a pleasantly curious expression.

The other housemaid, Stella, had a serious face with a kind smile, but when Clara's eyes landed on the scullery maid, Tess, she blanched. The girl was far too young. She couldn't have been more than fourteen or fifteen years old. Whereas the rest of the staff looked comfortable and at ease, Tess looked out of place and scared. She had almost certainly left her family recently to go into service here. Clara empathized more than the girl could ever know.

She nodded greetings to the staff gathered at the table, but one role was curiously missing from the entourage. She had to ask; her curiosity demanded it.

"Where is Lord Ashworth's valet?"

Mrs. Malone sighed and rolled her eyes to the heavens. "The earl prides himself on his independence. That is one thing you will learn quickly. He has refused the services of a valet. I have begged him to conform since he is in charge of an earldom and has more important things to worry about, but he resists. He is quite self-sufficient, much to our dismay." She huffed in frustration.

Clara nearly laughed. The idea of an earl performing his own daily grooming was astonishing. Who set out his clothes each night, and brushed his jackets? Did he truly bathe, shave, and dress on his own, with no help at all? Suddenly, she had an image of Lord Ashworth in his bedchamber shrugging out of his jacket, with cravat untied at his tan throat, his white shirt unbuttoned down the front. She nearly choked on her ale, a spiral of heat swirling through her.

She thought of the pompous, preening lords she had met in London. She doubted most of them even knew how to brush their own teeth, let alone shave or dress. It was one of the many reasons, she was sure, she had been unable to attract one as a suitor before the scandal: they could detect her disdain. It was difficult for her to abide the strong opinions of men who were so completely dependent upon others to sustain their very existence.

Of course, peers required servants to keep their estate running smoothly, but Clara would never forget Lord Wexley, and how he had demanded his valet be allowed to stand near him at the dinner table so he could gently dab his mouth with a napkin when necessary. Which was often, as it turned out, since Lord Wexley was a rather sloppy eater. His poor valet had gone through many napkins that evening. She shuddered with the remembrance.

Clara glanced curiously at the group. "Is he not concerned with maintaining a conventional reputation?"

"It is of the utmost importance to him. Never forget that," answered the housekeeper sternly, her gray eyes flashing at Clara in the candlelight. "He may not follow every rule, but as the sole remaining heir to the earldom, his family's image concerns him a great deal."

The table became quiet, and Clara absorbed the magnitude of what had been said, and how she might feel, were she in Ashworth's position. She had seen her family endure painful circumstances, certainly. But having to watch them die, and then be forced to carry on in their name afterwards? A chill chased across her skin.

"We were just so glad Lord Ashworth survived, although it wasn't clear that he would at first," added the housekeeper solemnly. "How he suffered for that title."

Mrs. Malone's eyes shone with the force of suppressed emotion. Briefly turning her head to the side, she sniffed. Thankfully, Matthew broke the somber mood with a friendly pat on Clara's arm.

"Well, his lordship is much improved now, healed as he is, and his sister is nearly out of mourning. I say it's about time for things to finally start looking up."

"His lordship came downstairs earlier," Clara started, then paused. "Is that normal behavior for him? I haven't seen it before in other households."

She saw many of them nodding, then Matthew laughed.

"It happens more than you'd think it would. He's caught me by surprise many a time. Why this one day, Charles and I were playing cards and . . ."

"He will ring the bell if he needs us," interjected Mrs. Malone dryly, casting a sideways glance at Matthew. "But often he prefers to be present among his staff, and the most efficient way for him to do that is to come belowstairs."

Clara was confused. "Why do you think he wishes to interact with staff so personally, when most peers refuse to even acknowledge the existence of servants at all?"

"He's lonely," said Amelia, who had been silent until now. She peered over at Clara with contempt. "Perhaps you should keep him company."

Clara's mouth fell open at the unexpected retort. Well, it seemed that catty women could be easily found in both London ballrooms *and* servants' quarters. But she couldn't deny the sting of receiving such a comment from Abigail's own sister.

Matthew said, "Oy! What's that for, Amy?"

Mrs. Malone stood abruptly.

"Amelia, in my office, *now*." The surly maid rose and stalked out of the dining room. The housekeeper examined the rest of the faces at the table. "Everyone, tidy this place up. Charles," she said to the blond footman, "ensure the earl requires nothing else this evening. Then off to bed with the lot of you." She turned on her heel and walked briskly away.

Charles left immediately to go upstairs, and the group fell silent. Clara focused on the scarred surface of the table in the uncomfortable silence that followed. This was not precisely how she'd hoped her first meal with the household staff would end. Mrs. Humboldt clucked her tongue sympathetically.

"Just ignore her, dear. She can be a bloody grouse when she wants to be," she said.

"That was very unkind," added Stella, the other housemaid. "Don't worry, you can partner with me tomorrow for your first day."

Clara nodded, and a small, cool hand slid lightly over her own. She raised her eyes to see Tess, the young scullery maid, standing next to her. A small glimmer of a smile touched one corner of her mouth.

"It'll be okay, miss," she said softly. "You'll see."

The journey back to her bedroom was long, and the stairwell black as night but for the candle in a candlestick holder that Stella carried, which helped immeasurably. Their shadows bounced and bobbed on the walls as they slowly trudged upstairs, appearing mysterious somehow, as if they were sneaking off to a clandestine meeting instead of just heading off to their respective beds. Amelia brought up the rear, keeping at least half a flight of stairs behind the rest of them. She had been prodded by Mrs. Malone into apologizing to Clara, which was awkward for everybody involved.

Clara wondered what it would take for Amelia to like her. Maybe that wasn't possible, but could she at least find a way to get Amelia to hate her a little less? She had no notion what she'd done that the maid had found so offensive. That was really the most upsetting part, especially given what Abigail had told her. She had always spoken warmly of her sister.

Unable to make any sense of the situation, she was glad when a loud creak of hinges announced their entry into the uppermost hallway.

They whispered good nights as Stella escorted each girl to her room—the one benefit of being understaffed was that they each had their own—lighted her candle, and moved on to the next. She performed this task according to hierarchy, beginning with Amelia, since Mrs. Malone lived in her own quarters in the servants' hall, and working down through the other girls.

"Don't forget," Stella whispered when she finally reached Clara's room. "Five o'clock tomorrow morning . . . I'll rap on your door when it's time to go."

"I'll be ready," said Clara, trying to seem cheerful. She was not a late riser by any means, but five o'clock was early for her.

The maid smiled. "You look nervous, but you'll do fine. I'll be with you the entire time!"

And with a small wave of her fingers, Stella floated away into the darkness.

With weary legs, Clara stepped inside her room and softly closed the door behind her. She placed the candle in a holder on the bureau and turned to survey her new lodgings, now dimly flickering by candlelight. She was suddenly utterly exhausted, and she knew five o'clock would arrive in the blink of an eye.

Clara again struggled with the row of tiny buttons on her dress, an exercise in precision she hoped would get easier with practice. Not even her time spent on needlework had prepared her for this tedious task. With a quiet cheer, she was finally able to shed the garment. She unhooked her corset, untied her skirts and drawers and slid them off, until all that remained was a crumpled chemise that hung to her thighs. Not having packed a nightgown, she supposed it would have to suffice.

Her first night in Lawton Park. Clara could hardly believe she was here. She removed her servant's cap and freed her thick hair, then glanced down at her new bed, which was thin and a fraction of the size of her old bed at home. The mattress appeared old but clean, and the light blanket provided would give plenty of coverage given the heat of late summer. The cooler weather might be something to worry about, though.

Crossing to the window, she opened it, admitting some much needed refreshing night air, when out of the corner of her eye she saw something moving in the shadows between the strips of moonlight on the lawn below. It was a figure. A man.

Who would be outside at this time of night? She stared unblinkingly into the darkness. The figure moved quickly and confidently out of the shadows, the light turning his blond hair silver. The pure white shirt and broad shoulders confirmed that it was the Earl of Ashworth crossing the gravel drive. She watched him, stepping slightly back from the window even though she knew he couldn't possibly see her, until he rounded the side of the house and disappeared out of sight.

Clara felt an unexpected pang of longing, swift and sharp. How ironic her life had become! In order to flee the baron, she had sacrificed everything that would have made her an eligible match for this particular man. He, with his tragic past and heated glances, would have made the London season an infinitely more fascinating experience. If only they could have met each other in Mayfair . . .

Her body warmed at the thought of dancing with him. Clara could imagine the clasp of his fingers upon her waist, and the incendiary feel of him pulling her close for a spinning turn. Or meeting outside in the gardens beneath a softly glowing moon, kissing wildly amidst the faint sounds of the orchestra drifting outside . . .

With a jerk of her head, she sternly checked her thoughts as they had no place in this tiny garret room.

Turning away from the window, she climbed into her bed.

CHAPTER FOUR

William stood next to the carriage as his father boarded, then he cast his eyes skyward. The inky sweep of night overhead was a reminder of how long their meeting had gone, and a light drizzle now fell to dampen the roads.

Despite the lateness of the hour, the group was eager to start the long journey home from Manchester. Lucas slapped him on the arm and grinned before vaulting into the vehicle, and his brother-in-law paused with one foot on the step before joining them.

"Is something the matter, William?" he asked.

He stared at Cartwick mutely. The answer, of course, was no, but somehow that answer didn't quite feel true. It was just a feeling, though. One he couldn't voice to his family without some fraction of logic to back it up.

"No," he finally replied. "I'm just surprised by how quickly it grew dark."

Cartwick nodded and joined him in surveying the sky. "It seems there is a storm moving in," he agreed, pointing to an incoming mass of heavy clouds, burgeoning with water and barely visible in the failing light. "No matter. We'll make it as far as we can, and find an inn if we must."

"William! Reginald!" Lucas called, scoffing lightly from the interior of the carriage. "I'd like to get home sometime in the next month."

Cartwick smiled and gestured for William to proceed before him. His father spoke up only when everyone was seated and the carriage was moving at a swift pace, bouncing evenly along the road out of town. He had to raise his voice, for the rain that had threatened only minutes before now struck the roof with ferocity.

Casual conversation ensued, with Cartwick sharing news from Eliza's latest letter. It seemed their young daughter had grown tired of her daily oatmeal, deciding that rather than eat her breakfast, she would prefer to paint the table with it instead. The earl suggested serving her meal on a canvas, even committing to hanging the masterpiece in the gallery at Lawton Park—a suggestion that had incited riotous laughter. When the group's amusement had finally subsided, he then broached the topic at hand: their potential investment in a northern cotton mill.

"I think we should proceed," the earl said, his dark gaze searching their faces for a reaction. "Scanlan said a lot of things that made sense. What say you?"

"I agree," answered Cartwick readily.

William glanced at his brother before replying. "Of course, Lucas and I would never stand in the way of a venture you deem sound, Father. I think only that perhaps we would like for there to be more discussion with Scanlan first. Namely regarding workers and the conditions at the factory, and the technology of the equipment, which would benefit from some improvements."

The earl raised his brow and stroked his bearded chin in thought. "I see. Well, I don't necessarily have an issue with that. What do you two have in mind?"

The brothers were cut short by a sharp bump in the road, one large enough to lift the vehicle off the ground for a moment before landing roughly once more, first the front wheels, then the back. The conversation stopped while the men stared at each other in silence, waiting to see if things would get worse. When the ride continued without event, Lucas breathed an unsteady sigh of relief.

"Perhaps we should pull over. Have the driver inspect the—"

The loud crack of the rear axle near William was unmistakable, and his heart stuttered, then tripled its pace when the carriage abruptly lurched backwards beneath him. The undercarriage dropped and scraped against the road, and he heard the remains of the wheel dragging loudly before breaking off altogether. Cartwick let out a shout. Lucas braced himself against their father, while William struggled desperately to right himself before being thrown further into the back of the vehicle. He could see his father's wide and terrified eyes, his hands stretched outwards.

"William!"

The force of the tilting carriage yanked the team of horses off balance, and their frantic whinnies could be heard through the noise of bending metal and shattering glass . . .

The harsh sound of his scream scraped its way up his throat and he wrestled through the bedclothes as if he were fighting off an army of demons. He didn't stop until he'd broken free of the sodden fabric to stand, disoriented and half delirious, in the middle of his bedchamber. Then he collapsed onto all fours, his chest heaving, each agonizing breath an attempt at regaining some shred of control.

William felt weak for even having the thought, but it was on nights like these when he wished he had someone he could rely upon. Perhaps a wife. Someone who cared enough to hold him in his moment of grief . . . stroke his brow until the tremors stopped.

An image of Helen flitted through his mind's eye. Annoyed, he banished the thought immediately and pushed himself up to a shaky stand. He slowly took stock of his body and the emotions that, so very recently, had run wild, then glanced wearily at the window. It was still dark but he could discern the faint sound of birdsong. The sun would rise soon.

Retrieving his robe, he shrugged it on. Regardless of his fatigue, he knew there would be no more rest for him this morning.

The sun was still sleeping when she and Stella entered the darkened study. Even with the warm weather, temperatures dipped in the early morning hours, and the room was cool. Stella quickly lighted the sconces on the wall, while Clara set down her tools with aching arms, kneeling with stiff, sore legs to spread a cloth around the fireplace grate. The work had been nothing short of backbreaking thus far. She dreaded Stella growing fed up with her clumsy fingers, her fumbling through tasks that ought to come easily for an experienced housemaid, and complaining to Mrs. Malone— but so far, the young woman had merely been friendly and encouraging, helping Clara when she faltered.

She glanced down at her morning dress as she slipped a pair of stained gloves over her now-calloused palms. The printed percale gown was plainly made, yet she was terrified to ruin it, despite the large apron she wore. Ruining it would mean losing a month's worth of wages to Mrs. Malone for a replacement, a consequence she'd never been forced to consider in her old life.

Stella came and knelt down next to her, sinking to her knees far more gracefully than Clara had. Although the earl was not present, it was considered standard procedure to speak as little as possible when working upstairs. Stella nodded in her direction, and Clara picked up a stiff wire brush and began scrubbing fire-charred debris and ash from the cast iron grate. It was difficult work, and she rocked back and forth, using her whole body to generate the force required to dislodge the soot. Black powder sifted down onto the drop cloth and floated into the air, making her cough.

Her arms were screaming in protest by the time she was done cleaning the front of the grate, and she was only halfway finished. Leaning in as far as she could, she worked towards the back of the structure, making certain to scrape thoroughly between each bar. That was when she first noticed the humming sound. Pausing briefly, she turned her head and listened.

"Did you hear something?" she asked Stella.

The maid's sober face broke into a grin. "You mean, other than your grunting and groaning?"

Clara returned her smile in good humor, but a sense of unease remained. She leaned back into the fireplace and resumed scrubbing away the grime. Minutes passed as she worked busily. The noise returned, except now it had risen to a high-pitched keening, and her head was plagued by an unbearable pressure. She squeezed her eyes shut and shook her head, then gritted her teeth, determined to finish the task.

Without warning, Stella shot to her feet. From the interior of the hearth, Clara could hear her muted voice as she spoke.

"My lord! We were not expecting you out of bed at such an early hour."

The Earl of Ashworth had entered the study, and Clara's backside was sticking out of the fireplace to greet him.

Hastily, she dropped her brush and lurched backwards, turning around to push herself into an upright position.

The earl was staring at them in shock. He was dressed in nothing but a pair of loose-fitting pants and a dark satin robe tied carelessly around his hips. With his golden hair disheveled and face unshaven as if he had just risen from his bed, he had an almost piratical appeal. It was abundantly clear he had not expected to encounter anyone at this hour.

The broad expanse of chest, half covered and half *uncovered*, was on display beneath the fluid drape of his robe. His extraordinary green eyes were filled with true surprise. The sight of all this in combination with the gleaming stubble that glinted on his unshaven face literally took her breath away.

But no, it wasn't just from the sight of Ashworth dressed in his robe. She really was having trouble breathing.

Clara touched her face, belatedly comprehending that her hands were covered in soot, and shook her head again, trying to chase a wave of dizziness away. What had started earlier as a hum had since escalated into a scream, and she noticed with a touch of panic that black spots were dancing over the walls.

The look of concern that crossed the earl's face was the last thing she saw as her knees collapsed, the floor zooming towards her as darkness overtook her completely.

Clara awoke with a start. From the feel of the fabric under her fingers, she could tell she was stretched out on the velvet settee on the far side of the room. Her gloves and apron had been removed. Humiliation burned through her. She had fallen unconscious from the exertion of her task.

In front of the earl.

Her eyes shot to Stella, who was sitting beside her patting her hand, and then locked on Lord Ashworth. He was standing above her, hands on hips, his green gaze scanning her face. She couldn't tell if he was angry or not—but she was suddenly very aware of the fact that her dress had been opened and her corset loosened. Her cheeks flushed; she wanted nothing more than to get out of that room. If one could die from mortification, she prayed the fatal blow would be arriving soon. Struggling to sit, she tugged at the back of her dress to keep it closed.

"Forgive me, my lord," she stuttered, as she attempted to stand. "I'm so sorry—"

"Sit," he commanded. Then less harshly, "You're in no condition to stand."

Slowly, she sank back down on the settee, wishing she could disappear. Her vision was a bit bleary still, but the room gradually became clearer, and she could see that, luckily, she must have pitched forward onto the carpet rather than backwards into the fireplace. And oddly enough, there were buttons on the floor. Which meant . . .

"My dress!" she cried, using her fingertips to verify the absence of buttons.

"Sorry," said Stella, with a note of empathy. "But we needed to get you breathing again and there was no time for buttons." She leaned forward and whispered, "I'll help you sew them back on later."

Clara tried to smile. "No, no, not at all. You were kind enough to help me. I will sew them on myself."

"Well, his lordship helped the most," said Stella, glancing deferentially back at Ashworth. "It was fortunate he was able to react so quickly and catch you. If it had just been me, you would still be facedown on the carpet," she tittered.

The earl had *caught* her? And she doubted that Stella had

managed to transport her unconscious body to the settee, which meant he had *held* her as well? Clara was torn between being humiliated and furious. Humiliated that she had fainted like a schoolgirl at his feet, and furious that she hadn't been aware and able to remember his embrace. Even if it had been accidental. And not truly an embrace.

She gazed up at him in dawning realization. Under her scrutiny, Ashworth's face changed, his eyes darkening in an unsettling way. He abruptly cleared his throat and walked towards the door.

"She was clearly unwell. Any gentleman would have done the same," he said, as if it had been of no consequence. He placed his hand on the doorknob and faced them once more. "Now, if she is recovered, I will take my leave of you both." Then speaking directly at Clara, "You seem to be exceedingly susceptible to accident. Do see that you take more care in the future. I refuse to scramble for smelling salts each time you clean a grate."

He turned and strode swiftly out of the study, leaving Clara to stare after him. The door closed, and she and Stella sat another moment in silence, then both burst out in nervous laughter.

"That was . . . so odd!" Stella struggled to say in between fits of hilarity.

Clara worked to keep her composure. "It was," she admitted with a soft hiccup. "But I suppose I deserved it."

"Yes," replied the maid, eyeing her uncertainly. "Has this happened to you before when scrubbing the grates?"

Of course, Clara had never cleaned a grate in her life. The

closest she had come was sitting prettily on couch cushions next to one in the afternoon. In all their preparation, she had not thought to consult with Abigail about the actual labor that would be involved.

Clara fidgeted, trying to appear casual. "Not that I remember . . ."

Stella chuckled despite herself, kneeling down to collect the stray buttons. She stayed Clara with a hand when she tried to help her.

"Sit and rest."

"Please," said Clara. "Let me at least change into another dress and come finish the grate."

"Certainly not," said the other maid. "You've caused quite enough excitement for one morning. If you're feeling well enough to walk, why don't you get my spare morning dress from my room and come watch me finish. If you're still fine when I'm done, I'll have you polish the railings."

Clara thanked her and stood on wobbly legs, when a thought occurred to her.

"I don't suppose . . . well, I would hate to create a scandal belowstairs that was attached to the earl, and so quickly after my arrival . . ." she began.

Stella shooed her away. "It will be our secret." Then she smirked. "Although I can't promise I won't tease you privately every chance I get."

"Thank you," said Clara, with a breath of relief. "I mean it. Even if you did rip all my buttons off."

"Oh," said Stella, her eyes dancing with mischief as she

placed the buttons into Clara's open palm. "I never said *I* was the one who tore open your dress."

Ashworth strode down the hallway, his relief gradually increasing as each step carried him farther from his study. Surely there must have been a better way to handle Helen's crisis, but in the moment, he'd been unable to think of anything other than what he'd done, which had been to rend her dress and loosen her corset with his bare hands.

He'd simply wanted to distract himself with ledgers, or by performing some mundane task. But instead . . .

He shook his head, trying to clear the image of her falling senseless into his arms. Forcing himself to forget the soft press of her body, and the enchanting blush that rose to her cheeks upon discovering her state of undress.

Would another peer have reacted similarly to a housemaid fainting on the floor before him? Probably not, but this difference alone didn't bother him. The most unwelcome surprise was the strength of his reaction. It was reminiscent of the way he'd felt that day in the village, when he'd found himself bolting across the street to tackle her out of harm's way. He hadn't been able to help himself then either.

And here, today, he was particularly troubled by the rush of satisfaction that had followed once her condition had improved and he could examine her at his leisure. It was not appropriate for him to greedily commit every inch of her exposed skin to memory after such an event, nor was it fitting that the silken feel of her beneath his fingertips seemed burned into his skin.

Not to mention his reaction had been witnessed by the other housemaid, Stella. He didn't believe her to be one of the worst gossips belowstairs, but couldn't say for sure that she would keep such an instance of drama to herself. Such talk had a way of spreading easily to other households.

The earl reached his chambers, slamming the door shut with more force than was necessary. Cursing himself in self-reproach, William swiped a hand impatiently through his hair. He tugged on the bellpull to summon Matthew for his morning coffee. With how the morning had unfolded for him thus far, the idea of staying upstairs, and away from *her*, seemed like the most prudent course of action.

The rest of the week passed uneventfully, at least in comparison to that disastrous morning in the study. Lawton Park had been swept, scrubbed and polished to a gleaming shine in preparation for the arrival of the earl's young niece, Rosamund, who was traveling to the estate a few days ahead of her mother.

Every servant filed upstairs and lined up on the front drive to greet her. The level of pomp and circumstance would have better suited the Duchess of York than a young girl, Clara thought. But clearly the earl's remaining family was more than precious to the entire household. Mrs. Malone very nearly glowed with pride, and her stubby nose was tipped ever so slightly up in the air as she kept an eye on the servants to ensure proper manners.

The late September afternoon was cool and foggy, and cold enough that Clara was able to see her breath. She stood with the others, stock-still, with her chilled hands clasped dutifully behind her back. But as the front entrance swung open and the earl emerged, she found she was no longer cold. He was dressed formally in gray trousers, dark blue jacket, crisp white shirt and a midnight blue cravat. Against the dark attire, his golden hair glowed. He was dazzling.

Out of the corner of her eye, she caught him, ever so briefly, looking her way. His face was not friendly, and the second their eyes met, he shifted his gaze straight ahead.

Her cheeks flamed. Luckily, no one else noticed the exchange, as a well-sprung carriage was rolling up the final length of the drive. It stopped before the house, followed by a man on a large black horse. Ashworth tipped a nod at the lone rider, then instead of waiting for the footman, strode right up to the vehicle and threw the door open. A tiny girl in a ruffled yellow dress launched herself out into his waiting arms.

"Uncah!" she cried as she wrapped her tiny arms around his shoulders.

Blonde waves, similar in their striking color to the earl's, bounced and swayed as Rosamund buried her face in his neck. The earl lifted her high off the ground, her chubby legs flailing and kicking, then set her gently on the ground and knelt beside her. He was grinning in a way that was almost boyish. Whereas one moment before his demeanor had been grave, now his eyes were alight with happiness.

Clara's stomach fluttered. She suddenly wished, uselessly, that she could be the one to bring such an expression to his face.

"Hello, my Rosa," he said, smoothing her hair and straightening her bonnet. "Did you have a pleasant trip?"

"Yes, Uncah," she said earnestly. "Louise slept a lot," she added, pointing to the woman who was currently exiting the carriage. "So I just played with Dolly." She held up a soft doll for him to see. It was clearly homemade, with dark yarn hair and a pretty pink dress, worn at the edges and obviously well loved.

The earl admired it gamely. "And did your dolly have a nice trip?" he inquired.

Rosa's shoulders sagged and she pursed her lips in a tiny pout. "Dolly was sleeping too," she replied, which caused the earl to laugh.

The rider who had followed the carriage dismounted swiftly and approached the earl. He was striking, tall, with jet-black hair and bright blue eyes. Ashworth stood, shook the man's hand and clapped him heartily on the back.

"Evanston, by God, it's good to see you," he said.

"Not nearly as good as it is to see you," said the man, laughing. "The back of a carriage becomes boring scenery indeed after the first twenty miles have come and gone."

Lord Evanston gestured towards the woman who had accompanied Rosa on the trip. "Lord Ashworth, this is Louise, Rosa's new nursemaid."

The pale young woman bobbed into a quick curtsy before the men. Light brown hair stuck out haphazardly from her cap, and she clutched her satchel tightly before her.

The earl's eyebrows rose. "Florence has cared for Rosa since birth. Did she find employment elsewhere?" he asked in astonishment.

"Not at all," replied his friend. "But she did take a bad turn and sprain her knee, making it necessary to find a replacement for this particular journey. With your sister detained by the entailment proceedings in Hampshire, I promised her I would accompany Rosa as far as I could, so we met in Brighton and I followed from there."

A shadow crossed over Ashworth's face, then vanished almost as quickly. Clara wondered if the shift was due to the entailment the viscount had mentioned.

The earl turned and gestured to the entrance of the house. "Let us go inside so we can get you both settled in." He took his niece's hand and the group started walking towards the house. Rosa's friendly little eyes were scanning the servants, and she was smiling at each of them. Most of them stared ahead, not even looking at her in order to avoid the temptation to return a smile, which would have been highly inappropriate. Clara, however, couldn't help herself. When Rosa's eyes reached her own, she impulsively grinned back. The little girl broke free from the earl's grasp and, to Clara's surprise, ran right up to her. Stella, adjacent to her in line, issued a quiet gasp of alarm.

"You look like my dolly!" Rosa said excitedly, holding it aloft so Clara could examine the similarities. "What's your name?"

Flushed with the embarrassment of attracting unnecessary attention, she glanced over at Mrs. Malone, who still stared straight ahead but was quite obviously displeased. She could see the earl slowly, almost reluctantly, turning and walking over to retrieve his wayward charge.

Seeing no other option, Clara smiled kindly down at her. "My name is Helen, Miss Rosa," she said softly. "Your dolly is lovely. I am flattered you see a resemblance."

She thought she heard Amelia snort from further down the line.

"You both have black hair and black eyes!" The girl frowned as she looked at Clara's dress. "You need a pink dress, though." She turned to the earl who had come to a stop behind her. "Uncah, don't you think she looks pretty like my dolly? Can you give her a pink dress so she will be dressed like her too?"

Lord Evanston chuckled from across the drive, clearly amused as he took in the earl's frozen expression. Clara felt her face turn scarlet; never before had she regretted being friendly to a child, but this was quickly becoming the one exception. Everyone's eyes were now directed at Lord Ashworth, awaiting the answer to the impossible questions.

Kneeling down next to her, he looked Rosa in the eyes. "I think your dolly is lovely indeed," he said warmly. Then he scooped her up quickly and stood. As he reached his full height, his eyes caught Clara's for a fraction of a second. As usual, it was impossible for her to tell if he was angry, or upset, or anything at all; his eyes were expressionless, his jaw clenched. As they looked at each other, a strange electricity seemed to crackle between them. She almost expected to get sacked right then and there just for putting him in yet another awkward situation, but he simply turned and headed to the house with Evanston, while the nursemaid hurried to match their pace.

As soon as they were out of sight, Mrs. Malone motioned her over. Her face was stern.

"Why did you smile at Miss Cartwick?" asked the housekeeper.

Abashed, Clara looked down at the tips of her shoes. "I don't know," she said meekly. "Truly, I apologize. I should not have made eye contact with the earl or his family."

"Do not make me regret taking a chance on you," said Mrs. Malone curtly.

As Amelia passed by them, Clara saw she was working to conceal a caustic smile. Matthew, in contrast, glanced over in sympathy.

As the other domestics entered the house, Clara and the housekeeper remained outside. "I'd have thought you would have learned that lesson at your other places of employment. Risking interaction with a peer, especially in public, is simply not allowed." Mrs. Malone was looking at her quite critically.

Clara dipped her chin in acquiescence, trying to keep her voice from shaking. She had worried the earl would sack her; she had not even given a thought to what Mrs. Malone would do. "Please forgive my mistake, Mrs. Malone. It won't happen again."

"No, it won't," agreed the woman. "For if it does, I'm afraid

I will have to let you go." Her gray eyes were cold and unflinching as she stared hard at Clara. "Do you understand?"

"Yes, ma'am," she answered quietly.

And with that, the housekeeper turned on her heel, gravel crunching beneath her sensible shoes, and walked briskly back to the house.

Clara worked to make herself as scarce as possible over the next few days. She could no longer afford to be so lackadaisical where the earl and his family were concerned. Her employment relied on her being capable of following convention, and without her employment she'd have no choice but to return home—and who knew what awaited her there?

Unfortunately, Rosa was making this difficult. She had proven quite adept at eluding her nursemaid, and the little girl not only sought Clara out, but seemed to prefer her above all other servants.

One day, Clara was dusting in the parlor, and she turned to find Rosa behind her, using her dolly to "dust" off a table leg. Another time, she had been on her hands and knees scrubbing the marble floors of the entrance hall, to discover she had again been joined by Rosa, also on her hands and knees, now clad in sopping wet skirts.

Clara had attempted to reason with her, explaining why she belonged abovestairs with the earl and her nursemaid, and not with her as she performed laborious tasks around the house. She had even enlisted the help of Matthew, who had acted very serious for a change, to convey the importance of staying upstairs. Rosa had nodded with wide eyes, only to sneak back down at her first opportunity.

Finally, Mrs. Malone said she would meet with Lord Ashworth to see if some solution could be found. Privately, Clara thought it would be ideal if Rosa's nursemaid could learn to manage the girl more effectively, but she knew it was not her place to say so.

Later that evening, Clara was wiping down the wooden table in the servants' hall. Supper had finished and she was tidying things up before following the others upstairs, exhausted and ready to tumble into her bed for a few hours' reprieve before waking again early in the morning. Gone was her normal leisurely routine from back home. Now she fell asleep in the black of night and woke to that same darkness, her aching body still crying out for sleep as she launched into another day of hard work. The fortitude required to just make it through the day made her admire the servants here at Lawton Park all the more.

She had just finished sweeping the last crumbs into the dustbin when she raised her tired eyes and jumped, nearly knocking over the bin. The Earl of Ashworth stood leaning against the door frame, silently watching her, arms folded across his chest.

"Pardon me," he said quietly, pushing off to stand before her. "I did not intend to interrupt your duties."

Bewildered, she hastily set her cleaning rag on the table, then curtsied low.

"My lord," Clara said nervously. She clasped her hands

together tightly to keep them from shaking. "I hope everything is in order?"

"There is a matter I wish to discuss with you." His tone was serious. "It is an issue that must be resolved immediately."

Clara's throat was tight with anxiety. She had caused a considerable amount of trouble for him lately—and now this situation with Rosa. He must have come to terminate her employment. Tears threatened and she forcefully willed them not to tumble down her cheeks.

"Yes, my lord. I understand," she said quickly, trying to get the words out before she lost her composure completely. "You don't need to explain. Please know that I tried my b-best . . ."

She moved to edge past him into the hallway, so she could hurry upstairs. But as she passed, the earl turned and grabbed her upper arm, firmly but gently pulling her back into the dining hall. His face was perplexed as he looked down at hers.

"Helen . . . stop," he said. "For God's sake, I didn't come down here to sack you."

She blinked at him. "You—you didn't?"

"No, I didn't." Ashworth's hand was still on her arm, warm and strong. "Although you do have a knack for getting in trouble." His green eyes glinted with amusement as he paused, searching for the right thing to say. "My niece likes you. And I . . . I think you are a hard worker," he concluded. His hand slid down her arm, releasing her at last. Her own hand moved to cover the spot where she could still feel the heat of his touch upon her.

Clara felt ridiculous. "Forgive me, my lord. I suppose I assumed—"

"Yes, I suppose you did," he said, a small smile lurking at the outer edge of his mouth. "Now, I want to discuss the situation with Rosa." He pulled a chair out from the table for her, then seated himself opposite side.

She sank down in stunned silence, grateful that she still held her position, and confused by his behavior. But then, it was difficult to think clearly when he was observing her so closely.

Ashworth leaned back in the chair and sighed.

"It is my understanding that Louise is a poor excuse for a nursemaid," he said plainly.

Clara had to laugh at his candor, and for the first time was able to look him directly in the eye without fear of discipline. The earl returned her gaze. It seemed the temperature in the room increased noticeably. She cleared her throat before speaking.

"My lord, I believe we have independently arrived at the same conclusion."

The earl nodded and folded his fingers together on the table. She resisted the impulse to reach over and slide her fingers on top of his. She wondered how he would react. Would he push her away? Or would he pull her closer . . .

"And I also understand," he said, yanking her out of her reverie, "that Rosa has been a problem as well."

"No, my lord, not at all," assured Clara. "On the contrary, she acts the way I would expect any curious young child to act. My only concern is that her actions might displease you."

"I see," he said, his eyes roaming over her as he pondered. "I believe the best solution, at least until her mother arrives, is for you to humor her as best you can. Quite honestly, I can't watch her every moment, and at this point, oddly enough, I trust you much more than I trust Louise. That is," he added with a subtle smile, "as long as you aren't cleaning a fireplace around her."

She smiled ruefully at the reference, but then frowned as she tried to make sense of his words. He tipped his head as he attempted to gauge her reaction. "Is that asking too much? I understand if you object."

Lord Ashworth had said he trusted her. For a housemaid who had plunged headfirst into both a carriage and the carpet in front of him not a fortnight earlier, that was saying a lot. Of course, he was comparing her to Louise. The standard was set low, so perhaps his trust wasn't as impressive as it seemed.

Regardless, she was relieved. "It will be lovely to have her company, my lord, particularly with your blessing. But what of Louise?" she asked.

Ashworth scowled. "I spoke with her tonight, just before coming to look for you," he said. "If it were up to me, she would be packing her bags forthwith. However, she is under my sister's employ and not mine to discharge. I will address the matter with Eliza when she arrives at the end of the week." He rose from the table and returned his chair back into its proper position. His features softened. "In the meantime, should Rosa find you, please care for her."

Clara stood as well, sinking into a curtsy. "Yes, my lord."

Surprisingly, the earl did not immediately move to leave

the room. Lord Ashworth examined her from across the table, lost in contemplation. He took one, two steps around the table, then stopped. She could feel the heat flowing off his body, and she swayed unsteadily as she looked up at him, unsure of his intentions.

It was impossible to be unaffected by him when he was in such close proximity. He smelled delicious—unlike any man she had met before. Most of London's aristocrats doused themselves with overly strong colognes, but Ashworth's scent was subtle, shaving soap and clean linen. Combined with his own masculine scent, it was nearly irresistible. She longed to grip his shirt to pull him close and breathe him in.

Instead she stared up at him, mute, until he laughed softly and shook his head.

"Rosa was wrong about you, you know." His deep voice was like a stroke of fingertips along her spine. Hesitantly, as if he knew better but couldn't stop himself, he reached out and lightly grasped a lock of her hair between forefinger and thumb. The errant curl should have been neatly restrained beneath her cap, but had managed to slip free of its pins at some point during her day.

"My lord?" she asked, in a daze.

"Your hair," he said. "Your eyes. They're not black at all."

Then, as if he'd encountered open flame, the earl jerked his hand away, turned and walked swiftly out of the dining hall.

CHAPTER FIVE

Clara, Rosa, and Louise made their way slowly towards the forest behind the estate. The weak light of the sun had broken through the morning fog to shine dimly across the grass, casting glistening reflections off the remaining dewdrops. Clara looked down at her skirts, noticing how the last inches of fabric at the bottom were becoming heavy and dark with collected moisture as they passed through the field. Rosa, in a state of childish bliss, had already tumbled to the grass numerous times, leaving green streaks on her dress that Clara knew she would have to scrub out later if she were to avoid the ire of the laundry maid. She would not have censured her playful romp for the world, though.

Inhaling deeply, she breathed in the scents of the season. There was the pungent smokiness released by nearby chimneys, and the sweet essence of leaves decaying in the crisp autumn breeze. It reminded her of her childhood. It reminded her of home.

She must have looked upset, because Louise glanced curiously over at her.

"Are you unwell?" asked the nursemaid. The tone implied the question was borne from obligation rather than concern, which was fortunate. Clara knew the least sign of empathy would cause her demeanor to crumble, an inconvenience she could not afford when pretending to be someone she was not.

She kept her eyes trained carefully on Rosa's quick movements. "No, thank you," she replied. "Just a speck of dust in my eye, is all."

Louise seemed satisfied with her answer and continued forward while the little girl leaped and giggled ahead of them, stopping frequently to pluck late-flowering weeds from the ground and scrutinize insects.

"Look!" Rosa exclaimed abruptly. "It's a worm!" She turned and thrust out her hand at her guardians, a fat pink worm writhing in displeasure from between her tiny fingers. Louise shrank back with a noise of disgust, while Clara stepped forward to kneel down beside the curious girl.

"Why, yes it is," she replied, admiring Rosa's captive. "And a nice big one, at that. Let's be sure to put it back where we found it, though, so it keeps the ground healthy. Worms have a very important job, you know."

Rosa stared at her, astonished. "They do?" She leaned over with an aura of respect and placed the wriggling creature back in between the long tufts of grass, where it immediately burrowed back down into the safety of the soil. Rosa clapped in delight and threw her arms around Clara. "He's going back to work!"

Clara squeezed the girl tightly. "Yes, he is. Well done!" She stood and took her hand, then hurried to catch up with Louise, who had left them behind.

The group had departed the estate twenty minutes earlier with the goal of reaching the majestic old growth forest to the east. Rosa, a firm believer in fairies, was buzzing with anticipation. She had even tucked morsels from that morning's crumpet safely away in the pockets of her dress, in the hopes they might tempt the magical beings to appear.

Clara and Rosa caught up with Louise at the edge of the forest. The nursemaid was reluctant to enter, although to Clara, the pathway leading in looked well-worn and inviting, lined with hazel and birch trees dressed in their brilliant October finery. She pictured the earl and his siblings as young children, exploring this forest by the very same route, then shook her head, annoyed. No matter how she tried to avoid the man, he always seemed to be hovering on the edge of her thoughts.

"Can we go in, Helen?" Rosa was gazing up at her with shining eyes, one hand gripping hers fiercely while the other had already dived into her pocket, readying the crumpet crumbs. Clara laughed and gave the little hand a pat in return.

"Yes, of course. We came all this way, didn't we?" She looked over at Louise, who was lifting up her skirts to examine something she'd found stuck to her walking boot. The look of revulsion on her face did not bode well for her footwear.

"Are you coming, or have you had your fill?" Clara asked, trying not to smile. Rosa was not nearly as conscientious, and laughed wildly as Louise scraped her boot along the grass to clean it off.

"I'll be there in a . . . *ugh* . . . of all the rotten luck . . ." With a final drag through a pile of leaves, the woman returned her skirts to their normal position and huffed over to join them as they entered the forest, their presence marked by the sudden dash of a hare across the path, so quick it could barely be seen.

"*Fairies . . .*" whispered the little girl reverently. Clara grinned and glanced over at Louise, who looked dreadfully bored. They continued into the thicket of trees, birds swooping and calling around them.

She was suddenly reminded of all the times that she and Lucy had ventured into the wilderness surrounding her family's Silvercreek estate. She could almost feel the swing of the wicker picnic basket in her grasp, full of tasty snacks from the kitchen. Could hear Lucy's laughter as they waded through the long grass, leaning over to smell the wildflowers . . .

"It certainly could be fairies," she said softly, willing the memory away. She missed her sister dreadfully still. But Helen the housemaid could not afford to get caught up in Clara Mayfield's recollections. "Let's see if we can find where they are hiding!"

They made their way further into the forest, the midmorning daylight dimming as the trees grew thicker and thicker. A sudden gust of wind upset the treetops, and leaves floated and spun as they fell from the canopy above their heads. It was the perfect crisp day for a magical hunting party.

Clara's daily chores meant her shoulders had become overly tense, and certainly more muscular than her days as an heiress. But she could feel them loosen now as she tipped her head up gratefully to bask in the narrow streaks of sunlight penetrating through the branches. The chance for a refreshing walk outside had been too good to pass up. How she'd needed this.

Up ahead, there was a rustling in the brush. Clara put a hand on Rosa's arm and crouched down, finger to her lips. Rosa's green eyes, darker than her uncle's but lovely just the same, went wide and still. Her mouth froze in an excited pucker. Louise rolled her eyes and stood behind them, waiting. The rustling continued, moved a bit to the right, continued some more, then stopped. Everyone waited, staring at the bushes, until a red squirrel leaped out at them, squeaking, tail whirling furiously in the air. They shrieked in surprise, then laughed as the squirrel hopped onto a rock and sat back on his haunches to gaze at them, its paws curled inquisitively beneath his fuzzy white chest. He possessed impressive ear tufts that stuck high above his head, giving him a profoundly dramatic appearance.

"Hello! Would you like a treat?" Rosa carefully tossed a chunk of the sweet bread in the squirrel's direction, and he wasted no time in jumping down to retrieve it. Picking it up in his tiny paws, he sniffed it and turned it first one way and then the other, before deciding it was suitable for consumption. The squirrel munched quickly and finished within seconds, then turned to Rosa again, staring at her with gleaming black eyes. She didn't hesitate, and tossed a fistful of crumbs at her new woodland friend.

"Rosa," said Clara. "Wouldn't you like to save some food for the fairies?"

The girl turned to look at her, her blonde hair lifting in the wind. "But he looks so hungry!" She tossed another handful of crumbs at him, and he made short work of them, scooting his mouth along the forest floor to collect every last bit, before standing again to gaze at her expectantly.

"Helen! Rosa! Over here!" Louise's voice echoed from some distance away, and the startled squirrel ran off.

Clara turned and guided Rosa through fallen leaves, until they were separated from the nursemaid by a low, ancient stone wall.

"How curious," said Clara, as she lifted Rosa to the other side. Louise was pointing to something on the ground.

"I've found the gateway to the fairy kingdom!" she exclaimed.

Surprised, a smile broke out across Clara's face. She hadn't thought Louise had been interested in their game.

Rosa gasped and approached the nursemaid, who was standing near a short stone cylinder that rose from the ground, sealed by an old wooden cover. Clara recognized it immediately. It was a well, boarded up and no longer in use. She glared in Louise's direction, and reached forward to pull Rosa firmly back against her skirts.

"No, Rosa, it's not." Then to the nursemaid, "Why would you tell her such a thing? She could get hurt playing near an old well."

Louise scoffed. "It's not as if she is unattended. She'll be fine."

"It's an irresponsible thing to say to a child," snapped Clara.

She lifted Rosa back over the wall, then hopped over herself and gripped Rosa's hand tightly as they journeyed back the way they came. Louise could follow, or not, for all she cared.

"You're not to play near the well, Rosa. It's dangerous," she said, as they walked briskly towards the light of the open field. "Do you understand?"

"Yes, Helen. But I ran out of food for the fairies," she said plaintively.

"The fairies can take care of themselves. It's *you* I worry about."

The sky had turned dark, but they made it back to the manor before the rain began. Rosa's dress was littered with twigs and dirt from their adventure, as was her hair. Clara looked down at her dress to find her own appearance just as unkempt. She ushered Rosa through the service entrance, up the narrow steps and into the hallway by the nursery. Satisfied at managing to avoid detection in their messy state, she let herself and Rosa into the room and turned to shut the door swiftly behind them.

"Uncah!" shouted Rosa in delight.

Clara nearly jumped. Surely, she had misheard. She faced the door for a long moment, then turned slowly.

There was the earl, glancing her way as he crouched down to wrap his arms around his filthy niece.

She'd done her best to avoid him these past few days, hoping to weaken the magnetic pull of her desire, the constant compulsion to catch a glimpse of him, be near him in some way. As she saw him now, Clara felt her entire body flush and she backed against the door. His hair fell in a disarray over his forehead, and the muscular definition of his arms as he hugged his niece caused her breath to hitch.

His eyes held hers and a notch formed between his brows as he scooped up Rosa in his arms and stood.

"Are you unwell?" he asked, stepping closer to her.

She realized it was the second time that day someone had asked her that question. Perhaps she wasn't well, and perhaps she was terrible at pretending she was.

"Yes, my lord. Forgive me—we rushed back and I've yet to catch my breath," she fibbed. It would be too ridiculous to admit that she simply needed more time to recover from the unexpected shock of seeing him.

But then he surprised her again. Instead of backing away and giving her space, or accepting her explanation and putting her out of his mind, he came nearer and offered his hand, saying nothing.

She stared mutely at the long stretch of his graceful fingers. As if in a dream, she saw her hand slide into his. In all her London seasons, her dances shared with men both young and old, she had never found herself so affected, and by the merest touch of hands. The feel of his skin was incendiary, and he curled his fingers more tightly around hers. Clara lifted her eyes to find his already looking down at her with the sober, contemplative expression she'd come to expect him to wear in her company.

Clara was unable to prevent her eyes from traversing the rest of his face—over the sweep of his dark lashes, down the strong line of his jaw, landing on the tempting curve of his mouth. Were he to lean in right now, she knew there would be no resisting . . .

She heard him catch his breath. It was almost as if he'd read her thoughts.

An impish chortle brought her back to the present. Momentarily lost in fantasy, she'd forgotten about Rosa. The child was staring at her, just inches away, from a comfortably perched position in the crook of Ashworth's other arm.

A nervous laugh escaped Clara's lips. Rosa was grinning from ear to ear, looking back and forth from her to the earl, with her eyes coming to rest on the former.

"You're funny!" she proclaimed loudly.

The earl ignored Rosa's declaration, and proceeded to lead Clara to a chair by the window. She sat and retrieved her hand as quickly as she could, then politely folded both in her lap to conceal the trembling. Had she imagined his reluctance as her hand had slipped from his? It was difficult to tell when her entire body was humming.

"Thank you, my lord," she said, her voice shaking audibly. "I appreciate your assistance."

Rosa leaned in towards Ashworth's ear. "She was fine just a minute ago, Uncah," she whispered loudly.

Clara wanted to melt into the floor. Rosa was just a child,

but the honest words still stung. Her face was hot with embarrassment and probably bright red, but the earl proved himself to be a gentleman by changing the subject.

"I'm actually quite pleased at the timing of your return from the forest," he said, then craned his neck to peer behind her. "Although I can't help but notice your numbers have thinned. Did we lose somebody to the fairies?" he inquired, his voice laced with mock worry.

"Louise should return shortly to resume her duties," Clara replied. "She was trailing behind us as we left."

"She found a fairy gateway!" exclaimed Rosa, clapping her hand over her mouth when she saw the frown on Clara's face. Lord Ashworth, perplexed, looked first at his niece, then back at Clara for an explanation, his eyebrows raised. She sighed.

"My lord, what she *found* was an old well, boarded up, just to the east of a stone wall."

The earl paused, his face blank, then recollection struck him. He leaned down to set Rosa on the floor, and straightened to shake his head with a quiet laugh.

"I'm surprised it hasn't crumbled into the ground by now," he muttered. "My brother and I spent many a day tempting fate near that old well." There was a pause, a moment lost in thought. Surely a remembrance of the brother he'd had, now lost.

He dragged his eyes up to meet hers, and cleared his throat.

"I came to advise you of my immediate travel plans," he said, changing the subject. "It should not affect you directly, but I will be departing for a short business trip to Hastings this afternoon. I will be gone for roughly a week. Lord Evanston will be accompanying me as well."

Rosa wrapped her arms around his leg and howled in disappointment.

"No! Don't leave me!"

Detaching himself from Rosa's grasp as best he could, he knelt beside her and pulled her close until their foreheads were touching.

"I will return in a few days, my darling," he said softly. "Until then you will have both Helen and Louise to keep you safe and sound." His amber-green eyes found Clara's. "I know you will be well taken care of."

Clara's chest grew warm as she watched him soothe Rosa's fears with his soft words and gentle embrace. There was something undeniably attractive about a strong and powerful man making the effort to comfort a small child.

He kissed the girl gently on the forehead before standing once more. "We leave for the village within the hour. There is some business to attend to there before we can continue south."

Clara rose from her chair. "I had not heard of this trip from Mrs. Malone. Is she aware of your departure? Should the staff prepare to send you off?"

Ashworth shook his head vehemently. "I require no ceremony when I leave my own estate, and Lord Evanston deserves none," he stated, with a hint of a smile. "As for Mrs. Malone, I informed her of my plans earlier this morning, while you were out."

The door suddenly flew open to reveal Louise, dirty cap

in hand and skirts covered in leaves. Her ill-tempered scowl dissolved into deference the moment she saw the earl, and she performed a clumsy curtsy.

"Begging your pardon, my lord—"

"It appears you are late," the earl interrupted crisply. "I'd like you to get Rosa set to rights straightaway."

Another hurried curtsy. "Yes, my lord."

Louise guided Rosa out of the nursery and, hopefully, into a fresh change of dress. And in that moment, Clara came to the startling realization that she and Lord Ashworth were now in the room, facing each other, alone. Her earlier light-headedness returned as he subjected her to a leisurely visual perusal, a small smile playing about his lips. She couldn't help but be embarrassed at the rumpled state of her morning gown, and as if to humiliate her further, a leaf fluttered down to the carpet from the tangles of hair that had come loose from her cap.

"Excuse me, my lord," she mumbled, clasping one hand to her head and ducking down to retrieve the errant piece of foliage. Her fingers had only just grazed the leaf when his fingers skimmed hers in his own attempt to help. A jolt of physical awareness shook her, and she glanced up in surprise to find the earl's devastatingly handsome face very close to her own, with him having lowered into a crouch beside her. There was no sign of the amusement that had been on his face before. Now he gazed at her eyes, her hair, her mouth . . . his expression inscrutable, but absolutely intrigued.

The roar of her heartbeat was deafening.

She shot back up to her feet. Ashworth's response to the unexpected closeness was more subtle, with him slowly curling his fingers around the greenery before rising to a stand himself. Casually, he extended it out to her.

"Perhaps you need a change of dress, as well."

The words themselves were entirely innocent. But the way his eyes lingered on her body suggested something else entirely.

She tried to remind herself that this kind of attention, however flattering, would only set her apart from the other servants. She was not Clara Mayfield any longer, and this was not a drawing room in London. It was absolutely not permissible for her to engage with the earl on any sort of meaningful level. Even if he found her attractive, and even if he might be willing to distract himself from his troubles with her company.

Clara attempted to smile in his direction before reaching forward to pluck the leaf from his fingers. She was careful not to touch him or meet his eyes.

"Thank you, my lord."

He simply nodded in her direction before striding past her and disappearing down the hallway. But not before Clara caught him stealing a lightning-quick glance back in her direction.

Clara had quickly tidied up herself and donned an apron in preparation for her afternoon duties. She rushed to enter the servants' hall and, not being especially careful, smacked right into Matthew. He stepped back and laughed, a pair of the earl's shoes in one hand and a polishing rag in the other.

"Ha! What was I telling you, Charles? The ladies just love me!" he called over his shoulder to the other footman.

Charles approached them, a pair of bright silver candlesticks in his hands. "How am I supposed to compete with that kind of power?" he asked, forlorn. "Women literally throw themselves at you." Shaking his head in a show of theatrical sorrow, he then straightened up and looked at Clara hopefully. "Maybe if I stand here long enough, a woman might collide with me?"

Clara laughed, and was about to make a sarcastic retort, when Amelia shouldered roughly past her.

"The only part of a woman about to collide with you is my fist, Charles," she said grumpily. Then she rounded on Matthew, who backed up against the wall, with hands—and the earl's shoes—raised in surrender.

"And you!" she began.

But before she could get any further, he smiled at her, his dark blue eyes twinkling. "Have I mentioned how lovely you are when you want to tear my head off?" he asked.

Instantly, Amelia's posture deflated. She actually smiled for a fraction of a second, before her eyebrows lowered again. She whirled around on Clara.

"What are you looking at? Why don't you quit causing trouble?" she muttered as she shoved past her the way she came, pausing briefly to straighten a painting on the wall before making her exit.

Matthew lowered his hands and gazed after Amelia with

something akin to fear. "It's too bad she's such a beast some-times." He ambled slowly down the hallway, shaking his head.

He may have found Amelia intimidating, but that cer-tainly hadn't kept Matthew from watching the swing of her hips as she'd left. Clara was curious if Amelia had any idea how Matthew felt about her, then realized she'd grown tired of wondering after Abigail's sister with such frequency. Par-ticularly since Amelia couldn't seem to care less. Furrow-ing her brow in annoyance, she edged closer to the picture frame, and using two fingertips, pushed it out of its recently corrected alignment. Surveying the crooked painting with a satisfied smile, she bent down to pick up her bucket and brush and went up the stairs.

Her day progressed slowly, as it usually did without Rosa to distract her. She realized that any time spent with the little girl was a luxury typically not afforded to servants, and she felt grateful for the occasional break in her routine. This afternoon was spent busily scrubbing the foyer, sweeping the carpets, and dusting the furniture and light fixtures.

When she was finished, she could already feel a pro-nounced stiffness in her lower back, and knew pain would follow in the morning, as it had every morning since her ar-rival. She stood and arched backwards, kneading the muscles with her fingers to loosen them. The daylight had weakened, and Mrs. Malone would be expecting the rooms to be lighted soon, so she gathered her tools to bring them downstairs.

Soon she was preparing for the impending dusk, balanc-ing precariously on the edge of a step stool, lengthening her body to light the wall sconces. The task was made difficult by her modest height, as even a step stool could not always provide the distance required to comfortably perform her chores. Even though the Earl of Ashworth and Lord Evanston were not in attendance tonight, Mrs. Malone insisted on lighting the public spaces, should an unexpected visitor come to call.

She had just lit the last candle, and was stepping down to survey the room, when she heard the sound of panicked footfalls growing louder as they came nearer to the drawing room. At last, the door flew open and Louise stood before her in frazzled disarray, her breathing loud and labored.

"She's gone missing!" she cried in distress.

"Who?" asked Clara. Her eyes widened. "*Rosa?*"

"Yes. I've checked the house. It's all I've been doing for an hour!"

Clara's blood turned to ice water in her veins. "An *hour?* And you're just now asking for help finding her? After an hour?!"

Louise's eyes shifted guiltily. "Well I'd hoped to find her on my own, before involving others . . ."

"I see," said Clara coldly. The inept nursemaid had wished to avoid attracting attention, and had likely only succeeded in making the situation much worse. "And how did you lose her in the first place?" she asked.

Louise actually stamped her foot, the sound echoing loudly through the room around them. Clara was sure she had not seen that particular show of temper displayed by a grown woman since . . . well, ever.

"Will you help me find her or not?" she demanded. "I don't need to be questioned, I just need help!"

Clara, too, was more eager to find Rosa than determine the particulars of the situation. Questions could come later. "Yes, certainly I'll help. You take the top two floors of the house. I'll take the ground floor and belowstairs." She paused. "Unless you have reason to believe she went outside?"

"No, no, I'm sure she's found some spot beneath a table and is having great fun laughing at my expense," Louise muttered as she stalked out the door. Clara didn't know how she could be so sure that the girl hadn't escaped the house. Rosa was so young, after all, and prone to exploring and finding adventure. She decided to patrol along the exits first before conducting the rest of her indoor search.

Beginning at the far end of the house and working towards the other, she thoroughly scanned the French doors in the ballroom and the music room. All appeared to be untouched. She entered the breakfast room and examined the doors there. They, too, were shut tightly, but as she turned to go check the library, her eyes happened to glance through the glass panes to the patio outside.

The last vestige of daylight shone, feebly illuminating a spot on the pathway. Clara approached the door, released the latch at the top, and twisted the knob to exit the house and venture into the twilight outside. Scanning the stone patio, she walked towards the spot and her eyes stopped on something dark and red. Blood? She knelt down and traced a fingertip through the sticky residue. No, not blood.

Jam.

She stood and her eyes traveled along the patio, finding bits of tart and jam along the way. Quickly, she followed the messy trail past the garden and in the direction of the field beyond the estate, where she paused.

The girl must have left by the service door. Clara faced the forest in growing horror, as the first huge raindrops splashed the ground nearby.

Chapter Six

Clara broke into a sprint, the pounding rain soaking through her skirts, causing them to wrap awkwardly around her legs. She increased her pace, racing around the eastern side of the house towards the stables. Rivulets of icy water trailed down her face, and she swiped a hand across her skin, blinking furiously to clear her vision.

By the time she reached the courtyard, it was flooded. She arrived at the stables a dripping mess, and shoved the doors open to storm inside.

Her body swayed, the strong smell of hay and horses assailing her senses, and she leaned forward to catch her breath. "Oscar?" she called between pants. She raised her voice. "I need a horse . . ."

The boy appeared from around a corner, pitchfork in hand, regarding her with shock. His pale blue eyes were wide, devoid of all comprehension.

"Aren't you a housemaid?" he asked in disbelief.

Clara had recovered and was already hurrying over to where the leather saddles were hanging neatly on the wall. As she heaved one off its mounting, Oscar rushed over in a panic.

"Hey! You can't touch those! What are you—" His speech trailed off as she whirled around to skewer him with a black look.

"The master's niece has run off to the woods, and both Lord Ashworth and Lord Evanston are away on business." She hauled the saddle through the stables, examining the horses in their stalls to quickly try and assess which one would best fit her needs. "I need a horse *now*, and a recommendation would be welcome since time is of the essence."

Oscar's eyes shifted from her face down to his shoes, as he weighed the consequences of caving in to her demands. "I dunno, miss. It could be my job if I give you a horse without any sort of approval first."

"You are right, of course," Clara conceded. "In this instance, though, I can honestly say that if you don't give me a horse, and some harm befalls the earl's niece, you will be more likely to lose your job than had you thought to trust me just a little."

The boy still stared at her with reluctance. Obtaining a horse would be much tougher without him on her side. She drew herself up and clenched her fists in exasperation. "Can't you understand? It's my neck I'm risking here as well. Were I not convinced of the validity of my request, I would not be making it."

This argument seemed to sway him the most, although he still looked uneasy when he finally nodded in ascension. He ran his fingers through his wheat colored hair and mumbled, "I suppose I don't have much to say against that."

He led her to a beautiful gray horse with shining black eyes. It looked to be the perfect size for her. It reminded Clara of her own horse, Philomena, that she had left behind in Silvercreek.

Oscar looked down at the saddle in her hands.

"Er—don't suppose you'd prefer a sidesaddle?" he asked, looking uncomfortable.

Refusing to acknowledge the irony of the situation, she stared at him and said, "Do I look like a lady to you?"

Perhaps wisely, he decided not to answer her, rapidly saddling the horse and helping Clara up. Her skirts were ill-suited for this activity, and they bunched and gathered around the saddle. Oscar managed to adequately ignore her scandalous riding position, along with the fact that her legs were exposed, by quickly turning to fit the horse with a bridle and reins.

The moment he'd finished, she steered the horse towards the courtyard, slowing to obtain a lantern on her way out of the stables, then turned once more to face him.

"A rider must be sent to the village . . . it is possible Lord Ashworth could still be there." A shadow crossed her features as she scanned the darkening horizon. "If I'm not back soon, we will need a larger search party."

And with a whirl of the reins and a kick of her heels, she was galloping furiously across the field.

Clara slowed her pace once she arrived at the woods. The pathway, so inviting just hours earlier, now looked dark and dangerous, the trees serving as dark sentinels on either side of the entrance. She shivered, wishing she had thought to bring a blanket or a cloak for Rosa. The temperature had dipped considerably in the last half hour.

"Rosa! Can you hear me?" she shouted.

The forest remained quiet. Indifferent.

Her eyes scanned the dim landscape, searching for any sign of movement. Occasionally, she would hear a noise and catch the shadow of a scared animal out of the corner of her eye, and each time her heart leapt into her throat. Fortunately, the horse she rode upon was exceptionally even tempered, only whickering softly at these disruptions. Clara leaned over and softly stroked her head.

"There's a good girl. We'll be there soon enough."

The pair continued. Clara kept calling out for the girl, her voice sounding loud and out of place in the quiet solitude of the woods. Her increasing panic demanded she charge forth and find Rosa in haste, but the rational part of her mind feared trampling the girl in the deepening gloom. She forced herself to keep a slow and steady pace, calling out to her in the hopes of receiving a response.

Finally, the light from her lantern shone on the stone wall ahead. Her heartbeat quickened as she clumsily dismounted and fumbled to tie the reins around the sturdy branch of a nearby tree. She approached the wall carefully, navigating over fallen tree trunks and other debris on the forest floor.

"Rosa!" she yelled. "It's Helen! Are you here?"

Silence greeted her as she stepped over the decrepit wall. She was fairly certain the well was about twenty feet to her left, so she edged her way carefully towards it. Her pulse was pounding now, and she forced thoughts of what she might find at the end of her quest out of her mind.

"Rosa, love! It's safe to come out!" Her voice was trembling now.

The dark shape of the well was discernible in the twilight. Clara inched closer until she could see it in more detail, then she shouted in hoarse denial, her fists rising to her mouth in terror. Half the boards on the wooden cover had been broken through, their spiky ends grinning at her like rotten jagged teeth. The breach appeared just the right size for a little girl to slip through.

Clara sank to her knees, distantly aware that hot tears were gushing down her cheeks. She crawled over to shine her lantern down the well, but it was too deep and her light did not reach the bottom.

"*Rosa!*" she cried, her face crumpling in despair. The thought of her bright little life being lost was too much to bear, and Clara sobbed until her lungs spasmed in her chest.

As she stopped to catch her breath, she heard a faint sound. A weeping to match her own, like some distant echo. She leaned forward at once, but the sound didn't seem to be coming from the well. Silencing herself, she stood eagerly on shaky legs and craned her neck to hear it better. The crying grew louder and it was only when Clara looked over the side of the stone wall that she saw a quivering shape huddled low against it. She inhaled the damp forest air to calm herself before speaking.

"Rosa?" she called, her voice even.

The shape raised its head, growing quiet. As Clara raised the lantern, she saw it was indeed Rosa, tightly gripping her doll. Without thinking, Clara leaped over the wall and gathered the girl tightly in her arms.

"Oh, thank God! I thought I'd lost you!" Clara cried. "Did you not hear me calling?"

The child sniffled and tried to catch her breath. "I did hear you, but I was scared. Then when I was going to call out, you started crying and scared me some more." Her eyes were huge and round in the darkness. "Am I in awful trouble?"

Clara couldn't help but let out a trembling laugh. She stroked the child's sodden hair and gazed at her affectionately. "No, darling, not at all. I'm just so happy that you're safe!" Her brows lowered. "Are you hurt anywhere? Did you injure yourself?"

"I hurt my leg when I tried to walk on that," she stated, pointing towards the shattered boards covering the gaping well.

Clara's eyes widened. "And you managed not to fall in . . ." She gently took the girl's leg in her hands and examined it. Scarlet gouges marked where the boards had pierced skin. Blood was still slowly oozing over the wounded flesh, appearing black and strange in the shadows. Thankfully, though, the injury appeared mostly superficial.

Clara reached behind and untied her apron. Quickly she

lifted it off over her head, wrapped it tight around Rosa's leg and tied it securely.

"We need to get you back to the house."

She stood and helped Rosa to her feet, then scooped her up in her arms and carefully maneuvered back to the horse. Once the reins were untied, she lifted the girl into the saddle then pulled herself up behind her. The horse immediately responded to the gentle jab of her heels, carrying them through the drippy confines of the woods, its hooves making soft sucking noises in the mud.

The world felt right again with Rosa safe in her arms. She squeezed her tightly against her body, attempting to impart some of her own heat to the shivering child. Clara couldn't bear to think about how close the girl had come to falling down the well.

She had no idea how Lord Ashworth would respond to the entire situation. Hopefully he would forgive her impetuous use of the horse, but she couldn't be certain he'd allow her the privilege of continuing to spend time with the girl, seeing as both she and Louise had been directed to watch her, and both had failed.

The trip out of the thicket seemed much shorter than the trip inside had been. Soon the horse was trotting out from the trees and into the field near Lawton Park. Up ahead in the distance she could just barely make out the light of multiple lanterns bobbing towards them in the night. Darkness had completely claimed the land, a tiny slip of a moon providing very little in the way of illumination. Her body was chilled through, and she knew Rosa felt the same. The thought of dry clothes and a blazing fire made her weary with anticipation. She pushed her wet hair out of her face; it had long since fallen from its pins.

The lights grew brighter until she could finally see the shapes of the men that held the lanterns, galloping swiftly towards them. The world suddenly became a thundering of hooves and commotion around them as the two groups converged. Her horse reared in panic, but a strong hand grasped the reins and Clara glanced up to see the earl right next to her, his green eyes dark and haunted.

"Uncah!" Rosa exclaimed. She was suddenly a wriggling mass in Clara's arms, and his eyes caught the movement.

"*Rosa*, my God . . ." He was off his horse in an instant, reaching up to gently grasp the little girl. Clara relinquished her hold as he pulled her to him in a crushing embrace.

Evanston was not far behind, swinging off his horse to approach Clara, his face grave.

"Let me assist you," he said.

Since there was no ladylike way to dismount from her current position, she simply swung her leg behind her, wincing as mud went flying, then turned to place her hands on his shoulders. Lord Evanston quickly lifted her off the horse and set her on solid ground. To her dismay, her legs wobbled, and she had to grasp his arm to steady herself. She saw Matthew and Charles lurking behind the two gentlemen, still on their horses, worry etched plainly on their faces. She nodded towards them in acknowledgment, and they tipped their heads grimly in return.

She and Evanston approached the earl and his niece to

find his arms still locked tightly around her. The viscount placed a hand on his friend's shoulder.

"Ashworth," he murmured, "we should get her back to the house. The doctor will be waiting there."

Finally, the earl pulled away, taking the girl's face in his hands and turning it from side to side as if checking for signs of injuries. When he spoke at last, his voice was rough with emotion.

"Are you all right, sweetheart? Are you hurt?"

Rosa sniffed, and Clara could now see rows of scratches covering her face. "I'm much better now that Helen found me. It was scary out in the woods, not fun like I thought it would be." She winced in pain and touched her wounded limb. "My leg hurts."

The earl reached down to lift her leg into view as she continued talking. He was looking closely at the makeshift dressing. Then he glanced at Clara sharply. "Is it serious?"

"I don't believe so. Nothing a good cleaning and a bandage won't fix."

He tipped Rosa's chin up gently. "We'll get your leg all taken care of, my love," Ashworth murmured.

Evanston reached a hand out to muss Rosa's sopping hair. Clara could tell the viscount had a great deal of affection for the little girl too, although he was more ill at ease in showing it. To his very obvious surprise, Rosa reached over to wrap her little arms fiercely around his neck. Within seconds, she had burrowed under the warmth of his cloak. Evanston glanced over at Ashworth, an awkward look upon his face.

"Er, I'd hate to extract her now. Perhaps she should return with me, on my horse?"

The earl nodded in reply. "That's fine," he said, smiling. "It is clearly what she'd like to do."

Turning to face Clara, Ashworth's eyes raked over her. Suddenly, she was aware of how tightly her wet clothing was clinging to her body. Her apron was still tied around Rosa's leg, so she couldn't even use it to cover herself. Biting her lip, she glanced down, unsure what to do. To her surprise, the earl stepped closer to her while he untied the laces of his cloak. She stared up at him, paralyzed, as he leaned forward to wrap the thick fabric around her shoulders, covering her completely. The garment was exquisitely warm with his own body heat.

"You may ride back with me, if you wish," he said. His voice was low, still rough with emotion, and it sent a delicious fire racing through every part of her body.

She swallowed, imagining what it would feel like to be held tightly against his broad chest . . . to feel the strength of his body wrapped around hers . . .

Which was why she could not say yes. To allow herself the luxury of physical closeness with this man, when she knew nothing could ever come of it, would cost every last bit of her sanity.

She lifted her chin. "Thank you, my lord, but I am able to ride on my own," she said, nearly choking on the words.

Ashworth's eyes widened, his expression an intriguing blend of emotions. Clara tried to decipher them, but they vanished as quickly as they'd come.

"As you wish," he replied. His tone was polite, but his jaw was clenched, as if he were restraining some particularly intense emotion.

He accompanied her to the patiently waiting gray horse, and took her right hand in his so she could pull herself up to straddle her steed. Again her legs were bared to view, and again she struggled in vain to adjust her skirts.

As he turned to mount his horse, she could have sworn she saw him smiling.

Clara immediately went to change into dry clothing. She returned downstairs wearing her dark pink morning dress, her damp hair pulled back into a proper bun. She felt much recovered, but still chilled to the bone. Stella ushered her to a place by the fire and pressed a steaming cup of tea into her hand, and the heat from both the tea and the fire soothed her icy flesh. Stella lowered herself into the chair opposite hers.

"The doctor has already examined Rosa," she whispered in a hushed voice. "I thought you would like to know—she will be fine."

Clara felt a layer of tension filter out from her body, and she sighed in relief.

"I'm so glad," she replied. From out in the hall, the sound of whispering caught her attention, and she turned in her chair to see the other servants gathered there to observe her from afar, murmuring amongst themselves. She laughed softly. "You must be the only one brave enough to associate with me right now."

Stella smiled and rolled her eyes. "There may be some truth to that, although I doubt the earl would sack me just for bringing you tea, even if you did help yourself to his stables."

"Do you think the earl will sack *me*?" asked Clara suddenly, sudden panic causing her heartbeat to thunder out of control.

"In this case, probably not. Your reasoning was sound even if your methods were questionable." She eyed Clara apologetically. "Although there's no way to know for—"

There was a rustling noise behind them as the servants gathered in the hallway straightened up and came to attention. The Earl of Ashworth, who had been conspicuously absent until now, walked into the drawing room, focused intently upon Clara as both she and Stella rose to face him. His hair was still wet from being outside, the normally gleaming, golden locks now rain-darkened and sleek. She felt the most inexplicable need to run her fingers through it.

Clara realized he was staring at her . . . watching her stare at him.

Mortified at being caught, she cleared her throat awkwardly. "My lord, I—"

"I need to speak with you in my study, please," the earl said in a low voice.

She felt the blood drain from her face and her eyes darted over to Stella's. "Of course," she replied, suddenly filled with dread. Stella gave her a little nod of encouragement before facing the earl herself.

"I can join the others if you wish, my lord."

"Yes, thank you, Stella."

He brushed past the housemaid on his way out of the drawing room and Clara followed, steeling her shoulders against the curious gazes of the other servants—who were busy acting like they weren't looking. Ashworth paused in a bit of annoyance.

"You are dismissed."

The group scattered, with Matthew and Charles going one way, Amelia and Stella scurrying off in the other, and the earl resumed his route to the study with a slight shake of his head.

Clara followed him, her legs working quickly beneath her skirts to keep up. She couldn't think of one thing she would have done differently that evening, and she would hold fast to that. Because of her, his niece had been brought home safely. If she was going to be reprimanded or dismissed, it would not be without a fight.

He ushered her into the study, and Clara came to a stop in the middle of the room, staring straight ahead as he closed the door behind them. Bracing for the worst, she jumped at the earl's touch on her elbow.

"Please be seated," he murmured near her ear, his closeness causing her pulse to escalate.

She glanced around nervously, then sank into a stately leather chair while he crossed to the sideboard to pour himself a drink. Agonized, she waited for him to finish so they could get on with things. At long last she heard the sound of the stopper being replaced in the glass decanter, and he walked to the front of his desk, turning and leaning informally against it to face her directly.

There were two glasses of brandy, one in each of his hands. She stared at him in surprised silence, then glanced down as he extended one to her.

"For you," he said, his voice low. "It will warm you up."

Clara hesitantly accepted the glass and stared at the swirling amber depths. Imitating the style in which she'd seen gentlemen take their brandy, she lifted the glass to her lips and took a modest swallow. A blazing trail tracked down her throat and into her belly, making her gasp and cough. She looked up at him accusingly with watery eyes.

"I apologize," he said, amused. "I should have warned you."

The earl lifted his glass and threw it back, draining it completely, before setting it down on the desk next to him. His long fingers gripped the edge of the desk as he surveyed her, but she did not miss the way they trembled there, or the flex of his jaw muscles in contrast to his nonchalant demeanor. Tonight's events had likely scared him much more than he was letting on.

"Thank you for bringing Rosa home safely tonight," he said, as Clara took another tiny swallow of her brandy.

"You are welcome, my lord. But there was plenty of luck involved, I'm afraid. Things could have ended quite differently," she said.

Ashworth averted his gaze to stare hollowly at his boots. She knew he could remember all too well how things can end when everything goes wrong. The fingers that curled around the edge of his desk suddenly tightened, causing his knuckles to turn white, and she glanced upwards in surprise.

He squeezed his eyes shut as if he were in pain and he twisted his head away from her with a quiet noise. Clara rose slowly and set her glass down, not knowing what to do and afraid of landing herself in more trouble than she already was. She desperately wanted to help him—although from what, she did not know. Her words came out in a concerned whisper.

"My lord?"

His lips were pressed tightly together and he shook his head in what seemed like despair. Her mind raced, trying to make sense of what was happening. The only conclusion she could come to was that somehow, tonight's events had caused some other, older turmoil to resurface. She had never seen it herself, but had heard stories of men from the local regiment back in Essex who'd seen battle and experienced similar struggles afterwards.

She supposed a deadly carriage accident was a lot like a battle.

Disregarding caution, at least for the moment, she took a step closer to place her hand just above his elbow. The earl's arm was hard beneath her touch, and it was shaking along with the rest of him. Her heart tugged at the feel of it. She squeezed tighter and leaned in.

"How can I help?" she asked softly.

With a suddenness that took her aback, his eyes flew open and he reached across his body to seize her hand. His breath rushed out in a pained exhalation.

"Don't," he commanded, his wild eyes mere inches away from hers. His grip on her wrist did not relent, however, and she remained where she was, willingly imprisoned by the blazing heat of his hand on her skin. He was holding her so close, and that same euphoria she'd felt the day he'd rescued her in the village came back with an intensity that caused her head to swim with dizzy pleasure. Clara knew she should pull away, but only wanted to sink further against him, to distract the troubled earl in some way. She saw the light gleam of perspiration on his brow, and longed to taste the salt that she knew lingered there, and on his lips, his neck. She leaned in closer . . .

He pushed away from the desk to release her, and she stumbled backwards until the back of her legs collided with her chair. Clara stared at him in horror. She'd just nearly kissed him, and worse, it had been at a moment when he was vulnerable. Perhaps it was seeing this strong, capable man exposed and defenseless that had caused her reaction—the need to comfort him in some way. Although in truth, every instance of closeness with him seemed to have a similar effect on her.

Ashworth's expression cleared and he sat back against the edge of his desk as if exhausted. When he spoke, his voice sounded rusty, as if he'd just woken from sleep.

"If that ever happens again in your presence . . . don't touch me."

Humiliation, sharp and swift, lanced through her chest. "Of course, my lord. I should not have presumed to—"

He shook his head. "It's not that. I just can't predict how I will react when I'm in such a state."

"Oh," she said, surprised. The hurt from a moment before

transformed into a warm, honeyed sensation in the pit of her stomach. He wasn't angry with her, only worried.

Ashworth's eyes rose wearily and he reached up to rub his temple. "I hope you can forget the display you happened to witness here." He sighed. "And I would appreciate it if we could keep the embarrassing particulars between us."

"Think no more of it, my lord." She paused. "But if you'd ever like someone to talk to, that is, if you think it might help—"

The earl lowered his brow and it silenced her immediately. Clara clasped her hands in her lap, remembering herself. They were not friends. He was her employer, and she had already broken the rules once tonight. To her relief, his gaze turned evaluative, then he leaned his long torso across the desk to retrieve her brandy and extend it to her once more.

"Back to your earlier point—yes, things could have ended differently for Rosa. And likely would have, if not for you. Lord Evanston questioned the nursemaid. She had a very interesting story to tell."

Clara's breathing stopped, her fingers suddenly nerveless against the glass. "Did she, my lord?"

"According to her, Rosa escaped while in your care."

She stared at him in disbelief. Of all the things she had been bracing for, this was not one of them. "That's a lie!" she finally managed, her voice unsteady with anger.

"I take it you have a different version of the events?"

Her entire body was shaking as she struggled to control her temper. Blood pounded in her ears as she gazed angrily up at him, and she forced herself to glance away and concentrate on her breathing. It would be of no benefit to lose control in front of the earl while he contemplated her with smoldering green eyes. Still, she could not make an answer.

"You know, sometimes you don't act like a servant in the least," he finally said.

Clara's eyes widened; she felt his gaze like a touch, and she knew this was not good. Not good at all.

"My lord, I—"

"Do you think any of my more well-behaved servants would have been able to accomplish what you did tonight?" he interrupted.

Clara stared at him, at a loss for words. She did not want to set herself apart from the other servants, but honestly couldn't say if one of the others would have done what she had done.

"I . . . I'm not certain."

"You go ahead and think about it," he replied, still looking slightly pale, but much recovered from his earlier episode. He crossed the room to deposit his glass on the sideboard. "And I'll tell you why I couldn't care less about what that woman says." He returned to his desk once more and seated himself behind it, folding his hands across his taut midriff. "First of all, Rosa told me Louise fell asleep while she was meant to be watching her."

Clara slumped backwards in relief as he delivered the news.

"And second, it was not your primary task to supervise Rosa at that time of day. Even if she had entrusted Rosa to your care, she would be the one ultimately who had failed." An expression of annoyance crossed his features. "She has been dismissed. Lord Evanston is currently making the necessary arrangements to get her off this estate as expeditiously as possible. I only wish I had done it sooner," he said, with a sigh of regret. Tipping his head, he asked, "Just to satisfy my curiosity, how did you become involved in all this?"

His scrutiny was almost too much to bear. Even after being absolved of blame, she found her hands were still unsteady. When she spoke, she was humiliated to discover that her voice was too.

"Louise enlisted my aid when she could not find Rosa on her own," she answered. "At that point Rosa had been missing for one hour."

Ashworth's gaze was unrelenting. "And how did you think to search for her out of doors?"

Clara shifted anxiously in her seat. "You might recall this morning's trip to the forest, my lord, and the fairy gateway Rosa mentioned in the nursery," she explained. "While I was checking the exits I found a trail of her favorite tarts behind the house, leading towards the woods, and I knew she'd gone back there . . ."

"To the well," he interrupted, his voice grim. "So then you, a housemaid, managed to coerce my stable boy into granting you access to a horse, which you used to ride, alone, in a storm, to find my niece." He looked incredulous. "Is this an accurate representation of the events?"

Her neck prickled in warning. She needed to downplay her actions or risk becoming overly conspicuous. "My lord, please know . . . I would have normally never . . . had not the circumstances . . ." She stumbled nervously over her words.

"Rest assured, the circumstances were extraordinary," he interjected, evaluating her solemnly from across the desk. "Not only were the measures you took warranted, they were necessary. And," the earl continued in a quieter tone, "I wholly acknowledge you risked both your personal safety and your position here to recover my niece and bring her home unharmed. For that, you have my eternal thanks." He paused. "However . . ."

Ashworth cleared his throat and looked away. Any security she had been feeling vanished.

"Unfortunately," he continued quietly, "I cannot leave these actions unpunished." The earl frowned, taking in her surprise, and added without enthusiasm, "I can't have my staff thinking there are no consequences for disobedience in my household. Even if that disobedience was used for the highest good."

His words hit her like a slap in the face. Clara understood Ashworth's perspective, of course. He wanted to maintain order in a household where she had created upheaval. The knowledge didn't make it hurt any less, though.

"Do you understand?" he pressed.

"I do understand that in most cases, what you say would be warranted, my lord. And yet—I can't see how you could find it in your heart to punish me, when a child's life depended on my willingness to break the rules," she responded unhappily. Clara stared at her shoes as tears pricked her eyes. She brushed at them angrily with the back of her hand, cursing herself for appearing weak in front of the earl.

Lifting her head, she found he had stood to approach

her from around his desk. His face was serious, his expression melancholy, and she became oddly aware of the sounds of their breathing in the quietness of the room. He lowered down to one knee beside her chair.

"My heart has nothing to do with this decision, Helen," he said softly. "This is business. I am grateful for your risk but must still assert myself as your employer." He shook his head. "You've put me in a terrible position. And you've also done me a great service," he added, his voice rich with sincere gratitude. She felt a sudden urge to reach out and stroke the side of his face—to touch him in any small way.

"Will I still be able to see Rosa?" she asked instead.

A small smile curved his lips. "I doubt I would be able to keep her away from you."

Her shoulders relaxed a fraction. She looked down at her hands.

"Then what is my punishment to be, my lord?" she ventured, her voice almost a whisper.

For a moment silence was her only answer, until at last he sighed. "You will lose your Sunday privileges for one month. Starting tomorrow."

It could have been worse. She wasn't happy, but it could have been so much worse. Dipping her chin in a small nod, she lifted her glass and drank the remaining brandy, this time enjoying the burn.

They both rose to stand, and she moved around him to collect their used glassware from the sideboard.

"I will take these downstairs. That is, if my lord requires nothing more of me tonight?" Clara couldn't help but allow a little sarcasm to slip into her voice. She hadn't meant to, but she was exhausted and unhappy, and being so near the earl was still wreaking havoc on her emotions.

"Helen," Ashworth said, a warning note in his tone. But when she met his stare, it seemed her words had affected him differently than she had intended. His golden-green eyes slid down the entire length of her body, snapping back up an instant later. Clara's breath caught in her throat as his gaze trapped hers. Fear and excitement flooded through her in equal measures.

Yes. Please . . . yes.

His expression changed quickly, a look of regret immediately stamped across his face. Ashworth took a deep breath and turned away from her.

"Good night," he muttered darkly, putting an end to the conversation.

Chapter Seven

Ashworth sighed in relief as he heard the door close behind Helen. He had just come perilously close to violating the same sacred contract between employer and staff that he had invoked in her punishment. What hypocrisy it would have been to reprimand her for her defiance of the rules, only to disregard every rule in the book by backing her against the wall and kissing her until she responded to him, pliable and willing in his arms?

Although he had an idea that, were it to happen, she would not just passively submit. He'd seen the flame flicker to life behind her eyes when he'd caught her wrist, even in the throes of his tortured state. The horror of nearly losing Rosa had only just resolved—a possibility that was all too real for him—and rather than being able to concentrate on the seriousness of the issue, he was busy contemplating Helen's reaction if he should tear her dress open once again.

William groaned and scrubbed a hand over his face. This would not do. It was why he should have sent her away. The danger was in her proximity. In the sparks that shot through his body when she was near, her hesitation at his presence. He was already aware of the attraction between them and that was problematic enough. But the concern she had shown him had not just roused him from his traumatized stupor, it had made him achingly aware of the beautiful woman in front of him as a possible source of comfort. This was not good, for comfort could take many forms, but none so tempting as the defiant housemaid.

Ashworth blinked. How long had it been since he had lain with a woman? Too long, apparently. Then again, he couldn't remember ever reacting to a woman this strongly, even women he had desired and bedded. It all seemed tame when compared to the need within him now for this . . . this odd, charming maid who was completely inappropriate for him.

As the solitary male left of his line, he could not afford to compromise his principles, nor would he. To do so would be a discredit to them both. To do so would be an absolute violation of his responsibility to his family, including those who'd been lost. A proper, highborn wife with a noble bloodline was what his earldom required, and he would deliver it. Eventually.

The earl crossed to the window, his view obscured by the darkness, tracks of falling raindrops on the glass the only visible indication of the weather outside. Sighing, he leaned his head against the cool pane and closed his eyes. There was no way for her to know how difficult it had been for him to discipline her. Especially when his thoughts on punishment strayed dangerously close to having Helen in his bed . . .

where he could tease her mercilessly until she writhed beneath him, begging for release. And only when he'd decided she had finally suffered enough would he finally take pity on them both by burying himself inside of her . . .

With another groan, the earl pulled away from the window and glanced at the door. He needed to leave, to find Evanston. Remaining here with the current turn of his thoughts was not an option.

He straightened his cravat and crossed to the door. His hand had just grasped the cool metal of the knob when it flew out of his fingers. Evanston stood before him, a look Ashworth didn't quite care for on his face.

"I've been looking for you," he said. "How was your meeting with the housemaid? I passed her on the way here," he added. "She seemed upset."

Ashworth frowned. "It went poorly. I had to punish her for doing the right thing tonight."

Evanston arched an eyebrow. "Wrong," he countered evenly. "You punished her for breaking the rules, which she did, regardless of whether it was the right thing to do or not." He lifted his broad shoulders in a shrug. "You had no choice. Besides, it's not as if you sent her packing."

Ashworth nodded in dispirited agreement. The viscount's eyebrow rose higher and he stepped backwards into the hallway to better examine his friend.

"You look like hell. What's been going on?" he asked.

The earl glanced at him in irritation. "My niece was in grave danger, I had to punish the one person who took it upon herself to help her, and you think I need another reason to be upset?"

Evanston said nothing at first, then a grin spread slowly across his face. "I know what this is about," he said slyly, raising his open palms up at Lord Ashworth in assent. "She is a pretty little thing, and fiery, to boot." After a moment's pause, he added, "You should take her to bed and be done with it."

The earl glared sharply at Evanston. "Is that how you handle complications in your household?" he asked acidly.

"Whenever possible," said the viscount, his grin wider still. "If you think it would help, I'll take her to bed for you. Maybe that would quell your interest . . ."

Ashworth suddenly lunged forward, shoving his friend against the far side of the hallway. A small gasp of surprise alerted him to another presence, and he released Evanston's shirt, turning to find Amelia standing a few feet away with a fresh pot of tea in her hands. William let out a low curse and dropped his hand, furious at himself for being discovered in such a way.

The maid bobbed into a quick curtsy.

"M-my lords," she stuttered. "I was instructed to bring some tea up to Miss Rosa, and thought perhaps . . ." she trailed off awkwardly.

"Yes," said the earl, cutting her off. "Allow me to bring her the tea in your stead. I was heading up there anyway."

Lord Evanston reached forward to grab his arm, his expression concerned.

"Christ, William, I said it in jest . . ."

Ashworth shook off the man's hand. "Then you'll know better than to make that mistake again," he snapped over his shoulder, as he took the tray from the flustered maid and stalked towards the staircase.

It was Sunday, and Lord Ashworth had taken his much-recovered niece out for a short trip to the village, while Clara was rushing to complete her chores before the rest of the staff left for their day off. She, of course, would not be leaving the estate due to her punishment. Instead, she was to report to Mrs. Malone in the library at noon to receive her extra tasks for the day.

With a weary sigh, she finished dusting the antiques in the drawing room. Noting that she still had five minutes until her meeting with Mrs. Malone, she gathered her tools and hurried downstairs, passing a grumpy-looking Amelia on the staircase. She was clad in a dark green walking dress that complimented her shining red hair, and a cream-colored bonnet dangled from her fingers.

Not for the first time, Clara thought it was unfortunate that Amelia wore such unhappy expressions. She could have been a beautiful girl but for her dour disposition. Clara had just rounded the corner when she heard the housemaid call after her.

"Helen! Did Mrs. Malone find you yet?" she asked.

Stopping in her tracks, Clara turned, narrowly dodging the stable boy, who avoided meeting her eyes, and craned her neck to gaze around the bannister at Amelia.

"No, I haven't seen her," said Clara slowly. "Why?"

The housemaid placed the bonnet on her head and tied

the ribbons neatly below her chin. "She cancelled her meeting with you in the library today."

Clara stared at her in surprise. "Really?"

"Yes. In fact, she had to leave the house earlier this morning, so she's not even here."

"Should I wait for her in my room upstairs?" asked Clara, worried.

"That's probably fine," said Amelia, briskly crossing the kitchen to leave out the service door, effectively ending their conversation.

Clara returned her supplies to the storeroom, thinking that might have been the first nice thing Amelia had done for her. She'd certainly saved her the hassle of waiting unnecessarily for Mrs. Malone to arrive. She climbed up the servants' staircase, coming to a stop at the entrance to the second floor. Rather than continuing up to the third, she pressed her fingertips on the wooden door and hesitated, then turned the knob to swing it open.

Lawton Park's immense art gallery loomed in front of her. Throughout the course of her day, she did not have much opportunity to come through here, as it was primarily Amelia's duty to maintain the hall where the Halstead family's treasures were kept. But she had longed for an opportunity to appreciate the priceless oil paintings, busts, and sculptures that made up the impressive exhibit. It was an opportunity she could no longer partake of in her new, meager existence.

Walking slowly along the south wall, she gazed at generations of patriarchs in their decorative regalia, staring with authority through the invisible lens of their artist. She knew the current earl was the fifth Earl of Ashworth, his older brother, Lucas, never having had the chance to fulfill his title. His father, Robert, would have been the fourth. She was awestruck seeing them here for the first time.

Robert's pose was elegant and austere, and where William's hair was a sandy blond and his eyes an intoxicating shade of hazel mixed with green, his father had possessed a wealth of brown hair and matching brown eyes. Despite the difference in coloring, Clara could still see physical similarities between the two men, and smiled at the ones she spotted—the same masculine build, the same appealing curve to the lips, the same intense gaze.

She continued further, to a painting of his brother. The brass nameplate beneath the portrait described him as Lucas Halstead, seventh Baron of Stratham. He appeared stockier than Ashworth, who was all lean muscle and athletic grace. Lucas's hair was also darker, like his father's, in contrast to William's head of burnished blond locks. But there was frankness to his gaze she found appealing. He was less shuttered than his brother. Less haunted.

Her eyes searched and alighted on the portrait of a beautiful woman, indicated to be Maria Halstead, Countess of Ashworth—William's mother, who had died giving birth to his sister, Eliza. She had been a true English beauty, fairhaired with large blue eyes and a sweet, secretive smile that Clara found enchanting. How devastating to have lost so many beloved family members. Tragedy had made its home here in Lawton Park for many years.

At the next painting, she heard herself gasp in surprise. Rosa, as a lovely young woman, stared at her from the precise brushstrokes of blended color, her wavy blonde hair and clear green eyes gazing outward with sincerity. Clara realized this must be Elizabeth, Rosa's mother. Each of the Halstead children had been blessed with dazzling green eyes somehow, a quirk of bequeathed traits since neither parent possessed them.

The earl's sister was beautiful. She would be arriving at Lawton Park soon, and Clara wished she could greet her as an equal, as a friend. There was something about the woman's expression that made her feel that they would have gotten along easily, had they met under normal circumstances.

She glanced at the rest of the gallery in confusion and cocked her head. Where was the current earl's portrait? Looking up higher along the wall, she thought she spotted a representation of him as a young boy, but it was unusual not to have his likeness displayed, especially now that he was the Earl of Ashworth.

The slam of a door jarred her from her thoughts, and she jumped, turning to see Mrs. Malone storm into the hall wearing an overcoat, an incredulous look on her face. Clara was shocked to see she had returned from her outing so quickly. She lowered into a hasty curtsy.

"Were you going to make me wait all afternoon as you whiled away your time here in the gallery?" she demanded. "Curious actions from one being punished for breaking the rules, I must say."

Clara opened her mouth to speak, but no sound came out. She tried again.

"But I—Amelia . . ." she stopped suddenly, arriving at the truth before speaking it out loud.

Amelia wouldn't have done her a favor, and she should've realized that at once. But it was no use kicking herself now. As infuriated as she was at Abigail's sister, she had to consider whether she had more to gain by pointing the finger in her direction, or keeping her mouth shut. Her chances of finally winning the girl's friendship might rely on Clara's judicious handling of the situation, even after being provoked.

Mrs. Malone's glance turned hooded at the brief mention of Amelia, and perhaps she could guess at the truth. But Clara would not give the housemaid one ounce of satisfaction. She met the housekeeper's gaze.

"My apologies, Mrs. Malone. I lost track of the time," she lied.

The woman stared at her. Clara wasn't sure if she believed her or not, but regardless, she turned and headed towards the servants' door.

"I am meeting a friend in the village at one o'clock," she said brusquely. "I have just enough time to hand off your tasks, so let's be quick about it."

Clara surveyed the library with a wistful sigh. How she wished she could take the afternoon to sink into a soft armchair and read one of the hundreds of books that made up Lord Ashworth's collection.

Instead, she would be rearranging them, first by language, then by last name. This involved the tiring task of emptying the shelves, sorting them, and returning them to their proper place. Many servants were not literate, or at least could not read very well, which was why this chore had been assigned to her.

The scent of ancient paper perfumed the air. She surveyed the piles of books that surrounded her on the floor. The stacks mostly comprised German and French texts, but there were also a few Russian and Italian books included, as well as some more exotic choices that were most likely collected for their eclectic value rather than anything else. She would be sorting through these heavy tomes until well after dark.

Setting the books aside, she leaned back on her hands and rolled her neck in a circle to loosen the tight muscles. Her back straightened as she heard Rosa's childish voice echoing down the hallway to disappear down the stairs beyond the green baize door. She and the earl had likely just arrived back from their trip to the village, and Mrs. Humboldt, having spent the morning at her leisure, would be downstairs working on dinner. Rosa would be eager to find out what she was cooking.

A man's footsteps echoed through the hallway, coming nearer to the library door. Clara smoothed the front of her apron and attempted to tuck several wayward locks of hair back underneath her cap just as the door flew open. The earl strode in, then paused to survey the messy piles of books, his eyes finally settling upon her with a glint of amusement.

"I suppose this is a case of things getting worse before they get better?"

He had the nerve to look incredibly attractive, as usual. She sniffed, and turned back to her work.

"If that is how you wish to see it, then yes," Clara muttered, placing another book into the Italian stack. "I see it as a necessary step in the sorting of many titles in various languages."

"A highly sensible approach," he said with an amused lightness in his voice. He retrieved a book from the French pile, then lowered himself into a plush velvet wingback chair. "Rosa and I just returned from the village."

"You didn't walk there, did you?" asked Clara, thinking of the injury to Rosa's leg. Immediately, she berated herself for offhandedly chastising the earl, but her question did not appear to upset him. He merely glanced in her direction, his wry gaze causing her heart to beat a little faster.

"What kind of person do you take me for?"

"I don't believe it's my place to have an opinion on that," she replied matter-of-factly, leafing through a book of Latin.

His mouth tipped into the barest hint of a smile. He flipped over the thick book in his hands to absently examine the binding. "And yet I believe you would tell me anyway, if the mood suited you."

Clara laughed. "Now what kind of a person do you take *me* for?"

"Hmm, good question," he answered. "I am still trying to work that out."

His answer sobered her instantly. Although it was impossible, she returned to her work, trying to behave as if he wasn't seated near her, although she could smell the fragrance of his shaving soap from her place on the floor. She also tried to act as if he wasn't watching her, but she knew he was. For a minute, the only sounds she could hear over the pounding of her heart were the shuffling of books and the turning of pages.

"Are you enjoying your task?" he finally inquired, breaking the quiet between them. "I'd thought you might."

Clara eyed him distrustfully. Had he deliberately assigned her a task he believed she would find amenable, or was he teasing her?

"Did you really?"

Ashworth leaned back in the chair. "What do you think?"

She shrugged. "I suppose it's possible. Although if you're taking requests, I'd probably like a walk through the garden better."

His laugh rang out, and she felt herself blush in sudden pleasure. There was a freedom in that sound, and something that seemed very foreign to the man who was making it. Strange as it was, part of her felt humbled at having been the cause.

"That could probably be arranged, but it wouldn't really be much of a punishment."

Her head lowered and she smiled. "Ah, that's right. You wish to punish me."

The silence that followed was her only indication that her comment had missed the mark somehow. She glanced up to find the earl contemplating her with an unfathomable gleam in his eye.

Clara's breathing paused while fire kindled in her belly, its luscious heat invading every cell in her body.

He cleared his throat.

"Can you tell me what that book is about?"

She'd almost forgotten about the heavy volume in her hands. Taking a breath to calm herself, Clara tilted her head to the side and flipped through the pages, piecing together enough words to determine the book was about the Battle of Waterloo, comparing the military strategies of both Napoleon and the victorious Duke of Wellington.

"Hmm," said Clara, feigning a lack of knowledge. "I don't read French," she lied. She snapped the book shut and held it out to the earl expectantly. "Perhaps you can enlighten me?"

Ashworth's fingers brushed against hers as she relinquished the book, and that same thrill she'd felt a moment before shot through her again. She could feel his eyes linger on her for a moment before he lowered his head to focus on the text.

"This is a book about the Napoleonic Wars. The Battle of Waterloo, to be specific," he replied accurately, closing the book to return it to her. Clara only shook her head.

"Would you read me a line?"

He looked down at her, then back at the book in his hands. "Very well," he said, opening it once again.

Scanning for a suitable passage, he ran his forefinger down the delicate pages of the book. Something about the small gesture excited Clara, and her temperature seemed to rise to an unbearable degree. Perhaps it was because she could envision the earl running that same fingertip along her skin. The nape of her neck, between her shoulder blades, the small of her back . . .

She closed her eyes, trying to reign in her thoughts. Finally, she heard him clear his throat.

"*J'aime le façon dont vous souriez,*" he recited in flawless French, his voice deep and sultry.

Clara's eyes snapped open in shock, and found he was staring right at her. She worried for one terrible second that she might faint again in his presence. Surely she couldn't have heard him correctly . . .

She realized she was about to reveal herself to him. Damnation! He couldn't possibly guess she spoke French, could he? She plastered a false smile on her face and laughed weakly, doing her best to act unaware of his scandalous words.

"What did you say?" she forced out, doing her best to appear ignorant.

At this question, Lord Ashworth had the decency to look a bit guilty. "I said, '*The army withstood repeated advances,*'" he replied blandly. His eyes betrayed the real tone of his message.

Clara coughed. She knew if the earl were to linger here much longer, she would find herself in terrible trouble. "My lord, I'm afraid if I continue at my current pace, I won't complete my work before tomorrow morning." She gazed up at him, willing him to go.

Lord Ashworth seemed to understand the source of her urgency. Perhaps he felt it too.

"You are right, of course. I will take my leave."

With a small nod, he turned and exited the library, stealing one last glance before the door closed quietly behind him.

The Earl of Ashworth had just flirted with her. Albeit, in a different language, one he hadn't thought she'd known, but he'd flirted just the same. And now, how was she to concentrate at all with the remembrance of his perfect French declaration ringing softly in her ears?

J'aime le façon dont vous souriez.

"I love the way you smile."

Frustrated beyond measure, she tossed another book into the French pile, then leaned forward, covering her face with her hands.

Stiff and aching from her hours spent on the library floor, Clara took her lighted candle and trudged up the narrow staircase to her room. It was late and she was tired, emotionally spent, and wished for nothing more than a few hours of peaceful sleep in her tiny bed.

Her room was cold, the warmth of summer but a memory, fallen prey to the persistent chill outside. She quickly stripped down to her chemise, then unpinned her hair and kept it loose so its thick layers would help to keep her neck warm. Diving under the covers, she struggled to get comfortable, but the light blanket was not nearly sufficient to warm her. She missed the warm, soft weight of her thick blankets back home, and with a shivering sigh, curled her legs up against her stomach.

The sound of the hallway door clicking open raised her head from her pillow. If it was Stella, perhaps she could point her to any spare blankets they might have. Scrambling out of bed, she hurried across the cold floor and opened the door to peer into the dark. Amelia's face, illuminated by candlelight, glared up at her in the murky hallway. Of course it was Amelia.

Clara smiled at her, making sure it appeared genuine. She would not give her an ounce of satisfaction for setting her up the way she had.

"Oh, hello," she voiced pleasantly. "Did you have a nice day out?"

The girl flinched and looked at Clara in confusion. "I, er, well yes, I did," she replied hesitantly.

Clara beamed at her. "It was a beautiful day outside, wasn't it?"

Again, Amelia faltered, gauging the authenticity of Clara's goodwill. "Yes, but it's cold now," she said slowly.

"It certainly is," Clara agreed, wrapping her arms tighter around herself. "Well, I'd better get to bed. Good night, Amelia." And she softly shut the door, excessively enjoying the girl's bewilderment.

She opened her drawer and removed both her morning and evening dresses from within. Laying them out on top of her meager blanket for more insulation, she huddled down in her bed, a pleased smile on her face.

Despite everything, it had been a good day.

CHAPTER EIGHT

Clara worked to breathe through her mouth while Stella patiently supervised her attempt at mixing furniture polish. It was a pungent concoction of linseed oil, beeswax, and turpentine, and the smell was causing her stomach to feel queasy. She was tired after having slept poorly, the air in her room cold, but her body somehow overheated as uninvited thoughts of Lord Ashworth invaded her dreams.

"Wait, not so much turpentine," said Stella quickly. Clara jerked her hands back just in time to halt the flow of the pale liquid. "There, that's better," said the other housemaid with relief. She looked up at Clara curiously. "Were you chilled last night? You look tired," she observed.

Clara set aside the bottle of turpentine and reached for the beeswax. "Oh," she said dismally, "I'm sure I'll be fine." Although thinking of the long winter months to come, she couldn't be certain. She was hesitant to inquire about extra blankets if none of the other servants required them, but was sure the position of her room in relation to the rest of the house was the problem. Her room was the farthest one from the bulk of the main house, closest to the west wing, which was not currently in use. Heat from the few lighted fireplaces would not reach her there.

They worked together carefully, adding ingredients and slowly stirring them together with a wooden spoon, adjusting amounts as needed. Finally, after the long process, Stella felt that the mixture had reached the proper consistency and she left the room to fetch Mrs. Malone for her approval. The noisy jingle of the massive keyring signaled the housekeeper's initial location in the kitchen, as well as her musical progression down the hallway. Both women entered a moment later, Mrs. Malone's hair pulled back severely and her black dress looking pressed and pristine. She glanced at Clara, then leaned over and peered down into the pail, raising the spoon into the air to examine the polish that clung to it.

"Very good for your first try," said Mrs. Malone with a brisk nod. "Divide it up into these jars, and you two can use one of them to polish the furniture in the study." She paused in thought, then frowned. "No, not the study. Lord Ashworth is meeting with his land steward. Work in the drawing room instead."

Both maids dipped into a curtsy. "Yes, Mrs. Malone."

Clara was curious about how the earl managed his estate and its affairs. Her father had owned numerous properties, some of them quite large, but he was far removed from the process of maintaining structures and gathering rent. Many times, her parents had despaired of her inclination to join the land steward on his rounds, but she had discovered first-hand that the best way to know what your tenants needed was to meet them yourself—not a popular concept among the landed gentry. She was interested to know if Ashworth, with all his idiosyncrasies, was of a similar mind.

Sharply, and seemingly for the millionth time, she reminded herself of her resolution to be indifferent to the man. Regardless of any memories of softly uttered French phrases.

The housekeeper departed. Clara focused her thoughts and started on her task, packing the mixture into the small glass jars with the spoon, then screwing the lids on tight, wiping the outside to ensure none had collected on the exterior. Stella returned the containers of turpentine, oil and wax to their respective places, and when finished, came to Clara's side to lend her assistance with the polish. She took a deep breath through her nose, exhaling with satisfaction.

"It doesn't smell nearly as bad when it's been mixed up," she commented.

Clara gave her a doubtful look, then tentatively inhaled through her nose. She was relieved to discover that it was true. The beeswax had done wonders to mute the repulsive acrid quality of the turpentine, but the scent was still quite intense. She knew that the dress she was wearing would smell like it for days, and she felt a twinge of displeasure. She missed the delicate floral scents of her past.

It was fascinating, though. Since she'd been employed at Lawton Park, many household smells she had taken for granted in the past now made sense to her. The furniture polish, the tea leaves used to sweep the carpets, the starch on the linens. All of these subtle scents mingled to create an atmosphere of crisp refinement. Despite her long-standing friendship with Abigail, she had not been fully aware of the hard work required to maintain such an impression.

Her chest clenched at the thought of her friend back at Silvercreek, and the family she had left behind. The familiar scents brought forth unbidden memories. Giggling with Abigail over tea in the kitchen belowstairs. Her mother plaiting her hair before bed. Chasing her sister through the orchard on a hot summer's day. The stricken expression on her father's face upon realizing Lucy had eloped . . .

Her eyes snapped shut. She must be Helen. And Helen's memories encompassed this house, and the people in it. Period.

Clara sighed softly.

"Headache?" asked Stella. "I have some willow bark powder in my room if you have need of it."

"No, thank you," replied Clara, leaning back down over her chore. "I'm just tired, is all."

Once she had finished packing the last jar, they were loaded onto a tray and placed in a cabinet in the storeroom, save one, which Stella put into a tool caddy loaded with polish, rags, and brushes. Clara took the caddy and they left the storeroom, encountering Amelia on the staircase. Her thick morning apron was dark with soot, and she was lugging her own caddy, which was heavy with blackened tools and brushes. Stella proceeded up the stairs while Clara paused, pressing her back to the wall to give the housemaid more room to pass.

"Morning," she said with a pleasant nod.

Amelia glanced upwards at Clara in surprise, then rapidly averted her eyes and shuffled clumsily past her. It wasn't a greeting, but it wasn't a hateful scowl, either. Clara was glad she hadn't risen to Amelia's challenge the day before, and hoped that maybe someday the girl would thaw just enough that they might be friendly to one another. Not friends, per se, but friendly.

Stella shook her head in amusement.

"Why you are nice to Amelia, I'll never know."

The corner of Clara's mouth tipped up in an ironic smile, thinking of Abigail and hoping her sister would come round soon. "Just giving her a chance to be nice back, I suppose."

"That's a fool's errand, if you ask me," Stella muttered.

They entered the servants' staircase, which was cool and dim on the chilly autumn day. Creeping quietly up to the first-floor entry, both girls stopped at the door leading into the drawing room. Clara grasped the knob and pushed the door open slightly, peeking her head around to ensure the room was vacant before entering with her collection of polishing implements.

A pair of bright green eyes peeked back.

With a shocked cry, she fell back against Stella, just managing to regain her balance before she could drop her supplies. Rosa bounced around the door.

"I found you!" she laughed.

Stella eased Clara to an upright position. "I'm not sure you should be alone in the house, Miss Rosa," she said.

The little girl released Clara and ran back into the drawing room to throw herself upon the settee. "Please don't tell

Uncah," Rosa begged, her face muffled by a powder blue cushion. "His meeting was so boring!"

"Boring it may be, but imagine your uncle's worry at finding you missing, especially after what happened last week," said Clara with a pointed look. "Come. I'll take you to the study myself."

This mission was not entirely altruistic. The thought of seeing the earl set a spark of excitement racing throughout her body. Clara glanced at Stella, hoping her enthusiasm wasn't too obvious. "I'll return in just a moment."

They had just reached the study door, and Clara's heart was already pounding at the thought of seeing Lord Ashworth. So she nearly jumped out of her skin when the study door flew open with a bang and the earl rushed out, slamming bodily into her.

Ashworth made a noise of astonishment and reached out to steady Clara, preventing them from toppling over onto the floor. She felt one of his hands clutch her arm while the other squeezed the curve of her waist. The earl pulled her up against him for more stability, and they stood there for a second, staring at each other in shock.

In a ballroom, in another life, they could have been dancing.

No . . . she thought desperately. Sensual awareness flooded through her at the close contact. It was difficult enough to try to ignore her attraction to him under normal circumstances, but it was absolutely impossible when his hands were on her. Hands that were strongly constraining her against his solid chest. Attempting to right herself, increase the distance, *do something*, she only succeeded in feeling much more of him, her fingers skirting in panic over the hard planes of his arms, his abdomen, his back . . .

Suddenly aware of their inappropriate proximity, he pushed her away, nearly sending her tumbling yet again. His face was contrite as he steadied her . . . this time from a more appropriate distance. Behind his shoulder she could see another man, most likely his land steward, watching the events with some amusement.

"Helen, what in God's name . . . and *you*," said Ashworth, directing an irate stare at his niece, who now appeared quite ashamed of herself. "After last week, you disobey a direct order from me to stay put?"

He broke off, and it was then that Clara noticed just how stressed his expression was, with dark circles under his eyes and the faint sheen of stubble on his cheeks. It seemed obvious that his Rosa's near miss still disturbed him greatly, unless there was something else going on that was affecting him this way. She wanted to find out . . . but how?

"My lord," interrupted Clara with a quick curtsy, trying to conceal her concern, "Rosa found me in the drawing room. She had not been gone but a minute or two, and I brought her back immediately."

His dark glance jumped over to her, and she tensed in anticipation of his wrath. But his features finally softened with gratitude.

"I appreciate your help," he replied, holding her gaze.

A thousand butterflies took flight in her stomach.

Turning away, he knelt down and grasped Rosa by the shoulders. "I need to know you are safe at all times," he stated earnestly.

Rosa lifted her eyes to meet his, then wrapped her arms around his neck and pulled herself close. Lord Ashworth laughed softly and patted the girl's blonde waves, then stood to face his steward.

"I apologize for the interruption, Paxton, but I believe we were mostly finished here," he said. "Be sure to convey my concern for the flooding situation at the Dunby and Howard farmsteads, and find out what can be done to resolve the matter."

The man bowed. "Of course, my lord. Right away."

The steward turned to leave, casting a brief glance at Clara over his shoulder as he did. She returned his smile, but as she looked back to the earl, she felt it falter. Ashworth stood in silence, watching his man depart with a curious expression on his face. Then he turned to her.

"Do you know my land steward?" he asked.

Clara looked at him, astonished. Was the earl . . . could it be possible he was jealous?

She scoffed at herself. The very notion was ridiculous. And yet, as she studied him, she could not quite decipher the look on his face . . .

"No, my lord," she replied, an embarrassed heat working its way up her neck. "I've never seen the man before today."

Before he had a chance to respond, Stella appeared in the hallway, a slight frown of confusion on her face.

"Begging your pardon, my lord," she began, "but I was

expecting Helen in the drawing room and wanted to see if everything was all right . . ."

The earl glanced at the other maid, and Clara again noticed the expression of strain and weariness etched on his handsome features. Something was wrong. She wished she could help.

"I have need of her today, Stella," he said, surprising her once again. The words had no ulterior meaning, and yet she couldn't help the delicious shiver that chased down her spine. "I must finish these letters and decide how best to deal with the flooding down near the village." He cast a sardonic look at his niece. "Clearly Rosa requires the full attention of a guardian."

"Certainly, I will watch over her. She can join me for my morning tasks." Clara turned to Stella and ushered Rosa in her direction. "Perhaps I could meet you in just a moment? I'll be along shortly."

Flummoxed, Stella nodded, curtsied, and left with the little girl who waved over her shoulder until they rounded a distant corner. Trying not to lose her nerve, Clara faced the earl, who seemed somewhat surprised by her actions. Steeling herself before she could lose courage, Clara whispered, "My lord, may I have a private word with you?"

She knew she was about to act brashly. But in that moment, she couldn't bring herself to care.

A notch formed between the earl's brows as he stared at her, bewildered. His singular green eyes held a mixture of fascination and restraint. Clara knew she was pushing the boundaries between them.

After a long moment, Ashworth took a step back and

extended a hand, gesturing for her to enter the study. Her heart was pounding so hard she could barely hear herself think, but since she had chosen to disregard any semblance of reason, she didn't think she was any worse off for it.

Clara proceeded to the middle of the room, and twisted around to face him only after she heard the click of the door behind her. To her surprise, he hadn't followed her all the way in, but remained nearer to the door so he could observe her from afar. She couldn't blame him, really. This was all very unconventional.

She cleared her throat.

"My lord, are you well?"

Ashworth's hand slowly dropped from the doorknob and he stared openly at her, his expression unreadable. Clara guessed it could have been weeks or months since he'd had a loved one or a friend ask him that question.

He cocked his head to the side, eyeing her curiously. "Do I appear to be unwell?"

Clara bit her lip. Of course, he appeared very well indeed. She couldn't stop her eyes from scanning over him and felt herself flush hotly in response.

"Yes . . . *no* . . . that is, you look distressed. As if something is wrong."

Ashworth stepped forward. "I am in charge of an earldom. There could be many things wrong." He paused. "And this concerns you because . . . ?"

"Well, I am aware it shouldn't concern me," she answered nervously. "But—I find it does."

He mulled this over in silence as his restless gaze roamed over her, starting at her cap, alighting on her face, moving down the dark rose-colored fabric of her morning dress, skimming over her apron, and landing on her sturdy black shoes. His eyes snapped back up to hold hers in their sway.

"I appreciate your concern, but rest assured, it is misplaced." The earl took another step in her direction. "However, since we're on the subject of appearances, I would tell you that you seem tired today." The corner of his mouth lifted in the barest hint of a smile. "Is there something amiss?"

Clara's lips parted in surprise. "That was neatly done, my lord. You managed to avoid answering my question while directing one at me instead." She hesitated. "Well if you must know, I *am* tired. My room is like an icebox at night."

He blinked. This time he really did look concerned. "Is it?"

"Yes," she replied. "But that's really beside the point. You are under no obligation to confide in me, I only thought perhaps—"

"And I told you," he said, cutting her off, "that I appreciate the concern. But you and I both know it's against all proprieties to discuss personal matters—"

"Have you always been so set on adhering to the proprieties, my lord?"

The earl straightened, eyes widening in disbelief, and she immediately knew the conversation had been taken too far.

Clara lowered her head and tried to avoid him, skirting

around the edge of the room towards the door. "Forgive my intrusion. It was wrong of me to insert myself where I do not belong."

She passed Ashworth and his hand shot out, securing her wrist in his hold before she could flee.

"Was that an insult? Or simply an observation?" he inquired.

She swallowed, weighing her response with caution. "No, my lord. On the contrary, I think it an admirable quality in a peer to be willing to break with tradition." Ashworth's gaze drifted from her face to the place where his fingers were wrapped around her arm. After a moment, he gently released her. Disappointment flooded through her as the heat of his hand evaporated off her skin.

Stepping backwards, he spread his arms wide in mock invitation.

"Since we are ignoring decorum, is there anything else you wish to ask?" Then he added wisely, "I may or may not choose to answer."

She considered this in silence, her hand moving to cover the wrist that still tingled from his touch. This game had already started. Why stop now?

"Yes, my lord. There is one thing." Clara took a deep breath. "Has your steward much experience with flooded farmlands?"

"Pardon me?" His voice was low. Possibly annoyed.

"My lord, your land steward is another servant, regardless of his accomplishments. I'd wager your tenants would value a visit from you, the Earl of Ashworth, along with the opportunity to discuss their thoughts on resolving the flooding."

She had managed to say the words, but she had also begun to tremble uncontrollably. She clenched her hands into fists and held them tightly at her sides to conceal her shaking.

Lord Ashworth stood stock-still. He simply stared at her as if she had spontaneously recited the Russian alphabet. When he did speak, he sounded calm, but his voice was hoarse.

"What do you know of flooded farmlands, Helen?"

A trickle of sweat raced down her back.

Ashworth stepped closer to her, his face expectant. Clara's breath came in gulps as she attempted to maintain her composure. "I—my father had experience in such matters."

"Your father?" he asked, intrigued.

"Yes, my lord," she responded hastily, hoping to change the subject. "I've no wish to interfere, but I was thinking a meeting might help connect you more closely to your townsfolk."

The earl's eyebrows arched. "Why do you take such an interest in my affairs?"

"I'm not. I don't," she stammered. "I'm only thinking as a commoner. Speaking as a commoner . . ."

"Speaking as a commoner," he interrupted thoughtfully, taking another step forward. "A commoner would know when to hold her tongue, and yet you, somehow, do not." Another step. The alarm bells she had chosen to ignore earlier were now clanging again, more insistently.

His words were true. She was being Clara Mayfield right

now, and she needed to correct her course immediately. Before he was close enough to touch her.

"Of course, you are right, my lord," she forced out, hoping to put an end to the conversation. "I only meant to help. I can see now that I've overstepped my bounds."

A huff of amusement escaped him. "A habit of yours." Then softly, "And how can you possibly help me?"

The earl took one last step in her direction, and it wasn't until Clara felt her back collide with the far wall that she realized she had also been retreating. He was only inches away, so close she could feel the heat radiating off his body. Being at eye level with his broad chest, he suddenly seemed far too large, far too close.

Ashworth had an incomparable sensual grace, unmatched by any man she'd ever seen. Without thinking, Clara reached out and placed her fingertips on his chest—whether a defensive reflex or an invitation, she couldn't be sure. At her touch, he tensed and closed his eyes, a small gasp hissing through his teeth.

Any lingering doubts melted away as she witnessed his reaction. He wanted her hands on him. She flattened her palms across the lawn of his shirt, feeling the contrast of hard muscle to soft fabric.

Clara had always believed her inexperience had caused her to be shy with men, but now it was apparent part of the problem had been that she had not yet been with the right man. Here, with Ashworth, fire flowed through her veins as she allowed her hands to roam. His clenched jaw and fists were an indication of resistance, but his refusal to halt her caresses challenged her to continue.

What could she possibly do to help him?

He had asked, and now she burned to find out.

Her fingers traced along the length of his blue satin cravat, and he made a sound low in his throat.

The sound raced through Clara like wildfire. Disregarding everything . . . the woman she was, and the woman she was pretending to be . . . she rose high up on her tiptoes and brushed her lips against his.

Chapter Nine

Holy hell.

Ashworth's eyes fell shut and he exhaled, struggling to control the desire that pumped through him. He was no saint, but knew that to indulge this fantasy could result in nothing good for either of them. But as her lips moved softly over his, her hands traversed the expanse of his chest, delicately testing and teasing. Unsurprisingly, his primitive brain started bargaining with him.

Just once, it pleaded.

Ashworth darted forward to nip at the wet lusciousness of her lips and she moaned against his mouth, sending a lick of fire straight through to his core. He clenched his hands into fists.

Don't touch her. Don't you dare touch her.

He ought to shove her away. He needed to get her away, but found himself submitting to her touch instead, hoping she would take it farther while dreading the consequences.

Ashworth's thoughts were shattered by her light tug on

his cravat, and he squeezed his eyes shut even tighter. How he yearned for her to untie it, slip it off from around his neck. All too easily, he could imagine her undressing him right here.

The earl heard a muted groan, belatedly realizing it had come from him.

Control.

He needed to master himself before things went too far. The Earl of Ashworth was destined to be with a different kind of woman. Even the notion of a disreputable dalliance made him feel like an unworthy son and brother.

William reminded himself that he also had a responsibility not to debauch his own employees. While not every peer held himself accountable this way, he did. And regardless of this intolerable need, he *would not* do her the dishonor of violating that trust. Even if she wanted him to.

Her sweet smell drifted around him, a faint trace of furniture polish barely detectable. His body was galvanized by the sweet taste of her; all his imaginings could never have captured her plush perfection.

Control!

The earl was shaking with the effort of his restraint. Helen trembled at the insistent searching of his mouth on hers, and he responded by exploring further until her lips parted, allowing his tongue to slide inside. Heat surged through him again, and he realized he was very close to simply ignoring all the reasons he shouldn't just take her against the wall. He tensed against it, determined to resist, when she moaned and tugged on his jacket to bring him closer, the tip of her own tongue flicking against his. Helen pressed against his chest and he was nearly undone by the soft weight of her breasts.

You need to stop–

He moved his hands to encircle her wrists and lifted his head to break the kiss. Helen's lashes fluttered up and a pretty pink blush crept over her cheeks and chest. Her dazed eyes were a mesmerizing contrast to her skin. Too dark to be called brown, but much warmer than black. A lock of the same indescribable color escaped her damnable cap to tumble across the pale curve of her cheek.

He wanted her.

He could never have her.

"Helen . . ." His voice was rough with emotion, something he hadn't expected. He cleared his throat and her anxious eyes met his for one moment before lowering her focus back down to his mouth. She wanted to kiss him again, with lips that were swollen and reddened from the first time. And he wanted to let her.

Damn it!

Releasing her completely, Ashworth retreated, defying every instinct screaming for him to take her with his mouth once more. Instead, he turned swiftly and strode across the room to seat himself behind his desk, raking his hands restlessly through his hair.

He stared numbly at the smooth surface of his workspace while she remained frozen. He needed to drive her away from him. If he wanted to avoid ruining Helen, he would need to hurt her.

Ashworth drew in a deep breath. "Your attentions are unwelcome," he stated soberly, hating himself but saying it anyway. "I believe Stella is expecting you in the drawing room."

A soft intake of breath disturbed the ensuing silence in the study, and pain lanced through his chest.

He was such a bastard.

William heard the swish of her skirts, perceived the breeze as she rushed past his desk, and lowered his head into his hands as the door clicked shut behind her.

Your attentions are unwelcome.

Clara stumbled through the machinations of her tasks, lost in a fog of disbelief. The Earl of Ashworth had soundly rejected her. Moments after responding to her kiss.

True, she didn't possess an excess of experience with men, but discerning when one desired you was another thing altogether. Clara flushed thinking about the way he'd tried to hold back at first, only to have his carefully cultivated self-control slip away with every kiss that followed. But somehow, she must have been mistaken. Their kiss probably carried no more weight than any other meaningless flirtation he could have—and probably did—with multitudes of women. Scorching tears filled her eyes at the thought.

Clara ducked her head and focused on buffing the leg of a richly sculpted rosewood table. She needed to hide her strained emotions from Stella, who was occupied in the opposite corner of the drawing room, polishing windows.

As if on cue, Stella swiveled on her feet and gazed out the

windows, which faced south along the circular gravel drive. After a moment's observation, she turned to look at Clara.

"Did the earl mention anything about a trip today?"

"No," replied Clara slowly, rising to her feet. "I know Paxton was heading to the village to speak to some tenant farmers, but that's all I can recall."

Clara approached the window and caught sight of Lord Ashworth on his horse, riding like a man with a purpose. Even from this distance, he looked resplendent in his riding gear. She averted her eyes before they could linger on the way his breeches molded to his powerful form, striving to appear indifferent before her fellow housemaid as he traveled out the gates of the estate. "Wherever he's off to, he can't be planning to stay for long. It's probably just a day's trip to the village."

She returned to her work, pouring all her energy and attention into it in the hopes of keeping her thoughts from wandering dangerously to the earl. With her tasks completed for the afternoon, Clara decided a visit to the stables was in order. She figured an apology was due to Oscar, the stableboy, after his unwitting involvement in her scheme to help Rosa. She tugged her thin cloak more tightly around her shoulders to ward off the cold and ventured out from the rear servants' door to cross the courtyard.

Lawton Park's flower gardens had been put to bed for the winter, and as Clara gazed at the woods surrounding the estate, she saw the brilliant orange and rust colors of fall had faded into dingy brown hues. Few leaves remained clinging to withered branches, the lush abundance of color transformed into a sparse kind of beauty instead. She could hardly believe she'd been living here long enough to see the seasons change. With a pang she thought of her parents and wondered what they had made of her long absence.

Shrugging off a wave of guilt, she ducked her head down and walked faster, entering the warmth of the stable gratefully after taking a quick peek around the door. Normally, for an earl with a house this large, there would be upwards of five dozen horses housed in the structure. But Lord Ashworth, not interested in entertaining society with shooting parties and the like, owned a meager twenty-one. Even then, she doubted many of them were exposed to the kind of usage considered common at most country estates.

"Hello?" she called, pausing near the huge wooden doors. The familiar scents of cut hay and horses filtered through the air. The boy emerged from a stall, pitchfork in hand. His wide blue eyes showed unwelcome surprise at again being confronted with Clara.

"Hello, miss. What do you want?" he asked cautiously.

Clara walked towards him through the stables, and stopped to stroke the nose of her cohort, the beautiful gray horse she had ridden on that cold and stormy night. The animal whickered softly in response.

"I'd like to apologize for what happened, Oscar," she said. "It was never my intent to cause trouble for you."

A reluctant smile flickered across his face. Most likely, he'd been anticipating another unconventional request. He twitched his head, sending a lock of blond hair out of his eyes.

"Aww, miss. It ended up being no trouble, especially since

you were able to help the earl's niece." He surveyed her sheepishly. "I heard you got it worse than me."

"Yes," she said, smiling. "But it was all worth it in the end, right?"

"That it was," he agreed.

A tiny whinny caught her attention from a nearby stall, and Clara peeked over the gate. She gasped in delight at the small spotted horse that stood there, gazing back at her with huge black eyes. "Oh, what a dear!" she breathed. "What's his name?"

"Goliath," replied the boy, resuming his chores with a sweep of his pitchfork.

Clara burst out laughing. "Who, pray tell, was responsible for naming Goliath?"

He looked as if she had lost her senses. "The earl, of course."

Her smile faltered, and she tried to quell the frisson that passed through her. She wasn't certain why evidence of his sense of humor would affect her, except it was appealing to think of the normally straitlaced earl as finding amusement in the naming of a pony.

Stop it. Stupid girl.

She leaned over to pat Goliath on the nose, chortling as he nuzzled her hand. The muffled sound of horse's hooves clattering in the courtyard alerted them to a rider's presence outside, and the pair stopped and stared at one another.

"You should leave," he whispered urgently.

"Be at ease, Oscar," she replied, trying not to laugh. "If the earl still trusts me with his niece, surely he trusts me with his horses."

Ignoring her, the boy rushed over to the broad doors of the stables and was greeted not by the earl, but by his friend, Thomas, Lord Evanston. The man swung off his horse and landed gracefully on his boots, handing the reins of his horse to Oscar a moment before noticing her presence nearby.

"Ah, Helen! How nice to see you again. You're not aiming to steal another horse, are you?"

She averted her eyes and smiled. "No, my lord. Not today."

Evanston's eyes scanned over her provocatively, but she felt this was standard behavior for him with most every female. If the tales circulating belowstairs were to be believed, the viscount had a tendency to indulge in gratuitous hedonism whenever an opportunity availed itself. This was no surprise to Clara, as she had heard similar tales of his prowess throughout the *ton* during her time in London, thought she'd never chanced to meet him, herself.

"I have news which may be of some import to you," he said.

She wondered what it could possibly be. "Yes, my lord?" she inquired with a curtsy.

"You will need to draw a bath for the earl."

Clara stood in mortified silence and cleared her throat before speaking.

"My lord?"

Evanston looked up at her, taking in her confused expression, and laughed. His deep tones rang out through the wooden walls of the stables.

"Our Earl of Ashworth has spent the better part of the

day digging a drainage channel with his tenant farmers to ease their chronic flooding. He even coerced poor Paxton into lending his assistance. I passed them on my way through the village." The viscount shook his head. "The man is covered head to foot in mud."

Shock and disbelief rooted Clara to her position. She felt her jaw drop.

"I see you are surprised," he said wryly. "Could you make appropriate arrangements with the staff?"

Clara dipped into a brief curtsy. "Yes, my lord." She turned and hurried out of the building, nearly knocking down a flustered Oscar in the process.

Her mind raced as she swept towards the service entrance of the main house. The earl may not have appreciated her uninvited affections, but he had taken her advice to heart, even assisting with the labor. Of course, the idea of him digging a ditch in front of the entire town was outrageous. News of his scandalous behavior was sure to reach London society, including the very people he had already managed to offend. She should have kept her mouth shut. But who could have predicted the earl would take such a rash approach to the matter?

Rapping twice at the heavy door, she did not wait for an answer before barging through to the kitchen. Mrs. Humboldt and her kitchen maid, Gilly, looked up in surprise, a fine plume of flour surrounding them as they busily rolled out the dough for that evening's pies.

"Mrs. Malone?" she asked breathlessly.

Eyes wide, Gilly pointed down the hallway. "In her room,"

she said. Clara nodded her thanks and headed towards the housekeeper's room, where she found the woman taking tea and going over menus for the next week.

"Excuse my interruption, Mrs. Malone, but I happened to meet Lord Evanston outside. He communicated that Lord Ashworth would require a hot bath upon his return."

Mrs. Malone's cool gray eyes held Clara's as she placed her teacup on its saucer with precision. "Do I want to know what the earl has been up to?"

Clara twisted her hands nervously. "Well, you see, apparently he spent the afternoon digging a drainage ditch. The viscount saw him on his way through the village."

The housekeeper's mouth puckered tightly in disapproval. "Which means that every other person traveling through the village could likely see him too." Standing abruptly, she brushed past Clara to the servants' hall where most of the domestics were busy quietly mending clothes and polishing shoes. The woman clapped loudly and the staff snapped to attention. Amelia pricked her finger with a needle and sighed loudly in annoyance.

"Charles and Matthew, bring the slipper tub into Lord Ashworth's chambers. Amelia, Stella, and Helen will run pails of hot water upstairs." Leaning backwards out of the room, she shouted down the hall to Gilly. "We need bathwater on the stove, now!" The kitchen maid's immediate reply of "Yes, ma'am!" floated back to the dining hall.

Mrs. Malone stepped back as the servants set about their new tasks. The footmen rushed upstairs to retrieve the earl's bathing tub, and the housemaids tidied their belongings before heading into the kitchen for the heavy pails of heated water. Again and again, the three women voyaged up and down the stairs with their pails, Amelia glowering at Clara as if she had purposefully intended to make her evening more inconvenient.

At long last, the copper tub was nearly full. Matthew positioned himself outside the chamber to wait for Lord Ashworth, should he require assistance. Stella and Amelia emptied their final buckets and returned downstairs. Clara leaned over to deposit the contents of her bucket into the tub, and with a jolt realized she was alone in his room. Given the current circumstances, she did not wish to encounter the earl at all, let alone in his room near his bath.

Hastily, she draped a plush towel over a nearby chair and bent down to retrieve her pails. She turned around just as the door flew open, thudding unceremoniously into the wall.

The earl stood before her, clad in his riding breeches and a shirt. His muddy coat and boots had likely been spirited away by Mrs. Malone to be brushed and polished anew. As Evanston had foretold, Ashworth was indeed covered in mud. His face was streaked with dirt, his clothing clung to every muscular curve of his body, and his blond hair was damp with sweat. If her heart palpitations were any indication, his state of dress had probably caused a frenzy down in the village.

She could hear Matthew behind him, offering his service and suggesting ideas for how to disrobe without creating any further mess. Ashworth silenced him with one sharply raised hand, his dark, unreadable gaze on Clara. Despite his unkempt appearance, the cultivated tones of his low voice betrayed him as an aristocrat of the bluest blood.

"That will be all, Matthew."

Matthew bowed and turned down the hall. Clara bobbed into a curtsy filled with false cheer and darted to the side, hoping to escape through the open door. He sidestepped to stand in front of her, blocking her path, and she jumped back just in time to maintain a proper distance. She dreaded the idea of looking at him, but found herself gazing upwards anyway, and what she saw on his face startled her beyond words.

Ashworth looked like he wanted to devour her.

Finally, he blinked. She took this as her cue to leave, holding her breath and trying to skirt around him with her buckets.

"Helen."

She stopped abruptly. All she wanted was to reach the security of the servants' hall. It wasn't that much to ask, really.

Instead, she slowly pivoted around to face him.

"My lord?"

Lord Ashworth took one slow step in her direction before coming to a stop. "Thank you."

Bewildered, she ran through the potential reasons for why the earl would choose to thank her—for being concerned for his welfare, for watching Rosa, for suggesting he meet with his tenants, or . . . kissing him in the study?

Surely not that.

Deciding further conversation would be an unnecessary risk to her sanity, she simply nodded in reply and turned to leave. She was stayed again by his voice.

"One more thing."

Clara's heart sank. She stared longingly at the hallway.

Glancing over her shoulder, she was once again arrested by the sight of him, somehow more accessible in his dirt-streaked clothes, his golden skin flushed from his exertions. "Yes, my lord—"

Ashworth came forward. He gripped her shoulders and spun her around, crushing his mouth onto hers. Clara dropped the empty buckets she'd been holding and they clattered noisily across the floor.

He took her lips with his, tasting her deeply, groaning in satisfaction. Unable to ignore the desire he stoked within her, she reached up, fingers diving into his normally gleaming and golden hair, now muddied and wet. The urgent pressure of his mouth traveled, down her jawline to her neck, making her gasp. His hands slid against her back, bringing her flush against him.

Clara turned her head, and suddenly realized the door was still wide open. "My lord, we mustn't," she said, panicking.

At her words, the earl must have regained some awareness. He released her and swore, stepping backwards, his breaths swift and unsteady.

"I know," he finally said.

After a long, silent moment, Clara cleared her throat awkwardly. Ashworth blinked, but refrained from meeting her eyes. A terse nod gave her permission to leave.

Bending down to gather her buckets, her head whirled in confusion, body still blazing from his touch.

She wordlessly exited his room and closed the door, leaning back against it for a moment to catch her breath. Only then did she glance down and notice the condition of her uniform. It seemed a stop at her room for a quick change would be necessary before returning belowstairs.

Otherwise, she might have a difficult time explaining how her dress was now covered in mud.

An unexpected meeting was called by Mrs. Malone the following day. Stella poked her head into the music room, where Clara was busily polishing the pianoforte, to inform her that servants were expected to finish their current duties before hurrying downstairs for the assembly.

"Do you know the purpose of this meeting?" she asked, intrigued.

Stella shook her head. "Not yet, although I do know the earl received a letter earlier today." The maid's eyes gleamed with excitement. "I think perhaps we will be receiving visitors soon."

Clara diligently completed her task, then loaded her tools onto the rolling cart and returned it to the supply closet in the hallway. She rushed down the servants' staircase to the dining hall, where most of the other domestics were already seated and awaiting the housekeeper.

Her eyes scanned the faces at the table. Beth, the stout laundry maid, was laughing raucously at something Mrs. Humboldt had said. Amelia's red hair could be spotted midway down the table, Stella's profile was a few seats from her, and the young scullery maid, Tess, sat quietly with her hands folded neatly in her lap. Clara gazed across the table to see Matthew and Charles conversing animatedly over an empty chair. Matthew caught sight of her and grinned.

"Helen!" he hailed, gesturing at the empty seat next to him. Charles sat on the other side of the seat, waggling his eyebrows mischievously at her.

"I promise the company from this side of your chair would be far superior," joked Matthew.

"Surely, you did not reserve a seat just for me," said Clara in a chiding tone.

Matthew glanced sideways at Charles, then back in her direction.

"I make it a rule never to sit next to Charles, as he gets up to all sorts of tomfoolery. Plus, you smell better than he does."

The footman in question was undoubtedly offended. "I smell fine!" he raged loudly.

A scrape of a chair interrupted the friendly banter. Amelia had risen from her spot to stare incredulously at the two footmen.

"Let me end this farce of a contest." She glanced over at Clara with obvious irritation. "Helen, sit here," she said imperiously, pointing to her now vacant seat.

Amelia's condescending attitude did not sit well with her, but regardless of the annoyance, she reminded herself that Amelia outranked her belowstairs. All eyes followed her wordless procession over to where Amelia stood, tapping her foot. She sank down into the chair and smiled up at the peevish housemaid.

"Thank you for offering your seat, Amelia. How kind of you."

The look on the girl's face was priceless.

Clara ventured a glance across the table at Matthew. His eyes were overly bright with the burden of suppressed laughter, but all emotion vanished from his face when Amelia rounded the table in a huff and flopped down into the seat between him and Charles.

The jingle of Mrs. Malone's keyring could be heard down the hall, and the staff straightened up and gazed attentively at the doorway. The appearance of the housekeeper came only seconds later, and in her arms she carried a large stack of blankets. She made her way to the head of the table, setting them down and placing her hands possessively on top of the pile.

"This," she said, "is not something I have ever seen in my days as a servant. However, we will accept the earl's generosity gracefully, and with thanks." Mrs. Malone started passing the blankets to Mrs. Humboldt on her right, who continued to pass them further down the table, a blank look of confusion on her face.

"It is Lord Ashworth's impression that the staff is in need of additional coverage at night." The housekeeper shook her head. "He bade me issue one additional blanket per each domestic servant. You will bring them up to your rooms before continuing with your daily chores."

As Clara's fingers slid over the soft material of her new blanket, she could feel the blood draining from her face.

Words exchanged between her and Lord Ashworth in the study the previous morning came back to her with sudden clarity.

This had to be some kind of odd coincidence. Otherwise, it would mean that the earl had gifted his entire staff with extra blankets based solely on her comment. It not only wouldn't happen, she felt preposterous for even thinking it. Still . . .

"Now, on to the true order of business," said Mrs. Malone, her sharp voice interrupting Clara's musings. "This morning, the earl received a letter from his sister, Lady Eliza Cartwick. She has finished with her dealings at home and is anxious to join Miss Rosa here at Lawton Park. We anticipate her arrival in three days, and there is a lot to accomplish before then."

The lecture continued, but Clara vaguely registered the commands being barked out by Mrs. Malone. Open and clean Lady Cartwick's old chambers. Prepare a room for her lady's maid. Process the additional goods purchased for the revised menus. Ready the servants' hall for an informal celebration . . .

The list of tasks was long, but soon the meeting came to a close. The servants stood with their blankets either held tightly against their chests or bundled under an arm. There were many smiles all around her, but she could not quite partake in their cheer. She scooped up her blanket, hurrying towards the exit while trying to ignore the lump in her throat, but a tap on her elbow stopped her just short of the staircase.

"What luck!" exclaimed Stella, beaming. "Why, you were cold just the other night and now here you have an extra blanket."

Clara's eyes shifted to the nearby servants, trying to assess whether anyone had heard Stella's words, before returning to settle back on her friend. The last thing she needed was someone believing that the earl was doing her favors. She could only imagine the kind of trouble Amelia could cause with that idea in her head.

Stella eyed her carefully, and a thoughtful expression passed over the maid's face.

"You were cold the other night, and now you have an extra blanket . . ." Stella repeated slowly, staring at her.

Clara quickly pulled Stella in for a hug before releasing her with a bright smile.

"And now so do you. What luck!"

Heart pounding, Clara brushed past her friend, retreating up the shadowy staircase to her room.

CHAPTER TEN

Clara finished dusting the fixtures in Eliza's room, then set down her duster upon noticing a wrinkle in the bedclothes. With a crisp tug the wrinkle was removed, and she stepped back to smooth her hand over the counterpane. Stella's head appeared suddenly from around the open doorway.

"Mrs. Malone would like everyone downstairs to help with preparations for tonight's dance."

Reaching across to fluff the decorative pillows adorning the bed, she glanced worriedly at Stella. "But I'm not finished in here yet."

The maid waved off her concern. "You can finish the bed, of course. But I wouldn't make Mrs. Malone wait more than a few minutes if I were you." Stella tipped her a smile, then hurried down the hallway.

The housekeeper had approved an informal gathering tonight belowstairs to celebrate Eliza's return to Lawton Park. Festivities such as these would be considered quite out of the norm in a grand house such as this, where servants were generally expected to remain unseen and unheard. The earl did not seem to mind this divergence from the normal routine, however, and it was entirely possible that he would be attending himself.

The thought of seeing him again made her nerves alight with tingling anticipation, although she knew very well that they should not dance with one another tonight. Not when she was plagued by memories of him, tall and looming, his body coiled and powerful. The only thing that had shocked her more than the ferocious hunger of his kiss was the way she had returned it. How her hands had dived through his mud-matted hair to bring him closer, kiss him harder. For a fraction of a second, she thought they might end up in that tiny tub together.

Even worse, she thought she might be the one to pull him in.

Clara lowered down onto the chaise longue stationed below a huge window that overlooked the gardens, wishing she could take a walk outside right now to clear her troubled mind. This was all very new to her, and so hard to understand. She'd never been driven by such a thing . . . never met someone who could fill her with such need, yet leave her feeling empty, as if she would never be satisfied. What she did know was that she was in no position to kiss anyone—especially the earl—and that even the smallest intimacy could open her up to something far more sensual. Something that was absolutely off-limits.

Bleak, gray afternoon light filtered in through the gleaming panes of glass, and she heaved a sigh. She knew she should get downstairs before Mrs. Malone noticed her absence, but the sound of approaching footsteps surprised her. She stiffened in alarm as Lord Ashworth came into view, his frame easily filling the doorway. It was a not unpleasant reminder of how large he was. She shot up to her feet with a soft exclamation as he glanced around the room, his gaze dancing over the bed, before coming to settle back on her.

"What are you doing?" he asked.

"I—I was just tidying in here, my lord." She hoped he hadn't noticed her sitting. "What are you doing?" she asked, unable to think of anything else to say and immediately feeling foolish.

His eyebrows raised in surprise, then he laughed softly. "Well, I suppose I am putting off a task I find cumbersome. Otherwise, I can't really explain why I decided to change my coat."

He ran his palms over the chest of his forest green morning coat and Clara stared, wishing she could do the same. Instead, she retrieved her feather duster and began dusting the porcelain figurines upon the bureau.

"Which task would that be, my lord?"

Ashworth paused, then crossed over to the window. He seemed to be debating whether or not to speak of his troubles with one of his servants, even one he'd seen fit to kiss. She almost thought he'd forgotten her question entirely until hearing his murmured reply.

"There is someone I must invite here—the tradesman I'd been going to meet when Rosa went missing."

Clara turned, confused. "But why would you find that bothersome?"

He twisted his lips. "The last time I met with him, I lost most of my family on the return trip home. The next time I went for a meeting, Rosa nearly fell into a well." Scoffing, he looked away. "I'm not certain if Mr. Scanlan is the bringer of bad luck or if I am, but I owe it to my father to at least see this through to its conclusion, whatever that may be."

She stood in shocked silence, not missing the way his hands had curled tightly at his sides. Clara wanted to go to him, but knew that such a thing would only be an invitation to further temptation, something a woman in her situation could not afford.

She found herself doing it anyway.

Setting her duster aside, she joined the earl at the window. A small tremor passed through him when she slid her fingers around his, but she could feel how his hand loosened and relaxed, finally allowing her fingers to slip inside, warm and secure. It was terrifying in her triumph, standing there holding his hand, and she could hardly believe her own audacity. Part of her feared that he would snap and turn her out of his house that instant, but for some reason she didn't think he would. And this was not truly about her. Not right now, anyway. Clara rose up on her toes to whisper in his ear.

"You are the only bit of good luck your family has seen in all of this, my lord," she breathed softly. "Never forget that."

Ashworth swallowed hard, his gaze still transfixed upon the garden below. He remained frozen, his long fingers wrapped around hers, as if not entirely certain how to proceed. Her heart suddenly felt like it would pound out of her chest and realization slammed into her. She was not at her family's home in Essex, and this man was not courting her. She was his housemaid, and soon she wouldn't even be that if she kept breaking the rules. Clara tugged at her hand, but to her surprise, he held it fast.

"Sometimes I feel cursed," he said quietly, almost as if he hadn't meant to utter the words aloud.

Clara thought of her sister's elopement, and of the ruinous season that had followed. She remembered sitting at the Mayfair ball, waiting with watchful hope, for a suitor to appear and rescue her from that purgatory. But the man beside her now, greedily clinging to her hand, had been busy fighting demons of his own that night. Had he shown himself, would he have been willing to fight hers too? She would never know.

Oh yes, Clara knew what it was like to feel cursed.

She blinked and glanced away, her eyes stinging with the effort to keep her emotion in check. The slight movement caught his eye and he turned to study her face, the golden flecks in his serious gaze catching the afternoon light.

"This is not your burden," he said in slow wonder. "And yet you act as if you care. Why?"

She shook her head and pulled harder at her hand in another futile attempt at freeing herself.

Because I do.

"Forgive me, my lord, if I've offended you somehow—"

He frowned. "It's just that I've tried to figure it out. I need to know . . . what is it about you that's so different?"

Trying to comfort him had been another mistake, as she'd known it would be.

A soft pull brought her forward and she gazed up at him helplessly, highly aware that his lips were only inches from her own.

"I'm not sure what you mean," she said, increasingly desperate.

"I think you know exactly what I mean."

His head lowered slowly until his mouth hovered above her own, just close enough for the warm whisper of his breath to caress her lips. She stood there in a daze, her eyes drifting closed, every inch of her body alight with the anticipation of his kiss. Still, he withheld it in what must have been an attempt to drive her mad. Clara shifted restlessly in his arms, her cheeks burning as her breasts accidentally brushed against the hard surface of his chest. She felt a momentary flare of delight at his murmured response, and his lips lowered once more to hungrily seek hers. To her dismay, he tore himself away at the last moment, stepping backwards to release her. He ran his fingers through his hair with an anxious sigh.

"No. I will see you tonight and I need to be able to act . . . normally . . . in front of the others."

She realized that he was talking about the dance. With a sense of dread, she realized she would have to act normally too.

"I, no, of course not," she forced out.

The earl shook his head and stared down at the patterned carpet. "I appreciate your time, but I should not have interrupted you at work. Pray, excuse me—"

Clara lowered her gaze to watch the polished leather of his boots as he walked swiftly out of the room. She waited until she could no longer hear his footsteps, then sank down onto the bed hoping to calm her overexcited nerves. She wondered if the earl really had just happened by, or if perhaps he had ventured back upstairs hoping to meet her along the way. She couldn't be sure, but he had certainly not refused her offer of comfort. He'd almost kissed her again too, but she tried not to think about that, or the fact that there'd been a bed nearby.

Suddenly, she frowned. Her head cocked abruptly. A servant had not passed in quite some time, nor had she heard one at work in another room.

Oh no . . .

Clara had forgotten all about Stella's reminder to come belowstairs, and now she was *very* late. Hastily she stood and smoothed the bed, then grabbing her tools, rushed out into the hallway. She deposited her feather duster and polishing cloths in the supply closet, then untied her soiled apron and jerked it over her head, only to realize that the ties had hooked on her cap.

In a panic, she worked to loosen the tangle of ribbons and hair, to no avail. Gripping the apron, she yanked, ignoring the tears that rose in her eyes. It finally came free, taking her cap with it and sending her neat knot into disarray.

Clara dropped the tangled fabric in the closet beside the other implements, kicked the door shut and bolted to the grand staircase. She raced down the stairs and rounded the balustrade, heading towards the rear of the house, then paused, craning her neck to listen. A man's footsteps could be heard from the direction of the dining room.

Heart sinking, Clara turned towards it. She really didn't want the earl to see her in such disarray, but when she reached the pristine dining room, there was nobody inside.

"Greetings, Helen," came a man's voice from behind her.

She whirled around to find Paxton, the land steward, standing at the opening of the green baize door. Clara smiled at him in relief.

"Hello, Paxton. What a pleasant surprise to find you here . . ."

"And not the earl?" he asked with a glimmer of mirth in his eyes.

She shrugged. "I must admit I would rather him not see me in my current state," she said, gesturing hopelessly at her appearance.

"So . . . it looks like you have been hard at work doing, er, something rather laborious," he finally managed while smothering a laugh.

Clara glared at him in good-natured embarrassment, just as Amelia emerged from the open doorway behind them. Paxton jerked around at her sudden appearance, and Amelia's mirrored expression of surprise seemed disingenuous at best.

"Oh my," she said, her eyes wide as she looked inquiringly to the land steward, then took in Clara's bedraggled condition. "What's happened here?"

Clara looked at Paxton, wondering if he had registered the not-so-subtle insinuation.

"I was rushing downstairs and . . . my cap became tangled in my apron."

The land steward snickered under his breath and she shot him an accusing glance.

Amelia arched a slender red eyebrow. "Could it be possible you are wearing your aprons wrong?" she asked sardonically.

"Oh, for heaven's sake . . . I was trying to remove it, when it got stuck . . ."

"It's of no consequence," Paxton interjected, placing his hand around Clara's shoulders in an attempt to guide her through the doorway. "We will see you tonight, Amelia," he called back to the maid, ignoring her ensuing huff of displeasure.

In surprise, Clara glanced at him as they made their way down the stairs. "You have come for the dance?"

He scoffed in mock offense. "I was invited, I'll have you know. And by the earl, himself."

The earl.

Clara swallowed. She was starting to think that since Lord Ashworth would be at the party tonight, she would need to find a way to be otherwise engaged. There was simply no version of events where she could see them being at ease with one another, and if any servant had reason to suspect something untoward—Amelia, for instance—she was as good as unemployed. Not that Amelia needed concrete proof to fuel her suspicions.

They stopped at the bottom of the stairs, and Clara glanced at Paxton, forcing a smile upon her lips. "Then I suppose I shall see you tonight," she said, trying to sound cheerful.

The steward tipped her a friendly wink. "I may even ask you to dance."

She laughed lightly. "Well if I don't find Mrs. Malone soon, she'll sack me before you have the chance." The threat carried some weight, but she knew full well that her lack of timeliness was the very least of her punishable offenses.

The other girls had long since gone down to the servants' hall for the dance, but Clara anxiously remained in her room. Stella had loaned her a dress of coarse, dark blue muslin, and it fit her rather well once she had pinned up the hem to account for their difference in height. Her thick sable locks had been reassembled into their typical arrangement minus one very important detail . . . the starched white cap that marked her as a housemaid.

She caught a glimpse of her reflection in the mirror and sighed wistfully. It was a far cry from her wardrobe of seasons past, the delicate lace, tulle, and satin from her former life—the becoming fit of her gowns, the exposed shoulders, the complimentary necklines. Glumly, she stared down at her hands, dried and roughened from too much time spent in mop buckets, the palms calloused from gripping heavy wooden brooms and brushes. Even were she to don one of her old dresses, her skin would be sure to snag and catch upon the fragile fabrics. She might not be wearing her white cap at the moment, but she still carried the unmistakable marks of a servant.

Feeling low, she turned her back on the mirror. If only she

could find a way to avoid the event entirely. But Clara knew she had to at least make a brief appearance to avoid raising suspicions among the staff. She made her way down the staircase, her steps causing the cold boards to creak beneath her feet. Before she had reached the bottom floor she could hear sounds of a lively fiddle tune, and a chorus of accompanying clapping and laughing. Slowly, she opened the door and entered the hallway. To the left was the servants' hall, and the source of the cacophony. But to the right, she heard other sounds coming from the room past the kitchen.

Happy for an excuse to prolong her arrival, she ventured down the long corridor into the scullery and found Tess, the young scullery maid, standing on a wooden platform in front of two large stone sinks. She was hunched over and hard at work, busily scrubbing the last of the day's dishes.

With a small rap on the doorway to signal her presence, Clara entered with a smile. "Hello, Tess."

The girl, who couldn't have been older than fourteen or fifteen, looked up and pushed a matted lock of hair from her face with the back of her hand. "Oh, hello. Why aren't you at the party?" she asked.

"I could ask the same of you, but judging from this stack of pans, I think I know the answer." Clara took a step forward, unhooking an apron from the wall. "Would you like some help?"

Tess's eyes grew wide. "Oh no, miss. That wouldn't be right. I'll be done eventually."

"Yes, and by that time the festivities will have ended," said

Clara as she rolled up her sleeves and joined her at the sink. "What would you have me do?"

After a moment's hesitation, the young girl threw her wet arms around Clara in a sudden show of gratitude. "Thank you so much. If you could help rinse and dry . . ."

"I am at your service," said Clara with a laugh, leaning over to retrieve the nearest pot.

Normally, Tess had her duties well in hand, but Mrs. Humboldt and Gilly had been very busy that day, cooking anything that could be made safely in advance of Eliza's arrival. There were cake pans, pie pans, roasting pans, mixing bowls and dishes from the earl's evening meal. Tess scrubbed each one with all her might, and only when it gleamed would she pass it down to Clara. When the cooking pans were finished, Tess placed a copper bowl in one of the sinks and washed the earl's fine dishes in that vessel, so as to not chip the delicate china on the unforgiving stone basins.

Finally, the washing was complete. Clara righted her sleeves and smoothed her hair, noticing with a sigh that her skirts had gotten wet despite her protective apron.

"I'll be back," said the scullery maid excitedly, opening the door to the staircase. "I need to change out of these clothes . . . do you think Oscar will be there?" she asked after a moment's hesitation.

"I'm sure he will be," replied Clara, keeping her face straight despite her urge to smile. "I'll meet you in the dining hall upon your return."

The girl sprinted up the stairs, and Clara walked slowly

back towards the servants' hall, from where the music and laughter still flowed. Lifting her chin in an attitude of confidence she did not truly feel, she entered the hall and surveyed the gathering from a distance. The sight that greeted her was a surprise.

Matthew was standing on an old wooden stool at the far side, energetically playing a fiddle. The long table had been pushed to one side of the room, creating just enough space for the crowd of people that had gathered, although it was still a tight fit even then. Nobody seemed to mind, though, and Clara stared in wonder at Matthew's unexpected display of talent, and how deftly he was able to maintain his balance on such a precarious stage. Given the amount of his perspiration, she could safely assume it was hard work.

It was nearly impossible to hear herself think amid the festive din, with the rustling of skirts and stomping of boots providing the only circulation in the sweltering room. Clara fanned herself with a hand as she scanned the crowd, where most of the servants were clapping a lively beat to Matthew's tune, but many were also dancing in the middle of the room. Even Amelia was managing to enjoy herself, caught up in dancing with the groom. The stable boy, Oscar, was there as well, although it did not appear he'd worked up the courage for dancing quite yet.

She found Paxton on the opposite side of the room, quenching his thirst with a mug of ale. Rosa's blonde curls bounced up and down as she cheered next to Stella, but what she was excited about was a mystery. Clara continued to scan the crowd for signs of Lord Ashworth, for surely he had accompanied Rosa. Then with a jolt, she discovered why he could not be found near his niece.

He was in the middle of the room . . . dancing.

Clara's mouth fell open. The fifth earl of Ashworth was twirling Mrs. Humboldt around the floor, and the woman was moving with such competent agile grace, she could have been a debutante. In fact, Clara had never seen the cook look so young or carefree. Certainly, the earl had been raised to dance the refined quadrilles and sumptuous waltzes of high-society ballrooms, but here he displayed none of the pomp of his elite position, pulling away to clap briefly before swinging her back around the dance floor.

He laughed, and a stab of what felt like jealousy pierced through her. She may have kissed the man, but she had never made him laugh with such abandon.

The last notes of the fiddle died away, and the earl bowed deeply to his partner, who grinned from ear to ear and curtsied in return. The surrounding crowd clapped wildly in good-natured approval. Tess appeared in the doorway, looking renewed in a clean dress, and Clara pulled her aside before anyone could take notice.

"Oscar is in want of a partner," she whispered with a wink.

Tess stared at her, wide-eyed. "It wouldn't be proper of me to ask him, though . . ."

"Don't be silly," replied Clara, laughing. "This isn't Grosvenor Square—it is the servants' hall and *the earl is dancing.* Surely if he is willing to bend the rules, you can as well."

The scullery maid looked at the dance floor in disbelief. Upon seeing the earl wiping his brow following his dance with Mrs. Humboldt, Tess let out a nervous laugh and glanced in Oscar's direction.

"Well, perhaps I could stand near him to gain his attention."

Tess made her way into the crowd to strategically position herself near the boy. Clara tried to follow her through the crush of people, but was interrupted by the sudden appearance of Paxton bowing before her.

"We meet again," he said in a jovial tone. "Perhaps you would like to start the evening with a dance?" he offered, extending a friendly hand in her direction.

"Helen!"

Stella's cry came just a moment before she lunged forward to hook her hand around Clara's arm. Paxton grinned and took a step back to avoid getting caught in their path.

"You should dance with Lord Ashworth. He's danced with every woman here!"

Coming off of the dance floor to skirt behind their group, Amelia eyed Clara with a dismissive huff. "I suppose that dress is tolerable on you. But as Stella said, he's already danced with every *woman* here."

"Amelia," came the earl's rich, deep voice, suddenly beside them, "it's best to not muddy your compliment with an insult."

Stella eyes grew huge and she hid a sudden laugh behind her hand. Amelia's cheeks turned as red as her hair. The maid lowered into a brief curtsy before retreating, annoyed, to the refreshment table, and a bloom of fire spread through Clara's chest when Ashworth's eyes flicked over to meet hers. She reeled inwardly at his sudden nearness, trying not to stare at the light sheen of sweat glistening on his throat, or how he had loosened his cravat in the heat.

"My lord," she said with an accompanying curtsy, praying she sounded normal. "I hope you have been enjoying yourself this evening."

He may have felt relaxed and lighthearted with her fellow domestics, but as she'd feared, his demeanor shifted back into guarded reserve near her. "Indeed. You were late to the party," he replied.

Indicating the water on her dress, she said, "I stopped at the scullery to help Tess complete her chores."

"Is this something you do often?" asked Ashworth, his eyes drifting ever so slightly down the length of her skirts.

"No, my lord. I only wanted to ensure she arrived at the party before it had ended for the evening."

The earl stared at her then, in the midst of all the voices and noise. "That was very kind of you," he said softly. He then turned to survey the dancers on the floor. "And your kindness paid off, for she has found herself a dance partner."

She looked over his shoulder to see that shy Tess had managed to secure Oscar after all. Clara's face beamed at her success, and for one moment, she caught a flash of the earl's answering grin before he censored himself back into an attitude of stern indifference. A disbelieving thrill raced through her at the sight. It was disturbing how profoundly she was affected by his smiles.

The first notes of a new song rang out from Matthew's fiddle.

"My lord," cried Stella, "you should dance with Helen—they just started a new one!"

Clara stiffened at Stella brazenly suggesting such a thing to the earl. She had a suspicion that the usually reserved maid must have been partaking of the ale.

Ashworth's eyes darted to Stella, the surprise in his golden-green eyes transforming, crystallizing into rejection. They returned to settle on Clara.

"I've finished dancing for the evening, but I'm certain Helen will have no trouble finding another partner."

Clara heard an unbecoming snort come from behind the earl, and knew that Amelia must have been lurking nearby. Her entire body went numb as humiliation coursed through her. Was this how the earl intended to act *normal* after their earlier encounter upstairs? By actively shunning her in front of her peers? Despite her lowly position, she found herself unable to leave his insult unchallenged.

She would have *no* trouble finding another partner, indeed.

Clara forced herself to smile until it felt halfway genuine. "How amusing . . . the earl has finished dancing and I've yet to even get started!" She stretched out her hand to Paxton. "I believe you offered to dance, sir?"

After all, Clara had suggested that Tess have courage in asking a man to dance. Now she would draw on that same bravery to dance with each man present.

She felt this particular flavor of revenge was best served blazing hot.

William escaped the happy gathering belowstairs and headed outside in the dark, stripping off his jacket as he walked. The air was cool and clean and refreshing. He inhaled deeply and attempted to clear his mind of thoughts of Helen, twirling merrily in the arms of other men.

He glowered at the landscape, now blanketed by night. It was true he had panicked at Stella's suggestion of a dance with Helen—perhaps he could have handled that better. But the contrition he had initially felt upon rejecting her had been extinguished somewhere around her third dance partner, and it had taken every ounce of restraint he possessed to keep from throttling any man near her after the sixth.

He tossed his jacket over a wrought iron chair and strode around the garden. He needed to walk off this frustration. How strange that a housemaid could bring him to such a state of emotional upheaval. While the reality of it was unsettling, he couldn't deny her pull. He'd given in to it earlier that same day, even seeking her out on the way back from his room. William couldn't regret it, foolish as it was. He'd risk being discovered a thousand times over if it would mean holding her once more, or seeing the way her eyes softened when they spoke.

He imagined part of the appeal was the distraction she

provided from the worry and sadness that had become a pervasive presence in his life. There had been countless days since the accident where the only motivation for him to even open his eyes, let alone get out of bed, was his sense of duty to his family. The need for him to carry on, no matter the cost. After all, they had already paid the ultimate price—

Christ.

Lowering down to sit on the stone wall that circled the rear garden, he worked to reign in his emotions before they got out of hand. William could recognize that this was not simply a matter of battling against his desire for Helen. Somehow, the emotional scars he'd suffered had become entangled with his feelings for her.

Standing, he scooped up his jacket from atop its iron perch. Then with a growl of anger, he hooked his fingers around the cold metal and hurled the chair across the garden, sending it to clatter noisily across the ground. The cacophony was unseemly and out of place in the chilly quiet, but incredibly satisfying. If only it were that easy to rid himself of the memories that had been burned into his brain, the guilt of surviving when no one else had, the need to deny himself the thing he wanted most . . .

With an irritated sigh, he walked back towards the house, scooping up his jacket on the way. He had come outside to sort through the tangle of his thoughts, yet only succeeded in twisting them further. Grabbing the door to the service entrance, he crept into the dimly lit kitchen, feeling like an intruder in his own home. The whoops and cheers from the party down the hall continued unabated, and he took advantage of their merry distraction to slide unnoticed into the servants' staircase. Staring down at his feet, he vaulted the stairs two at a time, in a sudden rush to be upstairs. He would just proceed through the hallway near his bedchamber—

A soft exclamation caught him by surprise, and he whirled around to find Helen, barely illuminated from the yellow glow that shone weakly from her candleholder, flattened against the wall in an attempt to avoid him. Anticipation and turmoil affected him in equal measures at her appearance. Her upswept mass of hair appeared black in the poor lighting. William longed to sink his fingers into it and hold her immobile for his kiss. Instead, he straightened up to his full height and scoffed at her in irritation.

"I'm surprised to see you so soon. Are your feet sore from all of your dancing?"

She glanced at him guardedly in the flickering light of the candle. "You dance very well yourself, my lord," she replied acidly. "Please, excuse me."

Helen curtsied then brushed past him, and although he told himself not to, he reached for her as she passed. His hand slid across her waist to restrain her gently, and he was rewarded by the soft intake of her breath.

"Certainly, there may still be a few men who did not receive the pleasure of your company tonight," he murmured near her ear, loving the way her breathing had accelerated.

She tipped her chin into the air and glanced away with a sniff. "There was only one, my lord, but he was feeling rather disinclined."

He felt a flash of annoyance at having realized she had indeed danced with every man at the party. "I'm still disinclined, if that's what you're wondering," he growled.

"Not at all," she replied pertly. "I'm only curious as to why you are detaining me if that is indeed the case."

Despite yearning to bring her closer, he released her and observed her very obvious relief.

Stepping to the side, William gave her ample room to pass, yet she remained there as if unsure of how to part ways. After evaluating each other in silence, he raised a brow in her direction.

"So you admired my dancing?" he asked, hoping to provoke her.

It was too dim to see her clearly, but he could almost feel her rolling her eyes. "It was rather capable."

He gripped the railing along the wall and leaned against it to survey her. "It was my first time since before the accident."

Helen's head snapped over to him, her eyes widening.

"I . . . oh. Have you . . . you have not been out in society at all since then?" she asked.

"Not when I could avoid it," he admitted. "I'm not certain that the company of Lord Evanston counts as society—not polite society, at least."

Her gaze held his, the cool anger that had lurked there before having dissolved into something warmer now. "May I ask, my lord . . . were you injured in the accident?"

William resisted answering her question, the familiar surge of adrenaline coursing through his veins—his prelude to panic. But as usual, and even despite their disagreement tonight, he could detect nothing in her question but the most genuine compassion. He exhaled slowly.

"Broken leg, broken ribs, dislocated shoulder. I did not wake for a week. All minor things." He glanced away in grim contemplation. "When I did wake, I found I'd acquired my family's titles and lands. I'd survived to become the fifth earl of Ashworth, and it only took burying all the other men in my family."

Helen's dark eyes shimmered with compassion. "I'm so sorry . . ."

"Eliza's husband, too, was such a loss." His mouth twisted in remorse and he pushed restlessly away from the wall. "God, I don't know why I'm telling you this—" The poison of his trauma crept in once again, and he felt his breath catch as a sickening sense of unreality took hold.

She moved closer, her eyes solemn, still carefully gripping her candleholder in one hand. "Perhaps it helps to unburden yourself in some way, even if it causes distress?"

"Not particularly," he uttered through gritted teeth.

Her other hand lifted, gently touching his shoulder, running along the jacket seam then further to brush against his cheek. The smooth satin of her skin was a soft contrast to the stubbled scrape of his jaw. His eyes fell closed in something that felt like . . . relief.

"I think it must," she whispered.

Helen stroked his brow, his cheek . . . soothing him. Although he knew better, he allowed it because her touch was proving more curative than those weeks spent languishing in bed had ever been.

She eyed him curiously. "You stop breathing when you are upset, my lord," she said. "Try remembering to breathe."

William had never really thought about it before. He tried it, breathing in deeply, then releasing. The fresh intake of air immediately helped to invigorate his mind, and he opened his eyes to regard her in hesitant surprise. She brushed a sweaty lock of hair away from his forehead.

"Again," she demanded softly.

Another inhale, another exhale, and each time he felt more refreshed, more like himself. He sighed and felt a hint of tension ebb out of his shoulders. When her fingertips danced lightly across his lips, an answering surge of pleasure flooded his loins.

"You shouldn't," he managed, while doing nothing to stop her, praying for her to continue. "I told you once before; you shouldn't touch me when I'm like this."

"I know," she murmured, with another teasing brush of her thumb.

He recognized his own words to her, from that day he'd kissed her in his room, muddy and angry and exhilarated from his time in the village. He wanted to kiss her now . . . kiss her everywhere. Craved the taste of her on his tongue. He could never have enough. Even if she ended up naked and breathless in his bed, it would never be enough . . .

His hand slid around her wrist, and her eyes went wide. He was ready to tug her upstairs to his bedchamber. Ready to satisfy his fascination. Ready to end the sleepless nights, spent occupied with thoughts of her, and days devoted to catching even just a glimpse of this woman . . .

A raucous shout from the other side of the servants' door yanked him out of his reverie. Someone was approaching, and the shame of being discovered like this with his servant was something he could not bear.

Releasing her, he shouldered roughly past. The inevitable confusion and hurt flashed in quick succession across her face, and he couldn't bear to see it, especially after the way she'd seen him tonight. How she'd helped him. Sparing her any kind of farewell, he turned on his heel and launched up the stairs to his chambers, slamming the heavy door behind.

He sank back to lean against the solid wood, desperate for some stability. He berated himself for having been so careless with his feelings, knowing something had shifted tonight . . . and that it frightened him. For months, he'd felt like an imposter in his own home, a pretender. And in an uncharacteristic lapse of judgment, he'd invited Helen, briefly, to see a side of him that very few had seen. He had made himself vulnerable to her.

Worse, it had felt good to do it. It had been like coming home, like being cared for.

Or like falling in love.

Chapter Eleven

Lord Ashworth glared down at his skewed cravat in irritation, then jerked it roughly from his neck to begin tying it anew. He was exhausted and irritable, and he knew it was because of the party the previous evening.

Clenching his jaw, he yanked the cravat into a precise knot. His refusal of Helen last night had been unavoidable. In fact, her continued presence in this house was becoming an unnecessary peril. Eliza would be here this morning, and she had already hinted to him in her letters her plans to initiate his search for a suitable wife.

Two light raps brought his attention back to matters at hand. "Enter," Ashworth commanded gruffly, and his bedchamber door opened to frame Matthew, looking sharp in his livery.

"Good morning, my lord. We've received word from the village that Lady Cartwick will be arriving shortly."

The earl nodded in acknowledgment. "I will be down soon." He paused to glance sideways at the man. "Excellent playing last night, by the way."

Beaming at the unsolicited praise, the footman nodded politely. "Thank you, my lord. I am pleased you found it to your satisfaction."

Lord Ashworth proceeded down the grand staircase and strode through the front doors out to the drive. Matthew followed behind him, then made his way over to assume his position near Charles beside the rest of the domestic servants. The earl's eyes unwittingly sought Helen and found her easily—the print dress, apron, and cap in no way diminishing her allure. A now familiar heat surged through him, and he tamped down his desire with an irritated sigh.

The sound of the incoming carriage caused everyone to straighten where they stood, except Rosa, who began jumping for joy. Placing his hands gently on the girl's shoulders, he was able to exert enough pressure to subdue her sufficiently for a civilized greeting.

Once the vehicle had come to a complete stop, Matthew approached and pulled open the door. Lord Evanston was the first to disembark and Ashworth greeted him with a handshake and a perfunctory nod before shifting his gaze to Rosa, who had ducked around the viscount to scramble up the steps of the carriage.

A great jostling could be heard from the carriage's interior, hidden from outside view. Ashworth and Evanston exchanged small smiles with each other, then Matthew stepped forward to assist as Eliza's lady's maid clambered hastily out of the vehicle. Looking a bit frazzled, she smoothed the front of her skirts and adjusted her shawl before glancing up to curtsy politely in Lord Ashworth's direction.

"Hello, Patterson," said the earl with a grin. "Did the carriage suddenly become too small for you?"

She laughed with good humor. "It certainly seemed to, my lord." The woman took a step backwards, waiting patiently for her mistress to exit.

A few moments later, Rosa emerged triumphant with her dolly. Following just behind her was Eliza, shining blonde curls catching what little sunlight had managed to break through the clouds that day. Lord Ashworth came forward, first guiding Rosa off the steps, then reaching up to take her mother's hand. Eliza's previously happy green eyes shone with tears at the sight of his face.

"Dear William, it is so good to be home," said Eliza, her voice cracking perceptibly on the word *home*. He quickly wrapped his arms around her and brought her close.

"All will be well," he murmured reassuringly. "Both you and Rosa will be taken care of. I can promise you that." He stroked her hair and pulled back, bending down to her height so he could meet her eyes directly. "You will stay at Lawton Park as long as you choose." William reached into his pocket and offered his sister a clean handkerchief, patting her comfortingly on the arm.

Eliza took it and dried her eyes, glancing awkwardly at Thomas, who was now busily scanning the landscape, acting as if nothing had happened. After a moment, she smiled down at Rosa, then stepped aside to survey the attending staff. The earl knew what was coming.

"Which one is Helen?" she asked her young daughter. Ashworth's gaze flicked over to the lovely maid in question, who suddenly appeared very nervous. Rosa smiled and pointed in Helen's direction.

"That's her, Mama. Doesn't she look like my dolly?" She raised her doll for an easy comparison.

His sister smiled and cast her gaze between the two figures, noting the similarities. "She certainly does, my love." She walked purposefully over to Helen, who curtsied respectfully before lifting her gaze. Eliza surprised her by taking her hands and pulling her close to place a kiss on her cheek.

"You and I are already friends, you know," said Eliza, squeezing her fingers warmly. "You saved my precious girl, and I will never forget it. Thank you, Helen."

Helen's face flushed, clearly pleased at his sister's approbation. "You are very welcome, my lady. I am only happy I was able to help."

William watched the interaction, puzzled. Aside from her initial nervousness, Helen seemed rather at ease in conversation with a lady of superior rank. Then again, she had certainly displayed a willingness to break boundaries with him, and damn it all if that hadn't spurred him on to breach propriety, himself.

His sudden scowl gained the attention of Thomas, who, noticing the change in his demeanor, stepped forward to touch his arm.

"Shall we head inside?" he asked in a low voice.

Ashworth nodded. "Let us get you settled in, Eliza," he said, interrupting their conversation with as much tact as he could muster. It wasn't much. "You and Helen will have the opportunity to converse later."

Eliza looked at him with some surprise, then glanced back towards Helen. "Yes, of course. No need to chat idly here in the cold," she said with a smile. "In fact, Rosa has requested we ride to the Gilded Rose for a spot of tea later on today. Perhaps you could join us?"

The earl clenched his teeth until pain shot through his jaw. Christ, it was one thing to have the woman living under the same roof, tormenting him with her nearness. It was quite another thing altogether to be subjected to her company while being forced to act normally in her presence. He tried to think of a polite way to object to Eliza's wishes, but came up with nothing.

The housemaid seemed taken aback as well. "I . . . I am honored, my lady. I will ask if Mrs. Malone can spare me once my afternoon chores have been completed."

"Very well, then. I hope to see you later." With a parting smile, his sister took Rosa's hand and proceeded towards the main entrance, Evanston following closely behind her. Ashworth forced his gaze forward as he marched past Helen, ignoring the way her eyes followed him as he accompanied the small group into the house.

Glasses and plates clinked merrily at the Gilded Rose, and an occasional boisterous laugh broke the conversational hum inside the establishment. The innkeeper had been sure to seat the earl's group at his most attractive table, nestled quietly towards the rear of the dining room, adjacent to a score of foggy windows. A tea-dyed lace tablecloth and a fine china tea set adorned its surface, adding to the charm.

Observing quietly, Clara studied the interaction between brother and sister from her chair in the corner. Rosa had requested the seat between Clara and her mother, and was now carefully drinking her tea with her pinky finger splayed out demonstratively.

Clara admired Eliza's satin frock. It was a lavender shade that suited her well, and was also in keeping with society's expectations for widows in half mourning. Her polished refinement made Clara feel quite plain in comparison, and she glanced down at her hands in forlorn contemplation. Her dry skin and broken fingernails did nothing to help her mood, and she sighed, bringing her eyes up to the tablecloth instead. Despite her own pensive thoughts, she couldn't help but be curious about Eliza's troubles at home. While Clara had not been close enough to hear their dialogue outside the carriage, the young woman had clearly been upset. The earl, too, had appeared agitated.

She found it interesting that despite his blunt rejection of her last night at the dance and afterwards, Lord Ashworth had been ignoring her today as though *she* were the one who had perpetrated a great offense. Gazing covertly at him from across the table, Clara couldn't help but feel some slight satisfaction at his intimations that watching her dance last night had made him jealous. His painful confessions on the staircase had been surprising, but the sorrow she had felt for him had been muddled by his peculiar treatment of her.

One moment he was divulging personal secrets, while the next he was shoving her away as if his breach of conduct had somehow been her doing. Now he was being forced to endure her presence after his abominable behavior, and she enjoyed watching him squirm.

With a start, she realized Eliza was looking in her direction. Ripping her eyes away from the earl, Clara promptly snapped her attention back to the discussion at hand.

"The earl has told me that you are sorely needed below-stairs, Helen, or else I might be tempted to claim you for Rosa's nursemaid, at least until Florence is fully healed and with us once again." Eliza shrugged and smiled. "Since I can't poach your services, perhaps you might be available to assist as need be, and join us upstairs on occasion?"

Clara stared at Lord Ashworth's sister in humbled gratitude. "Thank you, my lady. I would be honored."

"I know Father gave servants half a Sunday, every other week, for their time off," Eliza continued thoughtfully. Tipping her head towards her brother she asked, "Has that policy been altered over time, William? It seems domestics could do with a bit more than that, I feel."

Ashworth shifted to lean back in his chair, folding his hands over his flat stomach. "As it turns out, I happened to agree with you. Servants receive a full day off, after morning duties are finished, every Sunday."

"No," Rosa contradicted, reaching across the table towards a plate of tiny cakes. "Not Helen. You have her do more chores."

Eliza's luminous green eyes grew even larger. She turned to face her brother incredulously. "Surely not."

The earl stared across the table at them and shrugged. "Actually, yes. But only for a short while."

"May I ask to what purpose?" Eliza's beautiful features were now a mask of thinly concealed irritation.

Clara stared at the tablecloth and lifted her cup to her lips in an attempt to hide her amusement. Deciding to risk a glance upwards at the earl beneath her lashes, she caught him staring at her, his dark gaze unreadable.

"No reminder necessary, sister. I am quite aware of the steps Helen took to ensure Rosa's safety," he rejoined, shifting his eyes towards Eliza. "But as I explained to her after the incident, her measures were extraordinary. I could not proceed without disciplining her in some way, even if only to assert myself as master of this estate."

Clara felt an inappropriate thrill at the notion of Lord Ashworth asserting himself as her master. Unfortunately, the reality of the situation had not been nearly that exciting.

"And on this point," added Lord Evanston, "I must agree with the earl. You cannot leave a servant unpunished for taking a horse, no matter how heroic the circumstances."

Silence filled the air, and it became obvious that Eliza had not been made aware of the details of her daughter's rescue. She blinked at Evanston in surprise, then slowly rotated in her chair to address Clara specifically. "*You stole a horse?*"

Suddenly feeling uncomfortable under the intense scrutiny of the peers at the table, Clara managed a shaky reply. "I—er . . . well, yes, I did. But I returned it, obviously," she stammered. "So . . . so it was more like borrowing."

"She did, Mama!" said Rosa, reaching towards the cake

plate once more. "And she tied her apron around my leg when it was bleeding, too." She stuffed another cake into her mouth.

The earl's sister stared at Rosa, then at Clara, then finally at the men seated at the table. "How long has this punishment been in effect?" she asked.

"Since the incident occurred, two weeks ago," answered the earl.

Straightening her spine, Eliza looped a finger through the delicate handle of her teacup and raised it to her lips. She lowered it to rest on its saucer with a small yet deliberate *clink*, and glanced pleasantly at her brother. "I feel that should be sufficient, don't you?"

Clara could sense the earl's temper simmering quietly. He did not like his authority questioned, and yet his sister was probably the only person on the planet who could manage to do so without fear of consequence. She held her breath and stared at her fingers, anxiously awaiting his answer. Finally, he sighed. "Perhaps I could revisit the matter."

Eliza shot a satisfied glance in Clara's direction, and Clara longed to throw her arms around the woman in a tight hug.

"I'm sorry to say," declared the viscount, "but this type of mishap is one of the reasons I can't ever imagine having children." He paused, noticing that Rosa had halted in mid-slurp of her tea to regard him curiously. "No offense intended, of course," he assured her. "It's only I can't see having the energy to worry about anyone but myself."

Lady Cartwick scoffed and regarded him cynically. "There is plenty to worry about with you. This is true."

Evanston looked ready to make a biting retort of his own when a rider burst through the door, laughing heartily at the sodden state of his attire.

"The storm came out of nowhere! Save yourselves!" he brayed loudly to the other customers, before wetly stepping up to order a fortifying pint of ale from the innkeeper.

"Perfect," muttered the earl under his breath, standing abruptly. He crossed the dining room to open the door, surveying the inclement weather with a wary eye, then closed it and rejoined them at the table.

"It doesn't seem likely to let up soon, so we either spend the afternoon here or ride out now," he said, shaking his head. "I'm wishing we would have brought the carriage, after all."

Evanston rose from the table with a sideways glance at Eliza and her daughter. "I will ride to the estate and return with the carriage, if you wish."

"No," answered Eliza, placing her napkin on the table and standing with Rosa. "I can't think of a more rousing welcome home than a ride in the rain. It's not a long trip back to the house. I'm sure it won't be anything a change of dress and a half hour by the fireside can't fix."

Clara stared at her shoes. She had walked to the inn by herself to meet them, and had no horse to ride. This would not be an enjoyable voyage for her, but there likely wouldn't have been enough room for her in the carriage anyway. She tried to imagine what her family might've done in similar circumstances. She surely would've let Abigail into the carriage with her, but then, she wasn't exactly conventional.

With a sigh, she stood, only to find Lord Ashworth eyeing her thoughtfully.

They stepped out into the stormy weather, and the inn-keeper and his son rushed to retrieve their horses. William lifted Rosa, her cloak already soaked, onto Evanston's horse, while Thomas assisted Eliza as she mounted her steed side-saddle. Clara saw a blush rise on Lady Cartwick's cheeks when the viscount placed a steadying, and perhaps not entirely necessary, hand upon her waist. He then turned expectantly to Lord Ashworth, who stood in the rain, staring with indecision at Clara.

"Ashworth?"

"You three go on ahead," the earl yelled above the pounding rain.

Evanston nodded and rode off with the ladies, but not before grinning and casting a knowing glance at his friend that made Clara's face grow warm. The earl appeared to ignore the silent communication. Instead, he acknowledged the innkeeper and his boy with a brief tip of his head.

"Thank you for your assistance. I can manage from here."

"Yes, my lord," said the men in tandem, dashing back into the steamy warmth of the building.

Squinting amidst the deluge, he glanced at Clara, then at the surrounding streets, which were suddenly empty.

"You will ride my horse," he commanded. Streams of rain trickled down his face to drip down off his nose.

She shook the water out of her eyes to stare at him, mortified at how it might appear if anyone saw her on the earl's horse. "I will not."

"Pray, do not forget yourself," he said, his eyes narrowed. "I am master of this estate, and I am ordering you to ride." He swiped a hand over his face, displacing the moisture that had collected. "And quickly, before we catch our deaths."

"My lord, indeed it is you who is forgetting yourself. You are the Earl of Ashworth. I am a housemaid. You should not even be in my company right now, let alone allow me to ride your horse." She tried to put more distance between them, but her attempt was frustrated by the mud sucking against her boots.

Ashworth's angry sigh was punctuated by a thick cloud of steam, foggy and white in the frigid air. "I am not allowing it, I am demanding it. And since when have you needed my permission to ride one of my horses?" he asked sardonically. "Now mount up. Your hem is already covered in at least six inches of mud."

Clara faced him directly, shaking the raindrops from her eyes. "My dress is worth nothing. You should ride your horse to spare your fine clothing, my lord. I won't have you ruin your garments on my account."

"I possess an extensive wardrobe, whereas your dress may well be the only one you own aside from your service gowns." He glared at her. "Get on the horse. *Now.*"

Clara bristled. He made a very good point but rather than conceding, her annoyance from the previous evening's snub provoked her into losing her temper instead.

"I'm curious," she said crossly, "as to why my welfare concerns you so very much, when just last night you couldn't even be bothered for a dance." The words slipped out before she could censor herself.

The earl reared back in shock, then his brow lowered, his eyes turning molten.

"You," he said in barely more than a shouted whisper, "have become a nuisance." Ashworth leaned in close, his rain-soaked hair sleek and dark. "I am not obligated to explain myself to you, Helen. I will dance with whomever I choose, and you will stay silent on the matter, regardless of your infatuation with me." Sparks shot from his eyes. "Perhaps the better idea would be for you to find employment elsewhere instead."

The rain fell heavily all around them, drowning their exchange in steady white noise. Clara opened her mouth to speak, but no words came forth. Fear, mortification, and heartache burnt her spirit to ashes from the inside out. She had been so foolish. Not only had she mistakenly convinced herself of the earl's preference, but her inability to conform to life as a servant had just ended her days of service at Lawton Park.

Hot tears spilled past her lashes to stream down her cheeks, mingling with the chilled tracks of rain. She wanted to die. If he sent her packing tonight with nowhere to go, she very well could, either on the streets or at the hands of the baron.

She willed herself to be strong, but regardless, Clara felt her face crumple, a choking sob escaping her despite her attempt to hold it back. The earl's expression changed dramatically, but she was too distraught to pay it close attention.

"My lord, please forgive me . . ." Clara managed to say, before turning away to cover her face completely. She had managed to make a home for herself here these past few months, though it hadn't been easy. It had been hard enough leaving Silvercreek. What would she do now?

Immersed in her misery, she didn't detect the earl's approach, but her senses were jarred back to reality by the protective slide of his palms over her arms. Clara froze in confusion with him standing silently behind her, her heart beating like a hammer.

Ashworth said nothing for a long while, then pulled her gently back against the hard surface of his chest to wrap himself fully around her in what could only be described as an embrace. An intoxicating heat surged through every part of her, and she swayed dizzily in his arms.

"My lord . . ." she said, her voice unsteady.

Choosing not to reply, his strong arms tightened their hold and he leaned forward to rest his cheek against the side of her head.

"Helen." He spoke softly, his breath hot against the delicate edge of her ear. "Ride with me back to the house."

She lifted her head to protest, but the earl interrupted her.

"We will travel along the woods to the west. I will take care not to be seen."

Clara was suddenly tired of fighting. She simply nodded in acquiescence, and Lord Ashworth slowly released her to cross over to his horse, placing one hand on the saddle, then turning to stretch his other hand out to her.

The sight of him standing in invitation caused her heart to thump painfully. She joined him, slipping her hand into his. The touch of his skin upon hers was more than she could bear, yet his clasp was unyielding and she had no choice but to proceed.

She gripped the pommel and he helped her up into the saddle. Rather than sitting astride, as she had on her journey to find Rosa, she seated herself sidesaddle as best she could with her skirts drenched and caked in muck. The rich smell of leather mingled with the horse's musty aroma, and a thousand memories of home came rushing back to her. But these thoughts were eclipsed the moment the earl placed his boot in the stirrup and swung up behind her, swiftly eliminating the distance between them. The saddle, not truly created for two riders, made for a snug fit . . . one that took her breath away.

Ashworth tensed as he reached around her to take the reins; she could feel the muscles in his arms and chest contract. He set the horse off at a slow pace, which was reasonable given the conditions of the road and surrounding fields, and guided them to the wooded area along the southwest border of the estate. The canopy, although lacking the leafy foliage of summer, still provided some much appreciated shelter from the steady rain.

They rode in silence, the sounds of the horse's hooves and their breathing the only intrusions amidst the lull of the downpour behind them.

Clara's mind drifted as they made their way slowly towards the house. It was easy to dream with the noise of the storm and the heat of Lord Ashworth behind her. She rested against him, all too aware of the hard strength of his body brushing against her back.

Fat drops of glittering rain fell from the branches above to strike them with cold indifference. They came to the creek that ran west along the estate. What was normally a bubbling brook of diminutive size had changed into a fast-flowing waterway. After considering for a moment, the earl urged his horse onward with a jab of his heels. The horse plowed ahead but its hooves slipped on the slick surface of the rocks beneath the churning water. With a frantic whinny, the large animal pitched forward, upsetting Clara from her position in the saddle. She gasped and heard Ashworth utter a curse, yanking on the reins to right his steed, then quickly sliding one arm around her waist to haul her back against him. His horse scrabbled for purchase, then found his stride and pushed out on the opposite side of the creek, tossing his soggy mane and prancing a bit as he emerged victorious onto dry land.

Clara slumped against the earl in relief. She noticed his arm remained wrapped securely around her, although the danger had passed by then.

The shuttered west wing of Lawton Park became visible through the trees, but he continued further north to stop at a small wooden bridge that rose above the agitated waters.

Clara's breath caught as she felt the scrape of his jaw against the soft skin of her cheek. And then, the rain-wet heat of his lips brushed against the same place. Fire licked through her veins in an instant, and she remained still as he dragged his mouth back to caress the delicate lobe of her ear. Pleasure shot through to her very core and she gasped quietly.

With a growl, Lord Ashworth released the reins to pull

her body even tighter against his. He lowered his lips to the side of her neck, scorching the flesh with hot, openmouthed kisses that made her writhe against him. Frantically, she pulled away as far as the saddle would allow and twisted around to face him.

"My lord, we cannot," she said through trembling lips, placing her chilled fingertips against his chest. "You would grow to hate me for it. Indeed you probably already do."

His hands shifted to grip her upper arms, and he gave her a soft shake of remonstration. "You haven't been paying very close attention," the earl admonished. Pulling her forward, he whispered, "Let me tell you again."

Ashworth's mouth came down upon hers, and any further objections from her were kissed away with urgent ferocity. His lips were soft and sweet and tasted like tea, and his tongue was wickedly skillful. Bringing her hands up to the sides of his face, she returned his kiss with an intensity that had him pulling back in a daze, his breath heaving.

"Christ, Helen. And you wonder why I won't dance with you," he said huskily. "You're all I think about . . ."

His open confession shocked her beyond belief. It was everything she had dreamt of him saying, but instead of feeling glorious she felt guilty. He couldn't stop thinking about her—but in reality, he didn't even know her.

The earl could sense her change in mood, and did not seem surprised when she twisted back around, sliding off the horse to plant her feet on the soft ground. He quickly followed, landing easily on the forest floor before reaching forward to grab her wrist. With one quick motion, she was back in his arms, gazing up at him in frustration.

"Please don't, my lord. I am not worthy of you—"

"You are more worthy than ten of me," Ashworth said hoarsely, jerking her up against him. His touch gentled at once, his hands roaming slowly across her back, serving to enflame her and simultaneously preventing her escape. She could feel her curves molded against the hard planes of his body, and she sank into it, tired of fighting, wishing for defeat. Longing for him, and loathing herself.

"Nothing can come of this," said Clara, her voice barely discernible above the din of the rushing water beside them. "I can't—"

He lowered his head once again to meet her lips. This time, his kiss was slow, sensuous, thrilling her with the insistent pressure of his mouth over hers, soft flicks of his tongue teasing her unmercifully into shaking submission. Clara's knees weakened beneath her skirts and she slipped her hands beneath his soaked coat, seeking the heat of his body and pulling herself closer into his solid strength. Inhaling deeply into the kiss, she perceived the clean bouquet of sandalwood and citrus, along with his own, more subtle, male scent. She was dazed with the feel of him crushed against her, his incendiary warmth making her forget the frozen chill of the weather.

As her hands had begun exploring, so too did his. He stole her breath with his plunging kisses while one hand found her breast, compressed beneath the damp layers of her buttoned-up bodice. His tortured groan reverberated through her ears.

"I want to feel your skin," he murmured against her mouth. "I want to taste it."

She gasped at the thought, then his other hand found her backside and pressed his hips forward to meet hers, prompting a moan to escape her lips.

Ashworth hummed with pleasure, and Clara's head spun at the feel of his hand squeezing her breast, at the intimate press of his manhood through her skirts, at the way her entire body was clenching and crying out for more friction, more pressure . . . more of everything. She arched into his touch, her fingers curled possessively against the soaked shirt that did nothing to conceal the rigid flex of his muscles beneath. She wanted to feel his skin, too. She wanted it so much that it scared her.

Clara thrust him away and took a step back, staring blindly into the rushing water of the stream, trying to control her breathing. *Was she prepared to do this?*

She knew in that moment, the answer was yes.

But when she turned back to look at him, Ashworth was quiet. He scrubbed a hand over his face with a groan, and she knew at once that he was about to reject her again. At last, the hand dropped and he looked away.

"Please accept my apologies, Helen," he ground out with an attempt at formality. "You should proceed alone from this point. We cannot be seen together."

She blinked at the earl, humiliation spreading through her chest. He had the look of regret that she would expect from a man who had just made a grievous mistake.

She attempted to keep her voice even, but it had grown thick with the emotions roiling through her. "Yes, my lord."

He nodded, his eyes still affixed to some distant point. Clara clenched her fists and turned to stride briskly eastward. It was only until she was halfway across the field that the scalding flow of fresh tears made their way down her face at last.

Chapter Twelve

Christ, Helen. You're all I think about.

Clara couldn't get his words out of her mind. Nor the memory of the warmth of his arms, the weight of his body, and the skilled press of his lips on hers.

Something had changed. She felt different. A hunger had taken root deep within her, a desperate yearning to be intimate with this man. She'd found herself tossing and turning all night long beneath the warmth of her extra blanket, tormented by thoughts of what might have happened had she not broken the kiss.

She felt reckless and wanton. She felt unhappy and guilty. No matter how she viewed it, whether she was Helen or Clara, there was no outcome in which an affair with the earl was anything but doomed.

She struggled with the overwhelming urge to climb back into bed and bury her head beneath her pillow. But with a sigh, she forced herself to leave, shutting the door behind her and crossing the hallway to enter the servants' staircase.

Dismal, gray vestiges of light shone through the polished windowpanes above her, and her steps were slow and heavy on the narrow wooden stairs.

She yearned for her sister, for her family and friends back in Essex. She missed having the luxury of confiding in Lucy or Abigail, and even, on occasion, her mother.

Was she falling in love with him?

Reaching the bottom floor, she pushed through the door and walked down the narrow hall, past the dining room to a small room with a square, cloth-covered table in the middle of it. On top of the table were a mass of servants' shoes, lined up and ready to be polished. Matthew was already seated at the table, working on cleaning a pair of the earl's boots. With a jolt, Clara realized they were the ones he had worn yesterday.

Matthew raised his dark blue eyes to meet Clara's. "Oh, hello." He lacked his usual lively energy.

"Hello, Matthew," she replied, sitting on a stool to face him. Clara began sorting through the items on the table, finally settling on a pair of Mrs. Malone's serviceable black shoes. She reached for some polish and a cloth. "How are you today?"

He scrubbed the boots vigorously once more, then set the brush aside to retrieve his own polishing cloth. "I'm fine," he replied, applying himself to his work. Then, after a few more swipes with the cloth, he set it aside and shook his head. "No, I suppose I'm not fine."

Clara's eyes lifted and she, too, set down her polishing rag. "Oh?"

"You're probably not the right person to talk to about this," he began nervously. "But, well, you're a woman. You'll have a good idea."

Now her interest was truly piqued. "Go on," she prompted.

Matthew sighed. "It's about Amelia," he said, lowering his voice so as to not be overheard. "I don't know how to get her attention."

Clara smiled as she remembered how he liked teasing the red-haired housemaid. "I'd say you have no trouble gaining her attention."

"No, no. I mean, I fancy her," he whispered fiercely. "How can I *get her attention?*"

She stared at him, then clapped a hand over her mouth to stifle a giggle. He glared, clearly unimpressed by her reaction.

"I knew I shouldn't have said anything," he muttered.

"Matthew! I'm sorry . . . it's just that she's, well, so prickly," she replied bluntly, mastering her amusement. "I wouldn't have thought to match the pair of you together, but . . ."

"She's not always that way. In fact, she's usually only that way around you," he added thoughtfully.

Clara beamed at Matthew fondly. "I may not understand your preference, but she would be lucky to have you."

The footman stared sullenly at the boots before him. "I'm not sure she would share that sentiment."

Clara couldn't give two figs about Amelia's happiness, but if it made Matthew happy, then she would put her personal feelings aside and give him her honest advice.

She reached across the table to take his hands in hers. "Matthew, the first thing you need to do is to treat her a bit differently. Less like a little sister, and more like . . . like a woman."

"So, you think I should stop teasing her."

"No, not altogether," Clara replied. "I'd say that's part of your charm. But know when to stop, and try treating her like a lady more often." She smiled. "I don't think it would take much to convince her of your affection."

Matthew returned her smile and reached across with his other hand to give hers a gentle squeeze.

The sound of someone in the doorway made them jump, and they looked up to find Amelia staring at the two of them, her eyes focused on their clasped hands. Instantly, her face transformed into a scowl, and Matthew and Clara instinctively jerked away from each other, resuming normal postures on their respective sides of the table. The footman stood awkwardly to greet the fuming housemaid.

"Hi, Amy," he managed to say.

Ignoring him with a haughty turn of her head, she tossed a sealed letter onto the table in front of Clara.

"Abigail asked that I deliver this to you directly, although I can't understand why she wouldn't just address it to you and send it to the house. It can't be necessary for me to personally escort her letters into your hands. That is, unless there is something that bears investigation?"

Clara froze. She had written to her maid once since coming to Lawton Park, providing a hastily scribbled update and the false name she had adopted. But the fact that Abigail was sending a letter to *her* was a sign of some importance. She could not allow Amelia to indulge her suspicions. To do so could place Clara's life and Abigail's employment in jeopardy. She reached across the table to curl her fingers around the parchment, then drew it carefully into her lap, making an attempt at a genuine smile.

"I'm sure the letter itself is of no significance other than to inquire after my new situation. She may have assumed you wouldn't mind bringing it to me since you are her sister and she trusts you. But I will tell her to send it to the house next time if you'd rather not."

Amelia's eyes narrowed. Then with a scoff, she turned on her heel and stalked away.

Matthew sighed and ran his fingers through his dark hair, sinking back down into his chair with a defeated look.

"Perfect. Now she thinks I'm pursuing *you*."

Clara shook her head, wanting to empathize with Matthew but also wildly distracted by the letter now hidden deep inside her skirt pocket. "She'd be silly to think that. It might take a bit more convincing now, but it's me she loathes. Stick to the plan, Matthew. I'm sure she will forgive you."

He nodded despondently and resumed his task, but Clara found she could not wait a moment longer. Excusing herself with a friendly squeeze of his arm, she raced up to her room. Only with the door tightly shut behind her did she finally tear open the letter to read it by the light of her window. It would have to be burned immediately after, especially if Amelia was set on being nosy. The hastily scrawled lines written in Abigail's hand did not reassure her in the slightest:

His search is expanding, perhaps even to Kent. Stay safe.

   ~A

Clara's hands shook as she crumpled the parchment, though in rage or fear, she wasn't sure. She did know that the odds of Rutherford finding her—living belowstairs in a country estate—were laughably poor, but his tenacity was frightening. It was not unexpected, though, which was why she had taken such drastic measures in the first place. The fact that she'd had to at all inspired a fresh surge of hatred for the man.

Closing her eyes, she sent a silent thanks to Abigail for the warning, then she crossed over to the table and reached for a match.

The following day, Clara was summoned to breakfast in the morning room. She had managed to pass an entire day without encountering Lord Ashworth, but her luck had now come to an end at the personal behest of Lady Eliza Cartwick. Her fingers shook as she slipped her work apron over her head and removed her dirty gloves.

Stella, who had just finished the upstairs grates, eyed her with good-natured envy, a black smudge of soot marring her cheek. "It must be nice to be invited abovestairs with the earl's family."

Clara met the maid's eyes with an insouciance she did not feel. "I'm sure it's not nearly as exciting as one would expect."

In truth, it was unheard of for a housemaid to be asked upstairs when the family was breaking their fast. But with no guests present at the estate, she supposed Eliza felt she could do what she wished.

With a small smile to her friend, she nervously smoothed her skirts and turned to climb the stairs up to the green baize door, deafened by the frenzied pounding of her heart.

She entered the morning room, and was greeted by a shocked glance from the earl. His sister rose and turned with a smile, looking considerably less surprised than her brother. Rosa leaped out of her chair and hurtled towards the doorway.

"Helen!"

Clara knelt down to gather the little girl in her arms, laughter rising in her throat.

"Good morning, Miss Rosa," she replied, smoothing her golden curls with an affectionate stroke of her hand. Eliza had come to a stand beside them, and Clara rose, curtsying politely before her. "Good morning, my lady." It was a surreal feeling, curtseying to a young woman who, under other circumstances, might've shared punch and gossip with her at any number of parties.

Eliza was beautiful as usual, even restricted as she was by half mourning. The somber gray of her dress somehow worked to bring out the uncommonly lovely shade of her eyes, whereas Clara suspected it might have an opposite effect on most women.

"Good morning, Helen. I'm glad you could join us," Eliza said, glancing down fondly at her daughter. "Rosa was quite insistent that I invite you."

"I made cakes with Mrs. Humboldt! Would you like to see?"

Eliza laughed softly and placed a calming hand on the girl's shoulder. "There, there. Give Helen a chance to be settled, first." She focused again on Clara. "Are you hungry? Be sure to help yourself to a plate if you are."

Clara looked briefly over Eliza's shoulder. The earl was now standing, staring warily at the group of females on the opposite side of the room. Attempting to ignore his scrutiny, Clara considered Eliza's offer carefully. She was distracted by the sight of the sideboard loaded with coddled eggs, rashers of crispy bacon, and fragrant rolls fresh from Mrs. Humboldt's oven.

Coffee perfumed the air, and Clara was hit with a feeling of nostalgia so strong it nearly knocked her over. She used to love beginning every morning at home in the breakfast room with her coffee. Her family was welcome to join her if they wished—she and Lucy often laughed together about the latest gossip from their friends' letters—but even if they were busy she'd be in there regardless, savoring every second, and every last drop of her coffee. Now, her day started at five in the morning, and she was lucky if she had time enough to scald her tongue on some tea, let alone leisurely sip a cup of coffee.

Clara had already eaten earlier that morning, but the delicious scent of the food was making her stomach rumble—quietly, thankfully. She had to consider her fellow staff members, however. Coffee would be no cause for uproar, but an entire second morning meal, in the company of the earl and his family—that had the distinct potential for creating enemies.

"Thank you," she replied with a curtsy to the earl and his sister, "but I ate earlier this morning."

Eliza guided Rosa back to the breakfast table. "Please help yourself to a drink instead, then," she insisted as they resumed their places.

Clara turned back to the sideboard. She had not had coffee in months. The estate generously provided servants with a supply of tea in addition to their ale, but coffee was reserved for the family of the house. She stared longingly at the gleaming silver pot, then jumped as the earl's deep voice reached her from his place near the table.

"How do you take your coffee?"

She felt herself flush, and turned to face the table. Lord Ashworth's burning green eyes caught hers before she could look away. All at once, she was back on the horse with him behind her, the silken heat of his mouth scorching her chilled skin. In a panic, she tore her gaze away.

Even still, she could feel his vital presence come to a stop next to her. Without hesitating, Ashworth retrieved a cup and saucer, filling the former with steaming coffee. She was mesmerized by the graceful strength of his fingers, the way they flexed and moved. She could easily recall the slide of them across her back . . .

"Would you like cream?" he asked, his polite expression betraying a hint of amusement. She brought herself back to the present and saw that he now held a tiny pitcher, tipping it ever so slightly over her cup. "You'd best tell me," he added, sotto voce, "before I make a colossal mistake . . ."

She was intrigued to see the earl in such a playful mood, although it did nothing to settle her nerves. If anything, it only increased her sense of unease. Despite this, she couldn't prevent a reluctant smile from rising to her lips.

"Yes, please, my lord."

He expertly poured the cream then returned it to its station near the coffeepot. After a moment's careful pause, Ashworth removed the lid to the sugar dish and grasped the small silver tongs, proceeding to add two glittering sugar cubes to her drink. Clara's mouth parted and she looked up at him in wonder.

"How did you—"

"It just seemed right," he replied succinctly, stirring the hot coffee with a spoon and passing it over to her. As she took hold of the saucer, his fingertips came into contact with hers, sending a searing wave of awareness through her body.

"How long does it take you to pour a cup of coffee, William?" Eliza teased.

Thankful for the interruption, Clara broke eye contact with Lord Ashworth and moved towards the table. She hovered uncertainly for a moment, wondering if she ought to stand against the wall as a footman might during dinnertime.

Luckily, Eliza noticed her uncertainty. "Please be seated, Helen." She gestured across the table.

"Yes, my lady." Clara walked around the table and sat across from his sister.

Ashworth resumed his seat at the head of the table and

picked up his newspaper with practiced nonchalance. She tried not to notice how handsome he looked, or the way the morning light played through the variegated golden locks of his hair. Instead she focused on her coffee, blowing lightly before taking her first, luxurious sip. Her eyes fell closed in delight. The drink tasted rich and earthy, with the perfect touch of creamy sweetness she adored.

To her right, Ashworth cleared his throat, then turned a page.

Rosa retrieved a plate off the table and took great joy in showing Clara the tiny cakes she had crafted with the cook, while a conversation began between Lord Ashworth and Eliza, mostly about the everyday operations of the estate. The earl was focused on his sister, but occasionally Clara would catch him stealing small glimpses in her direction, which sent a rush of pleasure flooding through her.

"Can you walk with me later?" Rosa asked abruptly, crunching indelicately on a mouthful of bacon.

"I'm afraid Mrs. Malone will be keeping Helen busy today," interjected the earl, who had clearly been listening. "My business associate will be arriving this week, and there are preparations to be made."

Clara suddenly realized this must be the man he'd mentioned to her privately, that day when he'd seen her tidying Eliza's room. She was happy he'd been able to send his invitation after all, considering the task had brought him an understandable amount of anxiety. His sister nodded in recollection.

"Ah, yes. Was this the man you were to meet when Rosa went missing? The one you met in Manchester with—"

"The very same," he interrupted quickly. "He wishes to speak to me about investing in textile mills to the north." Ashworth turned another page, then set the paper aside. "I'm not entirely sold on the idea, although it has its merits, to be sure."

Eliza nodded, but her attention seemed caught by something in the abandoned newspaper, and she reached over to inspect it more closely. "My goodness. Did you see this article about the runaway bride? Oh, what's her name . . . here it is. 'Clara Mayfield, the daughter of prosperous banker, Robert Mayfield, has been missing nearly three months after leaving home on the eve of her wedding.'" She raised her brows and looked over at Clara with huge eyes. "Now that sounds like a sordid tale."

Clara felt the blood drain from her face in a sudden rush.

She cleared her throat. "Perhaps there were objections to the groom," she replied, as the room lurched sickeningly.

"Maybe he was *old*!" cried Rosa in horror.

Despite her emotional state, Clara had to laugh. If only that had been the singular issue, things could have turned out quite differently. She glanced over at Lord Ashworth to gauge his reaction to the story, and was met with a thoughtful gaze.

"Mayfield . . . why is that name familiar to me?"

Clara froze as she pondered the best course of action. While she wanted to avoid reminding the earl of any connections between her and her place of origin, the referral from Abigail had been provided from the Mayfield household. She could feign ignorance, but she quickly decided that was the riskier course of action.

Her fingers knotted together beneath the surface of the table. "My verbal reference came from a woman who serves under the Mayfields," she stated quietly.

Lord Ashworth's eyebrows raised in surprise. "Did it, really?"

Clara hitched her shoulders in a small shrug. "It did, my lord, but I never worked in their house, myself," she replied carefully.

"How fascinating," said Eliza. Straightening in her chair, she gently dabbed the corner of her mouth with a napkin and turned to face her brother. "And speaking of dodging marriage, William, I think it is high time you held a ball."

Ashworth's cup halted near his lips. His eyes briefly darted to Clara over the rim of his cup, causing her heart to skip a beat.

"I detest balls, and I can't abide the people who attend them," Ashworth said, gazing with some annoyance at his sister as he set his cup down.

"Oh, come now," Eliza admonished. "That can't be completely true. Besides, how else do you propose to continue the Halstead line?" She huffed in frustration. "At the very least, you would spend an evening dancing with some pretty young ladies. You might actually enjoy yourself."

Clara sank backwards in her chair, wishing she were anywhere but at this table, listening to a discussion on how the earl could meet a proper wife. Ironically, she was reminded of that last day in her family's drawing room, listening to her parents discuss her wedding with Baron Rutherford.

"I am uncertain why you would choose to discuss this at

the breakfast table, in mixed company, no less," growled Lord Ashworth.

Eliza was unruffled by her brother's anger. "The newspaper article happened to remind me of it. I'd been meaning to speak to you about it sooner or later."

"Let's make it later, then," said the earl with glowing eyes. He rose, tossed his napkin on the table and stalked out of the room.

Clara stared down at the tablecloth wishing she could disappear, but also thrilled at the possibility that the earl had resisted discussing marriage on her account. After a moment, Eliza broke the uncomfortable silence.

"Oh, dear. I didn't think he'd be quite so sensitive."

Clara smiled awkwardly. "He will likely warm up to the idea, my lady."

"Indeed," rejoined Eliza, but not before shooting Clara a thoughtful glance that was far more observant than she would've liked.

The afternoon light waned and Clara's back ached tremendously. She reached around to massage the aching muscles, then untied the apron strings from around her waist. Startled, she looked up to find Mrs. Malone standing before her, a grave look upon her already severe features.

"Helen, I need to speak with you in my office."

Wide-eyed, she nodded. "Yes, Mrs. Malone."

Confusion, followed by fear, shot through her. What could she have done that would warrant a private meeting with the housekeeper? Was it possible someone had seen her with the earl? She shivered at the thought. It would mean her immediate dismissal.

She followed Mrs. Malone into her office, and the woman closed the door securely behind her before taking a seat at her desk. Clara remained standing in the center of the room.

The housekeeper stared at her with gray eyes that were dark as stone. "You have been accused of indecent activity by another member of the staff," she stated flatly.

Clara broke into a cold sweat, nearly overcome by panic. Somebody had seen her together with the earl, and now she would have nowhere to go, no time to find another position elsewhere. She nearly choked on her next words. "Might I inquire as to the specifics of this accusation?" she asked hoarsely, dreading the response.

"You may. It was brought to my attention that you have been caught in a compromising position . . . with Paxton, the land steward."

Clara's mouth dropped open, first in relief, then in complete shock. She struggled to pinpoint the exact situation that could have motivated such a report. Then she recalled meeting Paxton near the dining room, after she had raced down the stairs, late to see Mrs. Malone. Her apron had snagged on her cap . . . her hair had been a mess . . . and Amelia . . .

Amelia.

So here it was, and she really should have expected no less from her, even if she was Abigail's sister. Rage churned as she faced the stoic housekeeper.

"I truly hope you don't place such value on Amelia's stories, especially the ones that concern my character," she fumed. "Have you interviewed Paxton yet?"

The housekeeper hesitated, taken aback by the magnitude of Clara's fury. "Not yet," she replied. "Since he resides in the village, it would take some time to arrange that."

Clara closed her eyes and took a deep breath to calm her temper. "Had you already spoken to him, his version of events would surely echo mine. I was working upstairs that day; it was the day of the servants' dance. I was in a rush to come downstairs, my apron got tangled in my hair, and I encountered Paxton on my way." She opened her eyes and met the woman's gaze directly. "That was when Amelia came upon us, near the dining room."

Mrs. Malone's mouth compressed into a thin line. "Thank you, Helen, that will be all. I will notify you if anything else is required."

Clara walked to the door, attempting to master her emotions before twisting the knob and exiting into the hallway. She needed to get out, to breathe some cool fresh air and clear her head. She walked briskly towards the kitchen and instantly spied Amelia. The infernal housemaid was near the stove, talking to Gilly, and she looked up at Clara's entrance, a tiny smile curving her lips. The smile vanished quickly, though, when Clara stormed right up to her.

"How dare you," she seethed. "I'm not certain what your grievance is, but I no longer care. I am done with you, Amelia."

She spun on her heel, leaving the kitchen staff in shocked bafflement as she pulled the servants' door open and walked out, slamming the heavy door shut behind her.

CHAPTER THIRTEEN

William lowered his brow and urged his horse faster with a jab of his heels, and the animal responded, hastening its pace until he could no longer make out the blurry landscape that surrounded them. Raising slightly off his saddle, he leaned into the motion, savoring the brisk wind that whipped through his hair. They sailed over the grass-covered hills that bordered the northern edge of his estate, then he pulled on the reins to turn back around.

The conversation in the morning room yesterday had affected him more than he'd shown, and considering his thunderous reaction to Eliza's mere suggestion of a ball, that was saying a lot. That night, as he'd lain awake upon his bed in unhappy agitation, he knew there was only one real course of action from this point forward. It was to go along with his sister's plans to find him a wife.

Surely these moments of weakness with Helen were an effect of being shut away from society for so long. He couldn't deny that he found comfort in her presence, not to mention a fiery need to possess her that plagued him constantly. Yet even in his weaker moments, when they were alone together and he was at his most vulnerable, he could not forget about his family members and their early, undeserved demise. And he could not continue to resist the need for him to fulfill his duties to the earldom—duties that included going to this damned ball.

He rode in silence for what seemed like forever, the rhythmic sounds of his horse's hooves striking the ground the only accompaniment to his gloomy musings. Easing up on his steed as they neared Lawton Park, he guided it into the trees for a well-earned drink at a stream, and with a jolt he realized he had guided them to the very place where he and Helen had shared their last kiss.

Muttering beneath his breath, he dismounted and allowed his horse time to recover while trying not to cave in to the temptation of reliving the experience. It would do no good to recall the way his hands had greedily sought to feel her body beneath the clinging, wet fabric of her dress, or how incredibly satisfying it had been once he did. Nor would it be of any use to remember how eagerly she had arched against him, or the sound of her moans as he'd pulled her close so she could feel how much he wanted her . . . how ready he was . . . that he could take her right there in the woods and no one would ever have to know . . .

"STOP."

William wasn't aware that he'd spoken aloud until seeing the startled reaction of his horse, who raised his muzzle out of the stream to regard him with an anxious whicker.

Unclenching the fists that had formed at his sides, he approached the animal and ran his hands along its flank until it cautiously lowered its head again to resume drinking.

By the time he arrived back at the house, dusk was starting to fall. He felt defeated and confused, but still determined not to waver from the plan set out before him. Be the earl. Find a wife. Pretend as if Helen were just another maid.

Hurrying through the halls, he was almost desperate for the quiet solitude of his study, but the soft intonations that drifted out from the drawing room caused his pace to slow.

Holding his breath, he drew nearer to peer around the door. Helen was there—of course it would be her—and he watched in fascination while she swayed gracefully from one side of the mantelpiece to the other, polishing the woodwork as she hummed her tune. She fell silent for a moment, causing William to tense in anticipation of his discovery, but it was simply that she had finished, starting once more from the beginning after her brief pause. The song sounded like a ballroom waltz. He viewed her in mystification, thinking that it was a curious thing to hear from a housemaid. Surely the distance between them was obscuring the sound.

William knew he should leave but remained there anyway, hypnotized by the slow twirling of her dance. But it was the haunted look, deep in the hollows of her eyes, that truly gave him pause. He'd seen that same sorrowful countenance in his own reflection every day for the past eighteen months, and with a vice-like squeeze around his heart, wondered what could have possibly brought her to such a similar state.

Her sudden jump made him realize that he had ventured forward while standing there, lost in his thoughts, and he mentally kicked himself for allowing such a thing to happen. Now there was no way to avoid talking to her.

"My lord," Helen exclaimed, eyes wide and obviously flustered. She gathered her supplies. "I beg your pardon, I was just finishing here."

He'd had every intention of just turning around and leaving, but his curiosity got the better of him.

"That sounded like a waltz," he said.

Helen stopped abruptly, almost as if she had collided with an invisible wall. The snow-white cap atop her head rotated as she turned to reply, hesitantly, stopping short of meeting his eyes.

"Not at all, my lord," she answered. "I'm certain the only waltzes to be heard in this house will be the ones at your upcoming ball."

Her tone wasn't defensive exactly, but given the current state of his mood, he found her comment did not sit well with him.

"I'm glad you brought that up," he ground out. "Eliza is right, you know. As the earl, I have certain . . . obligations."

The troubled look returned to darken her features. Perhaps it had never left. "I am aware of that, of course."

"They are duties that don't include you."

Helen recoiled, then narrowed her eyes. "Thank you for clearing that up," she replied bitterly. "You'll be relieved to know it is not my place to question you one way or the other."

William could hear the tenuous edge to her voice, sense

the heartache lurking beneath her biting exterior. He wished he could go to her now, as she had gone to him before, and take her hand. Assure her that it was better this way. That continuing with this madness was not a kindness to either of them. Instead, he backed away and attempted to bolster his own resolve with an authoritative lift of his chin.

"I'm glad we understand each other."

"As am I."

This was necessary, but God it hurt. He knew her pull on him had never just been about something as straightforward as lust. It had been his attraction to a like mind, a kindred spirit. Someone who, despite their vast difference in station, could somehow relate. A woman who could bring him out of his wretched thoughts with a simple touch of her hand, or a softly spoken word.

Remembering those times made him want to sink to his knees and beg for forgiveness, and his head dropped in regret.

"Helen, I—"

I'm sorry.

But Helen had already left the room.

Mr. Scanlan arrived two days later, presenting an impressive display in his richly decorated carriage and finely tailored suit, and accompanied by his own well-appointed valet.

Since the earl's meeting with him had been postponed due to Rosa's disappearance, Ashworth had chosen to invite the man to his home for a brief stay. The irony of avoiding Scanlan for so long after the accident, then entertaining him as a guest, was not lost on William. But he meant to move on with his life, and this was a good step towards doing so. He would be exploring the business venture his father had shown an interest in before his death.

Mrs. Malone had been simultaneously pleased that he was receiving a visitor, and disconcerted that the man was in trade. However, as she had commented to Clara earlier that morning, she took comfort in the fact that Scanlan was cousin to a distant noble acquaintance of the earl. This made the seemingly common guest more palatable, even if just by a tiny bit.

Despite Mrs. Malone's opinion on the matter, when Scanlan finally arrived, it was clear there was an undeniable air of charm about him. After disembarking from his carriage, the man bowed to the earl, then reached out to firmly shake his hand. He was roughly forty years of age, his black hair sprinkled becomingly with gray.

"My lord, it is a pleasure to meet with you again in person after so long." The taciturn acknowledgment of Ashworth's disastrous departure from Manchester remained unspoken between them.

William tipped his head politely in Scanlan's direction, although he suddenly felt a wave of nausea. "And you as well," he replied evenly. "I hope your trip from Hastings was uneventful."

Mr. Scanlan shrugged. "The weather on the coast cannot be relied on this time of year, although I enjoy the excitement of a good squall as much as anyone, I expect," he said with a small smile.

Ashworth stepped closer to Eliza and gestured to his guest. "Lady Cartwick, allow me to introduce you to Mr. Scanlan."

Eliza extended her hand in greeting while Rosa gazed up, clinging fast to her mother's skirts.

"A pleasure to meet you, sir, and welcome to Lawton Park," said Eliza. She looked down at her daughter with a wry expression. "This is my daughter, Rosa."

The man took her hand and bowed with a deferential flourish. "Lady Cartwick, such a pleasure. And Miss Rosa, what a delight. I was happy to hear you were brought back home from your recent misadventures, safe and sound."

Eliza bowed her head. "It was a relief to us all."

"Let us get you settled," William said, taking a step closer to the house and glancing at Mrs. Malone.

"Indeed. I thank you."

Mrs. Malone nodded at Matthew and Charles, and both men rushed forward to relieve the carriage of its trunks. Mr. Scanlan's valet joined them, and the group headed towards the side entrance.

As Clara stole a glimpse at the earl, she noticed that Scanlan's eyes drifted casually in the direction of the servants poised along the drive, then snapped back to linger on Amelia. More surprising was when he tipped his head in greeting to the red-headed maid as he passed.

"Why hello, Amelia."

She smiled at Scanlan in reply and dipped into a polite curtsy.

"Mr. Scanlan."

Clara glanced over to see Mrs. Malone scowl from across the drive. Scanlan returned his focus to the earl before him and resumed his pace.

"What was that all about?" whispered Stella, glancing over.

Amelia laughed lightly. "I worked in a household near Mr. Scanlan's a few years back," she replied under her breath. "We saw each other in town on occasion." She shrugged. "It was nothing. But I don't mind the chance to make Matthew a bit jealous," she added with satisfaction.

Clara had been intrigued, listening to the murmured discourse between Stella and Amelia, when the latter glanced over and pierced her with a black look.

"What are you looking at?" Her tone was not civil.

Clara rolled her eyes and turned away, wishing for a moment that she could reveal herself as Clara Mayfield and put the shrewish Amelia in her place. A small smile danced across her lips as she imagined the scenario. Then, with a sigh, she followed the rest of the servants into the house.

Due to the small party, dinner that evening was an intimate affair. Ashworth had taken the liberty of inviting Lord Evanston, to round out the number of guests, and he was next to him now as they received bowls filled with a creamy celery soup. The earl glanced over at Mr. Scanlan, who was conversing with Eliza while they ate. Her laugh rang out across the table at some amusing comment, and Evanston eyed them warily.

Ashworth's impression of the man was positive. It was

obvious he was well-versed in business dealings, and possessed much of the tact generally required to woo potential investors to the table.

"Lady Cartwick," Scanlan murmured after a sip of wine. "Forgive me for speaking so plainly, but I do know of your great loss, and I am sorry for it." He glanced at William. "For the loss *all* of you have suffered. I can see you are still mourning for your husband," he added, gesturing to the deep violet of her evening gown, "but also can't help but notice your enduring vivacity. Have you considered attending the London season next year? I feel society could greatly benefit from a woman such as yourself."

"Why do you ask?" Thomas demanded from his side of the table.

Ignoring the viscount, Eliza turned to face Mr. Scanlan. "It is something I have discussed with my brother," she said simply.

Lord Evanston choked on his soup, and William surveyed his friend with some amusement. "Surely, that is no surprise," he muttered under his breath.

"No, not at all," Thomas assured him reluctantly, his eyes watering. "I'm only shocked to just be hearing about it."

"That is excellent news," exclaimed Scanlan happily. "You are young, my lady, and it would be a waste for such beauty to hide away in the country forever."

"I am young, because I was married young." She brought her wineglass to her lips, taking a long swallow before returning it to its position on the linen tablecloth. "Mr. Cartwick was a good man, and a good father. While I detest the necessity of finding another husband, I cannot deny its importance, nor the security it will provide."

Scanlan nodded grimly. "Mr. Cartwick was a fine man. I had the privilege of meeting him briefly in Manchester. Please don't misunderstand me. I ask not out of disregard of your affection for him, but only because I am sure he would wish to see you and your daughter cared for in his absence."

Lord Ashworth glanced across the table at his sister with pride. He admired her greatly, not just for her poise in handling the social intricacies of her situation, but for the resilience she had shown over the past year and a half. While descended from noble lineage, Reginald Cartwick had not been of the peerage himself. As a member of the landed gentry, however, his ancient name and massive land holdings had gained him the significant respect of the aristocracy, and his pleasant demeanor had placed him highly in their father's estimation. She *had* been married young, a move he'd disagreed with at the time, but their father had been certain that the match would work well for her.

William couldn't say he'd been wrong; although not entirely a love match, the pair had grown into a mutual affection that had lasted until Cartwick's untimely death. Through it all, Eliza had shown an incredible fortitude—something he hadn't known she'd possessed. She would need to draw on this strength to sustain both her and Rosa in the trying months to come, as the final entailment of her late husband's property meant they were now losing their home in Hampshire.

Her letter months ago had spurred the earl into action, and he'd spent these many busy weeks making arrangements for them to relocate to the estate's Dower House, while she had worked to tie up affairs back home. Staying close to her remaining family was Eliza's preference. Financially, she was secure, but even if the late Earl of Ashworth had not made annual provisions for his daughter, which he had, William would not have permitted the awful event that took the lives of their father, brother, and her husband to cast her into precarious circumstances.

The disharmonious clank of a fork against a fine china plate brought Ashworth back into the present moment, and he followed the sound to his friend. Lord Evanston, looking displeased in the wavering light of the candelabra, flashed a bright blue glare in Scanlan's direction.

"I thought you came to discuss cotton mills?" he asked hotly, his eyes settling on the target of his annoyance.

Ashworth's head came up in surprise. Evanston knew the discussion was planned for the morrow. What on earth was he doing?

Well, he would sit back and see where Scanlan took this.

Eliza's fine brow creased at Thomas. "He meant no offense."

"No, no, it was a bold question and I take full responsibility for it," replied Scanlan. "I am willing to change the subject if the earl is amenable?"

William nodded at him, and Scanlan took a few seconds to compose himself accordingly.

"Well my lord, as we have discussed, Manchester has seen a great boom in textile mills, particularly cotton mills—"

His dialogue was interrupted by the arrival of the footmen presenting the next dish, which was poached fish in herb-scented broth with root vegetables. Scanlan took the opportunity to lean forward and breathe in the hot steam rising from his plate.

"Magnificent, my lord. Are these fish from your own estate?"

The earl nodded. "Nearly everything is from my estate." He gestured for him to continue. "You were speaking of cotton mills . . ."

Diversifying the family's interests was something his father had intended to do for quite some time. With the exponential increase in profitable mills and factories in the north, England had seen an increase in both population growth and profitability. Ashworth was still eager to find out more about investing in an endeavor that had the potential to provide jobs to so many, although he and his brother had both been concerned about the quality of living for the mill workers. Their tour of Manchester had been enough to convince him that, were he to finance a mill, either wholly or in part, steps would need to be taken to ensure health and safety for all.

Scanlan tucked his napkin more firmly over his lap and picked up his fork and knife. "Indeed. As you may remember, Manchester is happily suited to this type of endeavor. Water and coal provide affordable steam power for the mills, and through many technological advances, the production process is now fully mechanized."

"Yes, I know about Manchester, its canals and the ease of transporting goods and coal," said William. "What I need you to remind me of, however, is why I should invest in a mill with *you*."

Mr. Scanlan, unhurried, skewered a small piece of fish with his fork and ate it. "You should invest with me, my lord, because I have nearly twenty years of experience in manufacturing and textiles. I have factories throughout Manchester and the surrounding area, including Salford and Rochdale . . ."

"Right," interrupted the earl, "but you approached me this year with the notion of building a cotton mill on the level of Cambridge Street, with nearly two thousand employees. That will require an immense amount of capital and, you will forgive me, but your small factories of two hundred employees provide little in the way of assurance that my money will be well appropriated in this new venture."

Scanlan halted his meal and glanced at his host. He swallowed, then cleared his throat. "Of course, my lord, you seek precedents. In lieu of those, I hope you will find reassurance in the fact that I have found great success with my factories to date, and am well acquainted with many of the mill owners in the north. I feel they have established a productive model that we would do right to emulate—"

"Productive it may be, but I have seen these mills and the conditions are abhorrent," Ashworth replied evenly. "Any investment I am involved with in Manchester will have measures included to make improvements for workers. This is not negotiable."

Scanlan set down his fork and dabbed discreetly at his mouth with a napkin. "I will take another look at the numbers, my lord. But you should be aware that any additional improvements over and above the standard set by other mills will add to your expenses considerably." After a pause, he said, "Perhaps finding an additional investor would help ease your anxieties?"

At this, his attention shifted from Lord Ashworth to Lord Evanston, whose eyes widened. The viscount snorted.

"You've got some brass—" His black hair glinted as he glanced at the earl's sister, who was demurely attempting to conceal her amusement with her napkin. Rather than continue with that line of thought, he took a breath and started anew. "Fine. I'll tell you what . . . if you can present the figures for both scenarios, then Lord Ashworth and I will examine the numbers together. But for the record," he added, deftly raising an eyebrow at Scanlan, "I have never expressed an interest in this project. I make no guarantees or promises."

"Nor should you," Ashworth interjected. "The concern is not about the capital."

Scanlan was unruffled, looking first at him, and then to Evanston. "I will have both versions of the proposal ready for your review within the next two days."

Normally, Ashworth preferred investing with like-minded people. It worried him that Scanlan did not necessarily appreciate the benefits of improving conditions for factory workers, but he was not taken aback. There was very little concern shown at all within the current climate of Manchester. He was still willing to give the tradesman a chance given his experience and considerable expertise, with the hope that he could perhaps be swayed in time.

"We will review the matter then," he said, with a polite tip of his head.

Amber shafts of late-morning sunlight illuminated the stairwell as Clara journeyed to Mr. Scanlan's room with her cargo, the china tea set jiggling upon the silver tray as she stepped carefully up the stairs.

This morning, the earl had ridden out to meet with his tenant farmers, no doubt for an update on whether the flooding on their property had improved with the recent alterations. Ashworth's business associate had declined to join him on the excursion, instead choosing to shut himself up in his chambers and ringing the bell to request a pot of tea so he could continue working on his proposals in privacy. Since Eliza and Rosa had taken the carriage to spend the day shopping in the village, the estate had been left curiously devoid of family members.

As Clara neared the man's room, she heard a strange noise from down the hallway. It was an odd sound, akin to a muffled cry. She froze in place, gazing alertly in the direction of Eliza's bedchambers. The earl's sister was not in the house, which meant if anyone was in her room, it was likely a servant. She tried to recall whether Amelia or Stella was working upstairs this morning.

She reached over to knock on Mr. Scanlan's door, wanting to shed her burden so that she could go investigate. But she jumped in surprise as another shriek issued from down the hall. Quickly she crouched down and placed the tray on the floor outside his bedchamber, then hurried down the hall. Seeing the door was ajar, she curled her fingers around the edge and eased it open. She spied a discarded feather duster lying haphazardly on the floor, and peered in further.

Mr. Scanlan was there, using the bulk of his weight to press Amelia down onto the bed. The terrified housemaid was fighting him, but she was obviously about to lose this battle. One of the man's large hands was clamped firmly over her mouth while the other reached down to grab at her skirts. Amelia twisted and clawed frantically at his hair and face, and he relinquished his hold on her mouth to detain her wrists above her head instead.

She sobbed as she continued to fight him off.

"No! Please!"

"Quiet," he snapped, his voice guttural in a way that made bile rise in Clara's throat. "Be still."

Clara had heard tales of servants, especially women, being abused by their masters or even guests. But she had not thought Scanlan capable of such brutality. Until witnessing it herself, she could not have understood the awful reality of it, though her few moments with Baron Rutherford had given her some idea of the horror of such a situation.

Her eyes searched the room for something that would function as a weapon. The vase on the side table . . . too small and light. Letter opener . . . too lethal. Stepping backwards, she surveyed the hallway, spotting the silver teapot on the floor. That could work, but it contained scalding hot liquid that could disfigure him, or worse, harm Amelia. Then she spied the silver salver beneath it. It would have to do.

Quickly, she ran over and unloaded the tea set, placing each item noiselessly on the floor. Gripping the hefty tray, she entered the room once more to approach the pair from behind. Clara's stomach roiled hearing Amelia weep beneath Scanlan. Tasting the bitter flavor of her own fear, she swallowed hard and tiptoed forward. She needed to act fast—the element of surprise would be the only way for her to triumph over a man his size. Clara raised the salver over her right shoulder and it caught a ray of sunlight, gleaming brightly as she angled her arms for maximum force.

"Mr. Scanlan!"

Surprised, he rose upwards from his victim and Clara twisted her body with all her might, striking him hard on the side of his head. Scanlan collapsed next to Amelia with an unpleasant grunt, and sobbing, the maid scrambled off the bed to safety, taking refuge behind a bedpost. The man moaned and clutched his head, but still managed to push himself upright.

He spun around groggily to face them. Clara could see a large knot growing near his hairline as they stared at him, paralyzed, unsure of whom he would lunge for first. Both women started for the door simultaneously, but Scanlan reached out and snagged Clara by the arm before she could reach a safe distance. Furious eyes greeted her when she turned to look over her shoulder.

"Get back here, you bitch," he sputtered.

She cried out in distress and Amelia whirled around, her eyes wide.

"Go find help!" Clara shouted at her, just before he jerked her around to face him, his arm cocked back. With no time to dodge, she took the full force of his vicious, close-fisted blow. The impact caused bright stars to scatter across her vision, and she flew backwards to land in a heap. Stunned, she lifted her head to a spinning room.

He came at her again, but stopped abruptly at the sound of Amelia's screams echoing through the halls and receding. Knowing the remaining household would descend momentarily, he rose, enraged, and rushed from the bedchamber, leaving her laid out on Eliza's soft, beautifully patterned carpet.

Clara lowered her elbows and squeezed her eyes shut in relief, wincing at the resulting pain. Distantly, she registered the sound of approaching footsteps thudding down the hallway, before a greedy black void claimed her utterly.

When she awoke she was in the servants' hall belowstairs. She was seated on a bench at the far side of the room next to someone she could not see, the person hugging her tightly while holding a cool, wet cloth to her cheek. Many voices swirled around her. They were angry, worried voices, and in her bleary state, it was impossible to focus on the thread of the conversation. All she knew in this moment was that her face hurt and her head was pounding. She shifted uncomfortably as her regained consciousness brought a wave of nausea along with it.

"She's waking!"

"Helen, can you hear me?" cried a woman's voice next to her. Slowly, she managed to lift her head and behold the face of the person holding her in their arms. To her shock, it was Amelia. Clara furrowed her brow in confusion and struggled to sit upright, pushing away as Amelia tried to keep her close. Mrs. Malone's was the next voice she heard.

"You must relax, Helen. You've taken an awful blow to your head," she added quietly.

Clara gazed up blurrily at the housekeeper's serious face. Exhausted, she allowed her head to collapse back against Amelia's shoulder as the housemaid tended to her. The tense discussion continued to buzz until the intrusive clatter of footsteps interrupted, approaching from down the staircase and coming into the hall.

"His lordship's just arrived back at the estate," she heard Charles exclaim breathlessly.

"And Matthew is with him?" asked the housekeeper.

Charles nodded.

"Good. Don't leave him alone. One or both of you must be with him at all times . . ."

She was cut off mid-sentence by the sound of more footsteps now thundering down the staircase. The large group in the dining hall parted as Lord Ashworth pushed forcefully through them. Matthew caught up a few moments later to stand beside Amelia, out of breath, and shot an apologetic glance at the stern-faced Mrs. Malone.

"Sorry. He's quick."

With the arrival of the earl, Clara struggled again to sit up. Something important must be going on, she only wished she knew what it was. Amelia assisted her, gently gripping her arms and pulling her into a seated position.

The hall had gone strangely silent. And as she glanced blearily at the earl, she understood why.

He looked like he was about to murder someone.

Ashworth's fists were clenched and his chest heaved. His eyes were black, dilated pools, full of rage, and they darted from Clara to Amelia, not missing Amelia's ripped seams and mussed hair.

"Are you well?" His deep voice was simultaneously irate and sympathetic. Clara wasn't sure how he managed that.

Amelia nodded. "Just a few bruises, thanks to her." She dipped her head towards Clara.

Clara recoiled in shock at the housemaid's statement, twisting on the bench to stare at Amelia. She could remember nothing of what she was referring to, and icy spirals of panic began spreading through her chest. She gripped Amelia's sleeve tightly.

"What's happened?" she croaked.

The earl came forward to kneel before her. His hands reached out, seemingly to take both of hers, then he pulled them back with a subtle glance at the group of concerned servants.

Ashworth searched her eyes urgently, running a fingertip gently down her bruised cheek. Clara flinched and hissed in pain, turning away to avoid his inspection.

"Please don't. That hurts."

The earl frowned. "You've been injured and I need to examine you," he responded. "Do you know who I am?"

"Yes."

There was a slight pause. "Who am I?"

"You're the . . . Earl of Ashworth?"

Uncertainty crossed his features at her reply. "And do you know *your* name?"

"Of course," she answered. "I'm Clara Mayfield."

A collective gasp erupted throughout the room and Clara jerked in surprise, tears shining in her eyes. She could hear Amelia utter in awe behind her, "He hit her so hard, she thinks she's a Mayfield."

Ashworth tersely raised a hand to silence the servants, then reached forward to grasp her hand, his eyes fearful.

"What have I done wrong?" she whispered, her voice trembling.

"You've done nothing wrong," he murmured softly, reassuringly. "You need to rest."

Lord Ashworth remained crouched before her for a long moment. Mrs. Malone was staring mournfully at them, but snapped to attention when the earl rose.

"Fetch the doctor. For both of them," he demanded. "Where is Scanlan's valet?"

"Upstairs with his master, my lord."

"They'd better be packed," the earl spat. "Bring their carriage round. *Now.*"

With that, Ashworth turned and pushed back the way he'd come. The next noise they heard was him blasting through the green baize door.

"Go follow him before he kills the man!" Mrs. Malone yelped to the footmen in rising alarm.

Matthew and Charles snapped out of their daze and bolted abovestairs to catch up with the earl.

CHAPTER FOURTEEN

Ashworth propelled himself up the grand staircase, the harsh sound of his breathing echoing off the walls. Somehow, Scanlan had fooled him into thinking he was a decent man. Helen's bruised face was vivid in his mind, igniting a fresh surge of rage. He hadn't been there to protect her.

Couldn't protect her because she wasn't his to protect. Only if she were his countess, his *wife*, would she have the shelter of his power and title. Only if it were possible for him to claim her as his own, would there be no doubt of his exacting a swift revenge against anyone who dared touch her.

Ashworth's stomach lurched. The distress of seeing her, battered and bewildered belowstairs, was causing him actual physical pain. His revulsion at Amelia's ordeal only amplified the effect. He hurtled down the hallway with a roar. The coward's door was locked, of course. Ashworth leaned in close to the frame, his lip curled in fury.

"You have one second to open this door!" he bellowed. When no reply was forthcoming, he took a large step backwards and issued a massive kick with his bootheel, sending the door flying inward amidst a spray of splintering wood. Scanlan's valet, who had been tending to his master's wound, jumped back with a screech at the violent intrusion.

"What is the meaning of this, my lord?" Mr. Scanlan blustered indignantly, rising from his seat in a chintz armchair.

He did not pause to answer. He did not pause at all until he had locked his fingers around the man's throat and slammed him forcibly up against the wall, sending a nearby painting tumbling to the carpet below.

"You tell me," Ashworth seethed darkly, tightening his grip until Scanlan's face turned crimson.

The tradesman affected a raspy laugh as best he could under the circumstances. "Is this about . . . the maids?" he grunted incredulously, scrabbling to pry away the earl's fingers. "You ought to be apologizing for . . . their misbehavior . . ."

Ashworth, still gripping Scanlan by the neck, silenced him immediately by jerking him forward then slamming him back hard against the wall. Matthew and Charles appeared in the doorway, out of breath.

"My lord—" said Matthew, wide-eyed at the scene before him.

The earl ventured a quick glance in their direction before returning his focus to Scanlan.

"Stay back," he growled.

Despite his command, the two footmen ventured into the crowded room to stand within arm's reach of the earl. The valet was ineffectually cowering in the corner.

"We can't do that, my lord," said Charles. Matthew stepped closer, but his eyes were full of fire as he gazed at Scanlan.

"Let's talk about this, man to man," choked out the trades-man, eyes darting frantically to the angry faces surrounding him. "There's been some misunderstanding . . ."

The earl slid his hands down to grab Scanlan's shirt and flung him across the room, where he collided clumsily with the wall.

"Misunderstanding?" Ashworth uttered a harsh, humor-less laugh. "The only misunderstanding, here, is your belief that it is acceptable to enter my house and attack women under my employ." He stalked towards Scanlan. "And you want to speak man to man? A *man* doesn't force himself upon an unwilling partner. A *man* doesn't hit a woman, ever."

Scanlan had the audacity to look outraged. "She attacked me! That dark-haired whore got what she—"

With a gasp Matthew stepped forward, but Ashworth was quicker. He and Scanlan crashed into a bedside table, smashing it to pieces, then rolled along the carpet, the earl pummeling Scanlan all the while. Scanlan, by no means of small stature, was simply no match for Ashworth's muscular agility. William was lost in the jostling motion of their bodies as they wrestled each other . . . the pounding of fists . . . the pained grunts . . .

The loud crack as the wheel splintered and snapped off . . . the violent heave of the carriage . . . the groaning and creaking of twisting metal . . .

In horror, William tore himself off of Scanlan to land

heavily on the floor, his lungs seizing inside his chest. Grasping desperately at the memory of their meeting on the staircase, Helen's advice came back to him.

Breathe . . .

By the time Matthew and Charles managed to help him to his feet, the tradesman was bruised, battered, and gasping for breath himself. He pointed a trembling finger in their direction.

"How dare you," he cried, wiping his bloody mouth on his shirtsleeve. "I will call for the local magistrate! You cannot assault me this way . . ."

Now mostly recovered, Ashworth leaned in Scanlan's direction while his footmen struggled to keep him at bay. "I *am* the magistrate, and I will defend my estate and its people in any way I like."

Scanlan's eyes grew large and he glanced fearfully at his manservant.

"Pack my things, Rupert."

"If Rupert can pack your things in less time than it takes for me to throw you down the staircase, then by all means, proceed," snarled the earl.

Scanlan's valet managed to escape with just one of his master's trunks, laboring beneath its weight as he raced to the carriage waiting on the drive. Ashworth shook off his footmen and followed their exit, passing a concerned Mrs. Malone on his way.

Foolishly, Scanlan turned to deliver a parting retort as he reached the vehicle.

"You'll never gain a hold in Manchester. I know people!"

The earl knocked Scanlan backwards into his carriage.

"I know more people," he countered. "I will bury your mill. And I will bury you if you ever return here again."

Upon receiving the earl's summons, Dr. Chapman arrived from the village without delay. Both women were examined and treated in Mrs. Malone's office, while Ashworth waited anxiously in the servants' hall, seated at the worn wooden table.

Life carried on around him, with servants moving busily down from the hallway to the kitchen and back, continuing on with their duties for that evening's upcoming dinner. Their first task had been to straighten Eliza's room. He would not have her come home to that ugly spectacle, though he knew he'd have to inform her of the day's events.

Ashworth couldn't think about that right now, though. He was too busy trying to subdue his growing concern for Helen. Amelia had been treated already, and insisted on returning to work, saying she would rather be around people than left alone upstairs in her room to rest. Helen, however, was still in the office. She'd been there for the past half hour at least.

The creak of an opening door caused his back to straighten in anticipation. Dr. Chapman entered the hall, setting his heavy black satchel on the floor before rising again to address the earl. The physician's bespectacled eyes darted down to the earl's swollen, scraped knuckles. His eyebrows lifted.

"My lord, would you allow me to look at your hand?" he asked.

Ashworth jerked his hand off the table to conceal it from view. "It's fine," he stated flatly. "What news of the maids?"

Chapman nodded and removed his glasses, polished them with a cloth until the lenses gleamed, then replaced them on his face.

"Amelia had some bruising and scrapes on her extremities, but nothing more severe. She was fortunate given the circumstances. I gave her some salve and sent her on her way. Helen, however . . ."

Lord Ashworth leaned forward in his chair.

"Yes?"

The physician crossed to the opposite side of the table, pulled a chair out with a loud scrape, and seated himself with a sigh.

"I think time and rest will be the most effective remedies for her. She does appear to have received some brain injury, a concussion, from the blow to her head." Dr. Chapman tipped his head quizzically. "Do you know if Helen has any acquaintance with Clara Mayfield?"

For the second time that day, a tremor tripped up his spine at the utterance of that name. The earl censored his facial expressions before replying to the doctor.

"It is my understanding that she has a friend who works for the Mayfields." He paused. "She also observed my sister discussing Miss Mayfield the other day."

"I see," answered Dr. Chapman, steepling his hands beneath his chin and leaning thoughtfully back in his chair. "I am aware of the controversy in the papers surrounding Clara Mayfield right now, and it seems that, for a brief time upon regaining consciousness, Helen had grown attached to the idea that she was this woman."

Ashworth stared at the physician, deep in thought. "Clara Mayfield has been missing for three months. Helen came to Lawton Park three months ago." He felt the blood drain from his face. "You don't think—"

"The idea is preposterous, of course," Dr. Chapman said with a chortle, and dismissed the notion with a wave of his hand. "She is simply a housemaid who took a knock to the head and fancied herself a wealthy runaway bride when she woke. No, rest assured, my lord. Throughout my inspection she grew less certain of being Miss Mayfield, and more distressed at my repeated questions."

The earl was cautiously optimistic, although if he were being honest, something still seemed amiss. "You're saying she improved during your examination?"

"Yes, I'd say so. But an additional three days' rest would do her good, if you can spare the staff."

"I'll see what I can do," said Ashworth, standing to shake the man's hand. The physician returned the handshake gingerly, clearly not wanting to aggravate his wounds. After a moment's hesitation, he popped open his satchel and handed the earl a small container of salve.

He leaned forward conspiratorially, and in a hushed tone said, "If you're going to mete out your own justice, my lord, you'd do well to apply this afterwards."

Ashworth returned to Lawton Park after an unproductive excursion to the village, every bit as frustrated and discontented as he'd been since the attack. He hurled his coat over the back of the nearest chair as he entered his bedchambers and began pacing like a madman, pausing only every now and then to massage his aching hand. He would have gladly broken every knuckle to kill that man, although he supposed he was grateful to his footmen for stopping him.

A day had passed, and he longed to go to Helen. She was still badly bruised and confused, not to mention by herself. Only now he realized she'd mentioned her father once before, but never spoken of visiting him. She could be truly alone, and after the doctor's visit, Mrs. Malone had swiftly bundled her upstairs to rest. He hadn't even been able to see her for himself first.

Fury welled up inside him. He needed to do something to release the insufferable tightness in his chest. For the thousandth time, he reflected on the blatant stupidity of the situation. What could possibly prevent him from climbing his own set of stairs and visiting a member of his staff in her room? Was it so taboo simply to check on her condition? It seemed simple, but of course, it wasn't.

Besides the obvious impropriety assigned to visiting a female in her room, especially given the nature of Scanlan's assault, this situation was rendered even more improper by their difference in station. As it stood already, he knew that tales of his attack on Scanlan in would make him infamous, and most likely a target of derision, back in London and perhaps even in country society. Not that he was in their good graces right now, as it was.

The question was, did he care? He thought back to his willful shunning of the *ton* following his family's losses. Ashworth was not one of them, and there had never really been a doubt about that. He was invited to balls and soirées because he was a high-ranking, well-heeled bachelor from an old and noble family, not because he catered to the desires and demands of the aristocracy. His family tragedy had only served to make him a commodity, like some exotic creature from a far-off land to be admired simply for its strangeness. So why did he give a damn about them now?

William knew he was attempting to rationalize why a visit to Helen's room, alone, was somehow permissible. It never truly would be. Yet the need still remained.

He silently opened the door and strode to the end of the hall where a secret portal was concealed behind ornate wooden paneling. Stepping lightly, he made his way up the winding staircase to the attic level where the servants' quarters were located.

Ashworth emerged into the dimly lit hallway lined by doors on each side. He was thankful it was close to dinnertime for the staff, so he could go about this task without fear of interruption. Quickly, he thought back to one of their conversations in the study. She'd said her room was cold at night, so he supposed it must be one of the farthest rooms from the center of the house. His eyes fell upon a door to his right that seemed to fit the criteria, and he stepped forward to turn the knob.

As quiet as he could, he pushed the door open to see a room that was tidy and stark in its furnishings. The afternoon light was waning, but he was able to discern Helen's shape in the bed on the opposite side of the small room. Her hair, appearing black in the gloom, curled around her shoulders in long, thick waves.

His eyes slipped further down to the feminine curve of her hip, partially obscured beneath the blanket that covered her. A primal satisfaction filled him at the sight of the fabric wrapped so neatly around her body.

Ashworth took a deep breath, trying to clear his head before he made a mistake. He needed to think. Think about what in the world he was going to say to her if she woke up, shocked to find him in her doorway, which was likely to happen if he continued standing here. Now he questioned whether he should wake her at all. What right did he have to be here? Plans were being made to find him a proper bride, a woman who would not be Helen. He could make no offer for her. He hadn't been able to protect her from Scanlan. In fact, he'd unknowingly put her in harm's way by inviting the reprobate into his house.

Helen turned to face the door with a sleepy sigh, and his breath caught in his throat as he gazed upon her, taking in both her unmatched beauty and the disproportionately raised flesh of her blackened eye. She shifted beneath her covers again, moving languidly, as if starting to wake. He felt the abrupt and overwhelming urge to leave before she discovered him. He'd had no business coming here.

William started to inch the door closed, when a loud

creak of the hinges gave him away. His heart plummeted as her drowsy motions ceased and she froze in place. Suddenly, she sat bolt upright, wild eyes scanning the room. He took one hurried step forward so she could see him, cursing himself for frightening her.

"Helen, it's me," he said softly, waiting for some recognition, any recognition, to pass over her frozen features. A few seconds later, Ashworth could hear her rapid breathing slow slightly.

"My lord?"

He sighed in relief. "Yes. Helen, I'm so sorry to have scared you. I wanted to make sure you were all right, to see for myself . . ." He trailed off, unsure what else to say. *I just wanted to see you.*

Her eyes shimmered and her posture relaxed slightly. "You should step inside, before you're discovered."

Deciding she was right, he closed the door behind him and approached the bed. He paused for only a second, before sinking down and reaching out his hand. Despite their most recent, acrimonious parting, she took his hand, allowing him to pull her into a loose embrace. He did his best to ignore the fact she was clad only in her chemise.

She rested her head on his shoulder, settling into his arms. "You should not be here, my lord."

"Yes, well, I've not really been one to observe the proprieties, it seems," he replied against her hair, and heard her amused chuckle. She leaned back to gaze earnestly at him.

"Where is Mr. Scanlan?"

He was taken aback. "They didn't tell you?"

"Well, they might have . . . I don't remember."

His hands curled tightly. "I . . . sent him away yesterday, shortly after I arrived home."

"Is that where this came from?" she asked, lifting his right fist to examine the lacerations upon it.

Her skin was soft against his. "Yes."

"You shouldn't have. People will talk of this."

"People will talk, regardless," he rejoined. "I refuse to apologize for beating that man. My only regret is that I did not send him home sooner." He glanced down at the floor, guilt spreading through his chest in a sickening slide.

She blinked. "What could you have possibly done differently?"

"I should have listened to my instincts. After our discussion at dinner, I wasn't certain he could be trusted. He showed a lack of concern for the mill workers. That should've been an indication he'd have an equal lack of respect for my housemaids."

"Instincts are not always meant to be followed, my lord," Helen said with a touch of irony in her voice.

She had a fair point, but he ignored it. "No man will ever hurt you under this roof again."

"Aside from you?"

It could have been an accusation, except it wasn't. She was stating a fact. Hearing it still felt like a punch to the gut, though.

"Helen—"

She interrupted him with a hand on his arm. "It's fine," she said sadly. "You should go. I wouldn't want someone to find you here."

Ashworth wanted to say more, but took his cue and rose from the bed. He trained his eyes on the floor as she swung her shapely legs over the side to join him, tugging the hem of her undergarment down in a belated attempt at modesty. A quick pull of the blanket around her shoulders, and all that remained visible were her feet.

Those feet, though. They were lovely and petite, like the rest of Helen. His mind immediately transported him to his bed, with her, under the sheets with those perfect toes stroking the length of his bare calves.

He needed to leave.

Ashworth reached out to touch her cheek, brushing a trail around the ugly bruise that marred it. "I'll leave, but how are you feeling, truly? I wanted to ask you myself."

"I think I will be quite well by tomorrow," she answered, gazing up at him appreciatively. "Thank you for allowing me some time to rest today."

He shook his head, his expression serious. "The doctor said you should rest for three days, so I expect you to do so. *Clara.*"

Helen's dark eyes grew wide. "M-my lord?"

Ashworth had only meant to tease her and was taken aback by her reaction, but strove to maintain a neutral tone. "In the servants' hall you told me your name was Clara Mayfield." He thoughtfully caressed a lock of her thick, wavy hair, then smoothed his fingertips over her ear, tucking it behind.

Helen was still staring at him, a horrified expression on her face. "I did?"

"Yes. You did. It seems Eliza's conversation at the breakfast table made an indelible impression on you," Ashworth said solemnly. "So I want to ask you once more," he said, bending down to her level to meet her eyes. "Do you know who you are?"

Her pretty face was darkened by the shadow of some emotion he couldn't quite place.

"I know who I am."

Ashworth's fingers moved to slide lightly over her jaw, to her mouth, where he stroked the curve of her bottom lip with his thumb.

"And do you know who I am?" he asked softly.

She nodded, clutching the blanket tighter around her.

He leaned down, so close to her now. "Say my name."

The earl heard Helen's intake of breath. This was a mistake, he knew. With their gazes locked, he silently repeated his entreaty.

Say my name.

Her jet-black lashes swept down across the pale curve of her cheek.

"William—" she breathed.

It was all she had time to say before he brought his lips crashing down over hers. The intimacy of hearing her speak his name was more powerful than he could have imagined, and he struggled to maintain control, his tongue eagerly thrusting into her mouth to find hers. As before, in the woods, she responded with a hunger that drove him wild.

Ashworth's hands roamed over her body atop the blanket, down to the round curve of her bottom. Unthinkingly, he gripped her, pulling her up tight against his hips, the extent of his arousal undeniable through the thin fabric of her chemise. Her lips tore away from his and she gasped softly.

You should stop. She had not asked for this intrusion, not when she had been so violently mistreated.

Ashworth shook his head and released her. "Forgive me—" he managed to say.

Helen's eyes fluttered open, the glassy haze of desire still lingering in their depths. Her fingertips caught at his shirt, and he stopped. She appeared remarkably calm, but the slight tremor in her hands betrayed her nervousness. Her gaze bravely held his, and with a graceful shrug the blanket that had been wrapped around her shoulders fell in a pool around her feet. She stood before him in a state of near total dishabille, and he was lost.

Family. Duty. Obligation.

He clung to these tenets weakly as his gaze absorbed the lush shapes of her breasts through the thin fabric . . . the luminous skin of her thighs below the hem of her chemise . . . and in an instant, Ashworth felt his resistance crumble to dust.

He needed her. Regardless of all the reasons he should stay away, his soul yearned for her. His body burned for her.

With a groan, Ashworth buried his face in the dark veil of her hair. He pressed his mouth to the side of her neck, and inhaled deeply as her moan vibrated against his lips.

Nipping at the juncture of her neck and shoulder, he breathed her in. She smelled sublime, not of violets or jasmine like so many of the faceless debutantes he'd met before, but of her own sweet essence, more intoxicating than any perfume. The earl let his hands explore her again, but this time they coasted upwards to discover the roundness of her breasts. God, she was soft. So very soft. Helen arched against him, her quiet gasp urging him on as he kneaded gently, circling his thumbs over the sensitive peaks and squeezing them softly through the linen of her chemise.

"Yes," she murmured, rearing back briefly to catch her breath. "Oh, yes . . ."

Ashworth reached up to tug at the strap over her left shoulder, and Helen's breath paused in her throat. He kissed her ravenously, then raised his lips from hers, giving her time to protest if she wished. She said nothing, though, still holding her breath as he gave one last pull, freeing one voluptuous breast from the confinement of her slip.

"Remember to breathe," he whispered, tracing the heavy curve with his fingertips and brushing his mouth softly across her forehead.

She uttered a tiny, endearing noise of surprise.

"You are the loveliest thing I have ever seen," he murmured, gazing down at her hungrily, and another slip of his fingers sent the second strap sliding down her other arm, exposing both breasts to the chilly air of her tiny attic room.

Color crept into her cheeks as his gaze raked over her, but she made no move to stop him. She only closed her eyes, unable to keep herself from trembling beneath his touch. Her teeth chattered as she attempted to speak, then speech failed her altogether as he bent over her, the wet heat of his mouth closing over one rosy nipple.

Helen cried out as he tormented her relentlessly, suckling and kissing. Shifting his attentions to the other side, filling his hands with her breasts, he tasted her over and over. Her head fell back, dark hair cascading down her back, insensible to everything but the feel of his hands and lips. She tangled her fingers into his hair and pulled hard to bring him up for another scorching kiss.

Her hands slid from his hair to his waist, snapping him back into reality.

"We need to stop," he said, breathing harshly as she tugged his shirt up out of his waistband. "Helen—"

Her fingers found the flesh of his abdomen, and he tensed immediately at the feel of her touch. Helen was not in the mood for stopping, and she clearly wanted to feel him. Her hands stroked the muscled surface of his chest and she sighed before shoving the hem of his shirt higher to press her naked flesh against his. Now it was his turn to gasp, and before he could even process what he was doing, he found himself pushing her roughly against the wall.

Her breathing grew quicker when the hardness of his thigh slid between her legs. Helen's eyes were fever-bright, and she gazed at him with a desperate yearning that matched his own. A glow of color rose on her cheeks at the intimate contact as he brought his leg tighter against her.

William knew this was forbidden. Yet in the moment, with her in his arms, he couldn't seem to care. Against his better judgment, knowing it would end in disaster, he leaned down to claim her inviting, pink mouth one more time before . . .

The sound of a soft knock at the door interrupted them, and Helen froze in shock. Working to suppress the rising tide of his lust, the earl uttered a quiet groan and tore himself away from her. He stepped quickly into the corner as she frantically straightened her chemise. A voice came through, muffled by the wooden door.

"Helen, it's Stella. Are you awake? I thought I heard voices."

Tiptoeing over to perch on her bed, she glanced at him in panic before making a somnolent-sounding reply.

"Stella? I'm fine . . . just want to sleep."

There was no immediate answer, and Ashworth was beginning to wonder if she'd walked away when he heard her next words.

"I thought I heard a man's voice."

Damn.

At this response, Helen rose from the bed. She leaned down to retrieve her discarded blanket from the floor before wrapping it around her and cracking the door open a few inches. She eyed her fellow housemaid.

"In the women's wing? Are you joking?" she asked sardonically.

Stella chuckled from the other side of the door. "I could have sworn . . ."

Ashworth froze in the corner behind the door as Helen widened the opening, gesturing to the empty bed across the room.

"That's strange," said Stella, bewildered. "I suppose I was hearing things. How are you feeling, love? You look awful."

"How flattering," teased Helen. But he could see her fingers trembling on the doorknob, the only indication of how nervous she was.

"Sorry, it's just, your face—"

"I really should rest, Stella," she answered, allowing a hint of annoyance to seep into her tone.

"Of course, I'm sorry. I'll be back later to check on you again."

With a low exhale, Helen closed the door on her friend and leaned against it for support. Her eyes met his.

That was close, she mouthed silently.

She had no idea.

Chapter Fifteen

Self-consciously, Clara reached up to tuck her hair more firmly beneath her cap before letting her fingers venture gently over the left side of her face. Most of the puffiness had subsided by now, but the horrid black and purple bruises remained, and would likely take weeks to heal fully. This bothered her. Not because it offended her sense of vanity, but because the bruises served as a visual reminder of what had happened, and it was one more thing that set her apart from the other servants.

She was worried about the next time she'd encounter the earl. It was good they'd stopped when they had, but her body still tingled with pleasure at the memory of his mouth upon her bare skin, and at the feel of his powerful thigh pressed so intimately against her. She couldn't think about it for fear of shamelessly throwing herself into his arms when they next met. Even though his desire was obvious, it didn't change the fact that he would be marrying someone else.

Squaring her shoulders with a sigh, Clara emerged from

the staircase to make her way towards the dining hall. As she rounded the corner, she found most of the servants in the midst of a light breakfast. A multitude of surprised and pleasant exclamations greeted her sudden presence in the doorway.

"Helen!" cried Charles, his eyes alight with warmth. He rose from his seat to swoop in and encircle her in a tight hug. Amelia was quickly up on her feet as well, crossing over for an embrace.

"It's so good to see you up and about," said Amelia, pulling back to survey Clara. "Your face appears much improved."

Oscar, the young stableboy, looked up from his tea with widened eyes. "You mean she looked worse than *that?*"

Charles glanced at Oscar in irritation, lightly smacking the back of the boy's head. This earned him an indignant glare, although Oscar did have the sense to refrain from further commentary on the subject.

"That's enough, everyone. No need to cause a fuss," said Mrs. Malone curtly, making her presence known from the head of the table. She stood, folded her napkin carefully, and smiled at Clara. Coming from the usually stoic housekeeper, the gesture appeared slightly unnatural, as if her facial muscles resisted that specific expression. "Welcome back, dear. Sit down and have something to eat."

Clara dipped into a curtsy before taking the vacant seat between Stella and Tess. Tess smiled shyly at her approach and took the time to pour her a cup of tea, but Stella seemed to be avoiding her gaze. Clara's heart sank.

The simple breakfast offerings of bread and butter and

sliced ham smelled sublime, and Clara eagerly reached forward to load her plate. "Thank you, Tess. How are you doing?" she asked the young scullery maid, casting a deliberate sideways glance in Oscar's direction.

The girl laughed, catching the subtle meaning behind Clara's query. Her fingers hastily rushed up to her cheeks to conceal her delight. "I'm doing rather well. Glad to see you back, miss."

Clara grinned. "That's good. I'm glad to hear it." She took a sip of her steaming tea before retrieving another roll from the bread basket, buying herself time to gather the courage to look in Stella's direction. When she finally glanced her way, she found the maid's eyes already upon her.

"You look like you're feeling better."

"Yes," answered Clara. "It was nice to have time to rest, but I'm happy to be back. It's been quiet the past few days."

A contemplative look slid over Stella's features. "Has it?"

Clara's heart started pounding.

Oh God, she knows.

"I—I'm not sure what you . . ."

"Helen!"

Clara turned to find Matthew had just entered the room and was motioning for her to join him in the hallway. Thankful for the interruption, she slid out from her chair and joined the footman, walking down near the staircase to find some relative privacy. Curious, she cocked her head at him.

"What is it, Matthew?"

He swiveled around and pulled her into a tight hug. The sudden show of affection was surprising, but also welcome, especially after having been away from her family for so long. She'd missed the feeling of such amicable closeness, and her heart tugged inside her chest. Clara gladly returned the embrace then pulled back to smile at her friend, who was already grinning down at her.

"I'm so glad you're back, Helen. You're looking much better." His cheerful demeanor shifted into thoughtful remembrance of that night's events, and he glanced off to the side. "I wish I'd been able to pummel Mr. Scanlan, for both your sake and for Amy's."

"What stopped you?" she teased.

"Well, the earl, for one! Charles and I couldn't even get near the man. Lord Ashworth had already kicked his door down and tackled him." His brows rose and he whistled low between his teeth.

Clara stared at him. "He kicked the door down?"

"Yes, he did. Right after you told him you were the runaway Mayfield heiress." Matthew's face grew red with the effort to suppress his laughter, eventually losing the battle anyway with a loud guffaw. "That's a good one, by the way. I plan to use it if I ever manage to hit my head."

"How ridiculous of me." She laughed weakly, feeling sick to her stomach. Apparently she'd told everyone her real name. "How is Amelia? She seems much improved."

Matthew's eyes softened. "She is very well. We had a talk after the other day and I—I finally told her of my feelings."

"You didn't!"

"I did!"

"And yet, here you stand before me . . . alive!"

He laughed. "It's true. And," he added with a grin, "she says she likes it when I tease her."

Clara threw her arms around Matthew. "Well then, don't stop now." She squeezed him tightly. "I'm so happy for you!"

She pulled away to gaze up at the footman, and saw his eyes drop to her cheek. His expression turned serious and he ran his fingers near the bruised place in solemn contemplation of her injuries. "Now I wish to see you healed, with no more reminders of Mr. Scanlan."

Clara smiled up at him. "Don't worry, Matthew. I've already begun to—"

Above them, the green baize door opened and Lord Ashworth entered in a hurry, stepping quickly down the stairs. Clara glanced upwards just in time to catch the bewilderment on his handsome face, his footfall halting at the sight before him.

No, no, no . . .

Matthew's hand whipped abruptly back down to his side, and he took a giant step backwards to release her.

"My lord," he said a bit too forcefully, punctuating his words with a deep bow in the earl's direction. "I was just on my way up . . . to bring tea . . . for your meeting with Paxton," he finished awkwardly.

Ashworth's glance flicked over to Clara before returning to his footman. He cocked his head, eyes flashing.

"And yet here you stand, with Helen, and nary a tea tray in sight."

Dread settled into the pit of her stomach. The earl was upset, and there was no easy way for her to convince him that the encounter with Matthew was not what it seemed.

Matthew was struggling to renew his sense of professionalism. "Well, yes, that is true. I will go fetch that for you now, my lord, if you wish?" He cleared his throat guiltily once, twice, before raising his eyes to Lord Ashworth.

The earl stood immobile for what seemed like eternity before gruffly nodding in assent. "Fine. You can deliver it to my study."

Matthew hurried away on his task, and Lord Ashworth's gaze shifted to skewer Clara with a black look. "You should find something better to do with your time. I'm sure there are many tasks that *don't* involve Matthew."

Humiliation, dread, and the sting of his judgment all affected her in equal measures. Unfair judgment, if she were being honest. Her chin tipped upwards in defiance.

"My lord, you should know—"

"Yes—" he said in an angry whisper, cutting her off. "I should have known. Now if you'll excuse me, I have important matters that require my attention."

His sudden contempt shocked her into silence. She did not move until the earl's footsteps had completely died away on the stairs above her.

William stormed into his study and slammed the door behind him. He hadn't thought to find Helen so tightly wrapped in another man's arms this soon, but he supposed it was to be expected. Hadn't he been the one to cut things off with her? Hadn't he drawn the line between them in expectation of him finding a more suitable wife?

And hadn't that all been before he'd found himself in her room, begging her to say his name . . .

William—

He threw himself down into the chair behind his desk then buried his face in his hands. He'd rather liked Matthew before. It was too bad he'd hate him now, but he would certainly treat Helen well. And it was good to know that the depth of feeling did not go both ways. That she had already started to move on with someone in her own social circle while he, fool that he was, pined away for her in his study. It would make his search for a wife so much easier in the end. At least that was what he hoped.

Rage simmered dark and deep within his chest, but it was a laugh that finally issued forth, quietly at first then gradually becoming louder. What folly to believe that she had truly cared about him. It had been a convincing act to be sure, but in the end it had still just been an act. And now, here sat the Earl of Ashworth in all his glory, brought low by not just a woman, but by one of his damned *maids* . . .

With a furious sweep of his arms, he sent the items on his desk to the floor in a heavy slide. William rose to stand over the mess, chest heaving, no longer laughing. His inkwell was splattered across the numerous ledgers and books, now lying at his feet. The carpet was quite possibly ruined.

One of his servants would have to clean up this inky pile of papers and books—maybe it would even be Helen. He found he rather liked that idea.

A quiet knock signified Matthew's arrival with the tea.

"Come in," he barked angrily.

The wide-eyed look of Matthew's amazement at the scene that greeted him only heightened William's ire. He needed to get some air, take a walk, do something before he said something he would truly regret. Glaring at the footman, he pointed a finger at the floor.

"Get someone to clean this up, and tell Paxton I'll meet with him later in the week. I'm going out."

And without waiting for a reply, he shouldered past the stunned Matthew to escape the confines of his own home, which to his mind, had become increasingly less comfortable in the span of only a few short minutes.

Snowfall came early to Kent, the first flakes descending the next morning, before December had even arrived. Clara had once more been summoned by Eliza, this time out back to the gardens. The missive had been short, to the point, and her heart had leaped upon reading it: *Rosa requests your presence on the terrace.*

She couldn't be sure what to expect. She had not had the opportunity to speak to Eliza since the incident with Scanlan.

Taking the chilly weather into account, she donned a pair of gloves, cinched her walking boots tightly, and draped her plain brown cloak around her shoulders. Clara took one final dissatisfied glance at the looking glass before leaving to join them outside. No amount of fussing would make her battered appearance any more palatable, and she had to admit that, on occasion, she missed the glamour of her fancy gowns with their expensive fabric and lace ornamentation. They had provided her the armor she'd always felt necessary when facing uncomfortable situations.

She sighed wearily as she descended the staircase. This entire ordeal had become exhausting. More than exhausting. Sometimes she felt her very sanity was at risk. Pretending to be someone else was difficult enough, but with the added heartache of missing her family and knowing she was destined to lose the earl, if that hadn't already happened . . . it was nearly too much to bear.

But what choice did she have?

Her freedom from Baron Rutherford had now transformed into a prison of its own design. And by fleeing her fiancé, she had created a massive scandal that the *ton* had been hungrily feeding upon for months. If she were to be discovered living in hiding as a servant? There would be no recovering from that stain on her reputation.

William deserved better than that. His *family* deserved better. And so did hers.

Clara swallowed hard, working against the lump that had formed in her throat. She saw her future clearly, and there was no version of it where she and Lord Ashworth could be together.

Her best chance at an imitation of happiness was still for the baron to marry elsewhere—or expire, she thought hopefully—then return home to beg her parents' forgiveness. Her mother would be happy to see her, but Clara was less certain of her father. Surely he wouldn't exile both daughters for displeasing him, but even so, would he be willing to take her on as a spinster?

She could try turning to her sister, but even if Lucy wanted to help, her husband worked for what little they had and that meant limited means with which to assist her. Of course, having worked as a servant, Clara was now no stranger to the toil of a hard day's work. She would gladly earn her keep, if permitted.

Clara paused on the landing to discover her hand on the bannister in a white-knuckled grip. She breathed slowly, pulling herself together before opening the door to the first floor. She could not . . . *would not* . . . fall apart now. She'd risked too much and come too far for that. Seeing this to the end, whatever that might be, was the only option.

Clara stepped outside, swiftly closing the door behind her to prevent the warmth from escaping the interior of the house. Rosa's tiny form came bounding down the walkway until she was tugging on Clara's skirts.

"Helen! Where have you been . . ." Her inquiry drifted off into silence as she gazed up at Clara's abused face, shock replacing her natural curiosity. Clara knelt down to meet Rosa's eyes and smiled warmly.

"I had an accident, darling," she said. "I've been resting in my room, but I'm feeling much better now."

"You don't look better. You look hurt." Her petite nose turned pink from the sudden change in emotion.

Eliza approached silently, looking exquisite in a dove gray mantelet and matching bonnet. Her eyes, large and sad, met Clara's. She came to a stop just behind her daughter and placed her hands upon Rosa's shoulders.

"She *is* getting better, dear, but a hug might help her along."

Clara opened her arms and Rosa charged forward into them, burying her face against her neck and squeezing tightly. The dreary thoughts and feelings of that morning's reflections dissolved within the little girl's embrace, and Clara heard herself sighing in relief. When Rosa finally released her, she felt markedly improved.

"Rosa, love, can you make more snowballs?" asked Eliza. "There's a good drift by the fountain over there."

"Yes, Mama."

Rosa trudged across the terrace, her tiny boots making distinct, child-sized impressions in the snow. Eliza smiled and stepped closer to Clara, wrapping an arm around her shoulders.

"I thought perhaps you could use a respite from your duties this morning. That, and I wanted to see you." Her smile faded then, concern and regret in her clear green eyes. "Oh, Helen. I still can't believe Scanlan turned out to be such a monster."

"There was no way any of us could've guessed his true nature, my lady. It is difficult to know anyone's true nature, at that."

Eliza pulled back to give her an appraising look. "I suppose so, but I know that when my daughter's life was in peril, you risked everything to find her. I know that when Amelia was attacked by that awful man, you risked everything again, heedless of the consequences." The earl's sister squeezed her before letting her go. "I'd like to think I know you, Helen."

A jolt of guilt, swift and sure, rocked Clara on her feet. How would the earl's sister react to discover that the servant she had come to trust, even with the safety of her child, was a phony and a fraud?

She tried to smile, tamping her emotions down as the pair made their way along the snow-covered stone patio.

"How are you now?" Eliza asked, breaking the silence.

"I am feeling quite well, thank you for asking."

Eliza hesitated for a moment before her next question. "And are you . . . yourself?"

So, she had been told of Clara's bout with amnesia. Of course, the irony was that she had not forgotten herself because of her injury. She had *remembered*.

"Rest assured, I am myself," said Clara. "Although I can't say the thought of being a wealthy runaway heiress doesn't have its appeal." She managed a light laugh.

Liar.

Eliza's eyes gained interest. "It is a fascinating situation, to be sure. I am curious about Clara Mayfield." She paused a moment, in thought. "If she ran away of her own accord, however, she must be either very brave or very foolish. I honestly can't decide," she said, laughing.

Clara tried to respond in kind, but her smile was more like a grimace. She hoped it appeared more convincing than it felt.

"Perhaps she is both," she finally replied.

A thoughtful gaze passed over Eliza's face. Before she could reply, she was struck on the shoulder by a loosed snowball. Eliza's mouth dropped open in surprise, and she looked to Rosa, standing innocently by herself near the icy fountain. Rosa grinned and pointed to a hedge.

"It was him!" she said accusingly.

Clara scanned the frozen scenery, seeing no one. Eliza placed her hands on her hips, ready to take issue with her daughter for being dishonest, but she stopped short when the dashing Lord Evanston stepped out, smirking, from behind the tall shrubbery near the fountain. His black leather boots crunched in the snow, and he bounced a ready snowball between both hands, eyes alight with mischief.

"Thomas, you scoundrel!" cried Eliza, narrowing her eyes at her adversary. "Why are you here, anyway?

Evanston affected to appear hurt by her inquiry. "Now, now, Eliza. You're not being very nice," he replied, gazing down at his hands. "The truth is, I'm here to meet your brother. Some more nonsense about cotton mills, I imagine, and in the meantime I thought I would . . ."

Snow exploded across his chest. The viscount's retort had unceremoniously been cut short by Eliza's retaliatory snowball. He lifted his eyes just as she flung another in his direction. Her aim was true, but he nonchalantly leaned to one side, watching the missile sail past to crash into the bush behind him.

He glanced back up at her with his bright blue eyes, unimpressed.

"Is that all you've got?"

Eliza growled, incensed, and bent to gather more snow.

"Come, Helen. You're in this now, too!" she cried.

Clara dutifully joined the effort, and before long both women stood with an arsenal of snowballs, only to find that Evanston had taken the offensive, charging forward onto the terrace. Rosa was chasing him determinedly, pelting him with tiny frozen orbs along the way.

They were forced to retreat, firing snowballs as they went—although being a servant, Clara refused to actually hit the man. The pair ran the length of the patio, then split up, Eliza heading north to join forces with Rosa, and Clara racing west to remove herself from combat. She hid behind a shrub, clutching her snowballs, lying in wait. After a few minutes of listening to Rosa's girlish squeals and Eliza's hurried footfalls racing across the frosty ground, Clara tread to the edge of the greenery and peered around.

Craning her head forward to listen, she could discern some kind of commotion to the east. She followed the noise, skirting around the edge of the fountain and making her way noiselessly across the freezing stone path of the garden. Ducking around dormant trees and bushes, at last she came upon the source of the tumult.

It appeared that the Lord Evanston had cornered both Eliza and Rosa in the place where two hedges met. They clung to each other in mock fright as he lobbed snowballs at their feet. Eliza worked to form a snowball from the blanket of snow on the bush behind her but he acted swiftly, hurling one of his at her wrist, smashing her efforts.

"Say mercy!" he demanded.

Rosa giggled and scrounged together enough snow for a projectile. "Mercy!" she shouted, simultaneously striking his legs with the snowball.

Evanston laughed, doubling over in a fit of hilarity. "Saying 'mercy' means surrender, Rosa." He crouched down in the snow and opened his arms. "Tell you what. If you give me a kiss, I'll let you go."

The girl didn't hesitate, running into his waiting embrace and kissing him soundly on the cheek. Her mother huffed in amusement behind her.

"Traitorous child," she said accusingly.

He patted Rosa's bright red bonnet and rose, still gripping a snowball in his hand. Stepping forward, he eyed Eliza playfully.

"Say mercy," he insisted.

Eliza tilted her pert profile up in the frigid air.

"Never."

He took another step closer, nearly touching her now, a wicked grin broadening his mouth.

"Dare I request your surrender with a kiss?" Evanston grinned down at her and added quietly, "Perhaps I will elect to kiss you regardless of whether you surrender or not."

Astonishment washed over Eliza's features.

"Have your other conquests bored you to the point of harassing your best friend's sister?" she asked disparagingly. But she could not hide the color that rose to her cheeks.

Clara felt the need to help Eliza out of this awkward situation. She stepped out from behind the shrub and was startled when Lord Ashworth revealed himself from the other side of the enclosure, looking formidable in a black overcoat. Seeing her, the earl looked surprised as well, but he did not linger on Clara, returning his focus instead back to the roguish Lord Evanston.

"Stop making my sister blush, Thomas. You're surrounded," he said sternly.

Evanston pivoted to see both the earl and Clara on either side of him, and Eliza took in their sudden appearance with obvious relief.

The viscount didn't hesitate and hurled his snowball at Ashworth, who dodged it with a casual grace that caused Clara's pulse to elevate.

"Ah well, I can admit defeat," Lord Evanston said magnanimously, realizing he was out of ammunition and outnumbered. He reached out to brush Eliza's sleeve as she passed by him. "We'll save the romance for the earl's upcoming ball," he said in a low voice that revived the pinkness of her cheeks.

Clearly she was discomfited, but Eliza answered with confidence as she gathered Rosa into her arms.

"I'm certain my dance card will be full by the time you've finished flirting with all the ladies," she stated with an attitude of indifference.

His eyes grew sultry with challenge. "I suppose it's possible unless, of course, I set out to flirt with you first."

Clara noticed the way Eliza paused, almost in disbelief. Evanston's relentlessness came as a surprise, if her reaction was any indication.

"Stop," ordered Ashworth with a scowl.

Rosa shifted inquiringly in her mother's arms. "Why are we having a ball, Mama?"

Lady Cartwick glanced down at her daughter, most likely relieved by the change in subject. "Well darling, we're throwing a ball to find him a wife."

Rosa met Clara's eyes. "Oh," she said, her small voice containing a trace of confusion.

Ashworth turned to Evanston and clapped him on the shoulder. "We'd better get to it," he said, leading the man back to the house.

From behind, Clara heard the viscount let out a long sigh, his breathy steam rising in the cool air. "Yes. I suppose you made a promise to Scanlan and you're determined to keep it, aren't you?" Thomas glowered. "Would it make a difference if I told you that embarking on a considerable investment venture in the far reaches of northern England is bloody inconvenient for me?"

"No," answered the earl. "It would not."

"What if I told you I have plans with a lady friend this evening, and I intend to be on time?"

The earl viewed his friend with a sardonic lift of his brow. "If I arranged our meetings around your various affairs, Evanston, I'd never get anything done."

Evanston let out a laugh, and Lord Ashworth glanced back in Clara's direction briefly before continuing forward. It was frustrating to share his company, and yet be entirely unable to set the record straight. More than anything, she wished she could put him at ease regarding Matthew, but perhaps it was better this way. If he believed her to be involved with another man, it was more likely he would withdraw and move on.

That would be better, wouldn't it?

It most certainly would not, her heart disagreed.

Eliza set Rosa down and increased her pace to catch up with her brother. "William, I know you're busy, but I'd like your input on the menus for the ball by tonight. Mrs.

Malone requires sufficient time to make arrangements with the cook."

It was difficult to tell from her particular vantage point in the group, but Clara could have sworn Lord Ashworth turned his head to mutter an oath.

Clara felt Rosa's diminutive hand slide into hers. She grasped it tightly and looked down at the girl, so adorable in her winter outerwear. Rosa looked as if she had a secret to tell, and beckoned for her to lean down close.

"Yes, darling?"

In her excitement, it took Rosa a few moments to compose her thoughts. When she did, they came tumbling out in a fierce whisper. "Mama—well Mama told me not to tell you yet, but I just wanted to say . . . *I can't wait until you live with us at the Dower House!*"

Chapter Sixteen

Clara jerked her cloak roughly around her shoulders and lowered her head against the biting wind. The season's early snowfall had vanished almost as suddenly as it had arrived, but the chill from the north continued unabated. She didn't mind. The nasty weather suited her mood. It would have seemed wrong to feel so hopeless beneath the golden rays of an azure summer sky. This relentless gray ambience was certainly a more fitting backdrop for the current state of her life, such as it was.

She navigated through the people on the village street, who were swathed tightly in their own winter clothing. It was the day before the earl's ball, and Mrs. Humboldt and her kitchen maid, Gilly, were up to their elbows in cakes, biscuits, and sandwiches—all intended for the grand evening's refreshment tables. Mrs. Humboldt, her culinary abilities not having been put to good use for a number of years now, was the outward picture of confidence and expertise. Clara knew, however, that her inward composure was an entirely different situation. The cook's increasingly rosy complexion, accompanied by a noticeable surge in her use of profanity, reinforced this notion, although it also could have meant she'd resorted to taking nips off the cooking sherry.

Mrs. Humboldt had been surprised when they had run out of lemon curd before half the day's batches of cakes had finished, but not nearly as surprised as Mrs. Malone. The somber housekeeper and the raucous cook were normally good friends, but Clara had feared a great row would erupt over the miscalculation. Since Gilly was busy baking, Clara had offered to go into town instead to find the required ingredients, and since she'd already finished her morning chores, Mrs. Malone had grumpily given her assent.

The silvery tinkle of the bell suspended over the shop's door brought back memories of her mother and sister. Many times they had gone shopping together in Silvercreek. They'd shopped in London as well, but there was something Clara had treasured about the smaller, cozier shops of the country. Perhaps it was that they lacked the rigorous attention to poise and etiquette that London shops often demanded, instead treating their clients with warm, personalized familiarity. Time spent perusing lavish dress fabrics or satin ribbons for their bonnets had been a common way to pass an afternoon and, of course, money had been no object to her family. Itching to shake off his family's undesirable *nouveau riche* reputation, her father had insisted Lucy and Clara be clothed in all the latest fashions when attending the most exclusive soirees.

Clara traced her fingers along the smooth glass jars the

shopkeeper placed carefully in front of her. She passed her coins across the counter and made her way back out of the shop, unable to keep from feeling a pang of regret at her father's hopes, now disappointed on all fronts. There was no way for him to know how eager to please him she'd actually been, how much she had wanted to attract a man he would deem worthy.

But then, she thought her brother-in-law, Douglas Thompson, was a good and worthy man. A kind man. He loved Lucy with a reverence she'd never seen. And yet her parents shunned him for his lack of status. For his want of lofty connections.

If only the earl had just decided to go to the ball that night in Mayfair. If only Clara had managed to secure him as her husband. If only she could have brought her family back together . . . and avoided this entire mess.

Clara swallowed against the lump in her throat. She supposed she should be thanking him for exiling her to the Dower House, and really, it was for the best. She had no desire to watch this new chapter of his life unfold before her very eyes.

The tiny bell rang once more upon her exit from the shop. Remembering her earlier mishap in the village on that day when she'd first met the earl, she glanced both ways before stepping into the street, narrowly avoiding a pile of fresh horse manure as she did. She lowered her brow. Stepping in dung would certainly be appropriate given the way things were going for her right now.

"Helen!" called a man.

She froze momentarily as her brain processed the voice,

then turned reluctantly towards Paxton, who greeted her kindly. He steered his horse in her direction, dismounted, and tipped his hat.

"Hello, Paxton," she said with a feeble attempt at a smile. "What brings you to this side of town?"

He returned her smile, glancing out across the busy street while he spoke. "I've just received word from one of the earl's tenant farmers. The recent snowmelt flowed over our drainage ditches and flooded the farmland below."

"How unfortunate," Clara replied, deep in thought. "Of course, the ground will be cold and hard until the spring. Further ditches cannot be dug until then." She paused. "Do these farms have windmills?"

Paxton's eyes widened in surprise. "Well, yes. Currently they are used to grind grain into flour. But his lordship has previously suggested they be converted to pump water as well . . ."

"Yes," answered Clara. "I've seen this performed successfully on other farms. It may be too late for this season, but perhaps it could be accomplished in time to alleviate heavy rains next year."

He stared at her, nonplussed, and his expression forced Clara to remember herself. She still had an identity to conceal, not that anyone would believe that a gently bred, wealthy young lady had made it her business to follow her father's land steward on his rounds, then ended up in hiding as a housemaid.

A housemaid currently late in returning to Mrs. Humboldt's kitchen with her lemon curd.

Clara glanced at her basket and turned towards the estate. "I'm afraid I must get this back to the cook. Are you going there as well?"

"Why, yes. I'm on my way to discuss the farmsteads with Lord Ashworth." He smiled. "And I thank you for your input on the matter. I'm not exactly sure how you've come by your knowledge, but I appreciate it all the same."

She forced her face to remain neutral, but inside, her stomach was churning. "You are quite welcome," Clara replied nervously. A frigid gust of wind caused her to tug up the hood of her cloak.

"Perhaps winter is already here to stay," he observed, dropping the subject and pulling at his cloak as well.

"I believe it is," she answered, moodily reflecting that the icy claws that had come to settle around her had nothing to do with the change of season.

William shook Paxton's hand firmly before seating himself behind his desk. It was a cold day, made warmer, thankfully, by the fire that crackled and popped nearby.

"Would you like a drink before we begin?" he offered affably.

The land steward declined with a small shake of his head. "No thank you, my lord. I'm only happy we were able to meet considering your hectic schedule and the ongoing preparations for the ball."

He grimaced at the unwelcome reminder of tomorrow evening's event. "Yes, well I apologize for the lateness of our meeting, and the abruptness with which I called it off last time. Your flexibility is appreciated."

"I am at your service, of course," replied Paxton amiably. "Now on to the matter of the flooding at the farmsteads, which has unfortunately returned. I have just been at the village to meet with the tenants."

William traced a fingertip absently over the edge of his desk. "Glad to hear it. I wanted to meet with you before renewing talks with them, myself. Are they open to the idea of converting some of the existing windmills to pump water?"

"Yes. Conversion, or even building additional structures for that purpose. And I have recently had confirmation that this type of operation has been performed successfully, which alleviates some of my concerns about the process."

"And where did you receive such confirmation?"

Paxton shifted in his seat. "Well, it was from an unexpected source. I ran into Helen in the village, who told me she had seen this procedure work elsewhere."

William's head snapped up. A faint echo of her words to him that day in the study passed fleetingly through his mind.

My father had experience in such matters.

His brow furrowed. "Do you happen to know how Helen acquired this knowledge?"

"No," replied Paxton uncertainly. "It was a bit surprising. But I suppose perhaps it was something she simply noticed happening in her village."

William leaned forward to rest his elbows on the desk. "She told me once that her father had dealt with flooded lands before."

"She—she discussed this with you?"

"In passing, yes," he said with an imperial air meant to discourage further questions. No doubt Paxton was wondering when an earl and his housemaid would have occasion to speak about such things. Little did the steward know how much William and Helen had actually shared between them these past months, much to his regret. His jaw clenched. "It was nothing more than an errant conversation, but the comment did catch my attention at the time."

"I see," Paxton murmured thoughtfully. "It is possible her father was a land steward, like myself. Although why she wouldn't mention something so pertinent during the natural course of our conversation is a bit odd."

That was an excellent point. Why on earth *would* she be evasive regarding her family? What could an ordinary servant girl possibly have to hide?

No. He refused to care any longer. Helen had already moved on, and he would move on in similar fashion. But God, what he wouldn't give to just hold her once more—feel the rough fabric of her dress sliding beneath his palm as he stroked her back, or marvel at how effectively the hot press of her mouth could absorb his most painful confessions. What a fantasy it had been to be cared for and listened to by the little slip of a maid. And even though things had ended badly, she had still done him a world of good. He guessed it was why losing her felt more and more like he was losing a part of himself.

He forced himself to shrug indifferently while his chest felt like it was caving in.

"Perhaps she values her privacy, and it really shouldn't be any of our concern," he said quickly, glancing down at his desk to shuffle through his papers. "Now let's talk about when we can begin construction on these windmills in time to be ready come spring—"

The two men continued to discuss logistics, but William found his thoughts were rooted elsewhere . . . upon the only thing that he, personally, needed to accomplish with some urgency.

And that was getting Helen moved into the Dower House, and away from him.

The evening of the ball arrived, and after attending a hundred balls herself, now Clara finally knew what it was like to prepare the house for one.

This time, instead of arriving rested and at ease in her most luxurious gown with jewels at her throat, she would be working in the cloakroom, already sore from scrubbing the ballroom floor and dressed in her plain maid's uniform. Her time at a dance would usually be spent socializing beneath the soft glow of candlelight, but tonight she had been the one to strain her back while lighting the candles. Whereas normally she would be ready to dance with any number of gentlemen, now she could only stew belowstairs with her aching feet, restless in the knowledge that every lady here tonight had the eligible Earl of Ashworth in their sights.

The female servants gathered together in their upstairs hallway for a brief examination before Mrs. Malone sub-

jected them to her unflinching inspection belowstairs. Since
Lawton Park lacked the staff for an estate of its size, every
servant was required to assist in some capacity with the festivities. Matthew and Charles would be performing the lion's
share of the work nearest the guests, but it was regrettably
necessary for some of the housemaids to show themselves as
well. As it was not typically the norm, this did not please the
earl's sister or the housekeeper, who had tried, unsuccess-
fully, to convince the earl that hiring more male help from
town would be in his best interest. Lord Ashworth, true to
form, had scoffed at the notion of hiring more people simply
to make an impressive display, and Eliza had been forced to
be content that he was permitting the ball to be held at all.

Clara peered down at the women in their pressed black
dresses and white aprons, hair neatly pinned beneath their
caps. They appeared no different than they had on a thousand
other evenings, but there was an excitement behind their eyes
that was new. How she wished she could share in their enthusiasm, but all she felt was morose anticipation. She would not
be able to avoid seeing the lovely girls in their ballroom finery,
smiling and flirting with Lord Ashworth in an attempt to gain
his interest. That would be bad enough. But to see him perhaps return their attentions would destroy her.

Amelia ensured everyone looked their very best, dismiss-
ing each maid as she passed them. As the housemaid with
the most seniority, and having convinced Mrs. Malone of her
aptitude for both attention to housework and her ability to
work well with others, she had finally achieved her promotion
to head housemaid. A month prior, this would have been a

catastrophe, with Amelia abusing her authority purposefully to harass Clara. Now, however, there was no undue malice.

When she reached Clara, they were last two servants remaining in the hallway. The redheaded maid stared at her in the flickering light of the wall sconces, and her voice rang softly in the gloom.

"I don't think I've ever had the chance to thank you, Helen, or to admit that I was wrong." Amelia's glance sank down to the patterned carpet. "Abigail sent her letter . . . she insisted you were one of us, but when you arrived I didn't believe her. You were too pretty, too perfect, too willing to break the rules. And I hated you for it all, until you broke the rules to help me."

Clara didn't know what to say. Amelia had proven herself to be, quite possibly, the most observant and astute member of the household staff. Stella had picked up on Clara's unconventional relationship with the earl, but Amelia had been the only person belowstairs to detect that something was amiss, with both her story and her character, from the very beginning. She could not fault her for this. She hadn't enjoyed Amelia's ill treatment, but Clara was indeed every bit as duplicitous as Amelia initially claimed her to be. Heaven help her if the maid ever discovered the truth.

She shuffled uncomfortably, eager to leave the hallway. "Thanks are not necessary, Amelia. I'm just happy we could finally come to a mutual understanding."

"No, this *is* necessary, Helen," Amelia insisted. "After the way I treated you, I'm not sure I deserved to be helped." She shook her head, chagrined. "Anyway, I needed to say that to you. Also, Matthew was quite insistent about our having an honest conversation to clear the air."

"Was he?" Clara beamed, her dark eyes turning thoughtful. "I always thought it was strange that you could ever think Matthew preferred me, when it was so terribly obvious that you were the only woman he was even remotely interested in."

Amelia's eyebrow rose in a mischievous arch, and she smiled. "Perhaps I mistook his affection for you as something other than friendship," she stated, her color rising to nearly match the vivid shade of her hair.

Well, Amelia hadn't been the only person to mistake her friendship with Matthew.

They proceeded down to the bottom floor to join the rest of the awaiting staff in the servants' hall. The clattering of dishes and a subsequent litany of curse words could be heard from down the corridor in the direction of the kitchen. For once, Mrs. Malone didn't appear to hear any of it. Her face was taut and her eyes were sharp. Clara knew she had longed for the day when Lawton Park would again host a grand event. Now that day had come, and despite the shortage of staff, she was determined to have things off and running without a hitch.

The housekeeper walked their line, surveying her staff closely. She came to a halt near Clara to issue a quiet edict to fasten her hair more securely. Clara reached up to find her rebellious locks were already slipping from position beneath her cap, and pinned them aggressively until Mrs. Malone nodded her approval.

"Good," she said, then addressed the staff in clipped tones. "Listen, everyone. Matthew and Charles will be circulating throughout the ballroom and hallways with drinks. Since they will be quite busy, occasionally you may be called upon to replenish the food on the tables in the refreshment room." The housekeeper again paced up and down the line. "Amelia will station housemaids in various places—the ladies' dressing room, the cloakroom and the refreshment rooms will require constant staffing." Mrs. Malone puffed her chest out with pride. "As a servant of the Earl of Ashworth, tonight you will be representing both him and this estate. Do keep this in mind at all times." Her eyes darted over to Clara. "You are not to meet a guest's eyes, nor will you interact with them in any way other than to assist them as necessary, speaking only if called on to speak. Is this clear?"

The servants acquiesced in unison. In spite of her wretched disposition, Clara still found it amusing that Mrs. Malone had singled her out for that particular part of the lecture.

Mrs. Malone nodded crisply. "Excellent. I know you will all work to make his lordship proud." She targeted them with one last granite stare before excusing them.

The staff had gone in different directions, each heading off to finish their own last-minute tasks, when the earl strode unexpectedly into the servants' hall. Clara froze, taken aback at his sudden appearance.

Lord Ashworth was always the epitome of masculine perfection to her, regardless of his state of dress, or undress, as the situation may be. But tonight, the sight of him caused her mouth to fall open, and she had to hastily shut her jaw with a snap before anyone could glimpse her inelegant display.

Everything about him . . . from the black breeches clinging to his muscled legs, to his white waistcoat exquisitely framing the broad expanse of his chest, was flawless. A simple white cravat was tied with precision at the base of his throat, and his formal black coat accentuated the width of his shoulders, draping down to end in two graceful tails. The earl's boots gleamed in the light. He was nothing if not imposing, and she forced herself to breathe while his eyes scanned over everything. Everything but her.

Clara gazed at him intently while he conversed quietly with the housekeeper. He looked resolute at the prospect of tonight's ball, rather than joyous. Still, this did not comfort her. Did he fear losing control in front of his guests? It made sense to think he might be struggling with some of his old anxieties tonight, perhaps made even worse by having found her in Matthew's arms.

How she wanted to comfort him somehow. At the very least, she wished she could convince him of her true feelings. Apologize through some gesture or expression. Even if it served no other purpose than to spare him some of the hurt he obviously felt, close the chapter on their romance in an amicable manner, it would be worthwhile. But he refused to look her way.

He raised his arms as he spoke, his fingers working to adjust his gold cufflinks. Clara unwittingly recalled a time when those arms had been wrapped around her—when those long fingers had traveled over her body, trailing fire.

The mere thought of those heated moments in her cramped attic bedroom was enough to cause her to flush.

Say my name . . .

Clara glanced away in remorse and was surprised to see Stella staring in her direction. Stella had not been friendly since the evening Lord Ashworth had visited Clara's room, but right now she was gazing at her with something similar to pity.

He uttered some last instructions to Mrs. Malone, then turned and left the hall as quickly as he'd come. A jolt of panic shot through Clara's chest. He was going upstairs to, perhaps, meet a woman who would become his countess. She just couldn't let that happen without some sort of attempt to resolve the conflict between them, and inside herself.

Clara lunged forward, narrowly dodging Tess and Charles on her way out of the room. She prayed Mrs. Malone was too distracted to notice her following the earl. It would be a long evening for her if the housekeeper saw her already abandoning her promise to behave as a good servant should.

She caught him at the base of the staircase, the same place where he'd misunderstood her encounter with Matthew. Clara reached out desperately to touch the fine material of his sleeve.

"My lord, please . . . may I speak with you?"

He swung around and jerked in surprise. His eyes traveled from her hand to her face. She noticed with a sinking heart that he did not look pleased.

"What can you possibly have to say to me, Helen?" he asked stiffly.

Oh, he smelled good. It was irritating how easy it was for

him to drive her mad with longing. She knew there wasn't much time, so she leaned in closer, knowing it would cost her a bit of sanity to do so.

"I need you to know that what you saw with Matthew was not what it seemed. And that . . ." Here she faltered, her accumulated guilt and sorrow suffocating her under their weight. ". . . I wish you good fortune in your search for a bride."

At this, his brow rose and he stepped backwards to place more space between them. A flicker of regret flared to life in his amber-green gaze, and the muscle in his jaw worked as he glowered down at her, busily formulating his thoughts.

"Even were it so . . . if you and Matthew are simply friends . . . do you really think it makes a difference?"

"No, of course not, my lord. I only wanted you to know," she whispered, biting her lip to keep her tears in check.

Clara left before he could say anything else, could feel his eyes burning into her back. Her hurried footfalls echoed down the long hallway, and in her haste she ran headlong into Stella, who was exiting the servants' hall.

"Excuse me," she choked out, swiping at her face with her sleeve. When she tried to step around, Stella gently took hold of her arms and guided her into Mrs. Malone's office, which was empty. The maid closed the door and turned to face Clara, her severe features softened with sympathy.

"You are not the first woman to love a man above her own station, Helen. But it's foolish to believe you were anything but a distraction for him."

Clara's head snapped up, her eyes wide with shock. "Stella, I don't know what you . . ."

"I think you do," she replied with a confident tilt of her white-capped head. "And I think it was dreadful of him to take advantage of you in your weakened state, after the fight with Scanlan."

"No," Clara managed in barely more than a whisper. "It wasn't like that."

The maid looked doubtful. "Perhaps not, but think about that tonight while he courts the loveliest debutantes in the county. See if it still rings true then." She stepped closer to wrap Clara in a friendly embrace. "Falling for men like him will never end well for women like us," she said softly.

A truer statement had never been spoken, and not just for the reasons Stella was referring to.

The office door swung open abruptly, and Clara and Stella turned to find Amelia staring at them, looking dismayed.

"There you two are! Is there a problem?" she asked, a crease between her brows.

Stella squeezed Clara's arm and gazed expectantly at her. She had lied so much already, what could one more possibly cost her?

"Not at all," Clara said with a sniff. "We'll be right out."

Chapter Seventeen

Lord Ashworth bowed over what seemed like the thousandth daintily gloved hand so far this evening. Dragging his gaze upwards, he did his best to appear pleased at the introduction to this young lady, who seemed barely more than a little girl playing dress-up in her fancy gown and satin slippers. Her anxious mother stood just behind her, beaming with pride.

He pondered how Helen would look, wrapped in light, gleaming layers of tulle and gauze. With certainty, she would put every last woman here to shame. Indeed, he knew she could still outshine them all were she to simply walk into the ballroom in her maid's dress, apron and cap.

Unsurprisingly, his head started to pound. It was unwise to think of Helen right now. He had so far succeeded in burying his more difficult emotions, and he would not jeopardize that. Not now. Although he was furious at the idea of her becoming romantically involved with another man, the possibility of her finding a match within her own social sphere ought to have filled him with relief. It had provoked and distracted him instead, making the ordeal of tonight's hunt for a bride all the more taxing. He had not been inclined to listen to her earlier pleas on the staircase, but an inconvenient twinge of regret still remained. She seemed honestly mortified, and determined not to let the matter rest as a possible misunderstanding.

Had it all been just a misunderstanding?

He sighed inwardly, his anger dissolving into quiet wretchedness. What did it matter? He had already made arrangements to send Helen to the Dower House. The hollowness that filled his chest grew larger, threatening to swallow him whole. The thought of losing her for good was not something he could fully comprehend yet. William supposed the feeling would pass in time. He had to believe it would.

Forcing his attention back to the task at hand, he managed a weak smile at the girl standing before him now.

"A pleasure, Miss Morrell," he murmured in a low voice. He smiled politely, but as soon as the girl and her mother took their leave to enter the ballroom, the smile dropped and he squeezed his eyes shut tightly, fingers reaching upward to pinch the bridge of his nose. "Please tell me that's all of them," he muttered half under his breath.

Smothered laughter came from his right where Evanston stood, while a sharp elbow assaulted him on the left, courtesy of his sister.

"Do try to be civil, brother," she whispered sternly, green eyes flashing. "It's only the future of your earldom, after all."

Ashworth scoffed at her but felt the seriousness of her charge. Evanston gazed at the earl wide-eyed, in alarm.

"By God, that's a rather somber note to start the evening on." He lowered his voice conspiratorially. "Although, William, there are many lovely young girls here tonight that I would enjoy dancing with . . ."

"How surprising," interjected Eliza.

"Now, Eliza. I'm shocked," Thomas said. "If your brother does not wish to dance with the ladies who have assembled here for him, then *as a gentleman*, the burden must fall to me." He shrugged noncommittally, his eyes laughing. "I'd be doing God's work, if you think about it."

His sister's mouth pursed. "There is nothing *godly* about you, Evanston." She moved to brush past him towards the ballroom, the watered silk of her silver gown swirling out around her. "Come, William. If we don't succeed in finding you a wife, we can at least watch the viscount dance with countless—"

She stopped mid-sentence, and the earl looked over to see why. As she'd reached Thomas, he'd stepped forward to block her path. His face was serious, but his bright blue eyes were alight with mischief.

"Does the idea of my dancing with other women upset you in some way, my lady? It seems that it might."

Eliza's cheeks flooded with rosy color and she stared at Thomas in silence. William growled in warning. He would not have his friend target Eliza for his own amusement.

"Evanston—"

"You don't think it's a fair question?" Thomas pressed,

the corner of his mouth raised in a wry smirk. "It is a simple thing to resolve, if it does." He bowed ever so slightly, raising his right hand in her direction. "Will you do me the honor of dancing with me this evening, my lady? I'd hate for your dance card to fill before I've finished ravishing all the other females."

Eliza's hands flew up to smooth her intricately pinned mass of golden hair—something Ashworth recognized as a nervous gesture—and a tentative expression crossed her face as she gazed up at Lord Evanston.

"You're right, Thomas, I was being too harsh. You have my apologies." She glanced over her shoulder to Ashworth, resuming her forward momentum. "We should go inside . . . it is impolite to keep our guests waiting . . ."

Eliza's progress was again unceremoniously halted when she bumped into Lord Evanston's chest. She issued a tiny noise of surprise, but Thomas remained immobile.

"Am I to take that as a refusal?"

The earl knew that a lady could not, in keeping with strict ballroom etiquette, deny the invitation of a gentleman to dance if she had not already accepted the invitation of another. He was less certain if ballroom etiquette truly applied when the invitation was given in the hallway before the ball had even started, although it appeared that Evanston was going to hold Eliza to it.

Normally she might have laughed, maybe even swatted him on the arm for good measure, but for some reason she seemed uncharacteristically ruffled by his request. Thomas had been friends with William since childhood, and a regular fixture at Lawton Park for years, even more so after the loss of William's father, brother, and Eliza's husband. His sister was very familiar with him . . . though at present she was acting uncomfortable. Awkward.

Interested?

The earl bristled. He held his friend in high esteem, but the idea of Evanston attempting to court his sister was not acceptable in the least. The man was a rogue who prided himself on being able to charm his way through the London gaming clubs and into the bed of whichever woman pleased him most on any particular day. Eliza would not be lumped in with that disreputable lot. In fact, he would consider himself a failure as her brother if he allowed it to happen.

Before she was pressured into answering Lord Evanston's invitation, William slipped his arm through his sister's and steered the viscount over to his opposite side.

"Let us reserve the teasing for after the ball, shall we?" he said, shooting a warning glance at Thomas, who had the audacity to look annoyed.

Lord Ashworth clenched his teeth. This was going to be a very long night, indeed.

Clara was stationed in the cloakroom alongside Amelia. They busily received shawls and cloaks from arriving ladies, assisted with the repair of collapsing hairstyles, and mended torn dresses. It was not lost on Clara that all these girls, delicately perfumed and looking their best, were here to gain the favor of the earl. Her earl.

Ignoring the sick feeling in the pit of her stomach that refused to subside, she worked diligently. Each task blended into the next, as did the ladies who required her services. The only way to endure this evening successfully, Clara knew, was to remain emotionally distant, so she uttered no more than compulsory responses and kept her eyes trained on the specific demands of her occupation.

An older woman entered the cloakroom with a swish of her voluminous violet skirts, holding a long white glove in her manicured hand. She was accompanied by another lady, the owner of the glove if her solitary exposed hand was an indication, and they both leveled haughty gazes at the housemaids.

"I am Mrs. Levinthal. This glove needs mending." She relinquished the article to Clara, then raised her fingertips to check on the status of her coiffure in the mirror before moving her dark gaze to glower at Amelia. "Pin my hair too, and be quick about it." She sat at the vanity and smiled sideways to her friend. "I'm preparing to introduce a friend to the earl, Harriet. I think it will be quite the talk of the evening."

Mrs. Levinthal's companion appeared happily scandalized, and leaned in to whisper loudly, "I still can't believe it. And you said he's been staying at your estate this past week?"

Clara could see Amelia pinning the woman's hair with efficient motions of her fingers, her expression neutral.

"Oh, yes. Well, of course it would have been unseemly for us to arrive here together, as his whole purpose in visiting this part of the country is to continue the search. But I can tell you we've spent many recent evenings engaged in . . . *scintillating conversation*," she said with an immodest laugh.

The two housemaids met each other's eyes for a fraction of a second, just long enough to read their mutual amusement.

"I'm sure you'll make him forget all about his little lost fiancée in no time," snickered Harriet.

Clara's fingers paused in mid-stitch.

What did she just say?

Her eyes flicked up to the woman, rapidly assessing her. An abundance of silver threads wound through her otherwise black hair, and she guessed she might be roughly fifty years of age. The deep violet shade of her dress combined with the black lace flounces adorning it indicated she was in mourning, but not deep mourning. She was a widow, but it was permissible for her to attend this event and even, within reason, to dance. The oversized amethyst drop earrings dangling from her earlobes, along with the matching necklace, bracelet, and numerous jeweled rings, conveyed her wealth.

Mrs. Levinthal sniffed in displeasure. "Well I have tried in vain to convince his lordship that extending his sojourn in Kent would be of mutual benefit, but he is set to return to Essex on the morrow." She turned an arched brow to her friend. "It will be necessary to use all my available powers of persuasion tonight."

Her friend quirked her lips in a sinful smile. "I have every confidence in you, my dear."

Clara stood as if entombed in a block of ice, and her body felt nearly as cold.

Essex is a large county. Certainly, there could be numerous men experiencing difficulty with their affianced. It is only arrogance to think this has anything to do with you.

A small *ahem* broke the train of her whirling thoughts, and her eyes darted over to Amelia who was staring at her, confusion in her blue gaze as she continued rapidly securing Mrs. Levinthal's hairstyle. Luckily, the two women were still indulging in their vulgar brand of conversation and had not noticed Clara's conspicuous pause, or Amelia's attempt to regain her attention.

It can't be true . . .

But Abigail's furtive letter had warned her of the possibility.

Noticing Clara was still distracted, Amelia's eyes widened meaningfully, then sharpened to a consternated glare. Clara jumped and finally remembered herself, resuming her work on the torn glove.

Assuming he is in attendance tonight, he will never see me as long as I remain in the cloak-room.

It was this thought that gave her some slight comfort. And really, it was still so very unlikely to be the baron. She chided herself for jumping to preposterous conclusions and placed the final stitch in the seam, turning the glove right side out and presenting it for the approval of its owner, who did not deign to show any approval at all. The woman, Harriet, merely slipped the accessory back over her hand and continued chatting.

Taking one last, satisfied glance at Mrs. Levinthal's hair, Amelia stepped back. Both she and Clara curtsied, allowing the ladies and the extensive circumference of their skirts a wide berth as they departed to return to the evening's festivities. Amelia turned to look incredulously at her.

"What happened to you?"

Clara busied herself, unsure what to say, but before she could come up with something convincing, Mrs. Malone walked briskly into the unoccupied cloakroom. Her eyes scanned the racks burdened by lavish garments of different colors, shapes, and sizes.

"Good, I'm glad to see things have lightened up a bit here. We need help at the refreshment tables. Helen, you are excused to assist."

Cold fear rushed through her. Despite her resolution not to worry about the possibility of the baron being in attendance, she involuntarily shivered.

"B-but Mrs. Malone . . ."

"*Now*, please. *Thank* you," said Mrs. Malone tersely as she exited the room.

Clara stood motionless, finally turning to gaze at Amelia with huge eyes.

"What on earth is the *matter?*" asked Amelia, throwing her hands out in frustration.

There was no good excuse she could think of to explain herself to Amelia. Pasting a lukewarm smile on her face, she shrugged.

"It's just that this is my first big event. I suppose I'm nervous."

Amelia didn't look reassured, but reached out to squeeze her arm. "You'll be fine. I'll be waiting for you here when you're done."

Clara's hands trembled. She curled them into fists and ducked her head as she left the cloakroom.

"**A**re you enjoying yourself at all, William?"

Ashworth turned to find his sister staring up at him. Eliza's concerned gaze reminded him of her weeks of effort spent ensuring this evening was a success. She wasn't aware of the reasons for his unhappiness, nor could he disclose them to her. He would never be able to tell her that he, the fifth Earl of Ashworth, wasn't interested in any of these preening peahens. That the only woman he wanted was the utterly inappropriate, beguiling housemaid who had ensnared him upon their very first meeting in the village.

He could picture the look of solemn disappointment on his father's face.

Shaking off the image, he smiled warmly and reached down to squeeze her gloved hand in his own. "It's been a splendid evening so far."

Matthew stopped near them and extended a tray of champagne, carefully averting his eyes. Ignoring the obvious awkwardness, the earl lifted a glass to his lips, draining the contents in one swallow, then returned the empty glass to the footman's tray.

Eliza muttered under her breath as she watched Matthew hurry away.

"You are a terrible liar."

Ashworth sighed. "You should be socializing, Eliza. Don't waste your time concerning yourself with my enjoyment."

Before she could reply, an aging couple approached. The woman he recognized as Mrs. Levinthal, who lived on the opposite edge of town. His widowed father had often spoken of her marriage-minded tendencies, as he had been her target numerous times prior to her marriage to the wealthy Mr. Levinthal, now deceased.

She sank into a curtsy, and Lord Ashworth bowed politely in return.

"Mrs. Levinthal."

"My lord, it is delightful to see you after so many years!" she gushed vociferously. "Lady Cartwick," she said with an additional curtsy to Eliza.

His sister returned the gesture. "Welcome back to Lawton Park."

The woman's eyes were alight with excitement. "I thank you, my lady. I hope you will permit me to introduce my friend, who has just recently arrived in this part of the country." Her nose tipped up ever so slightly, and she held her hand out to the man beside her. "This, my lord, is Baron Rutherford."

Ashworth turned to greet the man, but hesitated at Eliza's small intake of breath. Her eyes were wide with hesitant curiosity, and she took one step forward.

"Forgive me, but you are—"

"Yes," interrupted the man in a gravelly voice. "The very same. I have traveled to Kent in search of my betrothed, Clara Mayfield."

Clara carefully entered the refreshment room, and placed a full tray of lemon cakes upon the table. Despite her nervousness about being seen, she took an extra moment to neatly rearrange the platters of food. She could hear the lively notes of a quadrille drifting in from the ballroom, and her heart suddenly felt heavy and leaden in her chest. Somewhere in that room the earl was very likely dancing with a beautiful woman, and only mere months ago, that woman could have been her.

The sound of laughter caught her attention, and she looked up to see two girls in their immense dresses advancing on the table. Not wanting to attract attention, she left the room by way of a hidden doorway, and with the door closed behind her she leaned against the wall and exhaled in relief. The anxiety she'd felt earlier in the cloakroom seemed laughable here, tucked safely away in the darkened hallway.

Her mind went to Rosa, who was spending the evening upstairs with Eliza's lady's maid, Patterson. She pushed away from the wall and set off, making her way through the winding maze of turns concealed in the depths of the house. Instead of heading back in the direction of the cloakroom, she chose to climb the rickety wooden staircase to the second floor. For a reason she could not name, the need to see that small, friendly face had become nearly overwhelming.

Clara crept noiselessly towards the nursery. A shaft of yellow light shone out from the door, left ajar. She entered, expecting to see Rosa and the lady's maid, but instead found the room deserted. A fire was blazing cheerfully in the hearth, which was good since she could feel the chill of the cold night air wafting in from the windows. A half-eaten crumpet was lying discarded on a plate near the foot of the bed.

Crossing the room, she moved the plate to the bedside table and brushed a handful of scattered crumbs from the coverlet. She supposed that Patterson's hands had been full these past few hours with Rosa begging to see the excitement downstairs. Allowing her to eat a messy crumpet in bed was probably the least of her concerns.

She parted the curtains, peering out the window to see a horse-drawn carriage being brought around the drive. A guest was leaving the ball already? It was late, to be sure, but too early for most departures. Perhaps they lacked the usual stamina required for this type of event. Clara remembered during the season—and even at country balls such as this—tumbling into her carriage beneath the weak, gray light of dawn, stifling her yawns in an effort to be polite to her hosts.

Part of her, the uncharitable part, wished she could call all the carriages to come around.

With a frustrated sigh, she exited the nursery and headed towards the main staircase. If she knew Rosa, the little girl would have talked Patterson into allowing her a closer look at the party.

Sure enough, she came upon them just above the landing, with Rosa clinging to a lacquered wooden bannister clad in nothing more than her nightgown and robe. Clutched tightly in her arms was her beloved doll, its rose-colored dress looking decidedly dingy after these past months' adventures.

Patterson turned at the sound of Clara's approach. "All the crumpets in the world couldn't keep her from wanting just one peek."

Clara smiled and lowered herself down onto the carpeted

step beside Rosa. The little girl slid her arm through Clara's and sank into her shoulder, all the while never taking her eyes off the grand foyer below.

"I just saw a lady in a purple dress," she sighed, enraptured. "It was so pretty."

"That sounds lovely," fibbed Clara, thinking of Mrs. Levinthal. "But now it's time to go to bed. Imagine how cross your mother will be if you stay up all night." She pushed up to a stand, extending her fingertips to the girl. "Let's go upstairs."

Rosa stood as well, raising her doll up as if preparing to dance.

"Look at me, dancing at a ball!"

She adopted what Clara assumed was her most elegant expression—eyebrows lifted, lids fluttering closed, mouth puckered into a tiny bow—and swung her soft cloth partner around in circles. The sound of approaching footsteps in one of the hallways below them caused Clara and Patterson to glance at each other in apprehension.

"Now, my sweet," whispered Clara urgently, tugging on Rosa's arm. "Up to bed this instant . . ."

The girl stumbled and lost hold of the doll, sending it sailing through the air to land on the smooth marble floor below. A collective gasp echoed through the two maids and the little girl simultaneously.

Clara stared at the stranded doll in horror as the footfalls grew louder still, steadily approaching the foyer.

She whirled around to stab a finger in their direction. "*Upstairs, quickly!* I'll get the doll."

The lady's maid scooped Rosa in her arms while Clara descended the final flight of stairs. Deciding speed would be best in this situation, she dashed out into the foyer, leaned over to seize Rosa's doll, turned back to sprint towards the safety of the staircase . . .

. . . And collided headfirst with a dignified guest.

The man must have entered the space while she'd made her frantic grab. He grunted at the impact and her mind whirled in a sudden state of panic. The worst had happened. She had been caught in an area of the house reserved for the peerage and their private amusements, and physically collided with an invitee.

Mrs. Malone's words ran through her thoughts, although in this frenzied context they seemed almost crazy, nonsensical.

You are not to meet a guest's eyes, nor will you interact with them in any way other than to assist them as necessary, speaking only if called on to speak.

She focused her gaze onto the man's polished leather boots and backed away, attempting a curtsy and gripping Rosa's doll tightly. If she could make it to the stairs, perhaps this man would pardon her atrocious clumsiness and allow her to escape.

"Forgive me," she said with deference, continuing her backwards progress until her heels had reached the bottom stair. Curiously, the man's feet stayed planted at their original location. She could imagine him staring at her in comical surprise, too stunned by her pitiful actions to move, but she refused to raise her eyes to verify if this was the case.

Clara tentatively raised her left foot onto the first step, and it was then that the guest's feet became a blur of motion, charging at her across the polished marble floor. It took a moment for her to realize he was coming after her with some violence, which seemed extreme given the circumstances, but only when his hands closed around her throat did she fully appreciate the danger of her situation. Rosa's doll fell to the ground as she reached up to pry at the vice-like grip circling her neck. He squeezed harder and black spots mottled the edge of her vision, her breath slipping from her lungs in weak spasms. She gazed up at the man in horror.

The wild eyes of Baron Rutherford stared back.

He leaned in, his breath heating her already flushed face.

"Found you," he snarled.

The surreal sound of screams mingled with the strains of the orchestra, and Lord Ashworth halted abruptly in the midst of an uninspired waltz with Miss Morrell. Alarmed, he released his dance partner and scanned the ballroom for Thomas, finding his friend standing near Eliza on the outskirts of the room.

"Evanston," he called sharply, twitching his head towards the door. The viscount nodded, his blue eyes wide with unease, and the music faded then died altogether as the two men weaved through the gathering of confused couples on the dance floor. Without the background noise of the music, the screams seemed louder and more shrill.

The earl and the viscount reached the door simultaneously. Thomas raised his hands and turned to face the inquisitive mass of people.

"Please enjoy some refreshment in the next room, as we excuse ourselves for a moment," he said, adopting his most charming smile. "We will return shortly."

Despite his impatience, William could see the sense in his friend's actions, if only to keep the crowd from interfering. Eliza joined them outside the ballroom, her eyes panicked, but was met with her brother's protective arm blocking her path.

"No. I don't know what's happening, but you will not . . ."

"I would recognize Rosa's screams anywhere!" she cried hotly and brushed past him, her pale gray skirts flowing behind her as she ran. Ashworth and Evanston raced to catch up, but none of them were prepared for the scene that greeted them in the foyer.

The lady's maid, Patterson, was kneeling on the cold floor, her arms wrapped securely around Rosa's waist in an attempt to detain the crazed child, who was flailing and swinging her doll as if attacking some invisible assailant. The front doors were gaping and an arctic wind gusted through the open portal, blasting Eliza as she lowered herself in front of her daughter.

"Rosa," she whispered vehemently, stroking the girl's face with her gloved hands. "What has happened?"

"He took her!" wailed Rosa, tears falling fast from her eyes.

"Took whom, my darling?"

"He took her! That bad man took Helen!"

Ashworth met Evanston's eyes, and Eliza turned to gaze up at them in frightened puzzlement. Dread, cold and weighty, rooted itself deep in his chest. He stepped closer to the crying child.

"Rosa, this is important. Where are they now?" he demanded, ice flowing through his veins.

"A c-carriage—" sobbed Rosa, sagging with grief, finally allowing her mother to fold her into a comforting embrace.

The earl's head snapped up as Matthew and Charles rushed into the foyer.

"My lord . . . ?"

He silenced them with a dark look.

"Horses. *Now*."

Chapter Eighteen

The baron's carriage raced down the drive, bouncing roughly over the bumps and stones in its path. The riotous motion sent its occupants jostling wildly throughout the vehicle's interior, and it was all Clara could do to keep Baron Rutherford at arm's length while struggling fiercely to maintain her equilibrium.

"Get your hands off me!" she spit, clawing at his face.

Clara fought him off with every ounce of strength she possessed, but he shoved her against the velvet upholstered seat, where her head collided with the lacquered wood panel above it. A brief explosion of stars illuminated the darkness behind her eyes, and her body involuntarily slumped from the blow. Rutherford used the opportunity to lunge forward and seize her white cap, yanking until it came free from its pins. The pain was white hot, shooting through her scalp and neck. He leaned close, trapping her to the seat with his weight. His face trembled with contempt.

"A servant. A servant! You jumped out a window on the

eve of our wedding and have been toiling away in some lord's estate *as a servant?* How dare you?" He eyed her in unconcealed resentment, and his face turned a deep, mottled red. "Then again, I will enjoy making you regret it."

"You'll never have the chance!" Clara snapped. "My parents will know of your cruelty for it's no longer concealed between us. You showed your true tendencies in front of the Earl of Ashworth's niece tonight!"

"That little whelp? Who would believe her? And what would it matter, anyway?" he sneered. "I'm still your father's best offer for your hand, and his shot at respectability."

Clara glared at him. "*I will never marry you!*"

"You have no choice," said the baron, a smug look upon his face. "I've instructed my driver to head north to Gretna Green. In a few short days, we will be man and wife, regardless of your feelings on the matter." He grinned in appreciation of her shocked reaction, then hooked his fingers around the edge of her apron, rending it with a violent jerk of his arm. She gasped, and he uttered a mirthless laugh as he tossed the ruined garment to the carriage floor.

Clara trembled, fighting off a tide of nausea. Even if she were to kick and scream through the entire service, chances were the marriage would still pass due to the baron's credibility as a peer. The journey to Scotland, however, would take days, and one thing was certain—she would not go quietly. At some point, they would be forced to stop at an inn for food and rest, giving her an opportunity to attract attention.

Unless she was bound and gagged, concealed under a blanket, she thought darkly. Which was likely.

"What about Mrs. Levinthal?" she sputtered at him in desperation. "Wouldn't she suit your needs as much as I ever could?"

Rutherford stared at her, surprised, then snorted in amusement. His gaze traveled down the length of her body and his mouth turned upwards into a wolfish smile.

"No. She would not."

With a cry of revulsion, Clara resumed her efforts to free herself from his grasp. Mentally, she calculated the potential extent of her injuries if she were to fling herself from the moving carriage. She quickly decided that there was no injury that could be worse than living as the baron's wife. If she could just make it to the door . . .

He withstood her exertions easily. Panicked, she felt her strength fading, when the vehicle pitched forward abruptly and jarred to a sudden stop. Lifting her head in bewilderment, she tried to gather her wits enough to dive for the door handle, but Rutherford recovered more quickly and subdued her with the pressure of his arm across her chest. He gripped his walking stick in a meaty fist and thumped it viciously against the roof.

"Barrett!" he shouted. "Why the devil have we stopped? Drive on!"

Clara could detect the sound of voices just moments before the door was torn open. She tipped her face into the welcome rush of cool fresh air, blinking to clear her eyes. The pressure of Rutherford's arm was suddenly lifted when he was brutally yanked from his seat by none other than Lord Ashworth, the strong angles of his face dimly illuminated in the flame from the carriage lamps.

She stared at him weakly in disbelief.

He came for me.

She could hear Rutherford blustering, and the earl's feral expression made Clara wonder if he would deal with the baron right then and there. Instead, Ashworth shoved him roughly into the restraining grip of Lord Evanston, and the next instant he was inside the carriage.

"Helen—"

The earl folded her into his arms and she melted against him, sobbing messily on his immaculate formal attire. She curled her fingers around the lapel of his tailcoat and nestled in against the warmth of his neck. Clara could feel his hands drifting over her back to pull her even closer.

"Did he hurt you, my love?" His voice was a low growl deep in his throat, and she froze in incredulity at the endearment before shaking her head. Ashworth responded with an inarticulate murmur and an affectionate brush of his palm over her hair, revealing her pale neck and the new marks on her skin, left by the baron's hands. His hand stilled immediately.

"*I'll send him to hell,*" the earl ground out in a guttural voice.

Rutherford hadn't hurt her, at least not in the way she feared most. But all it would take was a few words from the man to bring her life crashing down around her. She was about to be exposed for the fraud she truly was. Clara willed herself to maintain her already fragile composure. She could hear the men outside, including the baron's wordy protestations. It was only a matter of seconds before the Earl of

Ashworth, bent on defending her, would come to despise her instead.

"Here," he whispered, his hands shaking with rage. "Let me help you from the carriage."

"No, I'm . . ." Her face crumpled, and she dissolved into tears. "I'm sorry, William. Please, forgive me . . ."

His eyes, dark in the dismal interior of the vehicle, grew perplexed. "Forgive you? For what?"

Evanston's voice called from outside. His solemn tone made Clara wince.

"Ashworth, you need to hear this."

The earl stared at her, and the urge to bolt from the carriage became nearly overwhelming.

He reached out his once white-gloved hand, now stained from his horse's reins, and she accepted the offered assistance to tremulously lower herself down to the ground. When she raised her eyes, she saw Matthew and Charles standing beside the viscount, the baron locked in the latter's steely grip.

"You are about to owe me an apology, Ashworth," sneered the baron.

Lord Ashworth released her hand to approach, narrowing his eyes with each step. "Oh? Well, you first," he hissed, crumpling Rutherford's shirt in his fist to rip him out of Evanston's hold and throw him up against the exterior of his own carriage. "Tell me how you think it acceptable to enter my house under the guise of friendship, then proceed to kidnap and harm a most valued—"

"*Servant?*" Upon uttering the word, Rutherford erupted

into unsettling laughter. "You have been gravely misled by this woman, my lord."

The earl's eyes darted over to her, and she gazed helplessly back.

"This *housemaid*," said the baron derisively, "happens to be the daughter of one of Essex County's wealthiest families, and my bride-to-be, Miss Clara Mayfield."

Ashworth thought he felt his jaw drop, but couldn't say for certain since his entire body seemed to have gone numb all at once. Of course, it made sense. Hadn't she confessed to it herself after taking a blow to the head? And didn't it explain so many things about her that simply didn't add up otherwise?

Stunned, his eyes found her, standing near the carriage in her tattered black uniform. The earl took in her wild, dark hair and miserable countenance. Could it be? Could the woman he loved be that same wayward heiress of recent fame?

It seemed impossible, ludicrous even, that a lady of means would intentionally go into hiding as a domestic servant, working belowstairs to conceal herself. Even if she objected to her groom, which clearly she must, the dramatic flight from her marriage and the lengths she'd gone to in order to maintain anonymity were astounding.

His voice sounded rusty and unsure in the silence that had settled heavy among them.

"Clara Mayfield?"

It wasn't so much a question, as a request for confirmation.

Her long lashes lifted as she raised her frightened eyes. They shimmered in the wavering light from the lanterns, before she lowered her gaze to the ground once more.

"Yes, my lord."

His breath stopped in his chest.

My God.

Her admission elicited an answering smirk from the baron, who cast a vengeful glance at the earl before shaking off his hands. He tugged his jacket back into place, striding over to take Clara roughly by the arm.

"I require an apology for my mistreatment, my lord," he said pompously. "And I expect to resume my departure with no further interference from you or your friends." He pulled her close. "Miss Mayfield and I will be wed in Gretna Green before the week is out."

Gretna Green? No . . .

The earl stood frozen, locked in internal conflict. He, the fifth Earl of Ashworth, was furious with her. She had used him, after all, and the rest of the servants too, to mask her presence inside his house. Tales of this scandal would likely not leave his family name untarnished. It would be well within his rights to simply turn his back and allow Rutherford to reclaim his betrothed. And yet . . .

He, William Halstead, was painfully, exquisitely, and desperately in love with her. His reputation was already tarnished, but still he lived as honorably as he could, for his own sake and for his family. Even so, he hadn't spared a second thought about whether or not he would come after this woman and her captor.

And hadn't he also known what he would do when he found his housemaid—despite his elaborate farce of an attempt to find a respectable wife tonight—*hadn't he known?*

Yes.

He would make her his countess, and set the *ton* aflame.

Clara stood motionless in the baron's grip. The crystalline reflection of her tears caught the light as they fell from her eyes. No doubt she expected him to abandon her.

Ashworth's fists clenched and resolve hardened the muscles of his jaw. He took a step closer to them, eyes blazing.

"You will receive no apology from me," he said vehemently, pulling himself up to his full height to glare down at the baron. "And you should know that your claim on her is void. I insist you release her before I have you clapped in irons for kidnapping."

Clara gazed up at him in shock, while on Rutherford's face confusion gave way to hostility.

"How could my claim possibly be void? Her father has consented to the match—*we are set to be wed . . .*"

"Your betrothed has not consented, so far as I can tell," replied the earl sarcastically.

His argument was dismissed with a wave of Rutherford's hand. "A minor inconvenience, but nothing that will stop this marriage from going forth . . ."

Lord Ashworth stepped closer, leaning in to whisper fiercely, "*I have had her in my bed. She is mine to marry now.*"

The baron and Clara both gaped at him in shared outrage, while Matthew and Charles suddenly found themselves awkwardly preoccupied with the reflection in their boots. Conversely, Lord Evanston was assessing the earl with a mien of newfound respect.

Clara stepped forward, breaking free of Rutherford's grasp.

"My lord! I—"

Ashworth skewered her with a ferocious look. "You be quiet. Stand there," he commanded, jabbing a finger towards Matthew and Charles. He couldn't risk having her jeopardize her own situation merely to avenge the notion of her virtue.

Clara flinched at his harsh tone but ultimately did as he said, moving over to the footmen who stepped in front of her protectively as if to shield her from any further unpleasantries.

Baron Rutherford was looking to be on the verge of an apoplectic fit. He shook his fist in Ashworth's face, his entire body shaking with rage.

"Pistols," he spat. "At dawn."

Lord Ashworth eyed the baron skeptically. "I would win any duel between us, and you know it." He leaned down and lowered his voice. "You would be a fool to pursue this, Rutherford. The great pains she took to escape you would only serve to bring you shame, even if she were still your fiancée, which she is not."

"Would she not bring you humiliation, as well?" the baron demanded.

"Thankfully, I am beyond caring about that."

The man's face slowly turned purple. "I will have her examined by my personal physician! How do I know—"

"You will do no such thing," the earl interrupted coldly. "Let us not forget I could still have you arrested for kidnapping." He shook his head. "No," he said decisively, "the better course of action would be for you to quickly marry the very willing Mrs. Levinthal, and sweep all this disagreeable business under the carpet. You will have your wealth and your property . . . the only thing you will not have is her," he said, pointing to Clara, "for she is *mine*."

A primal surge of dominance flowed through him upon speaking those words. Clara's head whipped up at the shocking finality of his statement, and he wondered whether it had served to bring her a sense of relief, or stir her furious indignation instead. He couldn't worry about that now. William absolutely needed to assert himself over this man who would claim Clara for his own. There could be no doubt as to who was in charge, who was in control, and who would be marrying her when all this was finished.

Ashworth kept the full force of his attention on Rutherford, who was unusually quiet as he mentally digested the earl's words, weighing his options and the societal improprieties, and eventually . . .

Conceding defeat.

The baron's face twisted in bitter resentment as he wordlessly strode to his vehicle.

"Home, Barrett," he growled, throwing one last hateful glance at Clara. The driver, caught gawking at the spectacle down below, earned a scowl from his master as he scrambled up onto the carriage. Rutherford's walking stick could be heard striking the roof, muffled through the wood paneling. A short distance down the drive, he lowered his window and tossed out Clara's apron and cap into the frigid night air, where they fluttered and flapped like the liberated ghosts of her former self.

It was only when the rumble of the carriage had faded into the distance that Lord Ashworth dropped his defenses, the unwelcome drama of the evening's events finally taking its toll on him. He lowered his head for a moment and Evanston approached to place a strong hand on his shoulder.

"I must say, William, I was impressed," he said emphatically. "Especially the part when you told him you had—"

"I thank you for your assistance, Evanston, but do please shut up," answered the earl.

The viscount grinned and joined Ashworth as he approached Clara and the footmen. The earl could see that she was not dressed for the chill of this December evening, her torn dress doing little to protect her from the freezing cold, although whether she shivered from the night air or from distress, he could not say. He removed his formal black coat and draped it around her shoulders, keeping hold of the lapels as he bent closer to her.

"We need to talk."

Her lovely dark gaze flitted over to meet his, but her lips remained tightly sealed.

Ashworth stepped back to address Matthew and Charles. "I want to thank you for your help, and for your sensitivity with regards to this delicate matter." He looked meaningfully at both men. "I know of the talk that occurs belowstairs, but would ask that you say nothing of tonight other than to clarify that Helen is, in fact, Clara Mayfield. It is reasonable to expect that her fellow servants will expect some semblance of explanation, but all other details are private. Am I understood?"

Both men nodded and bowed.

"Matthew, you are charged with conveying Miss Mayfield back to the house and in through the servants' entrance," instructed the earl. "Lord Evanston and I will dismiss tonight's guests, but until the house is clear, I want her to remain in my chambers."

"Yes, my lord," replied the footman.

At this command, Clara's chin rose. "Have I been traded from one tyrant to another?"

He gazed at her sharply before stepping closer. "Any perceived tyranny on my part, Miss Mayfield, is regrettably necessary and borne of your deceptions. I have had quite a mess to clean up tonight, thanks to you."

Mollified by the flicker of shame that passed over her countenance, he walked swiftly to his horse and swung up into his saddle, unenthusiastically considering the task of explaining the situation to his sister as he dug his heels into his horse's sides and set off for the house.

Clara paced the earl's chambers, anxiously awaiting his return from the ball downstairs. If she'd known it would take him over two hours to join her, she would have requested a brief stop at her tiny attic room to retrieve fresh clothing. She had managed to smooth down her tousled mess of raven hair, but with buttons missing and torn seams, her black woolen dress was a shabby remnant of what it had once been ... similar to her current reputation.

While it was true that much of its tarnish was due to her unconventional method of evading marriage to the baron, she couldn't help but feel the stinging insult associated with the question of her virtue. Yes, she had been intimate with Lord Ashworth. But there was a vast difference between what they had done and what he had *claimed* they had done.

Despite the hurt and anger his words had stirred to life tonight, Clara was aware that those same words had also saved her from a forced elopement with Rutherford. Likewise, she knew that for Ashworth to admit having intimate relations with her constituted a risk to him as well. In fact, he had deftly cast aside how any question of her character might affect his family at all, which surprised her considering how much she knew it meant to him.

But she did have to wonder if his declaration of marriage would still have followed, had not the truth of her identity already come out.

The only thing you will not have is her, for she is mine.

Clara shivered, briskly rubbing her arms and coming nearer to the glowing fire. She wished she were still wrapped in his black tailed coat, but he had required it for his return to the party, even if only to send his guests home early. Guilt sliced through her at the thought of Eliza's ball, carefully planned for her brother, now laid to waste. She earnestly hoped Eliza would still count her among her friends when all this was said and done, but as it was, she wasn't even certain if she and the earl would be on speaking terms.

As much as it grated on her to be claimed by yet another man, she knew she still wasn't even close to deserving him. Although she had to admit that the idea of being claimed by this man held a significant amount of appeal.

Did he truly want her for his wife? The butterflies in her stomach demanded to know.

Her musings were interrupted by the sound of approaching footsteps from the hallway. She instinctively wrapped her arms more tightly around her midsection, as if to ward off the confrontation that was inevitable.

The doorknob turned and the door flew open to reveal the earl, looming large, his gaze angry and hurt beneath the dark sweep of his brow. Fear fluttered in her heart like a frantic bird, but she only watched him from her place by the fire, waiting to see what he would say.

After a moment, he shut the door tightly behind him, then turned to pierce her with another black look.

"You lied," he said accusingly.

She nearly choked in offense. "As did you!"

"You know very well why I had to lie," he countered furiously, stalking towards her. "Any lie I told tonight was only necessary because of you and your . . . pretending!"

"I never wanted this!" she cried. Hot tears of humiliation flooded her eyes and she swiped at them impatiently. "To be dishonest with my family, with your staff, with *you*." Clara held his eyes, silently beseeching for understanding. "You have to know . . . it killed me every single day. Especially when I . . . when you . . ."

Her composure dissolved. The fear, anguish, and heartache that had been held in check for too long came rushing out, and all she could do was cover her face with her hands to conceal the rising tide of her misery.

"No, stop—"

Ashworth's voice was hoarse, almost annoyed, as he came forward, his arms encircling her, his lips falling against her hair, her forehead, lightly against her cheek to send shivers of desire chasing over her skin. When his lips fell on hers there was a desperation to his kiss, the salty wetness from her tears mingling with the oaken brandied flavor on his tongue. She clung to him dizzily while he ravished her mouth, and only when she was completely breathless did he pull away.

"You should have told me," he admonished angrily against her temple. "*Why did you not tell me?*"

She shook her head vehemently. "I couldn't," she choked. "You might have sent me back to him. It's what any other man in your position would have done—"

"And what if the baron had found you walking in the village?" he said, cutting her off sharply. "Or if Rosa had not been there tonight? I mean, my God, you'd have disappeared without a trace and I cannot *abide* the thought—"

His fingers delved into her hair as he kissed her again, punishingly, and she allowed him to do as he wished, unwilling to resist him anyway. Soon though, his kiss softened as the force of his rage eased. The earl took her mouth slowly, stroking her with his tongue, the kiss transforming into a sensual exploration that caused her body to awaken in that now familiar need for more.

Ashworth pushed her away, his chest heaving. His eyes were brighter than she'd ever seen them, and the sight caused her stomach to do an odd little somersault. The muscle in his jaw jumped, showing his obvious struggle to master both his emotions and his desire. She took a chance and reached up to stroke the hard edge of his jawline with her fingertips.

"You didn't have to lie for me, my lord," she whispered.

Ashworth stared at her, incredulous. "I didn't lie for you. I lied for *me*. Can't you see that the very thought of losing you tears me apart?" He sighed in exasperation and raked a hand through his hair. "The only alternative was to allow that bastard to run off with you to Gretna Green!"

She shook her head, shivering in remembrance of how close Rutherford had come to doing that very thing. "This was not the first time he had treated me in such a way. The thought of spending my life with a man like him . . ." She swallowed hard. "It would have killed me. I had to escape, regardless of my father's wishes."

He tipped his head. "Which were?"

"My father wished to rid himself of our *nouveau riche* reputation. The clearest path to respectability was for my older sister to marry a man of the peerage." Clara took a breath before admitting the next part. "Lucy chose to marry beneath her station and thus failed him in that regard. I even helped her to elope," she added, laughing shakily beneath her breath. "But then my marriage became the last chance to repair the family name. I had accepted my part to play, but it was only when the baron cornered me at the end of the season that I knew I was in trouble."

The earl appeared puzzled. "So . . . you're telling me you were unable to secure a suitor during the season?"

"Yes, my lord," she replied sheepishly.

He stared at her, astonished. "Has every man in London gone mad?"

Clara felt her flush deepen, this time with an unexpected infusion of pleasure. Still, she hesitated before asking her next question.

"Do you think if you had seen me there, that you might have approached me? Regardless of my family's circumstances?"

"*Might* have approached?" He scoffed, his gaze turning sultry. "I would have gladly written myself in for every dance on your card."

A swell of emotion caused her throat to tighten, and she stepped forward to gently slide her fingers across his lapel. "I was in Mayfair, for the last ball of the season."

Ashworth's eyes widened. "The one that I—"

She nodded.

He tore from her grasp and stalked away to brace both hands against the mantelpiece as if seeking the strength to stand.

"To think all of this misery could have been avoided if only I'd have taken a chance—"

"You took a chance tonight," she reminded him quietly.

He raised his head abruptly and glanced over his shoul-

der at her. "Did you know this whole time that I'd intended
to be there?"

Clara bit her lip, knowing he might not like the truth. Finally, she nodded. "It was the reason I chose to come here for
work. I believed if the Earl of Ashworth was so resistant to
mingling with the *ton*, that there would be a certain amount
of safety for a woman who was looking to hide."

"You may have hidden yourself away from Rutherford for
a time," he said in a low voice, turning to face her. "But you
were not successful in hiding yourself from me. You were all
I could think about, day and night." Stepping forward, he
slipped one hand possessively around the curve of her waist,
while the other traced a lock of her hair, wild and loose across
her shoulders. "God, it was such torture."

She leaned in against his caress and her pulse started to
accelerate. "Yes. It was."

Ashworth's mouth met hers in one swift motion, hot and
slick and full of need. She squirmed against him in delight,
her head falling to the side as he lightly kissed his way down
the length of her neck.

She nearly jumped when his head suddenly jerked back,
his eyes black with fury as they fixated on her throat. Ever
so gently, his fingers brushed the recent bruises left there by
the baron. For a moment she was afraid he might step back,
might stop, but he shocked her by sweeping the wet warmth
of his open mouth against those tender places, traversing the
barrier between pleasure and pain. She gripped him tighter,
her fingers wrapping in the silky layers of his hair.

Despite his obvious need, or perhaps because of it, Ashworth gently eased her away with a fiery glance that betrayed the underlying current of his thoughts. He took a moment to collect himself before continuing. "Miss Mayfield, there is still a matter that we need to discuss—"

"No, that will not do, my lord," she said, clenching his coat in her fists to pull him back down. "I need to hear you say my name . . ." she whispered against his lips.

Months of frustration and longing surged forth and whatever needed to be discussed was momentarily forgotten again as she reminded him of his own words—a dark demand made in secrecy while hidden away together in her tiny room.

"*Clara*—"

Their lips tangled in another kiss, and she wrapped her arms securely around his neck to stretch the length of her body against his. Ashworth made a low sound in his throat and swiftly scooped her into his arms to toss her on top of the bed. Within seconds, he had joined her.

He tugged his jacket from his broad shoulders, then tore off his waistcoat and shirt. He reached for her, but Clara pushed him back, rolling over so she could kneel before him. Her eyes widened as she drank in the sight of his bare torso . . . the beautifully defined chest and the fine golden hair that covered it . . . the way his lean hips disappeared into the band of his breeches . . . how those breeches fit him so snugly . . .

An impatient, aching feeling grew hot, low inside her belly. Clara exhaled into the sensation and placed her palms flat on his abdomen. His skin was hot beneath her fingers as she roamed up his chest, relishing the feel of his muscles flexing, the sound of his groan. She leaned in to nip at his collarbone, feathering kisses up to his throat where she lingered, tasting him, loving how he responded to her touch. A new sense of power came over her. Fascinated, her fingers drifted down in exploration, sliding over the thick hardness beneath his breeches, yearning to feel all of him.

His entire body jerked at the contact.

Oh my . . .

Her hand was quickly snatched away in his strong grasp. "No," he said hoarsely. "Not yet."

"But—"

Ashworth silenced her with a dizzying kiss, taking advantage of her helplessness to flip her onto her back and unbutton her uniform. Her ragged black dress landed on the floor, with her corset, chemise, and drawers following soon after. Clara felt shy and not a little bit wicked lying on Lord Ashworth's bed in nothing more than her stockings, and she shivered as he rolled those down her legs, his touch like fire against the delicate skin. She stared up at him, feeling exposed and wonderfully vulnerable, and his breath faltered as his eyes traveled the length of her.

"I have pictured you in my bed more times than I care to count," he said. "But, Helen, my God—"

"Clara," she corrected with a soft laugh.

The earl lowered down to crush his lips against hers, the rasp of his chest hair tickling deliciously against her breasts. She bit back a moan.

"That habit, my love, will take a while to break." He smiled inquiringly. "And what, may I ask, prompted you to use the name Helen, anyway?"

Clara wriggled beneath him, savoring the feel of his weight pressing her into the mattress.

"It was during my first interview, in your study, when you asked my name . . ."

Ashworth moved down to draw her nipple into his mouth, and this time she couldn't stop herself from moaning, arching towards his mouth as he alternated between sly circles of his tongue and a devilish suction that caused her toes to curl. Still, she struggled to continue despite his efforts at distraction.

"I panicked and saw your copy of *The Iliad* . . ."

He raised his head, realization dawning behind his eyes. "Helen of Troy," he whispered. "The most desired woman in history . . ."

One hand traveled lower still and she cried out as his hand slid between her thighs to discover the warmth hidden there, unfamiliar pleasure blooming under his clever touch.

She writhed upwards. "William . . ."

With a muted groan, his fingers continued to circle, the pace quickening. Clara could not keep up with it all—the sensations were new and entirely overwhelming. But they suddenly coalesced into one glorious focal point at the very center of her being, and she felt herself climbing, ascending to some nameless, unexplored height. But before she could reach there, he removed his hand, laughing a little at her cry of frustration.

Clara lifted her head, her heart racing, a shiver chasing over her skin as a cool draught drifted through the closed windowpanes.

With tantalizing slowness, William moved further down her body, his lips gliding along her stomach, the curve of her hip, the sensitive skin of her thigh.

Surely, he won't . . .

Her brows furrowed a split second before his lips moved over the place his hand had occupied a moment before, his tongue tracing wicked patterns into her sensitive flesh. She buried her fingers in his hair, unsure whether she meant to stop him or urge him on, before collapsing back onto the mattress, the soft sweeps of his tongue causing every thought in her head to take flight like a flock of startled birds. She cried out, heedless of who might hear her. Never in her life had she felt a sensation so powerful. The delicious tension grew rapidly, reaching unsustainable levels until she found herself catapulted into the sky in a dazzling burst of release, shattered into a million burning pieces.

When she finally recovered some semblance of aware-ness, the earl shifted upwards to place a kiss against her forehead. Feeling a little self-conscious from the intimacy of the encounter, she felt her flushed cheeks turn warmer and turned her head to the side. He slid two fingers around her jaw to bring her back to face him, shaking his head.

"No. Don't ever feel uncomfortable," he murmured, his voice roughened in arousal. He rose up to his knees. "You have no idea what that does to me. How many months I have imagined it . . . you, in my bed, finding your pleasure . . ."

Any thought of her own insecurities was instantly erased when he stripped off his breeches, revealing a new expanse of hard muscle and golden skin that took her breath away. He lowered his body back down to settle beside hers, the thick length of his arousal pressing against her thigh, and he gazed down at her with eyes that were dark and full of need.

"I wish there were some way to avoid causing you pain . . ."

His hand slipped between her legs again, this time finding her most vulnerable place, and he teased her with a fingertip before slowly sliding it into her body. Her eyes widened in surprise and with a soft moan, she arched into the caress. She wasn't sure what he'd been talking about. This didn't hurt at all . . . it felt incredible.

"Oh, yes—" she sighed.

She could hear his breathing becoming more erratic as his desire heightened, and his slow exploration increased in its fervor. Clara's body responded eagerly, but she needed to feel his body too . . . wanted to become intimately acquainted with every part of him. She shifted her hand down to slide possessively over his manhood and he froze, his breathing halting at first, before releasing in staggered gasps. After a moment she also began exploring, moving her hand up and down the length, in awe at the satiny feel of his skin.

"*Christ*," he choked.

His gaze was molten as he watched her stroke him, until finally he tore her hand away in impatience and levered himself over to settle his hips between her thighs. He guided himself to her entrance with a last murmured apology, and she held her breath, the pain coming now as he sank into her, inch by glorious inch. He groaned loudly, and Clara reveled at the intimacy of the invasion even as she felt her body tightening against the stinging pressure.

"Forgive me, my love—" he managed, straining to hold still for her, giving her time to adjust.

But she couldn't bear for him to stop now. Gasping, she dug her fingers into his back and tipped her hips upwards, bringing him even further inside of her.

"No," she whispered. "William. Don't stop."

The earl's lips brushed against her hair as he lowered his head to find a rhythm that suited them both. Over and over he plunged, satiating the craving he had built within her, filling her in every way. She took him gladly, exulting in the feel of being claimed, the pain forgotten as her body steadily drove towards that shattering feeling of release once again.

She cried out his name as it crashed over her in a dizzying wave, and it seemed to drive him over the edge as well. He seized her hips in a punishing grip as he thrust slowly and more deeply. His lips found hers in a rough kiss, then he groaned against her mouth while his body tensed with the force of his release, the muscles in his back shaking from the intensity of the moment.

William finally collapsed on the bed beside her, utterly exhausted and in a daze. Clara rolled over to meet him, draping her leg over his as they struggled to catch their breath. Unable to resist, she tangled her fingers in the wild disarray of his golden hair, and his eyes fell closed at her touch. Her head dropped to rest upon his chest, and they lay like that for a while, enjoying the closeness between them, which had, until tonight, been so very forbidden. His husky laugh disrupted the silence.

"So, about that thing I wanted to discuss—"

"Oh yes, that," she replied sheepishly. "I suppose I interrupted you."

He arched a brow. "You did a fair sight more than interrupt me," he said, smiling faintly, "But this is important. I have a proposal."

Clara evaluated him in wry contemplation. "Does it involve moving me to the Dower House?"

His eyes flew open in astonishment, then he turned his head to the side in an effort to conceal a sudden grin.

"Rosa . . ." he said with an exasperated sigh.

Ashworth shook his head and propped himself up on an elbow to take both of her hands in his own.

"I'm sure by now you understand my motivation for wanting to send you away. Rest assured, I want something different entirely now." His expression grew serious. "First, your parents must know you are safe. I will write to them on the morrow, and we will leave for Essex shortly after."

Hope swelled within her chest and Clara nodded her head happily. The thought of returning home with the earl, strong and protective by her side, was an unexpected and wonderful conclusion to the wretched turn her life had taken once the season had ended.

"Second, I want you to know that tonight, when I'd realized you'd been taken, I set out immediately. My intent, once you had been recovered, was to make you my wife, *Helen*. Social status be damned."

Her mouth fell open. "William—"

He silenced her with a gentle squeeze of his hands.

"I realized very quickly once I'd lost you, that there was nothing I wouldn't give to have you back." His gaze softened. "You're the first dream I've had after a seemingly unending chain of nightmares, Clara. I'd give my entire world to be with you."

Clara felt tears sting her eyes, and she lifted their clasped hands to her lips. "That works out perfectly, then. Because there is no other man this runaway bride would marry."

His expression changed instantly and happiness flooded his face before her eyes. All the worry and care fell away, leaving him completely unguarded.

"Is that a yes? Tell me it's a yes," he demanded.

She laughed. "Yes, William! Of course, it's a yes."

Levering himself upwards, he leaned over her to kiss her soundly, thoroughly, lingering until her body flushed pink. When he withdrew, a sudden thought struck her and she couldn't contain her mirth, giggles falling from her lips though she tried to stifle them. A lopsided grin broke out on his face at her laughter.

"And what, pray tell, is so amusing?"

Clara gazed up at him, her eyes dancing.

"*J'aime le façon dont vous souriez,*" she whispered softly.

I love the way you smile.

He stared at her in astonishment. In a flash, he pinned her beneath him on the bed, and she shrieked in mock fright.

"You knew what I was saying!" His eyes darkened. "Why, you little minx . . . I'll make you pay for that."

And much to her delight, he did.

CHAPTER NINETEEN

Eliza's soft knock came early the following morning on Clara's bedchamber door.

She pulled his robe tighter around her flimsy chemise. The full-bodied thrill of her night spent with him still lingered, although part of her stubbornly refused to believe her nightmare was ending.

There were moments when she felt undeserving of her current happiness. Clara's deeds hadn't simply thrown her own life into chaos, it had affected the lives of everyone around her. The idea of explaining herself caused her chest to tighten with anxiety. How would Eliza receive her upon learning the details of her deceptions? Would the servants she had come to know as friends ever be willing to trust her again, and would they bristle at the notion of serving her? And how would anyone, except Stella perhaps, be able to accept her as the earl's choice, when up to this point there had been no outward indication of their romance?

She needed to start setting things to rights, which included meeting with her future sister-in-law on honest terms.

Clara opened the door to find Eliza, looking lovely in a lilac day dress, clutching another gown in her arms. Eliza cleared her throat quietly and flashed a nervous smile, her green eyes, just as striking but so unlike her brother's, moving to focus on the floor.

"Good morning, Helen . . . I mean, er . . ."

Eliza glanced up in helpless mortification, both women standing in silence for a long moment before dissolving into a breathless fit of mutual hilarity.

"I'm so sorry—" gasped Eliza. "I even practiced before I knocked on the door!"

Clara attempted to stifle her laugh and reached forward, touching Eliza's shoulder to gently draw her inside her chambers. "If it brings you comfort, you should know Lord Ashworth is struggling with the very same thing," she said, closing the door behind them as her tone sobered. "I have caused such trouble for you all."

The earl's sister made a sympathetic noise, draping her extra gown over Clara's bed, then turning to envelop her in a warm embrace. Clara relaxed against her with a sigh of relief and lowered her cheek to rest on Eliza's shoulder.

"You have been through a great ordeal." She pulled back to gaze severely at Clara. "Although you should have come to us sooner for help. My goodness, you even let me prattle on repeatedly about the mysterious *Clara Mayfield*! Not to mention, I made arrangements for the earl's ball . . ."

A tide of remorse crashed through her. "Forgive me, Eliza . . ."

". . . Only to hear from my brother that he has apparently been in love with you for quite some time," continued the earl's sister with a remonstrative shake of her head, her shining golden curls bouncing softly with the motion. "I'd wondered if he might have held a preference for *someone*, especially after the way he had resisted my efforts at matchmaking. But since I couldn't puzzle out who it could be, I never gave it much thought. Then to find out it was *you*! I'll never understand why you both let me go through with it."

"I suppose he could not publicly own his love for a housemaid any more than I could confess my true identity," she replied, feeling a current of sadness at the knowledge that she had come so close to losing him. "In my mind, there was no way for us to be together. The only redeeming aspect of staying here would have been living with you and Rosa," she added with a small smile.

Eliza gazed at Clara. "Well that certainly explains his sudden itch to be rid of you," she said. "I didn't understand it at the time, but now it seems obvious that the thought of loving you, yet marrying another, must have been killing him." The earl's sister reached up to gently touch the dark bruises that had formed across Clara's neck before dropping her hand. "Clearly Rutherford was the worst kind of man." She leaned forward to whisper conspiratorially. "My brother would not tell me what he said to break the baron's claim over you, but I can imagine the only thing that could have. I hope you can forgive him for that."

Clara blushed all the way up to her hairline and glanced away, tongue-tied.

"I . . . I will admit, I was shocked at first. But the earl had only my best interests in mind. Besides, there is much more to forgive on my side, in my opinion."

"Miss Mayfield, it is plain to see he had his own best interests in mind as well. I've never seen a man so smitten with a woman before. And by now you must know you are forgiven," added Eliza gravely. "Yes, you lived in this place under an elaborate pretense. But I would wager it wasn't an easy existence, working in service after coming from privilege, and it only attests to the desperateness of your situation. I'm still just puzzled at how all of this happened right beneath my nose, especially as it seems the only thing confusing Rosa was why her uncle was seeking a wife when he so *clearly* had feelings for you."

Clara laughed in spite of herself. "Rosa is very perceptive," she answered fondly. Her face grew warm with joy at the realization that soon she would be able to call her family. She crossed thoughtfully to the bed to admire the gown Eliza had brought for her to wear, tracing her hands across the lovely rose-colored muslin dress with ivory lace accents on the sleeves and neckline. Her eyes stung, and she lifted them to gaze at the earl's sister. "I'm so sorry I wasn't honest with you. Please believe me when I say there were many times I wished we could be confidantes, but my circumstances were dire, and I had already unwittingly placed your family in a hazardous position, as you discovered last night." She glanced away in regret. "I will never forgive myself for the way it ended, with Rosa witnessing the baron—"

"No," Eliza said sharply. "You will not feel a bit of guilt for that man's actions. Rosa will be fine. In fact, she will be even better now that you are to be part of the family." Eliza moved closer to wrap her arm around Clara's waist.

Clara stared at Eliza, awestruck. For months she had suffered with the idea of losing the regard of the earl and his family when the truth about her came out. But somehow, they seemed to have grown to love her every bit as much as she loved them. The truth slammed home, and Clara threw her arms around Eliza in a tight hug, grateful beyond words for her friendship.

"Thank you," she whispered fiercely.

Eliza shook her head. "This house has been joyless these past long years after losing so many loved ones." She squeezed Clara back. "I must say I am supremely happy to be gaining one for a change."

Clara's fingers reached up to touch her elaborate sable coiffure, now thankfully free of the white cap that had covered it for months, then fell down to pause over her trembling lips. She allowed herself a moment to appreciate the drastic change that had occurred.

Lord Ashworth had arranged a leisurely morning for his bride-to-be—an opportunity to remove any lingering vestiges of her time spent here as a servant. This had included a steaming bath scented with rosewater, ample time to brush her thick locks into a gleaming shine, and a chance to change into the dress Eliza had given her. The dark pink fabric provided a flattering contrast between the creamy paleness of her skin and the dark mass of her hair. It was the touch that completed her final transformation from Helen, the housemaid, into the future countess Clara Mayfield.

Almost as if on cue, there was a rap on the bedchamber door. She opened it to find the Earl of Ashworth, who seemed adorably nervous standing there in the hallway.

"My lord," she said with a shy smile. Stepping to the side, she allowed him to enter the room.

William came forward to close the door behind him, never taking his eyes off of Clara. She found she was many things all at once. Bashful, anxious, excited . . . but most of all, she was enamored with the man standing before her. What would he think of her now, seeing her like this? Her heart racing, she performed a little twirl to set her layered skirts fluttering, and he let out a soft sigh of appreciation.

"You are the woman I longed to see in that ballroom last night."

Relief washed over her and she felt herself flush in pleasure. "Yes, and it only took four hours to achieve the desired effect!" she joked.

"Obviously it wouldn't have taken anything at all," he quipped lightly, coming closer. "It wasn't as if I fell in love with an heiress who was primped to perfection. I fell in love with my housemaid, much as I tried to deny it."

She sank eagerly into his arms. "I'm glad you like it, my lord. I was half afraid you might prefer me in my uniform."

"Oh, I still like you in your uniform," he said, sliding his hands possessively around her waist. "I liked you in that tattered, old dress you were wearing when you nearly got hit by the carriage, too."

"Liar," she laughed.

The earl leaned down, his mouth nearly touching her own. "I am not a liar," he admonished, the warmth of his breath tickling her lips. "Why do you think I saw the carriage coming from where I was, across the street?"

"You—you were looking at me?" she asked, breathless now. Desperately, she rose up on her tiptoes to brush her lips against him, but he evaded her with a grin.

"That's putting it politely, Miss Mayfield."

William lowered his head to kiss her at last, and she was ready for him, for the slick thrust of his tongue against hers, for that seductive burn that flared whenever she was in his arms. He pulled away suddenly, causing her to moan in complaint. He shook his head in regret.

"Removing your dress now would be a shame, after all the effort you took in putting it on," he teased, even as his eyes turned dark with desire. His fingers caught at her skirts. "Although perhaps we wouldn't need to remove it completely . . ."

Her pulse jumped at his words, the hungry look on his face making her blush hotly. "No . . . I mean, I can't," she replied, shaking her head with a smile. "I need to go downstairs. I need to speak with them."

He stroked a thumb affectionately over her chin. "I'd offer to help," he said knowingly, "but you've shown that you are more than capable of helping yourself. So, what are you planning to say?"

"'They need to know . . . I just want them to know . . ." Her words faltered.

After a lengthy silence, the earl leaned down to meet her eyes reassuringly. "That you're still one of them?"

Clara smiled brightly at him, then frowned. "Well . . . yes?"

Ashworth drew her against his solid warmth and she closed her eyes, inhaling the intoxicating clean scent of him.

"You came into this house a stranger, and won every last one of them over—even Amelia," he added with a sound of amusement. "Doing it a second time won't be nearly as challenging. They know you're a good person. And despite the many things that will be changing, that particular trait will remain constant."

Clara melted against him again, burying her face in his shirt and wrapping her arms around his muscular torso. She wished she felt the kind of confidence he clearly did, but she just couldn't.

With a last, lingering kiss, she left him there in her bedchamber, soon finding herself belowstairs in the servants' hallway. The sounds of the staff in the dining hall reached her ears, and she felt wistful for a moment. Even if they forgave her, would it be possible for her to remain friends with them, as she had been before? To tease Matthew and laugh with Stella? She hoped so. She did not want to lose this small family she had found.

She glanced down at her skirts, smoothing the pretty pink muslin down nervously with her hands. Hesitantly, she proceeded forward, stopping one more time to calm her nerves before showing herself to the group as they chatted during their meal. The boisterous conversation halted abruptly, and the collection of faces stared at her in surprised anticipation. She was relieved to see that Matthew's mouth bore the smallest hint of a smile, and Charles tipped his head in her direction. Both men were privy to more of her secrets than the rest of the gathering, and she knew they could be relied upon to keep them. Tess looked a bit flustered, Amelia was smiling encouragingly, but Stella would not meet her eyes, preferring instead to focus on the wooden table before them.

Mrs. Malone glanced up from her tea to find Clara standing awkwardly in the doorway, and replaced her china cup hurriedly in its saucer so she could rise in greeting.

"Hello again, Miss Mayfield," she said with a smile and a nod before shooting an expectant glance at the rest of her staff, who were clearly frozen in shock. The sound of chair legs hastily scraping across the floor became deafening as the domestic servants shot up from their seats to greet her. The housekeeper gestured at an empty place at the table. "Would you like some tea?"

Clara was both relieved and surprised at the kind offer, and she nodded with a smile. "Thank you."

The group took their seats and she lowered herself into the nearest chair, with Matthew taking a moment to pour her some hot tea, then push the cup in her direction. It reminded her of the first time she'd met everyone belowstairs, here at this table while sharing a meal, and she realized that—in a way—she was meeting them again for the first time right now. Twisting her fingers around the delicate porcelain handle of her teacup, she pondered how to start. Finally, she sighed and gazed apologetically at everyone.

"I'm so sorry for having deceived you all. If I could convince you of just one thing, it would be that."

She felt the tension in the room diminish by a palpable amount, while the curiosity in the gazes that surrounded her actually seemed to increase. It gave her the encouragement she required to press on.

"And I want you to know that despite my altered circumstances, I still hope to be counted among your friends." She fidgeted uneasily with her hands. "At a time when I felt very alone in my life, hidden away from my family and loved ones, your companionship was often the only thing that prevented me from dwelling on that unbearable isolation." Clara allowed herself some solace in the fact that Stella had now raised her eyes and was looking in her direction. "I thank you for that. Most humbly.

"My real name is Clara Mayfield," she continued, glancing down the long table at Tess, seated next to Oscar, the stable boy, who appeared even more ill at ease now than he ever had in Helen's presence, were that possible. "You likely know of my situation from the papers these past few months, and there is very little I can add to that, except to say that I understand this state of affairs could prove awkward. I apologize for that as well."

"Will you be staying here, at Lawton Park?"

Stella's question rang through the hush of the dining hall, and the servants' eyes darted from the housemaid back to Clara in curious expectation. It was a fair question, just not one she had hoped to answer in mixed company, and so soon after the drama of the previous evening. She felt a sheen of sweat break out across her forehead, and her eyes flicked over to Matthew and Charles. Both footmen nodded at her.

"Well," she began, "although the earl and I will be leaving later today to journey home to my family in Essex, I should return sometime in the future."

Her cheeks flamed. While she wasn't comfortable making an announcement of any kind regarding her relationship with Lord Ashworth, they were welcome to draw their own conclusions. Indeed, she doubted anything could stop them, and if appearances were an indication, the outrageous look on Mrs. Humboldt's face meant she had already started.

Stella smiled knowingly and stared down at the wooden table.

"Why did you run from the baron?" asked Oscar from his position toward the rear of the group.

The table was silent. She was surprised that the apprehensive stable boy had managed to voice a question of his own, and he certainly deserved an answer.

"I ran because I was scared," she replied, tugging at the lace collar on her dress to reveal the ugly smudge of black bruises left upon on her neck. A collective intake of breath rippled through the servants. "The ball was interrupted last night when he attacked me. It was not the first time, and it would not be the last. *That* was why I leaped out of an upstairs window to escape on the eve of my wedding. Because the alternative was a lifetime of marriage to a cruel beast of a man, and it was more than I could willingly bear."

"I hope Lord Ashworth pummeled him," muttered Oscar with a scowl, and she repressed an affectionate grin.

Tess's soft voice reached Clara from the far end of the table. "Why did you hide here, as a servant?"

Clara debated how to answer, since the full extent of the truth would implicate Abigail. Amelia would have figured out the extent of her involvement by now, but she was also her sister and would not jeopardize Abigail's employment. In fact, the way Amelia had started playing with her fork likely betrayed her nervousness. The maid's eyes darted surreptitiously over to meet Clara's, and she gave Amelia a tiny nod of reassurance before facing the group once more.

"I thought the baron would never think to look for me belowstairs, and that was actually true. I'm not sure where he thought I was hiding, or whether he thought I'd be foolish enough to attend a ball, but it was only by chance that we met last night in the foyer."

"I'm glad you're safe now," Amelia said with a smile.

She gazed gratefully in Amelia's direction. Wrestling briefly with what to say next, she finally continued with pleading eyes. "Please . . . I really am not so different from the girl you knew as Helen. I hope we can stay friends."

She wasn't sure what she expected any of them to say, and for one terrifying moment, they said nothing. Clara shifted in her chair in the uncomfortable silence.

Then Matthew cleared his throat and took a bite of ham.

"Are you hungry?" he asked while chewing.

And before too long, laughter rang out in the servants' hall once more.

Clara stared out at the passing hedgerows, grassy fields, and bare trees through the cover of a low-hanging fog that had persisted since morning. Her head lay resting on the earl's shoulder and she snuggled against his solid warmth, a blissful peace settling in her soul as he murmured a noise of contentment, his arm curling more tightly around her body to draw her closer.

Ashworth's carriage continued, dauntless, across the muddy roads of the Essex countryside. The journey from Kent had so far been uneventful. Aside from the anxiety she felt at confronting her parents, she was calmer than she had been in months.

Clara couldn't anticipate her parents' reaction at seeing her after everything that had passed, so she tried not to think about her reception, and how there was the distinct possibility that things might not go well. They knew she was coming, at least, so they would be prepared in that regard. William had summoned the fastest courier in the village to deliver his notification of Clara's safety, and their impending arrival at the Mayfields' estate. They now knew she was safe, and in the company of the Earl of Ashworth. No doubt the baron may have been in communication with her parents as well, although given the earl's ultimatum to him, that would be risky indeed.

"We should be arriving shortly," whispered the earl against her hair, thankfully now free of the starched white cap that had plagued her for months. She tipped her face up to meet his and he kissed her slowly, thoroughly. She responded instantly and he laughed low in his throat, pulling back to break the kiss and place some distance between them. "Neither of us will be fit to greet your parents if we continue," he muttered huskily.

Clara knew he was right and yet she was reluctant to stop. She glanced up at him mischievously.

"I'll stop, my lord. But I blame *you* for starting."

"Fair enough," he responded with a boyish grin that made her pulse beat a little faster. The smile faded quickly, however, and he regarded her with a serious air, his handsome face turning solemn. "How are you feeling?"

Her gaze dropped to the polished gold buttons on his jacket. "Scared," she admitted truthfully. "Hopeful."

Ashworth's head swayed to the side as the carriage took a sharp turn around the drive, and he leaned in to touch his forehead to hers. "Choose to believe in the best possible outcome, Miss Mayfield, until they leave you no choice but to believe otherwise."

She nodded, gathering her bravery. "This will not be the worst thing I have had to endure these past months."

"No," he affirmed, "it will not." His gaze held hers as he pressed a final, lingering kiss onto the back of her hand. "In fact, I can promise you it will be the first in long lifetime of wonderful things for you."

"Not the first, surely," she said, eyeing him flirtatiously.

His lopsided grin caused her stomach to flutter. "No, not the first, and certainly not the last."

"I love you, William," she whispered. "So much."

His long fingers slid beneath the curve of her jaw, tipping her chin up to face him, as the carriage came to a stop.

"I have loved you from that first moment I saw you, nearly trampled by a carriage in the street," he said with a soft laugh. "We have suffered much to get here . . . to be with one another. You are so brave already, my little housemaid." He leaned down to kiss the tip of her nose. "Come a little farther with me, and let's start this new life together."

Silvercreek
Essex County, England
1846

Spring had arrived at last, and with it, the day of Clara's wedding. Per her request, it was to be a private affair. Given the excess of publicity her life had received during the past six months, she refused to wittingly provide more fodder for the gossips of London. In this instance, anyway, the *ton's* unsophisticated attempts at speculation would be their only entertainment.

She'd been due fifteen minutes ago to meet her mother and sister upstairs, but had been delayed by the enthusiastic well-wishing of her friends belowstairs. Not everyone had been able to make the trek north to Essex, and in the case of Mrs. Malone, had steadfastly refused to leave the house in less capable hands, no matter how grand the circumstances. A small crew of domestics had stayed behind to assist the stubborn housekeeper, and William had ensured transportation to Silvercreek for the rest.

These faces surrounded Clara now, beaming with eager delight. It was only appropriate for her friends to be present at the conclusion of her hard-fought and daring adventure, especially since they had been such an integral part of it. They were also more than pleased, and even honored, to help usher her into this new chapter of life as the earl's wife, the Countess of Ashworth.

The excited chatter flowed around her, and hugs assailed her from, what seemed to be, every direction. Stella, Gilly, Tess—they all wanted one last embrace, and she reveled in both their company and affections. The sudden appearance of Matthew on the staircase, however, was sufficient to disrupt the prolonged festivities.

"I beg your pardon, Miss Mayfield," said the dark-haired footman with a jaunty lift of one brow and an exaggerated flourish of his hand, "but the pleasure of your company has been requested upstairs. Repeatedly. By your mother."

"She's probably worried you've bolted!" Mrs. Humboldt exclaimed loudly, before clapping a hand over her mouth. "Apologies, miss. Mrs. Malone would have my head if she'd heard that."

With a laugh, Clara reassured the cook. "Not to worry. Given my history with betrothals, she would be right to worry—"

The sound of more footsteps on the stairs preceded the sight of her sister, Lucy, looking gorgeous in an azure dress with ruffled skirts that did little to mask the growing curve of her belly. Her hair, a light caramel brown, was swept up elegantly into an intricate arrangement of curls. She set her hand on the wooden rail with a thump, and sighed in a feigned show of annoyance with her younger sibling.

"Well, I thought you wanted to wear a wedding dress today, but I suppose that will just have to do," she said, eyeing Clara's plain dress doubtfully.

At this proclamation, Amelia grabbed Clara's left arm and Abigail seized her right.

"We'll be right up, Mrs. Thompson!" cried Abigail in a panic, pushing her way out of the crowd with Clara in tow.

Lucy nodded succinctly with a tiny smile upon her lips. "That's more like it."

Clara had convinced her friend to serve as her personal lady's maid at Lawton Park. She would share in Abigail's companionship once more abovestairs, and Amelia could share in it below. The sisters were beyond thrilled to be working in the same house at last, and Clara had no doubt it was the best solution for everyone involved.

The group came to the green baize door at the top of the staircase, and Lucy turned to smile at the small group before extricating Clara from their hold.

"I'm going to steal her for a moment. She'll be up shortly."

Amelia and Abigail drifted away. Lucy hooked her arm through Clara's and rested her head on her shoulder, leading her slowly toward the terrace. Clara huffed in amusement.

"I thought we were in a hurry?"

She could feel her sister's laugh against her arm. "We are. I just wanted you all to myself for a moment." Lucy sighed as they ambled through the dining room. "I was so worried about you, Clara. And I still can't believe how much things have changed for us now."

Clara leaned her head against Lucy's. "I suppose there's nothing quite like losing both your children to make you realize how much you love them."

"To be sure. I believe your flight from Rutherford was the only thing that could have helped bring Papa round that way." Lucy shook her head. "It's unfortunate it took such an event, although I daresay you might not have met your charming earl otherwise."

She knew the truth of her sister's words. Not only had their parents sought to reconcile with Lucy after Clara's hasty departure, they had welcomed both her and Douglas back into the family.

And Clara couldn't deny that during her journey she had managed to land herself a peer of the highest sort. One who was gentle, not cruel. An earl who would never strike her, preferring instead to argue his points with wit and intelligence. A husband who used laughter to diffuse her tensions. A man who would save the unfair tactics of persuasion for use in the bedroom, if need be . . .

"Well, yes," she answered, cheeks turning warm, grateful once more for her situation's unexpected outcome. "But it's been shocking to see how close Papa and Douglas have grown. In fact, I would never have guessed it possible."

Lucy rolled her eyes in Clara's direction, a sardonic grin spreading across her pretty features. "He has much more in common with Douglas than he may have thought at first. My husband is smart and ambitious," she said proudly. "It's part of why I fell in love with him." Her gaze shifted toward the windows off the terrace, where the men had gathered in discussion. "I knew that if he were given half a chance, our parents would care for him just as much as I do."

"I'm glad you were able to forgive them. There were moments after you'd left home when I'd had my doubts."

The pair came to a stop in the sunroom, the warm glow of mid-morning sun bright in comparison to the shadowy interior. Lucy turned to face her sister.

"One would need to be carved of stone to resist Father's pleas. He made it clear that he loves both of us, more than any kind of approval that the *ton* could provide," she said softly. "I am certain it was only after you left, though, that he truly came to know it. And oddly enough, once he stopped caring about society and their opinions, you came back to us . . . set to marry the Earl of Ashworth."

Clara swallowed against the sudden lump in her throat. After years of insisting that their happiness did not matter to him in the grand scheme of things, Mr. Mayfield actually found it did. In the aftermath of his choices . . . in the absence of his children . . . his priorities were found to be cold comfort, indeed.

"Girls!"

Clara and Lucy glanced up to find their mother approaching, skirts swishing wildly around her in her haste. She was accompanied by Eliza and her friend, Lady Caroline Rowe, who had journeyed in from Hampshire for the impending nuptials. Between Eliza's exquisite golden beauty and Caroline's striking auburn locks, the two women made for an eye-catching pair. Eliza winked at Clara as Mrs. Mayfield approached her, breathless.

"There you are, Clara, my goodness! Lord Ashworth has been ready for over an hour . . . I think he is very much in a hurry to be wed, while you have been dithering about below-stairs!"

"You are mistaken, Mother," laughed Clara, craning her neck to view the gathering of men standing outside behind the main house. "I am also eager to be wed, it's just—"

Her speech paused when her gaze found the earl through the panes of polished glass. He was standing, Rosa in his arms, his burnished gold hair gleaming, the fine angles of his face caught perfectly in the radiance of morning light. He was entirely relaxed among the gathering, engaged in conversation with Lord Evanston, Douglas, and her father.

She remembered the uproar he had created in Mayfair with his inability to attend the lavish ball. Could still see his waxen, haunted features, panic-stricken and pale. But there was no sign of that man here today. She smiled as he nearly doubled over in hilarity at something Douglas said, and could imagine him acting in much the same way before the accident. Handsome and at ease, lighthearted and charismatic, he stood dressed in his finest attire, talking and laughing with her family as if they were old friends.

Was it possible for a heart to burst with joy? She felt that perhaps it was.

In the midst of his sentence, Ashworth's eyes found hers through the glass, and he faltered. His incomparable green eyes turned warm, and his smile acquired a sultry overtone that caused her whole body to light aflame.

Just moments following his abrupt interruption, Rosa planted her tiny hands on Ashworth's face and manually rotated it back toward the group, who had already turned where they stood to determine the reason for his distraction. Viscount Evanston grinned and stepped to the right, effectively blocking his friend's view of his betrothed, while Mrs. Mayfield gasped in horror.

"He can't see you before the wedding! Upstairs, now . . ."

Lucy went to her mother's side and took her hand. "Be at ease, Mother. All will be well."

Her large blue eyes widened meaningfully at Clara and she tipped her head toward the dining room. "Lord Evanston is a pleasant man," she said in an attempt to divert her mother's anxiety as they made their way en masse inside the house. "You and he are closely acquainted, are you not?" she asked Eliza.

"We are," answered the earl's sister.

Lucy smiled good-naturedly. "I only ask because I see his eyes follow you quite often. I was curious if perhaps—"

"Oh, no. Not at all," came Eliza's amused reply. "We're just friends, and barely even that sometimes."

Lucy glanced at Clara with a suppressed grin. It was obvious she had detected the same heat whenever the viscount's gaze lingered on Lady Cartwick, but it seemed the only person who could not see it, or refused to, was Eliza, herself.

Upon arriving at the base of the stairs, Mrs. Mayfield slipped her hand into Clara's. "Allow me to walk you upstairs?"

Clara murmured in acquiescence and the ladies turned to retire to the drawing room. Her mother pulled her closer while they made their way up the staircase, leaving the commotion of the wedding preparations behind them for a moment of quiet.

"I'm so very sorry for what you've been through," her mother said in a low voice. "You told me . . . I know you did . . . but I just didn't understand. Didn't hear you the way I should have."

Clara shook her head. "No, no. We've moved past this now."

"Perhaps, but it still keeps me up at night. You should never have had to run away for us to understand how desperate you were."

Clara paused on the landing and turned to face her, squeezing her hand gently. "I won't disagree with that. But here we are, and it's all worked out for the best." A gleam of tears shone in her mother's eyes, and Clara hugged her close to whisper in her ear. "Sleep well tonight, Mama. Today I am marrying the man I love."

"Well, then you had better go and get dressed," her mother laughed, backing away to dab at her eyes. "Abigail and Amelia are already in your chambers, and as you saw for yourself, the earl is ready."

After one last embrace, Clara raced upstairs in a most unladylike fashion. Shutting her bedchamber door behind her, she glanced over at her wedding dress, hanging in the corner. A lovely dress, as it always had been. White satin, lace, pearls . . .

The memory of that fateful night came rushing back. Her dress had appeared like a ghost in the gloom, the crickets' song had bid her farewell, and she had known her life was about to change forever . . .

Clara also recalled the good-bye note she had tearfully pinned to the front of her wedding dress. With a start, she realized that the note was still there.

Except it wasn't quite right. She stepped closer for a better view.

The original note was still in place:

> *I cannot do this. I'm sorry. I love you.*
> *—Clara*

But to her surprise, there was now another note beneath it, pinned carefully to the shining fabric. She leaned forward to read it, then began to laugh.

> *I am so glad you didn't. Now come downstairs and marry me.*
> *—William, Lord Ashworth*

Acknowledgments

Behind this book is a literal army of people who have cheered me on throughout every step of the way, from my scribblings as a fledgling writer to the finished manuscript and its eventual release. I like to think of them as Team Tremayne, and I am so grateful to have had their support during this journey.

Thank you to my mom, Dorinda, who is by far my biggest fan and most voracious reader. Thank you to my father David, my brother Adam, and my nephew Connor, who never miss a chance to tell me how proud they are. Thank you to my husband, Gary, who gave me that little push I needed to stop doubting and start writing. Thank you to my mother-in-law, Patricia, for her test reads of my work. And thank you to my children, Elise and Reid, who understood why mom was a little cranky when I was working under my first big deadline.

It takes a lot of time and patience to be a beta reader. These people not only signed up for the job, they helped me send out a manuscript that was polished. Huge thanks to my writing partner Erika Bigelow, who was my first line of defense. Heartfelt thanks to my mother Dorinda for her attention to detail. Big thanks to Shannon Sullivan and Heather Bottomley, and many thanks to Rachel Whitaker, Anna Waller, Mary Murphy, and authors Samantha Saxon, L.E. Wilson, and Alexandra Sipe. I couldn't have done it without you!

To my fantastic agent Kevan Lyon, thank you for helping me navigate the business, for seeing something worth sharing with the world, and for the hard work in getting it there. Thank you to Priyanka Krishnan, my editor, for giving me that important first chance, for being so easy to work with, and for your invaluable and thoughtful input on my books. And thank you to the entire team at Avon/Harper Collins who have worked to help to make this dream of mine a reality.

Thank you to the members of my writing chapters, the GSRWA and the ERWA, for teaching me, guiding me, and for sharing in the joys of my success and allowing me to also share in yours. To author Jamie Michele, thank you for referring me to the Marsal Lyon Literary Agency. Thanks to Eryn Frank for her unflagging friendship. Thank you to Jane Austen for her inspiring work, and thanks to Kristi Beckley, who loaned me the copy of *Pride and Prejudice* that got this party started. I appreciate every last person who has been a friend and supported me, both in person and online.

And thanks to you, dear reader! I would be honored to have you join my team.

Fondly,
Marie

Dear Reader,

I hope you liked the latest romance from Avon Impulse! If you're looking for another steamy, fun, emotional read, be sure to check out some of our upcoming titles.

Love a little suspense in your contemporary romance? Be sure to check out Christi Barth's second Bad Boys Gone Good novel, NEVER BEEN GOOD. An ex-mobster in Witness Protection is bored to death in small-town Oregon and his beautiful, mysterious coworker makes for the perfect distraction. But they both have secrets from their pasts that could catch up with them at any moment . . . Christi's series about bad-boy brothers trying to be good will make you laugh and sigh!

We also have the next book in Mia Sosa's critically acclaimed Love on Cue series for all you contemporary romance fans! PRETENDING HE'S MINE is delicious, trope-y goodness about an uptight Hollywood agent who can't seem to keep his mind—or his hands—off his best friend's little sister. Mia delivers another laugh-out-loud, sexy romantic comedy and you don't want to miss it!

Historical romance fans will go wild for the new Cat Sebastian series launching in April! UNMASKED BY THE MARQUESS is the first in her new Regency Impostors series and it features a housemaid masquerading as a man and the notoriously stuffy marquess who can't seem to stop thinking about the impertinent scamp. But when her true identity is revealed, can these two stubborn souls find their way to happy ever after? One-click this incredible, passionate romance ASAP!

You can purchase any of these titles by clicking the links above or by visiting our website, www.AvonRomance.com. Thank you for loving romance as much as we do . . . enjoy!

Sincerely,
Nicole Fischer
Editorial Director
Avon Impulse

MARIE TREMAYNE graduated from the University of Washington with a B.A. in English Language and Literature. While there, a copy of *Pride and Prejudice* ended up changing her life. She decided to study the great books of the Regency and Victorian eras, and now enjoys writing her own tales set in the historical period she loves. Marie lives with her family in the beautiful Pacific Northwest.

www.MarieTremayne.com
Facebook.com/MarieTremayneRomance
www.avonimpulse.com
www.facebook.com/avonromance

Discover great authors, exclusive offers, and more at hc.com.